# Advance praise for Kevin O'Brien and *The Enemy at Home*

"Kevin O'Brien's new book takes us to Seattle in the opening years of the US involvement in World War II, when a serial killer is on the loose, targeting women who are contributing to the war effort by becoming Rosie the Riveters. The book is fast-paced, suspenseful, and intriguing, and it kept this reader guessing about the killer's identity nearly till the big reveal. Super enjoyable."
—Elizabeth George, #1 *New York Times* bestselling author

"A tantalizing whodunnit set in WW II Seattle with a cast of red herrings that had me guessing and turning pages right up to the final, shocking reveal—which I never saw coming. A perfect summer read!"
—Charlie Donlea, *USA Today* bestselling author of *Twenty Years Later*

"A sweeping, addictive story of bravery and sacrifice, told in Kevin O'Brien's cinematic style. Authentic period detail creates a suspenseful, chilling atmosphere in this grand historical novel."
—Susan Wiggs, #1 *New York Times* bestselling author

"A classic Kevin O'Brien page-turner, with a new historical twist. O'Brien takes us deep into Seattle during WW II, as his heroine juggles work, misogyny, solo parenting, and a serial killer on the loose. Nora is a heroine to root for, and the curves in the plot kept me reading late into the night (while checking the locks on my doors!)."
—Erica Bauermeister, *New York Times* bestselling author of *No Two Persons*

"Kevin O'Brien's latest is a compulsively unputdownable, keep-you-guessing-to-the-end, pages-flying whodunit, and as if that weren't enough, *The Enemy at Home* is also packed with compelling, complicated characters in a fascinating and meticulously researched time and place. World War II Seattle where women were newly considered workers, Japanese-American citizens were newly considered threats, and closeted gay communities were newly considering a place for themselves all combine to bring this timely novel vividly to life. A new Kevin O'Brien book is always cause for celebration, and this is his best yet."
—Laurie Frankel, *New York Times* bestselling author of *This Is How It Always Is*

"Nobody writes suspense better than Kevin O'Brien. Read *The Enemy at Home*, but do so w
—Robert Dugoni, *New York Ti*

T0020575

Books by Kevin O'Brien

ONLY SON
THE NEXT TO DIE
MAKE THEM CRY
WATCH THEM DIE
LEFT FOR DEAD
THE LAST VICTIM
KILLING SPREE
ONE LAST SCREAM
FINAL BREATH
VICIOUS
DISTURBED
TERRIFIED
UNSPEAKABLE
TELL ME YOU'RE SORRY
NO ONE NEEDS TO KNOW
YOU'LL MISS ME WHEN I'M GONE
HIDE YOUR FEAR
THEY WON'T BE HURT
THE BETRAYED WIFE
THE BAD SISTER
THE NIGHT SHE DISAPPEARED
THE ENEMY AT HOME

Published by Kensington Publishing Corp.

# THE
# ENEMY
## AT
# HOME

## KEVIN O'BRIEN

**KENSINGTON**
PUBLISHING CORP.

www.kensingtonbooks.com

KENSINGTON BOOKS are published by

Kensington Publishing Corp.
119 West 40th Street
New York, NY 10018

ISBN: 978-1-4967-3851-6 (ebook)

ISBN: 978-1-4967-3850-9

First Kensington Trade Paperback Printing: September 2023

10 9 8 7 6 5 4 3 2 1

Printed in the United States of America

*This book is dedicated to my dear friend and neighbor,*
*Ruth Young*

# Acknowledgments

I've got to start here with my good friend and brilliant editor at Kensington Books, John Scognamiglio. Thank you, John, for the inspiration, guidance and pep talks for the past twenty-three books. You're the best. And here's a great big thank-you to the terrific team at Kensington Books—with a special shout-out to art director Louis Malcangi for the gorgeous cover art!

A huge thank-you to my agent, John Talbot, and the team at The Talbot Fortune Agency.

Many thanks also to my marvelous writers' group: David Massengill, Sasha Im, Colin McArthur and Garth Stein. They were exposed to portions of this book in early draft form and always came up with great suggestions for improvement—whether I wanted to listen or not.

And speaking of writers who have always been there for me, I need to thank again my old Seattle 7 Writer pals, especially Dave Boling, Erica Bauermeister, Terry Brooks, Lynn Brunelle, Carol Cassella, Robert Dugoni, Bridget Foley, Laurie Frankel, Elizabeth George, Mike Lawson, Suzanne Selfors, Jennie Shortridge, Stephen Susco, and Susan Wiggs.

I'm also grateful to my proofreader and editor extraordinaire, Cathy Johnson.

And here's a special shout-out to the folks at ReaderLink Distribution Services. Without you, I'm nothing!

I'd also like the thank the usual suspects (along with a few new names), who have always been incredibly supportive: Dan Annear and Chuck Rank, Jeff Ayers, Ben Bauermeister, Dante and Pattie Bellini, A Book for All Seasons, the Book Stall, Amanda Brooks, Judine Brooks, George Camper and Shane White, Barb and John Cegielski, Barb and Jim Church, Marti Converse, Anna Cottle and Mary Alice Kier, Paul Dwoskin, Eagle Harbor Books, Elliott Bay Book Company, Margaret Freeman, Matt Gani, the Girls Gone Wild Reading Books, Cate Goethals and Tom Goodwin, Bob and Dana Gold, Pennie Clark Ianniciello, Island Books, Deborah Kamen and Sarah Levin-Richardson, the Kelly Family, Elizabeth Kinsella, David Korabik, Stafford Lombard, Susan London, Roberta Miner, Dan Monda, Deborah Neff, my terrific pals from Sacred Heart School, Mike Sack and John Saul, Eva Marie Saint, the cool gang at Shelf Awareness, John Simmons and Scott Hulet, Roseann Stella, George and Sheila Stydahar, and Marc Von Borstel.

A special thank-you to my high school Latin teacher, who turned out to be a friend for life, Tom Forrer (1944–2022).

And finally, thanks so much to my wonderful siblings and their families. Adele, Mary Lou, Cathy, Bill and Joan . . . I'm so lucky to be your bro.

# Chapter 1

*Sunday, April 4, 1943*
*11:27 p.m.*
*Seattle, Washington*

"Who's there?" Nora called out softly.

Clutching a fireplace poker, she cowered in the back doorway. Nora Kinney had thrown her robe over her nightgown before hurrying downstairs to investigate the noises that seemed to come from the backyard. The thirty-seven-year-old mother of two was alone—her husband stationed in North Africa.

On their secluded, tree-shaded block in the Capitol Hill neighborhood, the Kinneys' modest Craftsman-style home was dwarfed by neighboring mansions, some with garage apartments for servants' quarters. The Kinneys had a garage apartment, too—tucked behind the house at the end of the driveway. But it had been vacant for the past year, its windows boarded up.

Nora listened to the wind rustling tree branches.

"Is anyone there?" she asked, a bit louder this time, though she didn't want to wake the kids. She could see her breath in the chilly night air. She nervously glanced toward the garage—and the backyard, which dropped off to a wooded ravine. Past the gully's silhouetted treetops, Nora had a moonlit view of Lake Union and Queen Anne Hill. Because of the wartime blackout, the city looked desolate and eerie. Nora felt as if she were the only person awake in the darkened city—she and whoever was skulking around the house.

Nora had been lying in bed, unable to sleep, when she'd heard the noises outside. It sounded like someone—or more than just one someone—was in the backyard. She could have sworn she heard whispering.

They'd had nighttime disturbances before. They'd even had to call the police twice. But now she wasn't hearing anything. Nora stood in the doorway for another minute, looking out. The family victory garden—with a low wire fence around it to keep out rabbits and squirrels—was undisturbed.

At the start of the war, everyone had been encouraged to grow their own produce. Nora had heard that these private "victory" gardens would help lower the cost of vegetables needed to feed the troops, so money could go to other essentials. Everyone had become patriotic and planted victory gardens. Even apartment dwellers grew produce in window boxes. Mrs. Roosevelt had a victory garden on the White House lawn. Nora had planted lettuce, spinach, carrots and onions. The garden was good for about three salads or side dishes per week. But Nora thought the garden always looked so pathetic and scrawny.

She remembered how pretty the yard used to be.

There had been a patch of beautiful dahlias where the victory garden was now. Nora also remembered a trellis with climbing red roses on the north side of the garage. The garage apartment's former tenants, Takashi and Fumiko Hara, had been second-generation U.S. citizens, born in Washington State.

Gardening had been Miko's hobby. And Nora had always been hopelessly inept at it, so when her tenant had asked for permission to plant some flowers in the front yard, Nora had gladly given her the go-ahead. Miko had transformed the Kinneys' drab yard into a botanical showplace. She'd planted more roses and dahlias in front of the house and rows of daffodils and various colored tulips along the length of the driveway. At the height of spring, the vibrant colors had been gorgeous.

But all of that was gone now. Destroyed.

It was spring once again, and Nora still hoped some of the flowers might come back and bloom. At least the victory garden was intact. She could be grateful for that.

Ducking back inside, she closed and locked the door. She paused in the kitchen and realized she hadn't thought about what to cook for dinner tomorrow night. There was some ground beef in the refrigerator. Nora figured on stretching it out and making meatloaf. That would be easy to throw together with what they had in the victory garden. And "easy" was the way to go, since she'd probably be dead tired by dinnertime.

In just six hours, Nora would start her first day on the job as a riveter at Boeing's B-17 plant. She'd signed up, been fingerprinted for security, and gone through an orientation class on Friday. Over the weekend, she'd bought three different colorful bandanas to wrap up her shoulder-length, honey-brown hair while at work. Hollywood's Veronica Lake had posed for a photo in *Life* magazine, showing how women adopting her long, blond hairstyle—with that famous peek-a-boo bang—could get their tresses caught in the machinery at the war plants. So bandanas were essential for the job.

Nora had yet to hold a riveting gun. But if the ear-splitting racket the gun had produced during the orientation lesson was any indication, she might as well be operating a jackhammer.

"Remember, ladies," the mustached, wormy-looking instructor had told the class, shouting over the gun's noise during the demonstration. "This tool is a lot more powerful and dangerous than what you're accustomed to dealing with at home. And this gun is much heavier than the iron you use to press your husband's shirts." Then he'd smirked condescendingly. "Please, try not to kill anyone with it . . ."

This would be Nora's first job since she'd worked for kindly old Mr. Diggle behind a drugstore counter in Chicago eighteen years ago. Now she'd be working for Boeing. And it would be a hell of a lot more dangerous than operating a soda fountain. She was terrified she'd foul it up.

Switching off the lights, Nora headed back upstairs with the fireplace poker. Since her husband had shipped out, she sometimes slept with it at her bedside. She hadn't realized until Pete was gone how often she'd relied on him to investigate the things that go bump in the night. Now it was totally up to her. The poker by her nightstand gave her some peace of mind.

Upstairs, she peeked into her seventeen-year-old son's bedroom. The walls were covered with college pennants and scantily clad "Petty Girls" cut out of *Esquire* magazine. Nora couldn't very well object, since the artist George Petty's bathing beauties often decorated the noses of warplanes. Also on the bedroom walls, Chris displayed placards he'd collected over the years—everything from PRINCIPAL'S OFFICE to RAILROAD CROSSING to DANGEROUS CURVES AHEAD. Only God knew where he'd gotten them all. The bedroom reeked of Old Spice and BO. "Do all teenage boys smell like goats—or is it just our son?" she'd once asked her doctor husband. He explained it was the testosterone. So Nora had given Chris a bottle of Old Spice aftershave lotion for his last birthday—even though he wasn't shaving yet. He was still just a boy. And the notion that he'd have to register for the draft on his next birthday seemed unreal to her—and unthinkable.

In the darkness she couldn't actually see Chris; he was just a lump under the covers.

Moving on to the bedroom across the hall, Nora found her twelve-year-old daughter restlessly shifting under the covers of her canopy bed. On the wall, over her headboard, was Jane's shrine to Tyrone Power—with a dozen photos of him clipped from *Photoplay* and other movie magazines. Jane had a few strategically placed curlers in her red hair. She mumbled in her sleep—something she'd done ever since she'd first learned to talk.

Nora couldn't make any sense out of what Jane was saying. But she was certain it hadn't been her daughter's voice she'd heard earlier. The whispering had definitely come from outside—and there had been two voices.

Nora quietly closed the bedroom door. Stopping by the window at the end of the hallway, she moved the blackout curtain and checked the backyard again. She didn't see anyone out there. But she still wasn't satisfied.

In her bedroom, Nora set the poker upright—between the double bed and her nightstand. Then she went to the window, pulled aside the thick curtain and glanced out at the front yard. She was tempted to go downstairs again and turn on the front porch light. But they weren't supposed to leave any lights on outside because of the blackout.

On the West Coast, they'd started implementing citywide blackout drills months before Pearl Harbor. Cities would go completely dark by eleven at night, making it difficult for potential enemies to target major population centers. This meant all outside lights—streetlamps, illuminated signs, porch lights, everything—had to be extinguished. Like everyone else, Nora had installed shades or hung dark, heavy curtains to ensure that no light escaped from their windows. After December 7, these drills became an everyday reality.

It had been well over a year since Pearl Harbor, and the Japanese hadn't bombed or invaded the West Coast—at least, not with any major impact. There were exceptions—like the shelling of the Ellwood Oil Field west of Santa Barbara, California, by a Japanese submarine in February of the previous year. No lives were lost, and the damage was minimal, but people had gone into a panic. The notion that a Japanese sub could travel undetected across the Pacific, all the way to California's shores, was downright scary. What would keep them from invading? Another Japanese submarine had made it to the coast and bombarded Fort Stevens, Oregon, at the mouth of the Columbia River last June; and again, there were no casualties. The newspapers said the blackout had saved them. Then there was the invasion of the Aleutian Islands in the Alaska Territory— with two of the islands still occupied by Japanese forces.

Nora had to remind herself that the damage inflicted on the West Coast by the Japanese wasn't much at all compared with what German U-boats were doing to oil tankers off our Atlantic shores. Still, Nora lived in a perpetual state of dread. *God, please, let it be one of ours,* she thought whenever she heard the ominous buzz of a low-flying plane overhead.

A constant reminder of the danger and their vulnerability came with the helmeted local Civil Defense warden, who still pounded on doors and issued fines to anyone not complying with the blackout rules. At night, with the window curtains closed and the blinds down, Nora and the kids felt like they were living in a cocoon.

The blackout had led to a spike in crime and auto accidents, but abiding by the blackout regulations showed patriotism. And the Kinneys couldn't afford to look unpatriotic. Despite the small flag with the blue star displayed in their front window—signifying a family member in the service—the Kinneys were still considered by some as disloyal.

So Nora decided to keep the porch light off. She didn't want to give certain neighbors another excuse to despise them.

Crawling back into the double bed, Nora reached up and switched off the nightstand lamp. She still wasn't used to sleeping alone. Even in her slumber, she never rolled over to Pete's side. But all too often, she hugged his pillow, pretending it was him. Sometimes, it was the only way she could fall asleep—by making believe he was still there with her.

But then all it took was a strange noise in the night, and the illusion was shattered. She'd realize once again that he was gone.

Nora wasn't supposed to know where her husband was. The army censored all the mail before they photographed the letters and shrank the images onto microfilm for transport to the U.S., where they were printed up for V-mail. It was such a little thing, but she missed not having the actual piece of paper Pete had written on.

She and Pete had worked out a code in advance regarding his location. If they'd relocated him, the salutation on the letter would be "Hello, Sweetheart." Then the first letter of each sentence at the start of the letter would spell out where he was. In the V-mail she'd gotten on St. Patrick's Day last month, the letter had begun:

> *Hello, Sweetheart,*
>
> *Thinking of you & the kids. Unless I'm wrong, you'll be getting this note in about 2 weeks or so. Nothing much to report. I miss you like crazy. Seems like forever since we've set eyes on each other. I'm homesick. As the song says, "I'm Getting Sentimental Over You . . ."*

So she knew Pete was in Tunisia, where a great deal of the fighting was going on right now. And for a while, she'd gotten the impression that the Nazis were beating the hell out of the Allies—the green American troops especially. But apparently, Patton was starting to turn things around. She didn't tell the kids where their father was currently stationed. "Loose lips sink ships" and all that. But Chris had already guessed that his dad was in North Africa.

Pete was an orthopedic surgeon. He knew the army needed doctors and had told Nora he couldn't live with himself if he didn't do his part for the war effort. As the head of a household with dependents, he had a 3-A deferment. He didn't have to go. Nora argued that people in Seattle needed doctors, too. Plus, she and the kids needed him. But Pete couldn't be swayed.

That was just like him, so conscientious, so stalwart. Nora had heard people compare Pete to Gary Cooper. Tall, lean and handsome, he was quietly commanding, one of those people who whispered and everyone listened. Practically all his female patients fell in love with him. Of course, it helped that he was a brilliant surgeon. Because he was so dependable, Pete came across as solid and confident. But Nora knew about the little cracks of vulnerability that no one else saw in him. He was ex-tremely hard on himself. Sometimes, he could sink into a quiet depression and withdraw from everyone—especially after he'd lost a patient.

For Nora, it wasn't always easy being married to someone so good and so right most of the time. Arguing with him seemed impossible. It drove her crazy how he always seemed to have the final word on things.

Nevertheless, when Pete had mentioned joining the Army Medical Corps, Nora had fought him on it. She couldn't imag-ine trying to get by without him. At the time, the Germans and Japanese were clobbering the hell out of the Allies. The notion of an attack on the American front seemed very real. And here was Pete, announcing his intention to leave her and the kids so he could do his bit to help the war effort.

He seemed awfully pigheaded about it.

But last August, when he'd been getting ready to report for duty, he'd left his half-packed suitcase on the bed to run a few errands. Nora had been putting some clean undershirts in the suitcase when she'd noticed that Pete had packed his rosary. Pete was a good Catholic. The family went to Mass at St. Joseph Parish Church every Sunday and holy day. But Pete wasn't a rosary guy. He usually kept the string of beads—behind his handkerchiefs, cufflinks and tie clasps—in the top drawer of his dresser. Nora had never seen him praying the rosary. She couldn't imagine Pete packing it for this trip—not unless he was afraid.

She slipped it back in the sleeve along the inside of his suitcase and told herself to pretend she'd never found it.

That same night before Pete was supposed to catch the train for the East Coast, neither one of them could fall asleep. They lay in bed, holding each other, not saying a word. But Nora must have drifted off, because she suddenly realized she was in bed alone. It was nearly three in the morning. Switching on the nightstand lamp, Nora climbed out of bed and threw on her robe. She navigated the darkened hallway and crept down the stairs. A faint light came from the back of the house, and she heard a strange, muffled sound. She realized it was Pete crying.

Nora froze. She'd seen Pete cry only once before—when his mom had died. His sobs so unnerved her that she froze. She cleared her throat before she padded into the kitchen—so he'd have a few moments to pull himself together.

She found him sitting at the breakfast table in the center of the kitchen. The room was dark except for the stove panel light. Pete was in his pajamas. He had a glass and a bottle of bourbon in front of him. He quickly wiped his red-rimmed eyes before he glanced up at her. He, too, cleared his throat.

"Couldn't sleep," he said, his voice cracking a little. "Guess I'm prematurely nervous in the service." He nodded at the half-full bottle. "You want a hit, honey?"

"Hell, yes," Nora sighed. Taking a jelly glass from the cupboard, she set it on the table and sat down next to him.

Neither one of them was a heavy drinker, so for her to see Pete down straight whiskey was startling. But Nora said nothing. He poured a little in her jelly glass, and they both drank in silence. Nora felt the bourbon burn the back of her throat. She glanced down and noticed him clutching the edge of the table. His always-steady surgeon's hand shook slightly.

She put her hand over his. "It's going to be okay, honey," she whispered.

Pete let out a rasp and started to cry again. "I'm scared," he admitted. "I keep thinking this is the last time I . . ." His voice trailed off as he wiped his eyes. Then he took a deep breath. "I remember this guy down at the end of my block when I was a kid. His name was Jimmy Costello, a good-looking guy, worked at his father's grocery store. Everybody liked him. Whenever I came into the store, he'd say, 'Kinney, think fast!' and lob a piece of penny candy in my direction. When Jimmy enlisted to go fight the Kaiser, his dad posted a photo of him looking all spiffy in his army uniform. He kept the picture by the cash register for everyone to see. Anyway, Jimmy Costello came back from the Great War blind from mustard gas. His handsome face was all messed up, and he was half out of his mind. He barely left the house. Any kind of loud noise would set him off. I tried to visit. I came by the house with a bag of penny candy for him. But his mother wouldn't let me see him. The neighborhood kids who didn't know him before he left teased the hell out of the poor guy. They thought it was hysterical, watching him go to pieces. They'd sneak up to his house and shoot off their cap guns outside the windows, the little bastards. That's what Jimmy got for defending his country. Eventually, his parents moved him to the state institution in Elgin. Anyway, I remember how Jimmy Costello came back from the Great War—and I can't help worrying the same thing will happen to me."

Nora shook her head. "But you won't be on the front lines, Pete," she said, rubbing his arm. "You said so yourself . . ."

He nodded and wiped his eyes again. "I know," he sighed. "I guess I'm just a coward."

"You're not a coward. You're scared. There's a difference." She reached up and smoothed back his disheveled dark brown hair. "In fact, you know just how dangerous this might be, you know about all the horrible things that can happen, and yet you're still catching that train in five hours. That makes you brave. And it makes me very proud of you, honey."

He let out a sad laugh and then swigged some more bourbon. "Yeah, well, I've never been so terrified in all my life. I'm worried about you and the kids, too. I know you'll be safe. But what if I come back from the war all messed up, and you have to take care of me? And while I'm gone, you'll have to sacrifice and budget to get by on my new salary . . ."

Nora smiled patiently and squeezed his hand. "We'll get along all right, Pete. And you'll be okay. But if you have another sip of booze, you'll be sick as a dog on that crowded train tomorrow . . ."

That had been eight months ago. And since then, Nora had reminded herself over and over that Pete wasn't a medic, thank God. He wasn't there on the front lines dodging bullets to aid fallen infantrymen. He was at a clearing station, miles behind the lines with a group of doctors and nurses, sewing up the wounded. But the Germans sometimes bombed those first aid stations—even though the Red Cross symbol was clearly displayed on top of the tents. They weren't as bad as the Japanese, who hadn't signed the Geneva Convention pact and apparently targeted those Red Cross signs. At least Pete wasn't dealing with malaria, jungle rot and all the other horrors the troops were suffering through in the Pacific. But he had to put up with snakes, scorpions, insects and the unbearable heat of the desert. She knew the work was exhausting, the conditions primitive, and they were in short supply of everything.

But Pete didn't complain in his always-cheerful letters—just as Nora didn't tell him about her own worries. She imagined him composing his missives in spurts—whenever he got a break from the stream of incoming wounded. She could picture him stealing a few minutes in some makeshift mess hall tent, hunched over a rickety table, scribbling away to her—and then, overhead, the sudden shriek of a descending projectile.

Every time the doorbell rang, Nora couldn't help thinking it might be the Western Union boy or some soldier in his dress blues bringing her the news that Pete had been killed.

As she lay there alone in the darkened bedroom, Nora wondered if Pete was already dead. He could have been killed a week ago, and she wouldn't know.

She heard whispering again. It came from outside—this time from in front of the house.

Jumping out of bed, Nora threw on her robe and grabbed the fireplace poker. She ran for the stairs, but before she was even halfway down the steps there was a loud pop—and the sound of shattering glass. Nora stopped dead.

Her heart racing, she stood frozen on the stairway. For a few moments, she couldn't breathe. She heard the footsteps of someone retreating and then a car engine. The blackout curtain over the window in the door blocked any view outside, and it was dark in the front hallway. She wasn't sure what the sound of breaking glass had been. Had someone hurled an empty bottle at the house?

Nora finally caught her breath and hurried down to the hallway. She headed for the front door to move aside the curtain. But then, she stepped on something sharp. She heard an awful crunch and felt glass shards cutting her bare feet. Only then did she realize one of the panes in the front door's window was shattered. "Goddamn it!" she muttered, wincing in pain.

She switched on the hallway's overhead light and saw the shards and blood on the floor—along with a medium-sized rock. She felt so stupid.

Moving back the curtain, Nora glanced out the smashed windowpane. Through the trees outside, she couldn't make out the car, but then she heard its tires screech against the pavement as the vehicle peeled away.

"Mom?"

Startled, she swiveled around to see Jane in her nightgown, standing near the bottom of the stairs.

Nora put a hand over her heart and caught her breath. "Don't come over here," she warned. "There's glass on the floor, honey. You need to put some shoes on. While you're upstairs, could you get me my slippers? And from the bathroom medicine chest, could you bring me the iodine?"

Wide-eyed, Jane stared at her. "You're bleeding . . ."

She nodded. "Yes, I know. Could you hurry, honey?"

Jane retreated back up the steps.

Nora managed to unlock and open the door without stepping on any more glass. The cold night air hit her. What she saw out there was like a punch in the stomach.

Blotches of fresh red paint made a trail from the door's threshold along the porch floor to the walkway. And a message was painted across the front door: JAP-LOVER.

In their robes and slippers, Nora and her daughter cleaned up the mess. As Nora used the garden hose to wash the fresh paint off the porch, the watery red puddles reminded her of blood.

Jane idly wiped a rag over the water-beaded front door. "On Saturday, Ruthie McNally found out that her older brother, Mike, was killed in New Guinea," she remarked.

Nora glanced up from her work for a moment. "Oh, no, poor Mrs. McNally," she sighed. Then she went back to hosing down the porch floor. The McNallys had a boy in Chris's class, too.

*That explains it*, she thought. Her sympathy for the boy and his family was tinged with anger and frustration.

The neighbors—and, for some reason, the kids in Chris's high school—all seemed to know that the Kinneys had rented out their garage apartment to a Japanese-American couple for a few years. A general contempt for the Japanese had begun to take hold back in 1937, after Japan's invasion of China, with stories of atrocities—including rape, torture and mutilation. In the city of Nanking, estimates of the number of men, women and children slaughtered were as high as three hundred thousand.

Pete had had some serious misgivings about renting the one-bedroom apartment to Takashi and Fumiko Hara. But Nora had pointed out that the Haras were Americans. They'd never even been to Japan. In fact, Miko didn't know how to speak Japanese—except for a few phrases she'd picked up as a child listening to her parents. Nora had persuaded Pete to give the young couple a two-month trial run. She'd had a good feeling about them.

They'd turned out to be ideal tenants. Tak worked as a fruit and vegetable supplier and traveled all over the state. He was away every other week. Miko was the office manager and accountant for a boiler repair company. They weren't the only Japanese-Americans on the block.

At the far end of the street was a gated mansion. Its owner, a ninety-year-old widow, Mrs. Landauer, had a nurse-housekeeper named Sono Nakai, who was Japanese-American. Sono and her teenage daughter lived on the premises. No one objected to them. And after a while, most of the neighbors seemed to accept Tak and Miko, too.

But Pearl Harbor changed everything. Somehow, it got around—beyond just their block—that the Kinneys were "harboring Japs." In the predawn hours of Tuesday, December 9, Nora and Pete were awakened by a loud screech, and then a bang. After all the war news, Nora's first thought was that they were under attack. But then she realized the ensuing clatter was coming from the backyard. And she heard someone yell out, "Eat shit, Japs!"

Tak and Miko's trellis had been torn down and smashed to pieces. DIE JAPS! was painted on the garage door. A can of Dutch Boy had been kicked over, and red paint had spilled across the driveway in front of the garage apartment's entrance.

Tak and Miko had been terrorized. Fortunately, they'd remained inside the apartment throughout the incident.

That had been the start of the sporadic nighttime ambushes. Over the next few weeks, rocks were hurled through the Haras' windows and more messages of hate—often obscene—were scrawled on the garage in paint or chalk. Their garbage cans rarely made it through a week without getting knocked over. And every few nights, Nora could count on a car coming to a screeching halt in front of the driveway, and someone screaming out obscenities or *"Japs, go home!"*

Because of the blackout, Nora couldn't turn on the outside lights at night. So these "patriotic" vandals continued to harass the Haras under the cloak of darkness.

In mid-January, without explanation, a couple of government men took Tak into custody during one of his business trips. They nabbed him at an apple farm outside Wenatchee. Pete tried to look into why they'd taken him, but he got stonewalled. Eventually, he found out that Tak was being detained "as a precaution" at a temporary holding center in Puyallup, south of Seattle. They didn't give any other explanation.

Miko was frantic. She privately asked Nora to hide a couple of big photo albums and some family keepsakes—a couple of geisha figurines, a Hakata clay doll of an old peasant man, and a few other antiques. Many of Tak and Miko's Japanese-American friends were burning their mementos—anything that tied them to Japan. But Miko couldn't destroy these treasured family keepsakes. Nora put everything in a box and stashed it in the attic, behind the Christmas decorations. Yet she couldn't help feeling conflicted about it. In helping her friend, was she being unpatriotic?

The following day, when Nora was the only one home, two men identifying themselves as "U.S. Marshals" came by with a search warrant. They combed through the garage apartment, tagging and confiscating several items—including a tea set and a pair of bookends that appeared "oriental" to them, some maps, letters, a telescope and several books. Helpless, Nora stood by, watching them.

Tak and Miko weren't the only ones being persecuted. Down at the end of the block, the lampposts were broken and anti-Japanese signs were hung from Mrs. Landauer's front gate. Then Nora heard that the old woman had dismissed her live-in, Japanese-American nurse-housekeeper, and eventually, the harassment stopped—for her, at least.

In February, Miko had to report to King Street Train Station for "relocation." She'd been instructed to bring only as much as she could carry. Hoping she wouldn't be gone too long, Miko gave Nora four months' rent in advance. Nora promised to hold the apartment and their furniture for them.

Nora's heart broke for Miko. At the same time, she felt a tiny bit of relief that Miko's departure might bring them some peace—and she hated herself for it. Pete boarded up the apartment's windows and entrance—so people could see that the place was no longer occupied.

Miko and Tak were reunited at a holding center and then eventually sent to an "internment" camp in Idaho.

Though it had been over a year, Nora kept the garage apartment vacant for Miko and Tak. But the place continued to be vandalized. Then, last May, after Corregidor fell, someone came by at night and destroyed all the flowers Miko had planted in front of the house. The garden had been in full bloom—at the height of its dazzling beauty.

Once Pete joined the Army Medical Corps, word must have gotten around that the man of the house wasn't in. The blue star flag in the window was a dead giveaway, of course. So now the Kinneys' house was targeted, too. Whenever there was a decisive Japanese victory or someone—a neighbor or, in particular, one of Chris's classmates—lost a relative in the Pacific campaign, Nora could almost count on an unwanted visit in the dead of night.

This was the third broken window—and the second painted message—since the beginning of the year.

As Nora put away the garden hose, she figured the only way to discourage the vandals would be to rent the garage apartment again—to someone white. And then the Kinneys would be doing their part to fight the housing shortage in Seattle. Due to the influx of wartime workers at Boeing and the shipyards, apartments were scarce.

Nora reasoned they could use the extra money, too. It seemed pointless to hold the place for the Haras. The last time Miko had written her was in December. The prisoners in the camp had managed to improve conditions there and "make the best of it." They even had a small Christmas tree in the recreation hall. Nora remembered telling Jane about it. And she recalled her daughter's puzzled look. "I know Tak and Miko celebrated Christmas with us," she'd said. "But I didn't know they celebrated it in Japan."

"But they're Americans, honey," Nora had told her. "All the people in those camps are American."

With some cardboard and masking tape, she and Jane patched up the small windowpane in the front door. It was nearly two in the morning by the time they finished up and wearily headed upstairs to their bedrooms.

As she was about to sink into her bed, something occurred to Nora. How had Chris managed to sleep through everything that had happened in the past couple of hours?

She padded down the hallway to his room and checked in on him again.

Nora saw the same lump under his bedcovers. Uncertain, she crept around to the other side of his bed. One look from this angle, and she realized he'd stacked some clothes and an extra pillow under the covers in his place.

Nora had no idea when he'd snuck out or where he could have gone.

# Chapter 2

She wasn't the kind of girl who would go home with some guy she'd just met. But Jo Ellen Bryant had been willing to make an exception for the ensign. He was so handsome in his khaki uniform. He looked like Errol Flynn—right down to his rakish smile and the thin mustache. Were officers even allowed to have mustaches in the navy? Jo Ellen wasn't sure. She just knew that she'd been on the receiving end of that charismatic smile a few times earlier in the evening—even though it had come to her from across the crowded bar. She wasn't about to leave until she got a chance to talk to the man.

Jo Ellen was twenty-two, short and curvy with a cute, dimpled smile and wavy brown hair. She'd come to the J&M Café with her twenty-year-old sister, Loretta. The Bryant girls had grown up on their family's chicken farm in Prairie Grove, Arkansas, where driving twenty minutes to Fayetteville to mingle with college boys at the University of Arkansas had been about as good as it could get. Jo Ellen had considered the local boys backward hicks and had yearned to get out of Prairie Grove.

After a painful breakup with one of those college boys, Jo Ellen had realized that, while she was too good for the guys in Prairie Grove, she obviously wasn't good enough for those stuck-up college boys in Fayetteville.

When the war had broken out, Jo Ellen had looked into getting a job in a war plant, but Arkansas paid lower industrial wages than most other states, so Jo Ellen had convinced her kid sister that they should move to Seattle and work for Boeing. She'd gotten the idea from Bruce, the rat who had unceremoniously dumped her. He'd talked about joining the air corps after graduation and flying the B-17s Boeing manufactured.

The sisters were machinists in the wing section assembly at Boeing. At quitting time, they'd take the bus back to their one-bedroom apartment in Belltown, a working-class neighborhood just north of downtown. For their nights on the town, they'd change out of their work clothes and get dolled up. Painting their legs became part of this ritual now that silk and nylon were used to make parachutes instead of stockings. Jo and Lo (as they were often called back in Prairie Grove) would take turns meticulously drawing the fake seam lines down the backs of each other's legs with eyeliner pencil to simulate nylons. Their wardrobe was limited, but the sisters were both the same size, so they weren't forced to wear the same dresses over and over.

Unless one of them had an actual date, Jo and Lo always went out together. Unaccompanied women in bars could be hauled into the police station and held overnight—just because they *might* be hookers or Allotment Annies. As far as Jo Ellen was concerned, those Allotment Annies were too low for the snakes. They would scam soldiers into an engagement or marriage in order to get the serviceman's allotment money—sometimes scamming several soldiers at a time. The cops were also trying to curb the spread of syphilis and gonorrhea, and it was clear from the posters aimed at GIs that women were blamed for spreading it. Jo Ellen had seen a few of the posters—by the men's room doors in the backs of bars. They pictured normal-looking women—girls out for a good time—with warnings plastered below their likenesses: *She May Look Clean, BUT . . .* or *Don't Take Chances with Pickups! VD is not Victory!* Jo Ellen thought it was so unfair. As if horny drunk servicemen had nothing to do with the VD epidemic. But the local cops weren't dragging horny drunk servicemen out of bars and detaining them. That humiliation was reserved for unaccompanied women. Sometimes the women were even held and tested for venereal diseases. Fortunately, such a thing hadn't happened to either of the Bryant sisters yet.

Jo and Lo had arrived at the J&M Café together. The place was packed for a Sunday night, but the sisters managed to find a table for two in the corner of the bar. A lot of the customers were sailors, which meant the girls would be dodging passes all night—Loretta, especially. If Jo Ellen weren't there running interference for her kid sister, Loretta would have gone home with the first schmuck in white pants to buy her a drink. Loretta was prettier than she was and absolutely radiated Southern farm girl naïveté, which was like catnip for the servicemen.

Jo Ellen's standards were a lot higher than her sister's. She had a thing for guys in uniform, but if the guy wasn't a gentleman, he could go run up a tree as far as Jo Ellen was concerned.

The handsome ensign over by the window, deep in conversation with an older couple, struck her as the gentlemanly type. It was silly, but Jo Ellen imagined him kissing her hand at the end of their first date—and then sending her flowers when he asked her out again. She could tell his friends were classy, because the woman wore an expensive-looking hat with a net covering half her face, and they were drinking something in old-fashioned glasses. Every once in a while, Ensign Errol would sneak a glance past the couple and give her that captivating smile. And he was smiling at her—not at Loretta—which was a welcome change.

Maybe that was why Loretta wanted to go home.

"But we can't leave now," Jo Ellen argued. "I'm just starting to get somewhere with The Ensign!"

"Well, maybe he's waiting for me to leave before he makes his move," Loretta pointed out. She set a dollar down on the table. "Why don't you stay? Don't worry 'bout me. I'll be fine walking home alone." She stood up, and nearly every sailor in the vicinity turned his head.

Jo Ellen sometimes felt invisible next to her voluptuous, strawberry-blond sister. Maybe she'd have a better shot with the ensign if her sweet sister wasn't in the picture. "You sure you'll be okay?" Jo Ellen asked half-heartedly.

"Fine as frog's hair—as Grandpa used to say," Loretta replied with a smile and a little wave. She turned and sauntered toward the door.

Jo Ellen noticed her sizing up the ensign. Her sister glanced back at her. Wide-eyed, Loretta gave a little nod of approval and fanned herself as if she were overheated.

Jo Ellen giggled. Then she caught the ensign looking at her again. Jo Ellen smiled at him.

She heard someone clear his throat. "I bet my buddy earlier that you and the gal who just left are sisters . . ."

Jo Ellen turned to see a sailor standing at her side. He was no Errol Flynn. He looked about twenty-five and was lanky with a big nose and a weak chin.

"Well?" he asked. "Am I right? Was she your sister?"

Frowning, Jo Ellen shook her head. "No, she's my mother."

He laughed and then pulled out the chair Loretta had just vacated. "Well, since Mama's gone, maybe you'll let me sit with you and buy you a drink."

She shook her head again.

"You don't want to be sitting all by yourself . . ."

Jo Ellen stole a glance at the ensign, hoping he might notice that this guy was bothering her. Maybe he'd come to her rescue. He seemed like the chivalrous type.

But he wasn't looking her way.

And in that moment while Jo Ellen was distracted, the sailor sat down in Loretta's seat. "C'mon, wet your whistle with me," he said. He waved at the waitress.

Jo Ellen rolled her eyes. She was about to tell him to get lost. But then she figured maybe there was still a chance Ensign Errol would rescue her—if she gave just the right distressed look. Or maybe this sailor and the ensign were from the same ship. Maybe they knew each other.

A skinny, bored-looking waitress approached their table. "What'll you folks have?"

The sailor nudged Jo Ellen's arm. "I'm having a beer. How about you?"

Jo Ellen sighed. "Okay, I'll have a ginger ale, but just one. Then you'll have to go."

That was all the encouragement he needed. He gave the waitress their drink orders and then proceeded to talk Jo Ellen's ear off. She was only half listening. The bar was noisy, and she couldn't always hear him very well anyway. Their drinks arrived, and he raised his beer glass in a toast. "What's your name anyway?"

Jo Ellen told him.

He bumped his knee against hers. "And where did *y'all* get that cute Southern accent, Jo Ellen?" he asked coyly.

"From the South," she answered, moving her legs so that she was almost turned away from him. "Listen, there's an ensign over by the window, the one talking to that well-dressed couple. I think I may have met him before. Do y'all know him by any chance? He wasn't on your ship, was he?"

Sitting up straight, the sailor squinted toward the window. "Where?"

"Well, don't be so obvious!" she whispered, looking down at her drink.

"Who are you talking about—the guy who's leaving?"

Jo Ellen glanced over in time to see Ensign Errol stepping out the door with his friends.

Her heart sank.

"I don't think he's from my ship," the sailor said. "I didn't recognize him. But say, you're pretty good. You could tell he was an ensign from his uniform . . ."

The sailor kept talking while on the jukebox Dinah Shore sang "Blues in the Night." Jo Ellen couldn't help thinking, *How appropriate, how damn appropriate.* She felt so defeated, rejected before she'd even gotten a chance to say hello to her dreamy ensign. It was typical of her rotten luck. Or maybe she was just stupid.

Things hadn't changed much since she'd left the farm in Prairie Grove. She was still aiming too high, going for guys who were above her class. She pinned her hopes on ensigns when she should have settled for sailors—like this guy sitting with her. She told herself that he really wasn't bad-looking. At some point in the mostly one-sided conversation, he'd told her his name, but she had no idea what it was. He'd also mentioned where he was from—Wisconsin or Nebraska or one of those places. As nice and attentive as the guy was, Jo Ellen still wasn't interested in him. All she could think about was the handsome ensign who had slipped away.

The sailor chugged down his beer before Jo Ellen was half-way done with her ginger ale. He waved at the waitress again.

Jo Ellen didn't want to stick around and watch him get drunk. "Well, it's been nice, but I have work in the morning," she sighed. Then she got to her feet. "Thank you for the drink, sailor. You take care of yourself."

"You can't leave now," he argued. "We're just getting to know each other."

But Jo Ellen put on her coat. "Bye, now."

"Wait a minute . . ." He slapped a dollar and some change on the table.

Jo Ellen headed to the door and stepped outside. It was chilly out, and she stopped to pull up her coat collar.

The door opened behind her. "Wait a minute," the sailor said again. "How are you getting home?"

"My own two feet," she answered. "I live only a few blocks away."

"Well, let me walk you," the sailor insisted, throwing on his pea jacket. "It isn't safe for a pretty gal to be walking by herself along the waterfront at this hour. There's no telling what kind of trouble's waiting for you between here and your front door."

Jo Ellen gave him a skeptical sidelong gaze. The Elliott Bay waterfront was actually two blocks downhill to the west, and it was indeed sketchy, especially now, during the blackout. Though there were plenty of people out at this hour, a lot of them were drunken servicemen up to no good. She'd walked home alone late at night before—from this bar and others. And it could be a little scary. Plus, she was feeling especially lonely and vulnerable all of a sudden.

"C'mon, what do you say?" The sailor nudged her. "Let me be your naval escort home."

Jo Ellen worked up a smile. "All right, but you can't come in. My sister's probably already asleep."

"I thought she was your mother."

Despite her blue mood, Jo Ellen laughed. As they started walking down the street, he put his arm around her waist.

She pulled away and kept moving forward. "I said y'all could walk me home. I didn't say you could maul me . . ."

"Sorry," he muttered. The sailor shoved his hands in the pockets of his pea jacket and continued to walk alongside her.

They headed down the busy sidewalk together. To her left, Jo Ellen could see the silhouettes of the buildings along the waterfront and, between them, slivers of moonlight dancing on the indigo water of Elliott Bay. But just half a block down the hill, the area seemed completely deserted. It wasn't, though. She knew people were walking and going about their business down there—just as they were up here along First Avenue—but she couldn't see them because of the blackout.

She probably didn't need this sailor walking her home. Jo Ellen noticed a cop on horseback up ahead. She and the sailor passed other sailors, soldiers and civilians on the sidewalks—a few of them drunk to the point of staggering. On the street, people riding bikes outnumbered the cars, due to gas rationing. The few automobiles cruising down First Avenue had blue cellophane over the headlights—in compliance with blackout regulations. Some bar owners weren't as conscientious, and they left their colored neon signs on. Competing swing and jazz music echoed out the various open doors. The music plus the chatter, laughter and shouting from people on the street created a cacophony of noise. Jo Ellen figured she'd have been miserable walking home alone amid this hubbub, amid all these people who were drunk, happy or paired up with someone else. She felt grateful to have this dogface sailor distracting her—even if she was only half listening to him.

As Jo Ellen and her "naval escort" got closer to her home, the crowd of pedestrians thinned out and the noise died down. The sailor didn't try to put his arm around her again. But Jo Ellen felt him brush against her several times—his hand, arm and shoulder grazing hers. She figured, once they reached her front door, he'd try to smooth talk his way inside.

Jo Ellen and Loretta lived in a U-shaped Spanish-style two-story apartment building with a courtyard. Each unit had its own front and back entrance. The place was rundown, but cheap.

As Jo Ellen and the sailor turned into the courtyard, she noticed the window shades and blackout curtains for her unit were drawn. The sailor brought his hand up between her shoulder blades. "Wow, you live here? This is really nice . . ."

She got her key out of her purse. "Well, like I said earlier, I'm sorry I can't invite you inside. I'm sure my sister's asleep upstairs."

"Her bedroom's upstairs?"

"It's my bedroom, too. We share." Jo Ellen keyed the front door, but it was unlocked.

"Listen, if your sister's bedroom is all the way upstairs, and I promise to be as quiet as a little church mouse, do you think I could come in for a cup of coffee?" He still had his hand on her back.

Jo Ellen turned toward him, brushing his arm away. His hand fell to his side. "I told you already, sailor. My place is off-limits . . ."

He gave her a hurt puppy-dog look. "C'mon, please?" he whispered. "For the last seven months, I've only seen the insides of boats, barracks and bars. I haven't been in a real home since I left Indiana. I'd give anything to sit down in somebody's kitchen and drink a cup of coffee. I know it sounds like a bunch of corn, but I'm homesick and lonely. I think you are, too. Don't you miss your home in the South?"

Jo Ellen shook her head. "Not at all."

"Please? Just one cup of coffee for a lonely sailor . . ."

She was about to open the door, but hesitated. She wished she knew his name at least.

"I ship out tomorrow." He took hold of her hand and checked her wristwatch. "Or today, rather. I'm sorry I can't tell you where I'm headed—"

"Probably San Francisco or someplace like that."

He didn't let go of her hand. "Please, Jo Ellen, just one cup of coffee, and then I'll go . . ."

She pulled away and sighed. "All right, one cup. But we don't have any sugar."

Jo Ellen opened the door. From the foyer, she saw that Loretta had left the living room light on—along with the light in the upstairs hallway. "Lo, are you still up?" she called softly from the bottom of the stairs.

"Well, don't wake her," the sailor whispered. "Three's a crowd . . ."

A loud clatter came from the kitchen. Alarmed, Jo Ellen froze for a moment. Then she hurried past the stairs and down the hall, toward the back of the apartment. The sailor followed her.

"Lo? Is that you?" she called, a hand on her heart. "You okay? What happened?"

Jo Ellen stepped into the kitchen in time to see the screen door slam. A kitchen chair and a bottle of milk had been knocked over. The unbroken bottle was still rolling back and forth in a milk puddle on the gray and red checked linoleum floor—in front of the open refrigerator. On the kitchen table was a piece of cake on a napkin. Loretta had baked the cake last night, some kind of no sugar, no butter, no eggs "Victory Cake."

All Jo Ellen could imagine was that Loretta must have brought someone home. And in the middle of helping himself to a snack, the guy must have taken off like a bat out of hell when he'd heard her come in. Maybe Loretta had told him how much of an ogre her older sister could be when it came to her bringing strangers home.

The sailor chuckled, "Looks like we didn't wake up Little Sister after all."

"We talked about this just the other night," Jo Ellen murmured. "And we agreed. That's why you're not staying . . ." She headed down the hall to the foot of the stairs. She couldn't believe her naïve sister had left some stranger unattended in the house—even if only for a minute or two. "Lo!" she called—louder this time. "Loretta, are you upstairs?"

The sailor trailed after her. Jo Ellen didn't want him following her up to the bedroom. She briefly turned to him. "Stay down here, will you?" She didn't wait for an answer. She scurried up the stairs.

In the second-floor hallway, Jo Ellen found Loretta's work pants hanging from the doorknob to the half-open bedroom door. She stopped for a second. It was strange, because Loretta had hung her work slacks in the closet before they'd changed into their dresses earlier tonight.

Jo Ellen opened the door wider and saw her sister sprawled on the bedroom floor. Loretta wore only her panties and blouse. Her blue eyes were open in a dead stare, and her face was discolored. A small lamp from the nightstand between the twin beds was broken and lying beside her. Someone had used the lamp cord to strangle her little sister.

That same someone had then gone down to the kitchen and made himself a snack.

# Chapter 3

*Monday, April 5*
*10:28 a.m.*

"Okay now, so what are those?" the short, thirtyish man asked, shouting in her ear over all the noise. He pointed at the airplane's tail.

Squinting through her work goggles, which were so tight they gave her a headache, Nora studied the long copper studs that stuck out from the neat row of rivet holes along the tail's edge. They looked like rifle cartridges. She knew they were temporary holders for the airplane's outer skin. She would remove the cartridge-like pins before inserting the rivets. She'd learned about them in the orientation class on Friday—and again this morning—but the name of the damn things had slipped her mind for the moment. She pointed at them with the riveting gun, which had become oppressively heavy in her thick-gloved hand. "You mean those thingamajigs?" she asked, pointing to the pins.

"Ha! What a birdbrain!" the man laughed. "Yeah, honey, *those thingamajigs!*"

Nora stared at him. *Oh, give me a break*, she wanted to say. But then, giving her a break would have interfered with his mission to make the new girl feel like an idiot.

His name was Larry Krull, and he was training her this morning. At first, Nora had thought the dark-haired, swarthy-looking man seemed like a nice enough guy. She'd even found him attractive—even though he was a few inches shorter than her and kind of puny. But then she'd noticed Larry walked with a cocky swagger and never really smiled at her. He just smirked or sneered. And after a couple of hours with Larry barking instructions at her and criticizing her every move, Nora absolutely loathed him.

Larry had a work partner—a big, blond-haired oaf named Don, who was the bucker. He stood on the other side of the airplane's tail with a bucking bar in his hand. The bar was a piece of steel about the size of a big box of safety matches. Nora was supposed to insert the rivet into the rivet hole, press the gun to the rivet's dome head, and squeeze the trigger. Don would hold the bucking bar in place to flatten the rivet on his side. Nora had to be careful not to press the gun too hard against the rivet head; otherwise, she could dent the airplane's skin.

She hadn't yet put in a rivet by herself. She always had Larry on her back, practically grinding his slight, wiry body against her as he held her arms in place. They stood on a metal scaffolding ten feet above the floor of the vast assembly line, the fuselage and tail section of a B-17 in front of them.

From this viewpoint, Nora could see practically the entire shop. It was enormous—like five football fields under one roof. A huge American flag was suspended from the cross-beamed ceiling at one end. Nora couldn't make out anything at the other end of the shop; it was too far away. Between there and where she stood were rows and rows of plane fuselages and tail assemblies encircled by scaffolding. Big steel frames on wheels held engines or wings.

Busily hovering around each airplane section were armies of workers in coveralls, thick gloves, and goggles or face shields. The women wore hairnets—or bandanas like Nora. And everyone had a security badge. The massive shop smelled like smoke, electricity and sweat. There was so much going on—plane engines dangling and moving from cranes overhead, sparks flying from welding tools at every other station, people continually on the go—and all of it in sync. Nora tried not to get distracted. Half the time, she couldn't hear Larry—what with all the forklifts, drills and other machinery churning. It was even worse whenever Nora squeezed the trigger of her rivet gun. The searing blast actually hurt her ears.

"Hey, Don, did you hear that?" Larry shouted, with his hand lingering on Nora's hip. He kept pawing at her—in the guise of showing her how to hold and work the gun. "The plant's going to hell with all these stupid broads coming to work here. But at least, with this one, she's improving the looks of the place—and good for a laugh or two! *Thingamajigs!*"

The other man laughed. It was the cackle of a moron—or a bully, or both. Don obviously thought Larry was the epitome of cool. He nodded enthusiastically or laughed at just about everything Larry said.

"*Thingamajigs*, yeah, that's what they are, lady," Larry went on. He turned to Don. "She's never going to get it! I'd have an easier time teaching a monkey to do this work!"

"Yeah, as long as it's not a *lady* monkey, right, Larry?" Don seemed to think this a pretty damn clever remark.

Larry let out a laugh.

Nora felt her face getting hotter and hotter. The pipsqueak son of a bitch still had his hand on her hip. She wanted to kick herself for saying *thingamajigs*. How did she expect these creeps to take her seriously when she used words from Jane's vocabulary? Swallowing hard, she stared back at Larry and pivoted her body to brush his hand away.

This seemed to agitate him. "Maybe you should go back to your kitchen and start wearing a skirt again, honey—along with an apron. Stick to your cooking and knitting." He plucked one of the copper-colored studs from the plane's tail and shook it in her face. "If you can't even remember the name of this thing—"

"It's a cleco pin," Nora heard herself say. Then she yelled it: "They're called clecos!"

There was a crack in her voice. Nora told herself not to cry. For starters, she had goggles on. But more important, she didn't want to give Larry and Don the satisfaction of seeing her break down.

Yet she was at the end of her rope. Her foot hurt from cutting it on the window glass last night, and she'd been doing her damnedest not to limp all morning. She didn't want anyone thinking she was unfit for work on her first day. The damn riveting gun scared her, too, and not just the deafening noise it made. She was terrified the thing would slip out of her grasp and hurt someone or wreck something vital to the war effort. A part of her wondered if these two bullies assigned to train her were actually right. Would she ever get the hang of this?

She took a deep breath and looked squarely at Larry. "Would it be okay with you if I actually tried to do some riveting on my own? I think I can do it better if I didn't have someone crowding me and screaming at me the whole time. Could you let me do a couple?"

Stepping back, Larry gave a mock bow and handed her a rivet. "Why, yes, milady. Please, go ahead, and please, try not to put a dimple in the skin of the goddamn plane."

Don laughed again.

Bracing herself, Nora did her best to keep from shaking as she inserted the rivet in the hole and pressed the gun to the rivet's dome head. Squeezing the trigger, she managed not to flinch when the gun let out the earsplitting noise.

"How's that looking, Don?" Larry yelled.

His friend took away the bucking bar on his side of the tail, and then he inspected the results of her work. He looked disappointed. "It's all right, I guess," he replied.

Larry gave her shoulder a condescending pat. "Well, good for you, honey. You actually managed not to screw it up. Go ahead and try another . . ."

*I'll show him*, Nora thought. She inserted a rivet through the next hole down along the edge of the B-17's tail. Then she applied the gun to the rivet's dome head and squeezed the trigger again. It wasn't rocket science. These two clowns training her probably wanted to make the work seem a lot more complicated than it was.

She did another, and another, and then another. If this was all there was to it and the extent of what she'd be doing for eight hours every day, the job promised to be repetitive and dull. The instructor in her orientation class on Friday had said, "You gals are good at mindless, monotonous tasks—which makes you perfect for this type of work." He hadn't seemed to realize how insulting that had been to a roomful of women. Nora figured half the men in this place resented having females join their ranks. The two jerks training her certainly seemed determined to make her life miserable.

Nora wondered if every day would be this awful.

Then again, she was dead tired and that made everything seem bleak. She'd gotten less than three hours of sleep last night—thanks to the hellions who had vandalized her house, and thanks to her missing son.

After finding his bed empty, Nora had waited up for Chris to come home. She'd sat at the kitchen table and tried to read *Kings Row*. But she'd spent more time looking at the stove clock and getting up to glance out the front window every few minutes. She'd investigated each little noise, wondering if it was Chris or perhaps those hoodlums back to break another window. One minute she would be furious at Chris for disappearing, and the next, she'd be worried that something awful had happened to him. *Of all nights for Chris to sneak out of the house.* Nora kept thinking how, in just a few hours, she needed to be up and alert for her first day of work. She waited an hour and a half—until she finally heard footsteps outside the house.

Someone was coming around to the kitchen entrance. Nora prayed it was Chris. Because of the blackout curtains, he couldn't have seen that the kitchen light was on. Nora heard the key in the back door, and then it opened—as far as the chain lock allowed.

"Oh, shit," she heard him mutter.

Nora got to her feet, unfastened the chain lock and swung the door open.

Chris froze at the threshold. He wore his jacket open—over a dark sweater and jeans. He was slightly out of breath, and his wavy light brown hair was unkempt. Her son stood six feet tall, but he had a sweet, boyish face, which, at times, made him look like a lost lamb.

"Mom . . . what are you doing up?" he whispered.

"Waiting for you!" she hissed. "Do you know what time it is? Where in God's name have you been?"

"I . . . I couldn't sleep, so I went out for a little walk," he said.

"Seriously? You expect me to believe that? What do you take me for?" She opened the door wider. "Get in here . . ."

Stepping inside, Chris looked at the kitchen floor instead of her.

Nora closed the door and locked it. "You might be interested to know that while you were out gallivanting God-knows-where, we were vandalized again . . ."

At last, he looked at her, his brown eyes wide with concern. "Oh, no, what happened?"

"See for yourself," she said.

Marching him to the front of the house, Nora showed Chris the hastily patched-up broken windowpane in the door—as if what had happened was his fault. Keeping her voice down so as not to wake Jane, she told him how he'd left her and his little sister all alone while some thugs—probably classmates of his— had damaged and defaced their home. His father had entrusted him to be the man of the house in his absence. Was that a mistake? His dad was risking his life in North Africa, and how disappointed he'd be in him right now. Nora knew she was laying it on thick, but she was furious. She also drove home the fact that she was reporting for her first day of work in four hours— and he'd chosen that night to sneak out of the house. And then he'd lied to her about where he was. "Your school chums broke that window two and a half hours ago, and you weren't here. So don't give me this story about going out for a *little walk*. Where were you?"

"They're not my chums," Chris murmured, looking down at the floor again. "I really don't know for sure who's been doing all this stuff."

"All right, but where were you? I was worried sick . . ."

"I went out with Earl," he confessed quietly. "He borrowed his dad's Studebaker . . ."

"Oh, God," she grumbled. She couldn't stand his friend Earl McAllister. "What for? Exactly what was this pressing engagement you had at one o'clock in the morning on a school night?"

"Earl heard that a fleet of battleships was coming into the Naval Supply Depot at Smith Cove on Elliott Bay—y'know, by Interbay? Anyway, we wanted to see all the battleships."

Crossing her arms, Nora sighed in resignation. "Well, it's so good to know that you and your buddies are helping the war effort by not discussing troop movements and the like. That's just swell. Don't they have security guards posted all around that facility? How did you and Earl expect to get anywhere near there?"

Chris shrugged. "We ended up driving to a park in Magnolia. It had a good view of the bay, and we watched from there. Turned out to be only one battleship, and it wasn't all that spectacular. Anyway, I'm sorry, Mom. I figured if I snuck out, you wouldn't miss me. You could sleep and not even know I was gone. I didn't count on us getting vandalized tonight. And I didn't want to miss the battleships. Earl swore a whole fleet was coming in."

"That's what you get for listening to wartime rumors," Nora said. She shook her head and pointed to the stairs. "All right, just go to bed. I can't even look at you anymore, I'm so upset."

"I'm really sorry, Mom," he whispered—with his lost-lamb expression.

"Just go," she said, turning away from him.

Chris meekly headed up the stairs.

Nora returned to the kitchen and switched off the light. Then she went to switch off the light in the family room. Beside the lamp on the end table was a pair of binoculars that belonged to Pete. With the constant fear of invasion, she and the kids were always using the binoculars to look up at the skies—or out at the water.

Nora switched off the lamp, but she stared at the binoculars for another moment. Then she glanced toward the stairs. If Chris had snuck out to watch a fleet of battleships, wouldn't he have brought along the binoculars? Or hadn't it crossed his mind that he might need them?

Nora was too tired to analyze it. She left on the front hall light and wearily climbed the stairs. But despite her exhaustion, she was too keyed up to fall asleep. She must have tossed and turned for an hour before finally dozing off.

It was still dark out when Nora left in the morning to catch the bus. She usually woke the kids and made breakfast for them before they headed to school, but they were on their own today. She thought about that as she rode the crowded bus to the Boeing plant by the Duwamish River south of Seattle. She had her purse and her new lunchbox in her lap. She'd heard mixed reviews about the cafeteria food at Boeing, so she'd made lunch for herself last night and stuck it in the refrigerator. It had been one of the many things on her mental checklist in preparation for today. The kids were covered as far as lunch was concerned because they got hot lunches at school. And they both had keys to get back inside the house—in case she was delayed getting home. But she worried about them sleeping past their alarms without her there to wake them at seven fifteen—especially Chris, who'd been out half the night.

At work all morning, Nora had tried to stay focused on the new job. But she was worried about Chris, wondering if he'd told her the truth about sneaking out last night to watch a fleet of battleships. He'd probably just forgotten to bring along the binoculars. Or maybe Earl had brought a pair. Why would Chris lie about where he'd been?

"Hey, slow down, for Christ's sake!"

Nora froze and then eased her finger off the trigger of the riveting gun. She'd lost track of how many rivets she'd drilled into the plane's tail. But she was suddenly aware of Larry hovering behind her, barking in her ear.

"You're going off half-cocked," he yelled. "Pay attention to what you're doing—and to what Don's doing! You need to keep pace with your bucker! Were you asleep during training class? That's one of the first things they teach . . ."

"Sorry!" Nora said, wincing. She could see Don was annoyed with her, too—not that it was anything new; still, now, as her bucker, he had a legitimate reason to be upset. Nora didn't glance over her shoulder at Larry. But she still felt his hot breath—and a little bit of spit—on her ear and the back of her neck.

"Keep your mind on your work!" he yelled.

She nodded wearily.

A shrill bell rang. Nora wasn't sure what was happening.

"That's lunch," Larry said. He held out his gloved hand. "Here, give me the gun before you hurt yourself with it. You got forty-five minutes. Try not to get lost on your way back here."

Biting her lip, Nora carefully set the riveting gun in his hand. Then she started toward the scaffolding's stairs. She felt so tired and defeated. Taking off her gloves and tucking them under her arm, she rubbed her right hand. It was sore from holding the rivet gun for the past two hours.

Standing near the scaffolding's steps was an older man with kind eyes and a splotchy complexion. His name, *Ned*, was sewn on his work shirt—right by his plant badge. "First day on the job?" he asked.

She nodded glumly. "How could you tell?"

"Don't worry, it'll get better," he said with a fatherly smile. "Too bad some of these guys can't remember how tough it was for them on their first day. Maybe then, they'd be a little kinder." He patted her arm. "There, now, you keep your chin up, okay?"

Nora stared at him. She wasn't sure if she wanted to hug him or cry. "Thank you," she said with a tremor in her voice.

Then she hurried down the scaffolding's grated steps.

Nora had thought, with the staggered lunch breaks and a cafeteria that sat sixteen hundred, she'd be able to find a spot to eat. But for the last ten minutes, she'd been wandering around in the vast, crowded canteen, looking for a vacancy among the four-top tables. That was in addition to however long she'd waited in line for a cup of coffee. The coffee was probably cold by now. Some of it had spilled onto the saucer as she tried to keep from bumping into people. Her hand was also a bit shaky from operating the riveting gun. She held her lunchbox in her other hand.

Every time Nora saw an empty chair and zeroed in on it, inevitably someone at the table would tell her the seat was saved for a friend. A few of them were even hostile about it. The ones who really irritated Nora were the employees who weren't even eating. They used up perfectly good spots in the cafeteria so they could read the newspaper or knit or reapply their makeup. Nora wanted to tell them, *Hey, y'know, they have a break room for that.*

No sooner would a spot open up than someone would swoop in and grab it. The cafeteria's bus staff tried to keep up with the turnover as they collected the dirty dishes, glasses and silverware. Efficiently moving around the tables, the men wore white coats and the women had on waitress uniforms. Most of the cafeteria workers were black. Nora had noticed a few black people on the assembly line, but didn't see any of them in the cafeteria.

One of the men busing tables took pity on her. "Ma'am, are you looking for a seat?" he asked. He'd been pushing a cart stacked with containers of dirty dishes. He was in his forties and had a touch of gray in his hair.

Nora nodded eagerly. "Yes . . ."

He pointed to the wall to her right. "There are some empty spots at the tables in the section on the other side of the telephone booths."

"You're a lifesaver," Nora sighed. "Thank you so much. I thought I'd have to eat my lunch standing up. This is my first— "

"Boy!" a woman called from a nearby table. "Boy, could you take away these plates?"

With a quick, contrite nod at Nora, the man turned and hurried away to bus the table.

Nora nodded back, but he was already gone.

With a sigh, she headed toward the phone booths against one wall and noticed around the corner the annex full of long tables. She also noticed Larry and Don, seated with some friends at a four-top near the section. It looked like they hadn't seen her, and Nora gave them a wide berth as she took a spot near the end of one of the long tables.

Once she sat down, she realized that nearly half of the workers eating in this section were black. She hadn't seen any signs designating WHITE ONLY or COLORED in the cafeteria. But apparently, this was how it was—in some unofficial understanding. At least she wasn't the only white person in the section.

She sipped her lukewarm coffee and used a napkin to dab up the mess in the saucer. She kept thinking Larry and his buddies were watching her. Hell, she felt like *everyone* was watching her—so pathetic, sitting there eating alone.

If only she could have joined the war workforce with a girlfriend. Then this whole lonely, scary ordeal might have been a fun adventure. And she'd have someone to talk to right now.

For several years, her best friend had been Betty Garner, who had lived two blocks away. Nora didn't have much in common with the other women in her neighborhood or the wives of Pete's doctor-associates. Most of them were club-women with maids and bridge games and beauty parlor appointments. But Betty was like her. She was busy with housework and her four kids. She was also very down to earth and funny. They would call each other up in the middle of the afternoon: *"I'm going crazy. I need to get out of the house. Do you want to go for a walk?"*

*"I'll be ready in fifteen minutes."*

Then they'd meet up and walk a few blocks to Volunteer Park. They'd tell each other their troubles, and Nora would feel halfway human again.

Betty's second oldest, Danny, was Chris's best friend. The boys had practically grown up together. Danny was, in fact, Chris's only friend. Chris was like her in that way. He'd make one friend and stick with him—or he'd be by himself. Nora used to worry that Chris might get singled out and bullied at

school because, despite his lean, athletic build, he wasn't interested in sports. But Danny Garner was on the football and
baseball teams. So Nora was always grateful that Chris's best
pal was such a popular, sports-minded kid—and her best friend's
son, to boot.

But then the Garners had moved to Cincinnati in the summer of 1940—shortly before Chris had started high school.
Nora and Betty still faithfully wrote to each other at least once
a month. But the boys—being boys, and young—gave up on
letter writing after a few weeks, which, to them, seemed like an
eternity.

As she sat alone at one end of the long cafeteria table, Nora
figured this was how it must have been for Chris on his first
day of high school—without his best friend, Danny. She remembered asking him how he'd managed to get through the
day; Chris had told her he was fine.

And later, when she'd noticed him coming home with
bruises, he'd told her that he was fine, again.

Nora sipped her coffee and opened her lunchbox. Peeling
back the wax paper from her bologna sandwich, she found a
piece of paper. It was a note from Chris:

> *Sorry I snuck out last night. I feel like a stupid jerk*
> *for making you worry. Have a good first day of*
> *work!*

He'd doodled something beside the notation, and it took
Nora a moment to realize it was a pair of work goggles. She
couldn't help smiling. But then she thought of how hard she'd
been on him last night. With Pete away and her best friend in
Cincinnati, Nora knew she'd come to depend on Chris way too
much. And the poor kid had troubles of his own—not that he
ever told her about them.

Nora always had to second-guess when something was

bothering him. She figured he'd spent his freshman year friend-less and keeping a low profile at his high school. Yet he seemed content, alone in his room, reading Jack London and drawing cartoons. He'd even created his own comic strip, *Foley's Fighters*, an action-adventure epic inspired by *Terry and the Pirates*. In the one chapter that Nora saw, Chris had Foley and his mot-ley crew fighting diamond smugglers in the Belgian Congo. It was actually pretty good. At the time, his dad was home, and Tak and Miko were living above the garage. There was always something going on around the house, and Chris wasn't exactly starved for company. Besides, his grades at school were excel-lent, so Nora figured she shouldn't worry about him.

But then Arlene came into the picture early in Chris's sophomore year. Intelligent, off-beat pretty and rebellious, she seemed to hold a spell over him. Chris said they weren't ro-mantically involved, but Nora could tell that he had feelings for the girl. Chris would drop everything and run over to Arlene's house whenever she called. Arlene didn't come over to their house very often, but when she did, she rarely even acknowl-edged Nora was there. Nora would have to say hello first, and then the girl would roll her eyes, flick back her brown hair and sigh. "Hello, Mrs. Kinney," she'd mutter. Then she and Chris would head out the door again or upstairs to his room. Nora couldn't understand why her son was attracted to such a snob, but kept her mouth shut. Arlene also had a sharp, caustic sense of humor, which Chris picked up. He'd always been such a sweet kid, but he suddenly turned sarcastic and even defiant at times. Chris and Arlene never got together with other kids in their class. It was always just the two of them. When Nora asked Chris about it, he told her: "I don't have any other friends, and neither does Arlene. Most girls don't like her be-cause she's so smart."

Arlene lived nine blocks away. Apparently, Chris used to slip out of the house in the middle of the night to meet up with her. Pete caught him once, trying to sneak back into the house at three in the morning. Nora and Pete grounded him for two weeks.

"What do you think he was doing with her until three in the morning?" she asked Pete in bed the following night.

"Playing Monopoly in her basement, he told me."

"And you believe him?" Nora whispered.

"Yeah, I don't think he's even kissed her. She's not interested in him 'that way,' he told me. She's really got him dangling."

"I don't understand what he sees in her. She's not even that pretty. And she talks down to me like I'm a complete moron. Chris could do better. Is it too much to hope that he gets over her during these next two weeks while he's grounded? Or do you think the more we keep him from seeing her, the more he'll want her?"

"The latter," Pete answered, rolling on his side and resting his arm over her. "Let's leave him alone. Maybe he'll realize without our help that he'll never get anywhere with her—and that she isn't such a prize."

"That little snot is going to end up breaking his heart," Nora sighed.

"Yep," Pete replied, spooning her the way he always did right before dozing off.

That was last spring, when Pete started talking about joining the medical corps.

At the beginning of the summer, Nora learned that someone else was leaving. A forlorn Chris gave her the news: Arlene's parents had decided to send her to a private boarding school in Bellingham for junior year. Nora had to hide her elation.

Chris was determined to spend as much time as he could that summer with his friend.

But suddenly, Arlene didn't want anything to do with him. Every time Chris called, she was too busy to talk. Whenever he stopped by Arlene's house, she wouldn't see him. She didn't even bother coming to the door. Chris couldn't figure out what he'd done to displease her. He was already miserable enough over his dad's impending departure for God only knew where. The poor kid could have really used a friend at the time. Instead, all he got from that little drip was the cold shoulder.

After weeks of ignoring him, Arlene finally returned one of his calls. When he spoke with her, Chris took the phone into the broom closet under the front stairs. Nora was in the kitchen and could hear him murmuring. He didn't sound happy. When he finally emerged from the broom closet with the phone, Nora asked him what Arlene had to say for herself.

Chris listlessly explained that Arlene had met a guy at the beach early in the summer, and she was in love. His name was Dale, and he lived in Santa Rosa, but was staying with his cousins in Seattle for the summer. "Arlene has a whole new set of friends now," Chris reported with a pitiful shrug. "She said, 'No offense,' but she's 'outgrown' me."

Nora swallowed her anger. "And how did you respond to that?" she asked.

"I said, 'Who in their right mind would name a boy Dale?'"

In a way, Nora was almost grateful to Arlene. The girl's selfish antics were a distraction and kept Nora from completely distressing over Pete's absence.

Chris tried not to show it, but Nora knew he was hurt and heartbroken. She just hoped that little snot wouldn't come running back to Chris once her boyfriend had returned to Santa Rosa and forgotten about her. And of course, that was exactly what happened.

In mid-October, on her first weekend home from boarding school, Arlene called Chris. Nora did her damnedest to act disinterested. "So how's Arlene?" she asked—once Chris had stepped out of the broom closet with the telephone.

He just shrugged.

"Are you going to see her?"

"She wanted to get together, but I told her I was busy," Chris replied. He set the phone back on its stand in the front hall and wound up the cord. "I didn't go into it with her, but she was really a jerk to me last summer. Plus, just now, she didn't even ask about Dad. I'm not dying to see her again."

*Yes, thank God,* Nora thought, but she kept her poker face on until Chris headed up to his bedroom.

The next morning, after 9:30 Mass, when they stepped out of the church, a couple of girls who had been in grade school with Chris practically pounced on him. They pulled him away from Nora and Jane—seemingly to talk to him about something urgent and confidential.

Jane scurried off into a huddle with some of her friends. So Nora was standing alone for a few moments while other parishioners continued to file out of the church. One of them made a beeline toward her. It was Agnes Gibbs, a petite, wizen-faced woman with bright red lipstick that ran into the cracks around her mouth. She wore a silly hat that made her look tipsy and a fox stole, complete with heads and paws.

"Nora, did you hear?" she said, grabbing Nora's arm. People were passing them on the sidewalk. Agnes's voice dropped to a whisper. "Your son is friends with the Drummond girl, isn't he?"

"Arlene?" Nora said, and then she nodded. She remembered that Mr. and Mrs. Gibbs lived across the street from the Drummonds.

Agnes Gibbs pulled her closer, and Nora could smell her Chanel No. 5. With a hand over her heart, the older woman sighed. "It's so tragic. The poor Drummonds! Their only child . . ."

"What happened?"

"Three thirty this morning, Herbert and I wake up to the sound of a shot. And then, a few minutes later, we hear the sirens. Neither one of us has slept since. I mean, how could we?"

Wide-eyed, Nora stared at her. She was getting impatient with Agnes's buildup. "What happened?" she repeated.

Agnes frowned with disapproval. "The girl, Arlene? She killed herself."

"What?" Nora whispered.

But she knew she'd heard correctly. She glanced over at Chris, whose back was to her. The two girls talking to him looked appropriately solemn, but even at a distance, Nora detected a glimmer of delight in their eyes. They either didn't like Arlene very much or they were excited to share such a bombshell with someone who knew her—probably a combination of both. Nora could see Chris shaking his head over and over.

"The Drummonds were trying to act like it was an accident," she heard Agnes say. "Herb and I got dressed and went over there to see if we could be of any help. I heard one of the policemen say what they think really happened. He said that while the Drummonds were asleep, the girl snuck down to her father's study, dug his revolver out of the desk and shot herself in the head. They wouldn't let me in the room, but I guess there was blood everywhere."

She squeezed Nora's arm. "Her poor mother found her. Can you imagine? There wasn't a suicide note or anything. But I'm telling you, that Arlene was always a strange girl. In fact, I was genuinely surprised when I started seeing Chris over there so often. But then, he hasn't been by in the past few months, has he?"

"No, he hasn't," Nora murmured. She bit her lip and glanced over at Chris again. He still had his back to her while the two girls spoke with him. He finally turned away from them, and Nora saw the stricken look on his face. Chris tugged at the knot of his tie to loosen it. He anxiously glanced around until his eyes met Nora's.

"Excuse me, Agnes," she said. Then she threaded through

the crowd toward her son. She reached out to hug him, but Chris pulled back.

"I need to get out of here," he said under his breath. "There are too many people . . ."

Nora spotted Jane nearby, still chatting with her friends. "Jane!" she called. "Jane, come on, we're heading home!"

She realized several people were staring at Chris and her. Or at least, it felt that way.

Once she pried Jane away from her friends, Nora started home with her and Chris. St. Joseph's was a mile away from their home, but since gas rationing had started, they usually walked to church and back. Of course, new shoes were scarce, too, so it was always a draw how to get around.

That October Sunday morning, Chris stayed several paces in front of Nora and Jane. Nora quietly explained to her daughter what had happened. All the while, she kept an eye on Chris up ahead, the distance between them widening as he picked up his stride. Slump-shouldered, he had his hands in his pockets and his head down.

If he cried for his friend, he never let anyone see.

*The Seattle Star* ran a brief article on page nine about Arlene's death, describing it as the result of a "self-inflicted gunshot wound." The last sentence of the article stated that the funeral services would be private—for family only. Chris sent the Drummonds a sympathy card, which was very sweet. He'd shown it to Nora so she could check the spelling.

She kept an eye on him for the next several days. He was like a zombie and spent nearly every minute at home alone in his bedroom with the door closed. He didn't even listen to the radio programs he liked so much. It was as if he was punishing himself.

One night, Nora finally knocked on his door. Talking her way into his sanctum sanctorum, she sat down on the bed with him. "Honey, I can practically guarantee that what Arlene did had nothing to do with you," she tried to assure him. "It was probably because of that Dale person or problems at her new school. You don't know . . ."

"Maybe," he shrugged. "But she wanted me to come over, and I said no. I could have been there for her, and I wasn't."

Nora imagined Chris going over to Arlene's house—maybe even sneaking out in the middle of the night. She could see that girl persuading him to pull the trigger for her, or, perhaps, even making it a double suicide. Nora thanked God that her son had refused to see Arlene that night.

She put her arm around his shoulder. "Honey, I don't mean to put her down or speak ill of the dead, but Arlene dumped you. She cut you out of her life four months ago—and didn't even bother to get in touch with you when Dad shipped out. She wasn't there for you. And you'd been a good friend to her. She didn't even write to you when she went away to school."

Chris frowned. "So—in other words, I didn't matter to her."

"I'm not saying that," Nora sighed, stroking his back. "I'm just pointing out that she was a girl with a lot of problems, and she pushed you away. There's not much you or anyone else could have done to help her. It's okay to feel bad, Chris. Just don't blame yourself."

She kept thinking that Pete would have known what to say to him. But all she could do was keep a close eye on Chris and try to cheer him up as much as she could. Nora figured he probably wasn't getting much sympathy at school. Arlene didn't have any other friends.

That had been six months ago. And Nora was still worried about him. In fact, she'd been hesitant about taking this job because it meant Chris would be on his own even more.

It was strange, because she hardly fretted about Jane at all. Her daughter had a different, major drama every day. But she also had scads of friends. She was always telling Nora about her latest projects and activities.

Chris was different. His only friend was Earl, and he hardly told her a thing.

Nora gazed at the note he'd left in her lunchbox. She wondered when he'd snuck downstairs to plant the message in there with her sandwich. She hadn't heard him, and she'd been awake, tossing and turning most of the night after he'd come home. Had he ever gotten to sleep?

"You look positively grim," she heard someone say.

Nora tucked the note in her lunchbox and looked up.

"But then I shouldn't be surprised," said the woman standing across the table from her. "I saw you working with Larry Krull all morning. Condolences." She was plain-faced, skinny and in her late twenties. Her blond hair had been pulled back and tucked into a pink bandana with black polka dots. She carried a lunch tray that held a sandwich and a cup of coffee. "Larry loves to torture the new girls and make them cry," she continued. "He's a real woman-hater, that one. And he's watching us right now."

Out of the corner of her eye, Nora glanced over at Larry's table. He and his buddies were staring at her. He had a cocky grin on his face, and his pals looked amused.

The woman set her tray on the table and then plopped down in the chair opposite Nora. She smiled, revealing a pair of slightly crooked front incisors that somehow made her face more interesting and attractive. "My name's Connie," she said, extending her hand across the table. "Connie Wiedrich."

Nora shook it. "Nora Kinney. This is my first day here."

"I figured," Connie said. "Congratulations on having made it through the morning without running for the exit shrieking. Now say something to me, and we'll both laugh—so Larry realizes he didn't break your spirit."

" '*Break my spirit*,' " Nora repeated. "That perfectly describes what he did to me."

"You're still here, aren't you? So . . . he didn't succeed.

*Laugh*." She put down her coffee cup, threw her head back and cackled.

Nora forced a laugh and then stole a glance at Larry's table.

His friends had suddenly lost interest. Larry was scowling at her.

"What's so funny?" a second woman asked.

Sitting down beside Connie, she set her lunchbox and a glass of milk on the table. She was a big, sturdy-looking woman of fifty with wavy, short-cropped gray-brown hair.

"Fran DeLuca, Nora Kinney," Connie said. "It's Nora's first day. Three guesses who trained her this morning."

"Oh, God, not Larry." Fran sighed. She took a thermos, an apple and a spoon out of her lunchbox. "Listen, Nora. First, it's nice to meet you, honey. And two, whatever insults Larry threw at you, just ignore them. He's an insignificant little worm. I've stepped on better." She poured some soup from the thermos into the thermos top.

"That smells good," Connie said.

"Go fetch yourself a spoon, Con," Fran said. "There's too much for me here anyway."

Connie got to her feet. "You're the best. That Marty is one lucky fella to get your cooking every night. Be right back." She started toward the lunch counter.

"Is Marty your husband?" Nora asked Fran.

"No, my husband died a few years ago," Fran answered—with the spoon halfway to her mouth. "Marty's my son. He's twenty-three. He was wounded in the Solomon Islands."

Nora set down her sandwich. "Oh, I'm so sorry."

She nodded. "Thanks. They had him at that new naval hospital up in Shoreline for nearly a month. His ship was torpedoed. A lot of his friends were killed. He lost an eye. The navy gave him a glass one, and they stitched up his face. He was cut up pretty bad, but he's healing. He's been home for the last three weeks—sort of an indefinite sick leave."

Fran ate some of her soup. "What about you? Are there a husband and kids in the picture?"

Nora told her about Pete and the children. She was showing Fran their photos in her wallet when Connie returned with an empty bowl and two spoons. "Nora, I brought a spoon for you, too. You need to try this . . ."

"Well," Fran said. "You're awfully generous with *my* lunch, aren't you?" She poured some soup in the bowl and cracked a smile at Nora. "Seriously, there's plenty. The vegetables are from my victory garden. Give it a try."

"Thank you," Nora said, sampling the soup, which was rich, savory and thick with pasta and vegetables. "This is incredible . . ."

"I overheard some gals talking in the lunch line," Connie said. "They were saying that one of the machinists was strangled last night. Have you heard anything?"

Fran nodded. "It's all they were talking about during the coffee break this morning. You know who it was? It was that Loretta—whatshername—Bryant. You've seen her . . ."

Connie shook her head and slurped some soup.

"Young, blonde, pretty. She and her sister work in the wing assembly section. They're from Arkansas. A couple of good-time girls, but sweet . . . nice . . ."

"Oh, I think I know who you mean," Connie said.

"The older sister—I forget her name—she found the body in their apartment when she came home from a bar late last night. Their place isn't far from the waterfront. You know how sketchy that area can be. They were saying during the break that the police think Loretta might have picked someone up and taken him home."

"So—they haven't caught the guy?" Connie asked. "He's still out there somewhere?"

Frowning, Fran nodded. "I'm afraid so. I'll have to check tonight's edition and see if there's anything in there about it."

"Where did you say this happened?"

"Belltown."

"That's right next to Queen Anne. It's practically in my neighborhood!" Connie shuddered. "So—there's a strangler on the loose. This is too creepy for words. I don't know about you, but I'm double-locking my door tonight."

Nora said nothing, but she was thinking how Belltown wasn't very far from her house on Capitol Hill.

Connie pushed away the empty soup bowl. "Well, I don't mean to sound like a hard-hearted Hannah, but I hope they don't collect donations for a funeral wreath or anything. I'm strapped this week."

Nora reached into her lunchbox for another napkin to wipe her mouth. Chris's note fell onto the table. She dabbed her lips and read the note again:

> *Sorry I snuck out last night. I feel like a stupid jerk*
> *for making you worry. Have a good first day of*
> *work!*

Nora folded the note and slipped it back into her lunchbox.

# Chapter 4

"God, Kinney, you're such a dummkopf!"

Tying the sash of her robe, Nora stopped in the doorway of the master bathroom. She'd been soaking in the tub for the last forty-five minutes—during the last ten of which she could hear someone yelling in the backyard. With the bathroom door closed, Nora hadn't been able to make out the words, but she'd recognized Earl McAllister's loud voice. She'd tried to ignore the shouting from Chris's friend. After a humiliating day working under Larry, Nora had just wanted to take refuge in a warm bath. She'd been so damn tired, depressed and achy. Pete had cautioned her in a recent letter that the first day of a new job was always the longest and worst. Nora figured she could pat herself on the back for having survived it. And she might have also made a couple of new friends in Fran and Connie.

Nora couldn't help wondering what Earl had been shouting about. Now she heard him all too clearly. She lingered in the bathroom doorway for another minute, listening.

"Butterfingers! I passed it right to you, stupid! You're god-damn hopeless!"

Chris said something in response that Nora couldn't quite make out.

In her bare feet, she padded out of the bedroom and down to the window at the end of the hallway. The blackout curtain was open. Nora glanced down at the backyard, where Chris and Earl tossed a football back and forth.

She couldn't believe Earl had the guts to show his face around here today. Hadn't Chris told him that she'd found out about their secret excursion in the middle of the night? Chris certainly had to know he was pushing his luck to invite his partner in crime over to the house so soon after he'd been busted.

"God, Kinney, you're pitiful!" Earl shouted—after Chris fumbled a catch.

A few inches shorter than Chris, the handsome, fair-skinned boy had a more solid build. Earl wore a tan jacket, a pressed shirt, and spotless trousers. The McAllisters had a live-in maid, so Earl was always immaculately dressed. In contrast, Chris had thrown an old sweater over his school clothes. As usual, he had his back to the ravine—so every time Earl tossed him a high one, Chris would have to scurry down into the wooded gully to shag the lost football. Hadn't Chris figured out by now that he was getting the short end of the stick?

After Arlene's suicide, Nora had hoped Chris would recover and get to know someone nice—or maybe get involved in some after-school activity. But Chris would come home alone at 3:20 every day and head directly up to the second-floor bathroom. Then he'd shut himself in his bedroom until dinnertime. That was when Nora first noticed the bruises on his face. When she asked him about the marks, Chris claimed he'd banged himself up in gym class.

"I don't believe him, of course," she told Pete long distance. At the time, Pete was stationed at Camp Barkeley near Abilene,

Texas, and calling every weekend. Nora had taken the phone into the broom closet for this particular call because the kids were home. "Every few days, there's a new bruise," she whispered, "and those are just the bruises I can see. I'm sure someone's picking on him at school, but I can't get him to admit it."

"Sounds like it," Pete replied glumly. "If he heads right to the bathroom the minute he comes home, he's probably been holding it in all day. I'll bet he's afraid to use the bathroom at school. That's where bullies tend to do their bullying. At least, that's how it was back in my high school days." He sighed. "God, poor Chris . . ."

"What do you think I should do?" she asked.

There was silence on the other end of the line.

"Pete? Are you still there?"

"Yeah, I don't know what to tell you, honey. If he hasn't said anything to you or me about it, then obviously he doesn't want us to know. I didn't tell anyone when it happened to me back in high school. I just avoided the bullies the best I could, and when that didn't work, I tried reasoning with them. Finally, I ended up slugging it out with one of them. I got the crap kicked out of me, but they left me alone after that. It's a rite of passage for a lot of teenage boys. Damn, I hate that Chris is going through it."

Nora never got Chris to admit that he was being bullied, but she kept furtively checking for new bruises on his face when he came home from school.

Then, on a Friday afternoon in January, Chris was accompanied home by a nicely dressed, blue-eyed, blond-haired boy, who politely introduced himself to her as Earl McAllister. Later that afternoon, the boys went to see *Cat People* at a downtown movie theater.

Chris said that Earl was his lab partner in biology class. He lived four blocks away. He was an only child, and his mother had died from tuberculosis a few years ago. As far as Nora was

concerned, the boy was a godsend. At last, Chris had a friend—
and her son was actually getting out of the house. They went
ice skating at the Civic Ice Arena, bowled at D&L Alleys, and
trekked to a movie theater downtown to see the Technicolor
swashbuckler epic, *The Black Swan.*

On week three of their budding friendship, the boys went to
see Alfred Hitchcock's latest, *Shadow of a Doubt.* Nora remembered that one in particular because the theater owner
called her at 1:45 on a Thursday afternoon. An usher had caught
Chris trying to sneak Earl in a side door during the early afternoon matinee—when the boys should have been in school.

This, after Chris had just recently promised to buckle down
and do better in his studies. Since Arlene's suicide, his grades
had gone from nearly all As to Cs and Ds.

Nora grounded Chris for two weeks. Once he'd served his
fourteen days, he immediately got together with Earl again.
Nora warned him that he was on probation.

As far as she could tell, the boys didn't get into any trouble
for a while. But then, last month, after the winter thaw, Chris
and Earl took to tossing around the football in the backyard,
and Nora heard a sampling of Earl's foul mouth. But even more
offensive than the obscenities was the way he derided Chris for
every missed catch or bad throw. His favorite nickname for
Chris was *dummkopf.* Sometimes, it sounded like he might
have been kidding, but mostly, he just seemed cruel. Nora told
herself not to interfere.

Still, that was when she changed her mind about Earl McAllister being such a godsend. And when she decided the handsome towhead looked like a member of the Hitler Youth—and
he sounded like a little Nazi, too, the way he barked at Chris.
Nora kicked herself for initially being taken in by him with his
phony polite routine. She couldn't help cringing inside whenever Chris stepped out with the kid. She became very strict

about when Chris had to be home: 10:30 on weekends, and no weekday after-dinner outings at all.

At one o'clock on a Sunday morning three weeks ago, Nora had been awakened by the phone ringing. She staggered out of bed, threw on her robe and hurried downstairs. All she could think was that Pete had been killed in North Africa, where the U.S. was experiencing heavy casualties at the time.

But the call was from the Seattle Police. Chris was being held at the downtown station. Nora felt like an idiot. She'd thought Chris was upstairs in bed asleep. But no, he'd slipped out of the house after she'd gone to bed. Somehow, he'd gotten himself down to the waterfront, where he'd snuck into a bar and tried to order a drink—within earshot of a plainclothes detective.

The police took pity on him and only issued him a warning. Nora had to get dressed and go pick him up at the police station.

Chris insisted he'd snuck out and gone to the bar on his own. Nora knew he was protecting his friend. And forbidding him to see Earl might only compel him to sneak out at night to meet him in secret. The war had caused an epidemic of juvenile delinquency—especially among boys approaching draft age. But Chris had never before shown any interest in drinking or carousing. And he'd never been in trouble with the police before. Nora couldn't prove that Earl had anything to do with the incident. All she could do was ground Chris once more—for another two-week stint.

She remembered promising to ground him for a whole month if he ever snuck out of the house in the middle of the night again.

As she spied on Chris and Earl tossing around the football outside, Nora decided that, after the stunt they'd pulled last night, she should follow through with her threat. Chris was better off on his own—away from this little creep who kept getting him into trouble. Why did he let himself be manipulated and abused like this?

She watched Earl step back and heave a wild, wobbly pass that was too high and about ten feet to Chris's left. But Chris still made a run for it and jumped up with his arms extended.

"C'mon, you got it," Nora whispered.

The football deflected off Chris's fingertips. It hit the ground and rolled along the lawn. Chris grimaced and rubbed the fingers on his right hand.

"What—did you hurt yourself?" Earl called. "Sissy!"

"I'm fine!" Chris called, retrieving the football. He tossed it at Earl, who didn't bother moving an inch as the ball bounced on the ground a couple of feet in front of him.

"Jesus, what's wrong with you?" he barked. "Try throwing it *at* me, dummkopf!"

"You're one to talk, you little creep," Nora said under her breath. "Your last pass almost wound up in the ravine . . ."

"So like I was saying earlier," Earl went on. "I dragged this sack of bricks to the footbridge over Lake Washington Boulevard by the arboretum. And it was heavy as shit . . ." He hurled a pass at Chris, who actually caught the ball. "So I went to the middle of the bridge and waited for a car to come. This DeSoto was driving down the boulevard real slow, and I saw this stupid-looking old lady behind the wheel . . ."

He paused to catch the football, which Chris had thrown directly to him. "Just as she drove under the bridge, I dropped the sack, and—*wham*—it hit the old lady's windshield! You should have heard the glass smash. The old lady slammed on her brakes, and another car crashed into her rear end. God, you should have seen it! It was hysterical! You'd have shit. I could hear the old bag screaming and crying. She didn't know what hit her . . ." Earl let out a grunt as he passed the football to Chris.

Nora watched Chris fumble the catch, but she was too disturbed and distracted by Earl's story to care. She studied her son's face to see if he was chuckling or even slightly amused by the tale. But she couldn't read his expression. He retrieved the ball. "Earl, let me ask you something," he said, holding on to the football for a few moments. "Aren't you afraid you'll end up in hell for some of the stuff you do?"

Earl laughed.

Chris lobbed the football at him, and it bounced off the ground a few feet in front of his friend.

"God, you stink, Kinney!" Earl complained. Shaking his head, he fetched the football.

"I don't think it really happened," Chris said.

"What?"

"Your story about almost killing that old lady," Chris said. "I think it's a crock. I mean, I can't see you lugging a sack of bricks down that long path to the footbridge. Maybe one or two bricks, but not a whole sack of them. That's just too much work. And how could you tell from way up on the footbridge that an old lady was driving?"

"Oh, fuck you," Earl grumbled.

"C'mon, give me a break. Like you could really see inside the car from up there . . ."

"Fuck you!" Earl yelled this time. He hauled off and hurled the football at Chris—obviously aiming below the belt.

Chris dodged the ball, which skidded across the lawn behind him. He laughed. "I'm sorry! I know you like to think of yourself as a regular Dillinger. But I just don't believe you . . ."

"FUCK YOU!" Earl shouted—even louder. He reached down, grabbed a rock from Miko's old garden and flung it at Chris. This time he seemed to aim at Chris's head.

Chris ducked just in time.

Incensed, Nora pulled back from the window. She bolted for the stairs, raced down to the first floor and headed into the kitchen. She was barefoot and still in her robe, but she didn't care. Breathless, she threw open the door—just as Earl was about to hurl another rock at Chris.

"Earl!" she barked. "That's enough! If you throw that, you'll be sorry!"

Hesitating, he defiantly stared back at her. For a moment, Nora thought he might actually pitch the rock at *her*. But then he frowned and tossed the rock aside.

"I could hear you in my bedroom on the other side of the house," she said. It wasn't quite a lie because she'd heard him from the bedroom earlier. "I'm sure half the neighborhood got an earful of that language, too. It's time for you to go home, Earl." She shook her head. "Quite frankly, I don't know how you even have the nerve to show up here today after the prank you two pulled last night."

Earl squinted at her as if she were crazy. Then he turned to Chris. "What prank last night? What's she talking about?"

"Just go, Earl," Chris hissed. "Amscray."

The boy grabbed his football off the ground. He turned back to glare at Nora, muttered something under his breath and then stomped toward the driveway.

Catching her breath, Nora waited until he disappeared around the other side of the house. She opened the kitchen door wider for Chris. "Get in here . . ."

With a sigh, Chris came up the steps to the kitchen door.

"Just now," Nora said, "when I mentioned your little excursion to the Navy Depot last night, Earl acted like he didn't know what I was talking about."

Chris nodded and brushed past her. "Yeah, you're right, Mom. He *acted* like he didn't know . . ."

She closed the door, then turned and took hold of his arm. "Honestly, why you're even friends with him is a total mystery to me. He's more trouble than he's worth. He treats you like dirt. And I heard part of that story he was telling you . . ."

Chris faced her, but he wouldn't look her in the eye. "That was a crock, Mom. He was just grandstanding."

"Well, I don't understand why he'd think a story like that would impress you."

"It didn't."

"Why do you keep inviting him over?"

Chris finally looked her in the eye. "I didn't invite Earl over. He always invites himself. I know you're still sore about last night, and I'm sorry." He sighed and gently wiggled his arm from her grasp. "If you want to punish me, go ahead. You're off to a great start. Talk about embarrassing. Tomorrow, it'll be all over school how I needed my mommy to come to my rescue. Earl already thinks I'm a mama's boy. This just seals the deal. And you're in your bathrobe, too. Thanks a lot, Mom."

"What?" Nora asked, incredulous.

"Never mind, you wouldn't understand," he muttered. "I'm sorry . . ." Shaking his head, he turned and hurried out of the kitchen.

Nora listened to him stomp up the stairs.

"Seriously?" she said to no one.

Nora looked down at her terrycloth bathrobe and fingered the lapel. Then she defeatedly plopped down on the kitchen chair. She understood now. She'd humiliated him in front of his friend—worse, in front of a mean, malicious friend.

What was this strange power Earl had over her son? It was obvious that Earl was practically forcing Chris to pal around with him. What else was he forcing Chris to do? Nora was pretty certain the two of them hadn't been watching battleships in Elliott Bay last night. Why had Chris lied to her about that? What was he covering up?

Nora thought about that note he'd left in her lunchbox today. She told herself that, despite his problems, Chris was still a sweet kid with a good heart. He mowed the lawn for Mrs. Landauer down at the end of the block. After dismissing her Japanese-American nurse-housekeeper, the old woman had hired a Swedish woman who barely spoke English. So

Mrs. Landauer often depended on Chris to run errands for her. She trusted him with her car, an old Duesenberg. In fact, Chris was the only one who ever drove it.

Mrs. Landauer was childless and treated Chris like a grandson. She also paid him well. Since the Kinneys were now on a budget, Chris voluntarily gave Nora half his earnings: usually ten dollars a week. Mrs. Landauer often sent him home with an apple strudel she'd baked herself. The old lady sometimes included a note for Nora, scrawled in her shaky handwriting, saying how polite and kind her handsome son was, and how proud she must be of him.

She could hear him shuffling around upstairs in his bedroom.

Maybe she would ground him for only a couple of weeks.

Nora glanced down at her bathrobe again. She needed to get dressed and start thinking about dinner.

# Chapter 5

*Monday*
*9:30 p.m.*

*My dearest Pete,*

*The kids are in their rooms. The house is quiet. And I'm sitting at the dining room table, writing a few lines here before I go to bed. I think I'll be asleep before my head even hits the pillow. You warned me that the first day of work at a new job is always the longest and most draining, and you were oh-so-right, my love. But I got through it, and I think tomorrow will be easier.*

Nora paused, looked up and stared across the table at the dining room's rosebud pattern wallpaper for a few moments. She wanted to tell Pete about how awful Larry Krull had been to her. But why upset him?

She'd spoken a bit more with Ned Sprenger, the older man

who had been so kind to her just when she'd felt so defeated. He'd said that she reminded him of his daughter, who was a nurse, currently stationed in Australia. For Nora, it was like having her father nearby, looking out for her—ready to catch her if she fell. But apparently, plant management moved the new employees around from one workstation to another every day. So Nora wondered if she'd be working anywhere near Ned again. Fran and Connie had said *maybe* they'd see her at lunch tomorrow. Everything seemed so tentative at her new job. Everything was tentative—period.

Sometimes, when she wrote to Pete, she couldn't help thinking that he might be killed before her letter reached him. Or maybe he was dead already, and she was writing to no one.

Nora self-censored whatever she wrote to Pete. For example, she wasn't going to tell him that she'd just double-locked the doors and checked the first-floor windows because a Belltown woman had been strangled last night—and the killer was still out there somewhere. She didn't tell Pete anything that might worry or distract him too much. She wasn't going to write about the window in the front door being broken last night—or the trouble she'd been having with Chris lately.

She'd read an article a while back instructing women to be cheerful in their letters to their GI husbands and sweethearts, to remind them of home, family and the neighborhood—the things they were fighting for. Nora tried to comply with these guidelines, but it made for some pretty boring letters.

Back when Pete was at the University of Illinois, they had written each other long, candid, pour-your-heart-out, sometimes passionate missives—at least, she'd thought so back then. It had been a while since she'd reread any of those old letters. She still had them in a shoebox in the back of her closet.

They'd met in Chicago when Pete was visiting a friend during summer vacation between his sophomore and junior years at the university. Nora and her brother, Raymond, who was nine years younger, were living with their maternal grand-parents in Flossmoor at the time. Both her mom and dad had been dead for years.

Her mother had been beautiful and "fragile." At least, that was how Nora's dad had described her when she'd become so withdrawn and strange after Ray was born. "Your mother's too fragile to handle the baby and housework all by herself," Nora's father told her. "You'll have to help out, honey."

Every weekday, as soon as nine-year-old Nora came home from school, her mother would point to a wet, hungry and screaming Ray in his crib and say with clenched teeth, "You have to take care of him, because I can't anymore." Then her mom would take to her bed—and not emerge again until Nora had dinner ready. Pretty soon, her mother was spending all her time in bed, and Nora's grandmother had to come look after the baby until Nora took over at 3:30. On weekends, Nora had Ray all day. She loved her little brother, but sometimes she re-sented his very existence. Her grandmother and father called her "Ray's little mother."

Her father worked as a switchman for the Illinois Central Railroad. He made Nora feel cherished with his constant praise. He called her his *angel*, his *lifesaver*. In turn, she adored him and never wanted to let him down. He had enough to con-tend with.

Her mother spent the next four years in and out of sanitari-ums, where she was treated for melancholia. Nora thought *melancholia* sounded more like a flower than a mental illness. It was during one of the lengthier stays in a sanitarium that her mother caught and succumbed to the Spanish flu. Nora became fiercely protective of her toddler brother for fear that he, too, would fall victim to the deadly pandemic sweeping the country.

But it was her father who died less than a year after her mom—not from the flu, but in a freak accident in the railroad yard. He was struck and run over by a maintenance-of-way car being switched to the repair track. He was severed in two just below his chest.

Nora was devastated. She and Ray went to live with their grandparents in Flossmoor. Her grandmother was sweet and affectionate, but long-suffering. She was the first to admit that she wasn't very bright—or sometimes she was the second one to say it. "Stupid woman," Nora's grandfather would often mutter as soon as her grandmother left the room. The rail-thin, balding old man was stern and aloof. He'd never completely recovered from a stroke years before and struggled to get around—even with a cane. He spent most of his time sitting in the same chair in the living room, staring out the window or glaring at the two grandchildren he didn't want in his house. Ray was terrified of him. Nora often wondered if her mother had inherited the melancholia from her father. Was it hereditary? She worried about becoming that way, too, as she got older.

And she worried about leaving her nine-year-old brother alone with their grandparents once she went away to college. At the same time, Nora couldn't wait to get away—far away. She longed to travel and applied to colleges along both coasts. She figured her father's insurance would cover her education. She'd been working part-time as a clerk at Diggle's Drugstore for three years so that she'd have some spending and travel money while she was in college. She'd loved studying geography in school and dreamed of traveling after college, maybe even seeing Europe or the Orient.

But her grandfather had other plans. He claimed her father's insurance wouldn't cover the tuition to any of those "fancy" East or West Coast universities. And even if they could afford it, sending a girl to college was a waste of money. Once she finished high school, Nora was expected to get a full-time job and contribute some of her income to the household. It was time she paid back her grandparents for taking care of her and her brother for so many years.

So—the day after she graduated from high school, Nora started full time at Diggle's. She'd been working there full-time for a year—mostly behind the soda fountain counter—when she met Peter Kinney. She saw this tall, handsome, young man hold the door open for an elderly gentleman. While the old man took his time shuffling through the doorway, Peter's eyes met hers. Nora smiled at him. He smiled back, and that was it.

Nora thought it would be a summer romance. She had no idea how much she would have to give up.

Pete took the El and two different buses from his parents' house in Evanston to her grandparents' place in Flossmoor to see Nora three or four times a week for the rest of that summer. When he went back to school, 140 miles away in Urbana, they wrote to each other regularly. Nora took a bus down to see him as many weekends as she could get away. With her dreams of visiting Paris, London and Hong Kong, she'd never imagined dipping into her "travel fund" to pay for bus trips to Urbana. She always told Ray and her grandparents that she was spending the weekend with her friend, Claire, on Lake Shore Drive. She hated lying to Ray and her trusting, gullible grandmother. But Nora didn't give a hoot about lying to The Gargoyle, which was Pete's nickname for her grandfather. ("He looks like something they'd put on top of a building to scare away the pigeons.") None of them would have understood—or believed— that when she stayed at Pete's apartment off-campus, she slept in his roommate's bedroom.

Nora timed her visits for when the roommate, Walter, was away for the weekend, visiting his girlfriend. Pete always changed the sheets on the bed for her because Walter was a smoker and a slob. Nora remembered many a night, lying in that bed, unable to sleep from all the pent-up desire. She'd stare across the darkened bedroom at Walter's bookshelves—crammed with empty bootleg whiskey bottles that he'd collected, and she'd think about Pete in the bedroom next door, probably still wide awake as well.

Though Pete had "some limited experience," they were both virgins. Nora had had plenty of dates, almost-boyfriends and opportunities. But she'd decided to save herself for the right guy and marriage. She liked to think of herself as a "good girl," but a big part of her decision was her fear of getting pregnant. At age nineteen, she'd already spent over half her life looking after a child. She wanted a break from that. Whenever a guy started going too far, all she had to do was think about changing diapers and having her dreams of travel shattered, and she'd find the resolve to tell the guy to stop.

Even though she knew Pete was "the right guy," and he brought her so much overdue happiness, she still made him stop when things got too passionate in his Model T—and, later, on the sofa in his apartment. She must have trained him well because, pretty soon, Pete was the one to call it quits whenever they started going too far. Nora remembered those nights when they'd stop necking, and then wordlessly go about the tiresome task of stripping his roommate's bed.

One night in April, after nine months of dating, they didn't stop and change those damn sheets. They just couldn't make themselves stop.

After that, they were very, very careful. At first, Nora was uncomfortable whenever Pete pulled out a condom and inspected it for tears. But with medical school ahead of him, he was just as afraid as she was about a pregnancy. They tried to take every precaution.

Nevertheless, Nora still got pregnant.

"Now, we don't have to wait," Pete told her. "We can start our lives together. And don't worry, honey. You're going to be a great mom."

She knew that. She'd already been a great mom—to her kid brother.

Their wedding was a hasty little service in an annex of St. Nicholas Church—with two of Pete's college friends as the only witnesses. The story they gave their stunned families was that they hadn't wanted anyone trying to talk them out of getting married. They were in love, and their minds were made up. They came across as more determined than impulsive. Actually, it didn't matter much to Nora how they came across, just as long as no one ever suspected that they *had* to get married. And she didn't want their unborn child ever suspecting it later on.

They set up house in a tiny one-bedroom apartment near the university. The college girls dating Pete's friends seemed to envy Nora. In their minds, she and Pete were a blissful married couple. But in reality, there was a period of adjustment and a lot of morning sickness. Plus, Nora's travel fund had been drained to help pay the rent.

And then there was Ray. Nora felt as if she'd totally abandoned her eleven-year-old brother. Ray made it known that he resented being stuck alone with his grandmother and The Gargoyle. Nora didn't blame him. For most of their lives, they'd been there for each other. Now it must have seemed to Ray as if he didn't matter anymore. Nora frequently invited him to spend the weekend at their place in Urbana, but it was never comfortable with three people in those cramped quarters, and he'd never really warmed up to Pete.

Once Chris was born, there wasn't any room for guests.

Then Pete started his residency in Seattle. They had another addition to their family with Jane. Nora heard from her grandmother about Ray's defiant behavior and the trouble he got into at his high school. Some of it was typical teenage mischief. But he was caught a couple of times stealing from the local grocery store—and from Diggle's Drugstore, Nora's old place of employment. Fortunately, Nora's grandmother paid back the store owners and persuaded them to drop the charges.

In a move that irked Nora, her grandparents paid for Ray's college education. Suddenly, they had money—or maybe they were just desperate to get him out of the house. But Ray quit college after a couple of years—around the time their grandparents died. Nora wondered how he could have thrown away the chance for a college education.

Ray ended up moving around the country and going through several jobs. He visited Seattle from time to time, often showing up at their doorstep without advance notice. The kids adored him, and Nora was happy to see her little brother. But things between Pete and him remained strained. Ray did all sorts of little things to get on Pete's nerves—often on purpose. Ray never stayed for more than a few days. During practically every visit, there was an incident that made Ray's departure come not a minute too soon. Once, when he was nineteen, he borrowed their car for the night, then brought it back with a dented fender and a broken headlight. He was too drunk to recall what had happened. Then there was the time when Nora took him to a local haberdashery, where Pete was a regular customer, and Ray stole a couple neckties. When Nora found out, she went back to the shop the next day, paid for the pilfered ties and tried to convince the clerk that there had been some sort of misunderstanding. She was humiliated. On a few occasions, Ray dropped Pete's name at various local shops so they'd accept a check—only to have it bounce. The maddening thing about it was that no one from any of these shops had a bad thing to say about Ray. He'd charmed each one of his victims and they were quick to forgive him—especially after Pete paid them back. Sometimes, Ray stayed only one night, and then hit Pete up for money before leaving the next morning. But there were also visits when Ray showered them with expensive gifts and made a point of paying Pete back. Nora and Pete would wonder where he'd suddenly gotten his money.

Nora would also wonder how, when he had all his freedom and mobility, Ray could make such a waste of his life. Three months after Pearl Harbor, he knew it was only a matter of time before he was drafted, so he joined the navy.

Nora still longed to see the world, and she was oddly jealous of Pete and her brother, whose stints in the armed forces took them to faraway places—like North Africa and the South Pacific. It was ridiculous, she knew. But she still envied them.

Nora saved the postcards from Ray when he was stationed in Honolulu for four months. From what she could tell, the navy seemed to have reformed him. But just days before he was supposed to ship out for combat duty, Ray broke his arm and cracked a few ribs in a fall. The injury led to a serious infection that had sidelined him for a month. He was recuperating in a navy hospital in San Diego and would eventually be reassigned to a new ship.

When Nora had written to Pete about Ray's accident, he'd replied in a letter: *Well, it looks like Ray's really doing his part for the war effort.* Nora had decided to ignore the sarcastic remark. But if he'd said that to her in person, it would have led to a big argument. Pete bugged the hell out of her when he made out like he was the voice of authority—simply because he was a doctor. When he insulted her brother, he insulted her family. Still, he had a point, damn him. As much as Nora wanted to believe that Ray had reformed, she couldn't help wondering if he hadn't set up that accident to avoid combat duty.

Then it occurred to her that, like her brother, she wasn't doing much for the war effort either—besides planting a victory garden; helping Jane with various paper, rubber and scrapmetal drives; and buying the occasional war bond.

That was one reason she'd gone after the job at Boeing. She'd wanted to *do something*. But a few weeks ago, when she'd mentioned in a letter to her brother that she wanted to get a war job, Ray had fired back a note saying she was crazy:

> *Sorry, Nor, but I just can't see you in overalls with a blowtorch in your hand, putting together a B-17. You couldn't even figure out how to work the stupid latch on the bathroom door at Grandma's house. Remember?*
>
> *Have you run this past the good doctor yet? I'll bet it goes over like a pregnant pole-vaulter with him. No wife of his is taking a regular job—especially a MAN's job. But he probably wouldn't put it that way. Pete's going to say he's worried about you getting hurt . . .*

That was exactly what Pete had said in his V-mail after she'd written to him about the Boeing job. Her getting injured had been his number-one concern. Nora had written back that *his* getting injured was *her* number-one concern. *So now we're even*, she'd written in her letter.

> *I know you're not thrilled about me taking this job, honey. But I feel like <u>I need to do my part for the war.</u> I seem to recall someone we both know telling me the exact same thing when he enlisted in the Army Medical Corps. Besides, we could use the extra income around here . . .*

They'd gone from Pete's doctor's salary of $660 a month to the $54 a month from the army. Nora didn't want to deplete their savings while Pete was away. Plus, Chris was going away to college next year, God willing, and Jane, not long after him.

Pete eventually came around to her way of thinking. But he

still wasn't too thrilled about his wife working—just as Ray had predicted.

Nora wanted to assure Pete that, after her first day on the job, she was confident she could pull it off.

*There's a big sign overhead when you walk back to the assembly line from the cafeteria,* she wrote.

> *It says: 34 DAYS WITHOUT AN ACCIDENT.*
> *If you saw how absolutely huge this plant is, Pete, and how many thousands of people work there, you'd know that's a pretty remarkable record. And I don't intend to be the one to ruin it. So don't you worry—*

Nora heard something outside, and she stopped writing. It sounded like one of the garbage cans scraping against the driveway.

Springing to her feet, she hurried into the kitchen and switched on the outside light. Blackout restrictions be damned. She wanted to catch these hooligans in the act. She unlocked the kitchen door and flung it open.

Over on the far side of the garage, a raccoon standing on its hind legs clawed at the top of the garbage can. "Get out of there!" Nora hissed, clapping her hands loudly. "Get!"

The raccoon's eyes caught the light as it looked at her. Then it lazily returned to all fours and wandered back toward the ravine.

Nora's heart was still racing as she watched the animal disappear in the shadows. Gazing at the dark, wooded ravine, she suddenly felt as if someone was there amid the trees, staring at her. She thought about the woman who was strangled late last night, an assembly-line worker—like her.

Rubbing her arms from the chill, Nora shuddered and quickly ducked back inside. But as she locked the door, she sensed someone else in the kitchen. She swiveled around.

Chris stood over near the refrigerator, staring back and looking just as startled.

"God, you scared me," Nora gasped.

"Sorry," he said. "I heard something outside."

Catching her breath, Nora fixed the door's chain lock. "I heard it, too. It was just a raccoon." She looked him up and down. Chris wore a sweatshirt, blue jeans and his tennis shoes. He rarely wore his shoes in the house. "Where are you going?" she asked. "Why aren't you ready for bed?"

He looked at her as if she were crazy. "Mom, it's not even ten o'clock yet. And I was headed outside to check on the noise."

She took a glass from the drying rack. "Where's your sister?"

He shrugged. "In her room, doing her homework or clipping pictures from movie magazines or whatever she does in there. I don't know." He stepped aside as Nora opened the refrigerator. "Why are you still up?" he asked. "Don't you have to leave for work in about seven hours?"

"I was writing to your father." Nora took out a bottle of milk and poured a glass for herself. "I was just about to head up. I'll finish the letter tomorrow." Leaning back against the kitchen counter, she sipped her milk and gave him a wary look. "So can I count on you to go to bed at a decent hour and not sneak out again in the middle of the night?"

"Yeah, Mom," he muttered, looking at the kitchen floor.

"For last night's little stunt, I've decided to ground you for just a week," she said. "But there's a catch. You're going to help me clean out the garage apartment and move Tak and Miko's things to our attic. It occurred to me last night, they're not coming back for a while, and there's a housing shortage. I figured we'd rent the place out again. You'll help me get it ready for showing."

"So . . . I'm sentenced to one week of hard labor, swell," Chris said. He seemed to consider it, and he nodded. "Okay, I guess I have it coming. I'll start clearing out their stuff tomorrow. Well, g'night." He sheepishly kissed her on the cheek and then started for the front hallway.

"Oh, and, Chris?" she called gently.

In the kitchen doorway, he stopped and turned to her.

"Being grounded means no visitors," she said. "I don't want to see Earl around here this week."

He nodded again. "I figured as much. Night, Mom."

Finishing her milk, Nora listened to him head up the stairs. Short of tying a cowbell around his neck or handcuffing him to the bedpost, there was nothing she could do to make sure he didn't sneak out again tonight. She'd just have to trust him.

# Chapter 6

Sally Baumann felt someone hovering over her.

With a gasp, she opened her eyes and sat up in bed. She anxiously glanced around the darkened bedroom and, with relief, realized she was alone.

*It must have been a dream*, she thought.

Sighing, she sank back down and pulled the sheets up to her chin. She squinted at the clock on her nightstand. She always set the alarm for ten. How could she have slept through it? Had someone really been in her bedroom? Maybe the intruder had switched off her alarm.

*Yeah, blame it on an intruder*, she thought. She was still half-asleep and not thinking right. Obviously, an hour and a half ago, the damn alarm had rung, she'd turned it off, rolled over and fallen right back to sleep. She'd done it before.

Sally still didn't want to get out of bed, but she had to be at work in two hours.

It wasn't like she could sleep anyway, not with all the noise those stupid high school kids made outside. Even with her window shut and the shade down, she could still hear them. That was probably what had woken her up.

Sally had rented the one-bedroom apartment over a drugstore—two blocks from the high school—during the Christmas break. She'd had no idea the store would be a hangout for school kids during their lunch hour and after classes got out. Sometimes, there would be as many as fifty of them out there, gabbing away, laughing and yelling.

Wrapping her pillow around her head to cover her ears, Sally wondered if, as a teenager, she'd been as obnoxious as these kids were. Of course, she'd been. She hated to put down her own sex, but those teenage girls—with their high-pitched giggles and the way their voices carried—were the worst.

It was her own damn fault. She'd stayed up too late last night.

Sally worked the swing shift at Boeing: two thirty until ten in the evening. She told people she was a riveter, because most everyone knew what a riveter did, but they didn't have a clue what a bucker did. Sally herself hadn't known when she'd quit her job as an operator with Pacific Telephone and Telegraph and gone after a war job that paid better. "Big girls like you are good as buckers," she was tactlessly told by the milquetoast clerk who had signed her up during orientation. "Bucking requires more muscle and girth than riveting. You have the build for a bucker."

For Sally, losing weight was a constant struggle. She couldn't help it if she was big-boned—and tall. She had a pretty, dimpled smile, a porcelain complexion and close-cropped jet-black hair. She'd always assumed she'd be married by the time she turned twenty-five, but that had been two years ago and she was still single.

She just wanted to get married and start a family. It was one reason she'd left her job at Pacific Telephone and Telegraph, where she'd been surrounded by other women. She'd figured her chances of meeting some nice guy with flat feet would be better on the Boeing assembly line. But most of the guys there were married. Practically all the eligible men were away fighting the war, and her prospects were bleak. It was like the song said, "They're Either Too Young or Too Old." The only steady guy in her life right now was Lloyd Adalist, who was sixty-five years old. He was retired. Lloyd and his wife, Dorothy, lived down the hall from her and treated her like an adopted daughter. On the other end of the spectrum were the high school boys who swarmed the area, some of whom would whistle at her as she left for work.

After getting off work last night, she'd eaten alone at The Dog House Bar and Grill. She didn't want to go home, so she went to one of the all-night movie theaters and came in halfway through the new Lana Turner movie, *Slightly Dangerous*, but it was only so-so. She finally returned home at one thirty, poured herself the first of a few scotch and sodas, and read for a couple of hours.

Now she was slightly hungover and wishing those kids outside would just shut up. How many of them were out there? It sounded like thirty or so. Throwing back the covers, Sally climbed out of bed and made her way to the window. She moved the shade and peeked down at the sidewalk below. She saw only about fifteen kids, standing in the rain like idiots. A few of them were smoking.

Sally took her robe from the foot of the bed and put it on over her nightgown. Then, barefoot, she padded through her hallway to the front door to pick up her milk delivery. She started to unlock the door, but realized it wasn't locked. She froze for a moment. She always locked her front door before going to bed.

The chain lock had broken two nights ago. It had been the strangest thing the way the links had come apart in her hand when she'd tried to set the lock in place. She'd mentioned it to Lloyd yesterday before going off to work, and he'd said he would replace the lock for her this week. Sally wasn't in any hurry. The building seemed safe enough.

With the chain broken, she'd have made sure the regular lock was secure before going to bed. How could she have forgotten to do that last night?

Three scotch and sodas, that was how. She might have even had four.

Sally opened the door, stooped down and grabbed the bottle of milk. It had been out there since around six this morning. She hoped it hadn't gone sour. It was probably okay. The bottle still had a chill to it. Stepping back into the apartment, Sally closed the door and locked it.

She started toward the kitchen, but then stopped. Under her bare feet, she felt traces of water on her hallway's hardwood floor—like someone had just come in from the rain.

Sally glanced over toward the living room, which had green curtains on each side of the entryway. She didn't see anyone there. But what if somebody was hiding behind the curtains? She looked down at the floor, thinking she might spot the intruder's shoes sticking out at the bottom of the drapery—the same shoes that had tracked in the rain.

But no one was there. Sally reminded herself that it had been raining last night, too. She could have tracked in the rain herself. It was probably just taking a long time to dry.

She was fine, for God's sake. No one had broken into her place—not in the middle of the day, and not with all those high school kids just below her window.

Still, she warily walked through her living room to the kitchen. From the dry rack by the sink, she took the all-glass vacuum coffee maker and filled the bottom chamber with water. While it began to heat on the stove, she attached the top chamber. She was just starting to spoon in the coffee when she heard a strange noise from the bedroom. It sounded like hangers rattling.

Sally paused again and listened. What was with her this morning? She was so on edge. It was probably just those kids outside making noise.

But then she swore she heard the floorboards creak.

Taking a deep breath, Sally quickly finished spooning the Chase & Sanborn into the top of the coffee maker. Then she headed back toward her bedroom, determined to set her mind to rest that everything was fine.

She didn't even get as far as the bedroom door.

She stopped to stare at her work pants, hanging on the bedroom doorknob. She hadn't put them there. She remembered hanging them in her closet last night.

Again, she felt the wet floor under her bare feet. From where she stood, she couldn't see anyone in her bedroom.

Sally turned her gaze to the darkened bathroom at the end of the hallway. She noticed her reflection in the mirror over the sink. And she saw something else in the mirror—a man in a blue jacket, hiding behind the open bathroom door. His back was against the wall, and he seemed to be studying her through the hinge crack. She couldn't make out his face.

Horrorstruck, Sally couldn't move. She wanted to scream, but she could barely breathe.

She didn't know how long she stood there, but Sally finally got enough air in her lungs to yell out: "Help!"

She turned and rushed to her front door. She'd forgotten she'd just locked it and struggled with the doorknob for a few moments before fumbling for the lock. Out of the corner of her eye, she could see down the hallway. The bathroom door swung halfway closed as he came out of his hiding place. Sally didn't stop to look at the intruder, but she could still feel him closing in on her. She flung open her front door and screamed for Lloyd.

Sally kept screaming as she raced down the corridor to Lloyd and Dorothy's apartment. Frantic, she pounded on their door. All she could think was that they weren't home—and she was going to be murdered there in the hallway. Sally kept banging on the door until—at last—it opened.

She almost collapsed in Lloyd's arms. "There's . . . there's somebody in my apartment!" she cried.

The older man took hold of her hand and stepped out to the hallway. Sally glanced back toward her apartment in time to see the intruder in his blue jacket at the far end of the corridor. He ducked into the back stairwell. She still hadn't gotten a look at his face.

After that, everything was all a blur for a while. Lloyd told his wife to call the police. Then he and Sally hurried to the end of the hallway. From the window at the end of the corridor, they spotted the culprit in the blue jacket darting into the bushes along the side of the building. He was heading toward the high school when he disappeared from view.

Lloyd told his wife to stay inside their unit until the police came. He took Sally back into her apartment to check if the prowler had stolen anything. That was when Sally smelled something burning. Frazzled, she ran into the kitchen and found the coffee boiling over the top chamber of the glass coffee maker. She took it off the burner and turned off the stove.

Sally's heart was still racing as she and Lloyd checked the bedroom. Her purse was on the dresser, where she'd left it last night—along with a few dollars and some change. Her jewelry box—full of costume baubles—seemed untouched. Nothing was out of place except for her work pants.

"Those were hanging in my closet earlier," Sally said, pointing to her slacks, draped over the doorknob. She clutched the top of her robe near her neck. She was having a hard time getting her breath. "He must have moved them while I was in the kitchen making coffee. I heard the hangers rattling. I thought it was just my imagination."

"Do you have anything valuable in the pockets?" Lloyd asked.

"Of my work pants?" Baffled, Sally shook her head.

"What do you suppose he was after?"

Sally just shook her head again. She heard the police siren in the distance.

She wasn't sure what she would tell them. But she was certain now that this stranger had been watching her while she'd slept.

# Chapter 7

*Wednesday*
*6:19 p.m.*

"Guess what, Mom," Jane announced at the dinner table.

"What?" Nora asked, not looking up from her plate.

They were having meatloaf left over from the night before last—even though it hadn't been one of her best efforts the first time around. The ground beef had been eight ration points, so Nora was stretching it out for a few meals.

Everything was in short supply thanks to the war—gasoline, metal, rubber and most foods. Nora was no expert on government organizations, but she knew what the Office of Price Administration was. The OPA imposed restrictions on the amount of certain goods an individual could purchase—based on the number of people per household. Nora received her first ration card book in the mail last May. In order to buy sugar, butter or canned goods, she had to forfeit a certain number of ration points in the form of stamps from the book. A month ago, the OPA sent her another ration book—this one for meat.

In the butcher display case at her local Safeway, they had the ration points posted—alongside the prices—by the poultry and the various cuts of meat. Depending on demand, the required ration points were always changing. Nora's butcher confessed to her that he still didn't completely comprehend the ration point system.

With these restrictions, Nora had learned resourceful ways to repurpose their meals. But tonight, she'd been too exhausted to do anything creative with old meatloaf.

Having been on her feet all day at work, she'd come home to "the garage apartment project." Chris had helped her move furniture and clean. But by the time Nora had to start fixing dinner, she'd felt depleted. All she could do was shove what was left of Monday's meatloaf into the oven, then try to make it through dinner and dishes without nodding off.

"Chris was almost arrested today," Jane said.

"What?" Nora set down her fork. It clanked against her plate. Suddenly, she was wide awake. All she could think was that Chris and Earl must have gotten into some kind of trouble again. She stared at Chris, sitting at her side—across from his sister. "What's she talking about?"

Rolling his eyes, he squirmed in his chair. "She's throwing you a curve, Mom. It's a huge exaggeration."

"It is not!" Jane insisted. "My friend Kim Baldwin said her sister Lynne was there outside Hart's Drugstore when the police almost arrested him. Lynne saw the whole thing."

"Well, that's pretty interesting," Chris shot back, wiping his mouth with his napkin. "I'm surprised she recognized me. Every time I say hello to Lynne Baldwin, she acts like she doesn't know who I am."

Nora was starting to get impatient. She cleared her throat. "All right, so what exactly happened?"

"Kim's sister got the whole story," Jane said—almost gleefully. "Somebody broke into this lady's apartment. She's a riveter at Boeing—just like you, Mom. She lives above Hart's Drugs—"

"How do you know all this stuff?" Chris challenged her. "God, Miss Busybody! You weren't even there!"

"Like I said, Lynne Baldwin talked to the police. A guy in a blue jacket—the same as Chris's navy-blue gab jacket—broke into this lady's apartment like he was going to rob her or kill her or something. But she screamed and ran to a neighbor's place, and the guy got away. Lynne said the guy looked like Chris. And Chris was right there by the drugstore, so the police almost arrested him—"

"God, you're so full of it!" Chris interrupted.

"Hey, don't snap your cap," Jane said, reaching for her glass of milk. "I'm just repeating what Lynne Baldwin told Kimberly and Kimberly told me."

"Well, you and Kimberly and Lynne Baldwin don't know what you're talking about. So why don't you mind your own business?" Chris turned to Nora. "The police spoke to everybody who was outside Hart's Drugstore. And there were a bunch of guys wearing blue gab jackets. I wasn't the only one."

Nora figured that much was true. The wide-collar, zip-up gaberdine jackets were very popular right now. But she had a feeling there was more to the story than Chris was letting on. "Were you with Earl?" Nora asked him pointedly.

"No, I was by myself. I just went to Hart's to buy a Clark Bar. And when I was leaving, the police stopped me. They asked me where I'd been and if I'd seen a guy in a blue jacket like mine. So . . . I told them I was in the store buying a candy bar. A bunch of guys were in there—and outside—wearing blue jackets like mine. The cops talked to me for thirty seconds maybe." He shot his sister a look. "I wasn't *almost arrested*, stupid."

Jane stuck her tongue out at him.

"Well, that's real mature," Chris grumbled. "Why do you bring up stuff that's none of your stinking business? You're just trying to get me in trouble with Mom." He shook his head at her. "What's your problem anyway? What happens to me at school has nothing to do with you, understand? God, you're such an obnoxious, little brat. I'm serious, Jane. You really are a creep, y'know? *A miserable creep.* I wish you'd—"

"That's enough," Nora interrupted sternly.

With her mouth open and tears in her eyes, Jane stared across the table at him.

Chris kept shaking his head over and over.

"May I be excused?" Jane asked in a shaky, little voice. She didn't wait for a reply. Suddenly sobbing, she jumped to her feet and bolted out of the dining room. Nora listened to her running up the stairs. Then her bedroom door slammed.

Chris sighed. "She's throwing herself on the bed right now, very dramatic," he muttered. "And notice how she conveniently got out of washing the dinner dishes again."

"What was that all about?" Nora whispered. "Why did you—*attack* her like that?"

"Because she was annoying me—and trying to get me into trouble. Like I'm not already in it deep enough with you. I wasn't *almost arrested*. And I didn't break into anybody's apartment—"

"No one said you did," Nora pointed out.

With his fork, Chris idly moved around the few scraps of food left on his plate.

"You really hurt her feelings," Nora said.

"C'mon, give me a break." Frowning, he squirmed in his chair again. "She bursts into tears or has a temper tantrum about six times a day lately."

"Don't you know she looks up to you, Chris? Now even

more so with your father gone. How could you talk to her like that?"

With his eyes still downcast, a look of remorse passed across his face. He sighed. "Okay, I'll give her a few minutes to calm down, and then I'll go upstairs and apologize."

"I don't understand why you got so angry," Nora said. "Is there more to this story than you're letting on, Chris? We were working all afternoon in the garage apartment together. Why didn't you mention it to me then?"

"Because I didn't think it was worth mentioning," he replied edgily. "I didn't think it was important. God, I walk into a drugstore and buy a candy bar, and suddenly I'm a criminal." Standing up, he took his plate, walked around in back of her and picked up Jane's plate. Then he headed into the kitchen.

Nora thought it was strange that the police had been questioning high school kids about something as serious as a housebreaking. And the victim had been another assembly-line war worker—just like the woman who had been strangled.

She heard the dishes clattering in the sink, and the water went on.

"Are you saving what's left of these carrots?" Chris called tonelessly. "It's not even half a serving, and they're kind of mushy."

"You don't have to wash the dishes," she called back to him. But she was too tired to get up. "I can do them later. I'd rather you square things with your sister. And you have homework to do."

He came back into the dining room and took her plate and silverware. "It'll only take me fifteen minutes or so," he grumbled. "Besides, I've been sentenced to a week of hard labor, remember? So . . . what do you want to do with the carrots?"

"You can throw them away," she replied. "Thanks, honey."

He headed back into the kitchen.

Nora thought about how Pete had a way of talking to the kids and managing them. He could get Chris and Jane to smile or even laugh through some of their most difficult moments.

She stared across the table at his empty chair.

Chris had the water going in the kitchen, and he couldn't hear her. So Nora went ahead and cried.

# Chapter 8

*Friday, April 9*
*9:07 a.m.*

"Oh, I blame the war for this juvenile delinquency problem," Marge declared. With her elbow on the cafeteria table, she puffed on a cigarette.

Marge Chaffy was Nora's bucker this morning. They kept changing work partners on Nora every day. Apparently, it was something the plant did with trainees. She and Marge were having their coffee break together.

"Mind you," Marge went on, "it was no picnic dealing with my oldest, Mary, when she was a teenager. The same goes for Leo. But my sixteen-year-old, Ralphie, used to be an absolute angel. Didn't give me a speck of trouble. Then the war came along, and now, thanks to the gang of hoods he runs around with, I wouldn't be surprised if he ends up on the Ten Most Wanted list."

After three hours of working with her, Nora was just now learning that the robust, fiftyish woman with the blue bandana was a widow with three kids: a married daughter, the difficult teenage son, and a middle child, Leo, who was twenty and in the army—stationed in North Africa. Nora had promised Marge that, when she wrote to Pete tonight, she'd ask if by any chance he knew Leo. "The odds are pretty slim," Nora had said. "But wouldn't that be a kick if they'd actually met?"

Nora was also discovering that Marge was a bit of a chatterbox when not working a bucking bar. Nora had merely mentioned that she'd had a hard time falling asleep last night because she'd been worried about her teenage son.

This prompted Marge to tell her all about her three kids—while puffing her cigarette and slurping coffee. Nora barely got a word in edgewise. But she liked Marge, and it was nice to have someone confiding in her. Plus, she felt reassured knowing that Chris wasn't the only teenager out there getting into mischief lately.

She wanted to believe that Chris had told her the whole story about the police questioning him outside the drugstore on Wednesday. Certainly, if he was an actual suspect in a break-in, the authorities would have detained him and notified her.

"I swear, Ralphie and his pals on the football team act like a bunch of hooligans," Marge went on, stubbing out her cigarette. "They're always breaking training, always whooping it up. Thank God Ralph's got a sweet girlfriend—not just pretty, but smart and nice. I hope he doesn't mess that up and lose her, because she's a peach." Marge took off her shoes and rubbed her feet. "How about your son? Does he have a steady girl?"

"No," Nora answered—with a wan smile and a little shake of the head. How could she explain to her about Chris's "almost girlfriend" who had committed suicide? And her son wasn't on the football team. He had no friends at all—except a loudmouthed bully who treated him like crap. Next to Chris, Marge's son sounded so normal and adjusted. Nora didn't want to open up to her about Chris's problems. The woman might not have understood.

Nora watched Marge slip her shoes back on and noticed for the first time that she was wearing brown, open-toed pumps. They were hardly regulation footwear for their job. Nora had read Boeing's list of recommended clothes, shoes and safety gear. Last week, she'd gone out and purchased a pair of lace-up "Military Walkers" for $2.99. They weren't exactly flattering, but they were on the list of acceptable footwear. Nora had felt lucky to find them, since shoes had become so scarce lately.

Marge caught Nora looking at her shoes. She wiggled her toe, visible in the small opening, and then she cracked a smile. "I know, I know, I'm pushing my luck wearing these."

Amused, Nora shrugged. "Well, they're pretty."

"But impractical," Marge said, holding her leg straight out to show off the shoe. "And to tell you the truth, by the end of the day, they're not the most comfortable things around. But they make us hide our hair and wear men's pants or coveralls. I have to hold on to one little bit of femininity. My lead man keeps saying I'll get into trouble one of these days if some higher-up checking the line notices what I've got on my feet. Fortunately, no one ever really looks at a woman's shoes except other women. Still, I know I'm living on borrowed time." She glanced at her wristwatch. "Goodness, speaking of time, our break's almost over. We need to get back . . ."

Returning to their station, they slid right back into a comfortable groove, working together on the tail assembly of a B-17. From the other side of the tail, Marge would give a little nod every time she had the bucking bar ready for a new rivet. Because of all the noise, they had to communicate with signals and gestures.

Nora wondered if she'd ever see Marge again after today. Or would she disappear like all the previous buckers who had come and gone? Nora decided to ask Marge to join Connie, Fran and her at lunch today. She figured they'd like Marge, too.

Nora still hadn't gotten used to what it was like to have a job—and coworkers. Fran had told her in confidence that she never saw Connie outside of the plant. Maybe it was because Connie was about twenty years younger. But before Nora had joined them, they'd been eating their lunches together for several months. Nora couldn't understand how work friends could be so detached once off the clock. Then again, they had their own lives and their own sets of friends outside of work.

Nora wondered if it was too early or too pushy to invite Connie, Fran and Marge over for dinner on Sunday. The only times she had entertained at home had been for Pete's friends and their wives. It would be nice to throw a party for her own friends for a change.

"HEY!" someone shouted over all the racket.

Nora took her finger off the trigger of the riveting gun and glanced over her shoulder.

Larry hovered behind her. He pushed his work goggles up to his forehead and nodded at Marge, whose attention he had now, too. "The foreman wants you up in his office—now," he said, loudly. Then he turned to Nora. "You stay put. I have to scrounge up someone to work with you. It might take a while. Don't move. Don't do anything. Just wait."

Marge gave her a bewildered look. All Nora could think was that someone—maybe Larry—had complained about Marge's nonregulation footwear.

"C'mon," Larry said to Marge. "They're waiting for you up in the crow's nest."

Marge moved her work goggles up to the edge of her blue bandana. She gave Nora a nervous smile. "Well, it's been nice knowing ya . . ."

"Good luck," Nora said with uncertainty.

But Marge had already turned away to follow Larry down the scaffolding steps.

The "crow's nest" was the head foreman's office—up near the rafters. Along one wall, about three stories above the plant floor, a row of offices with windows looked out over the assembly line. Some of the blinds were shut, some were open. One office, smack dab in the middle, jutted out from all the others—with windows on all three sides. That was the office of the head foreman, Mr. Susco. He was like God; he could look down from his "nest" and see everything that was going on in the plant.

Standing beside the tail of the B-17, Nora watched Marge follow Larry into the cage-like elevator. Larry shut the accordion-style door.

Glancing up at Mr. Susco's office, Nora spotted him pacing around in there while two other men stood and watched him. It was too far away for Nora to read his expression. But one of the men was in an olive uniform. For a moment, Nora thought the uniformed man was one of the security guards, there to escort Marge off the premises. Were they really going to raise such a stink over a pair of nonregulation shoes? But then Nora realized the man wasn't a guard. His olive-green suit was an army "dress" uniform. The third man had stood with his back to Mr. Susco's window. But now, as he turned around, Nora saw he was an older man. She also saw the priest's collar around his neck.

Nora's heart sunk. She felt sick.

"Oh, no," she whispered, watching the elevator stop at the office level. The door opened. Then Marge and Larry stepped out and disappeared down the corridor.

All Nora could think was that Marge had no idea what was waiting for her. She wondered if it was too much to hope that Marge's son, Leo, had merely been wounded in North Africa.

But if that were the case, they wouldn't have called for a priest to console her.

Larry must have left Marge at Susco's door, because, from what Nora could see, Marge stepped into the office by herself. And once Marge realized who was waiting there for her, she had to know what had happened.

It was painful to watch, but Nora couldn't tear her eyes away.

Marge stood there with her hand over her heart.

The uniformed army man—his posture suddenly ramrod-straight—started reading something to her from a piece of paper. The priest gingerly put his hand on Marge's arm. But she staggered away from him. Doubled over as if in pain, Marge collapsed into a chair.

Nora watched Mr. Susco move to the window and lower the blinds.

Still staring up at the "crow's nest," Nora imagined the sobbing and wailing inside the office. She could almost hear it—past the deafening noise of the assembly line. Dazed, she glanced around at all the other workers at their stations, going about their jobs.

She couldn't help thinking that Pete was in North Africa, too. The Allies seemed to be sealing a victory there. Had the Nazis made a last-ditch effort to regain a foothold in Tunisia? She wondered if Marge's son, Leo, had been one among hundreds or thousands of Allied casualties. Maybe he'd been killed in an aerial attack or some other kind of indiscriminate bombing.

Nora imagined a man in an olive uniform knocking on her front door tonight.

She had no idea how long she'd stood there at her station, waiting for Marge's replacement.

Nora had been told to stay put. But she was so shaken up,

she just wanted to go home—or at the very least, run to the restroom, duck into a stall and cry.

"HEY!"

She swiveled around to see Larry standing behind her again—this time with an older, stocky black man with a kindly smile and gray flecks in his hair. His goggles were pushed up to his lined forehead.

"You're going to be working with this boy for the rest of your shift," Larry announced, shouting over the noise.

Nora nodded cordially to the other man and then turned to Larry. "Is Marge going to be okay? Was it her son in North Africa?"

"That's none of my beeswax, and none of yours either," Larry replied. "This is Willie. Try not to inflict any bodily harm on him. Now, you've just had the last twenty minutes to rest up and do nothing while the company paid you. So, shake a leg and try to make up for lost time, okay?"

He patted the man's shoulder and walked away.

After what had happened to Marge, the last thing Nora wanted to do was go back to riveting like everything was status quo. But she managed to smile at the man. "Hi, Willie. I'm Nora."

He nodded and adjusted his goggles over his eyes. "Nice to meet you, ma'am."

"The woman I was working with, Marge Chaffy," Nora said over the din. "Did anyone mention what happened to her? Was her son killed?"

Willie shook his head and gave a sad shrug. "I'm sorry, ma'am. I don't know anything about that. I was just told I'd be bucking at this station." He walked around to the other side of the B-17's tail and pointed to the first hole in the rivet line pattern along the tail's edge. "Is this where you left off?" he asked, setting the bucking bar in place.

They didn't waste any time getting to work. Nora tried to

focus on riveting, but she kept thinking of poor Marge—and wondering if Pete was okay. Willie was a good partner, working in sync with her, and every once in a while, nodding and smiling at her reassuringly. Past the resounding blast from her gun, she somehow caught him humming to himself. It took her a while to figure out the tune. She paused before putting in a rivet. "Glenn Miller, 'Moonlight Serenade,' right?" she asked over the racket.

He chuckled. "I'm sorry. I didn't know you could hear me."

"Well, it was a very good rendition." With a nod, she set the rivet gun in place, pulled the trigger, and they were back to work again.

Pretty soon, she heard him humming another familiar song. It was The Ink Spots' "I Don't Want to Set the World on Fire." Nora didn't miss a beat of riveting work as she called the song title out to him.

Laughing, Willie nodded. He kept pace with her and started humming another tune. It took two guesses before she finally got it right with Duke Ellington's "Take the 'A' Train." The little game went on for a while—and made the time fly by. It also made Nora forget her troubles for a while—and she almost felt guilty about it.

She started humming tunes for Willie to guess. She almost stumped him with "Tangerine," but he got "Somewhere Over the Rainbow" after only a few notes.

"That one was simply way too easy, ma'am," Willie chuckled.

Smiling, Nora paused for a moment while she loaded a rivet into the gun. "Okay, I'm going to get tough on you for the next one, Willie. And please, call me Nora. I feel like . . ."

She trailed off, once she realized Larry stood a few feet away, scowling at her.

Nora quickly got back to work—and so did Willie. She sensed Larry approaching, but she didn't look away from her riveting.

"Save the chitchat for your coffee break!" he yelled.

Not looking at him, Nora just nodded and kept focused on the rivets. Willie nodded contritely as well.

It didn't seem fair. Nora had seen other work partners chatting at their stations while they went about their duties. No one ever reprimanded them. Was Larry completely dedicated to making her miserable?

But he wasn't the only one. Once he walked away, Nora stole a glance around and noticed a few others on the line giving her and Willie dirty looks. She suddenly realized that no one liked seeing her get along so well with a colored man. It made her angry—and sad.

She and Willie didn't say anything. Nor did they look at each other or smile for the next hour. Nora hoped she hadn't gotten him into any kind of serious trouble. The people scowling at them probably blamed Willie for getting too familiar with a white woman. She might get the cold shoulder from a few people, but they'd be a lot harsher on Willie.

When the lunch bell rang, Nora didn't know what to say to him. She didn't even know if he was coming back. Maybe Larry would find another bucker for her.

"Thank you," she called to Willie over all the racket. She wanted to tell him that she enjoyed working with him and hoped she hadn't gotten him into trouble. But she realized people were staring.

"Thank you, ma'am," Willie said, backing away from her. Then he turned and retreated down the scaffolding steps.

Two men at the neighboring workstation stared at him with unveiled contempt. Larry wandered over to them. He threw her a look and said something to the two other men that made them laugh.

Nora figured she was the topic of a filthy joke. She waited until they headed down the scaffolding before she removed her gloves and pulled off her goggles. Then she started down the scaffolding's grated steps.

She found Ned waiting for her at the bottom of the stairs. She was grateful for the older man's kind, fatherly smile. "Hi ya, Nora," he said.

She knew her face was flushed, but she worked up a smile for him. "Hello, Ned. Ever have one of those days when..." She trailed off, because he was nodding like he already understood.

"Larry's gone just a little too far this time," he said. "I can't believe he paired you up with a coon. What was he thinking? I'm going to say something to the lead man. Willie's an okay sort, but they should stick him with one of his own people."

Bewildered, Nora just stared at him for a moment. She finally shook her head. "Th-that's okay, Ned. He's really very nice. I-I'm fine..."

But she wasn't fine. Nora was so utterly disappointed in this man she'd thought was sweet and caring, she had a hard time concealing it. She could tell he was disappointed in her, too.

Biting her lip, Nora turned and hurried toward the cafeteria.

"Anyway, I think you're right about Marge's son," Fran said, setting her cold, homemade meatball sandwich on the crinkled wax paper in front of her. She sat with Nora at one of the four-top tables near the cafeteria's annex. Connie had left her half-eaten lunch on the table while she'd gone to talk to someone. She'd said her friend in the cafeteria line might know what had happened with Marge.

"They wouldn't have had a priest there if he'd just been wounded," Fran continued. She wiped her hands with a napkin. "When it happened to me, there was no priest and no grim reaper military messenger. They called me into the personnel office, and this nervous-looking clerk with sweat on his upper lip told me that someone from the navy was trying to track me down because Marty had been wounded. Of course, I went into shock. All the clerk could tell me was that Marty was in stable condition and being transferred to a hospital stateside. I was supposed to wait for the navy to send me a telegram at home that night—with more details. Once I calmed down, I decided to go right back to work. I knew if I went home, I'd just fall apart or climb the walls. So . . . get this, come lunch-time, I'm sitting here with my egg salad sandwich, trying to keep myself together, and this woman comes and sits next to me. Her name's Bunny Something, one of the secretaries. She's around my age—maybe a little older. I used to think she was pretty nice. Well, Bunny says she heard that my son got wounded and oh, what a shame and all that. Then she asks if I'd heard of the National League of American Mothers. I'm think-ing it's some kind of organization for the mothers of service-men—or wounded servicemen. But no. Bunny cleared that up for me really quick. Turns out she's with some crazy isolation-ist group. She started telling me that it's the Jews and President Franklin D. *Rosenvelt*'s fault that my son was overseas fighting a war we have no business being in. Can you imagine—a Jew-hating Nazi sympathizer working and recruiting here?"

Setting down her peanut butter and jelly sandwich, Nora shook her head.

"I told her—first off—that my son was in the Pacific, not over in Europe or North Africa. And second, I said, 'Just be-cause he's fighting for your right to spout your stupid fascist bullshit, Bunny, it doesn't mean I have to listen, thank you very much.'"

"Good for you!" Nora said.

"Anyway, my point is—it takes all kinds, and just about every one of them is working here. So don't be surprised if some people you think are swell end up disappointing you. The funny thing about this Ned fella is I'm sure he doesn't consider himself a bigot at all." She picked up her messy sandwich again. "And don't worry about your friend, Willie. I don't think anyone's going to lynch him or anything—"

"Oh, Fran, don't even say that!" Nora winced.

"I'm sorry, me and my big mouth. But it struck me that's what you were afraid might happen. The sad truth is, you were rattled by the way people were reacting, but I'll bet he has to put up with that kind of thing five times a day. Not that it makes it any easier to put up with. Anyway, it's not your fault how people react." She glanced past Nora's shoulder. "Is that Connie? She's certainly been gone long enough . . ."

Nora turned and spotted Connie in the crowded cafeteria. Her pink and black bandana was a giveaway. Weaving through the tables and the people, she headed toward them.

"I got the story from my friend Kaye," Connie announced glumly. She plopped down in her chair and put a napkin in her lap. "You're right, Nora, her son was killed. But it wasn't in some battle or attack. He was driving a jeep and ran over an old mine."

"Oh, how awful," Nora murmured. "No wonder they called a priest for her. Good Lord . . ."

Nora took a deep breath and told herself that at least she could rest easy about Pete for a while. There was no last-ditch Nazi offensive in North Africa. Then again, in all likelihood, the army would soon relocate Pete to wherever the Allies made their next major offensive, and he'd be in the thick of all the fighting again—even if he wasn't exactly on the front line.

"I hope you appreciate this scoop, sad as it is," Connie said over her glass of iced tea. "It cost me a dollar."

"Your friend charged you for the information?" Fran asked, incredulous.

"No, Kaye hit me up for a donation. Marge's friends are all chipping in for flowers. I barely even know her, and I contributed. We better start winning this damn war. That's the third time I've gotten hit up this week."

Fran shook her head and turned to Nora. "She always complains about donating to these things."

"I have a right to complain. I just paid for the privilege." Connie took a bite out of her tuna fish sandwich.

"That reminds me," Fran said. "One of those donations this week was for that poor Loretta girl who was strangled. Have you heard from any of your sources if the police have a lead on the killer?"

Connie had her mouth full. But she gave them both a somber look and slowly shook her head.

Fran burst out laughing.

"What in the world is so funny?" Nora asked.

"Her!" Fran replied, pointing across the table at Connie. "With her mouth full and that serious pout on her face!"

"You're horrible," Nora said, but she started to laugh, too. So did Connie. "You're both horrible! And to think, I was about to invite you two monsters to dinner on Sunday night . . ."

"Yes!" Fran said. "A doctor's house in the rich section of Capitol Hill? Count me in. I'm dying to see how the other half lives."

Nora turned to Connie. "Can you make it—Sunday night?"

She had her mouth full again, and nodded—with an exaggerated serious look.

The three of them started giggling again.

After everything that had happened that morning, Nora felt guilty for laughing. She automatically glanced around to see if they'd attracted any attention. No one seemed to notice them—except for one person.

Larry sat alone a few tables away. He stared at them as he ate his sandwich. Nora couldn't read his expression. It wasn't his usual smirk—or the contemptuous look she'd gotten from him earlier that morning. He seemed to be studying the three of them.

He didn't look away when Nora caught him staring.

He just kept eating his sandwich and assessing them with that cold, detached gaze.

After her lunch break, when Nora returned to her station, she found a tall, stocky man waiting for her. He wore a face shield that cast a heavy reflection, so Nora couldn't really tell what he looked like or how old he was. "My name's Warner Nash," he said behind the shield. "I'm your bucker, and I'm not one for small talk. So let's get started, okay?"

"Fine," Nora replied. Then they started to work.

And neither one of them said a word for the rest of the afternoon.

# Chapter 9

*Friday*
*3:11 p.m.*

"*I'm Warner Nash, and I'm not one for small talk,*" Nora grumbled, imitating her bucker for the afternoon. "God, what a horse's ass. With my luck, they'll probably stick him with me all next week . . ." Carrying a bag of groceries, she turned down the block toward home. After getting off the bus from work, she'd swung by the Broadway Safeway and said goodbye to seventeen ration points for barely a bagful of necessities.

Nora told herself to cheer up. She'd survived her first week of work and didn't have to go back there again until Monday. And she was cooking dinner for her friends on Sunday night. Fran had asked if she could invite her son, the one who had been wounded in the Pacific. And Connie wanted to bring a date. It would be a regular party.

"Good God, what was I thinking?" Nora muttered. She'd just finished a major project, cleaning up the garage apartment. Instead of giving herself a break and resting up, she now had to clean the house for company, buy food and liquor, and cook.

As she started to turn up the walkway to the house, Nora was wondering what to serve for Sunday's dinner. But then she saw something that made her stop in her tracks.

Someone stood by her front door—with the newly repaired window. A tree branch was in the way, so Nora had only a partial view of a man in what looked like a dark blue uniform.

For a few seconds, Nora couldn't breathe. All she could think was that something had happened to Pete—and this military man had come to deliver the bad news. The kids weren't home from school yet. Nora imagined having to sit them down and tell them about their father.

With uncertainty, she took a few more steps toward the house. There was a seaman's duffel bag on the front stoop. The man's back was to her, but she saw the white cap and the sailor's collar squared off at his shoulder blades. Then the sailor turned around, and she saw her brother's face.

"Ray!" she screamed. Nora set down the grocery bag and ran up the walkway.

His arms outstretched, Ray grinned at her and stepped down from the front stoop. "Nor!"

Nora hugged him fiercely. He let out a little groan, and she quickly pulled back. She'd forgotten about his broken ribs. "Oh, God, I'm sorry! Did I hurt you?"

Chuckling, he rubbed his left side. "It's okay. Everything's healed. I'm just a little sore. I'm all patched up, honest . . ."

"I'm sorry, I-I'm in shock. I can't believe this!" Taking hold of his hand, Nora looked him up and down. "God, you look great, Ray, so handsome in your uniform. What are you doing here?"

"They let me out of the hospital," he said. "And I have a week of R and R before I need to report back to my outfit in San Diego. I just blew the first thirty-six hours of it coming up here on a crowded bus. Can you put me up for the next few days?"

"Of course," she said, getting her breath.

But then, in her head, Nora immediately tried to work out the challenges. They didn't have a guest room, so she'd have to put Ray in Chris's bedroom and exile Chris to the sofa in the family room. She was working now and couldn't keep Ray company during the day. And finally, most dauntingly, every time Ray had stayed with them in the past, it had turned into trouble. Nora couldn't help wondering if something was wrong already—if there was some other reason for this surprise visit. She adored her brother, but . . .

"What's the matter?" he asked. "Can't you squeeze me in? You've got a look on your face. Something's bothering you, I can tell."

"Are you kidding me?" she replied. "I'm just so happy you're here! We'll make room. The kids will be over the moon!"

She hugged him again, careful this time not to squeeze him too hard. Nora held on to him like that for a few moments. That way, he couldn't see her face—or her sudden, inexplicable apprehension.

"But it says right here on the menu that you have a twelve-ounce porterhouse steak," Ray told the mustached, middle-aged waiter.

"Yes, sir, I apologize," the waiter replied, standing at attention beside the table. "We're presently out of that item—as well as the prime rib, the beef tenderloin and the filet mignon . . ."

"Ray, there's a war on," Nora muttered.

Her brother nodded impatiently. "Yeah, so I've heard."

For his first night in town, Ray had insisted on treating the family to dinner at Von's Café in the theater district on Fourth Avenue. They didn't have reservations, but he'd used his charm with the hostess to land them one of the mahogany and brass booths. Nora sat with Chris beside her, and on the other side of the table, Jane was next to Ray. Everyone was dressed to the nines, and Ray wore his navy blues.

During the drive downtown, Ray had mentioned that he was in the mood for a big, thick, juicy steak. Nora had warned him that a lot of the restaurants were out of the high-end cuts of meat because of the war.

"I believe we have one lamb chop left," the waiter said. "If I put the order in now, it'll be yours. It's quite good, I assure you. I can also recommend the stuffed peppers . . ."

"Oh, c'mon now," Ray said, looking up from his menu at the man. "What are you giving me with the stuffed peppers? You've got some choice cuts of beef back there. You're just saving them for big shots, right? I'll bet if Clark Gable walked in here right now and he ordered a porterhouse steak, he'd get a porterhouse steak . . ."

Chris and Jane snickered. But Nora rolled her eyes. What confounded her was that the kids were always mortified if Pete so much as made small talk with the waiter or waitress in a restaurant. And whenever Nora asked for a doggie bag, the two of them would practically crawl under the table in embarrassment. But her brother was needlessly harassing this poor waiter, and they thought it was funny. Anything Uncle Ray did was just fine with them. He was like the Pied Piper.

Jane had brought along to dinner a wind-up toy Ray had given her this afternoon. It was a black Scottish Terrier that sat on its hind legs and played the cymbals. Nora had seen wind-up monkeys that played cymbals, but never a Scottie that was so musically inclined—probably because Scottish Terriers didn't have long arms or hands. But this one did. Nora imagined Jane's reaction if she'd given her the trinket: "God, Mom, do you think I'm a baby?" But Jane loved her musical Scottie because Uncle Ray had given it to her. She couldn't make up her mind whether to name it Fala or Toto. She must have wound it up and played it on the table a dozen times—with the cymbals going *ding, ding, ding*. Nora had finally told her to stop, which, of course, made her a complete and utter drag in her daughter's opinion.

"Party pooper," Ray had chimed in.

Typical of Ray, he'd shown up on their doorstep without any warning and wanted to stay for a few days. Fortunately, he'd found a solution as to where he'd sleep. And in a way, his timing was actually perfect. The garage apartment was ready for occupancy again, and he could sleep there without anyone having to give up their bed. Nora gave him the extra key to the house so that he could come and go whenever he pleased. With Pete gone, Nora didn't have to worry about the usual underlying tension between him and Ray. And her brother's presence was a much-needed morale booster for her and the kids.

Nora had last seen Ray over a year ago, when he'd taken the train up to spend one night with them during a four-day leave. He'd also used the visit to hit up Pete for three hundred dollars to pay off some creditors. Still, Nora had missed her brother.

But it only took a few hours of being with Ray again to remind her how much he drove her crazy sometimes. With his good looks and breezy, confident manner, so many people found Ray irresistible that he didn't realize when he was being downright annoying. Nora was always the one who had to point it out to him. It was a role she'd reluctantly taken on ever since they were kids.

"Ray, just order the lamb chop," she sighed.

Frowning, he handed the menu to the waiter. "All right, I'll have the lamb chop, medium."

"Very good, sir," the waiter said, tucking the menu under his arm with the others and making a hasty departure.

"I wouldn't blame him if he spit in your mint jelly," Nora said, cracking a smile.

Chris laughed. "Yeah, he's going to put a big honker in there, Uncle Ray."

Ray sipped his scotch and soda and then smirked at Nora.

"Remember the old man—when he ate lamb chops or pork chops?" He grinned at Chris and Jane. "This was your great-grandfather Whitlock. I've told you about that grouchy old fart—" He put a hand up to keep Nora from interrupting. "I mean, *coot*—grouchy, mean, old *coot*..."

Chris and Jane started to laugh.

"You guys wouldn't believe it," Ray went on. "Granddaddy would use a knife and fork on the chop—like a normal person—until he got to the bone. Then he'd pick up the bone and tear at the meat with his rotten old teeth. His chin would get all greasy. His fingers would glisten. It was absolutely disgusting to watch him. Swore me off chops for years. He ate corn on the cob and ribs the same way—gnawing at the food, slobbering and growling like a dog. I could barely eat a bite after watching him. It was enough to gag a maggot..."

He had Chris and Jane in hysterics.

Ray was laughing, too. As the kids quieted down, he shook his head and smirked across the table at Nora for a moment. "That's your great-granddaddy, guys. That's who your mom left me with when she went off and married your dad. I was eleven years old."

Nora said nothing. She just forced a laugh and tried not to squirm.

"What the hell do you think you're doing?" someone yelled.

Nora sat up in bed. She recognized her brother's voice—coming from outside.

"Shit! Let's get out of here," someone else said. Then Nora heard what sounded like two or three people running up the driveway.

Throwing back the covers, she bolted out of bed and grabbed her robe. While she wiggled her feet into her slippers, she heard another voice.

"Let go of me!"

There was murmuring, and then Ray again: "Do I look like a goddamn Jap to you, kid?"

"Lemme go!"

Nora ran out of her bedroom and saw Chris. They'd both come into the hall at the same time. He was fully dressed—with his shoes on. "Uncle Ray caught some guys by the garage—"

"Did you see them?" Nora asked, heading to the window at the end of the hall.

"Sounds like he's nabbed one..." But she could already hear somebody sprinting up the driveway. Nora looked out the window and saw Ray, standing in front of the garage. He wore a T-shirt and his sailor pants.

Jane's door opened, and she poked her head out. "What happened?"

"It's nothing, honey," Nora said, passing by as she headed for the stairs. "Go back to bed."

Chris followed her down to the first floor. As she hurried toward the kitchen, Nora glanced over her shoulder at him. "Did you see any of them?" she asked again. "Did you recognize anyone?"

"No, their backs were to me," he answered.

Unlocking the kitchen door, Nora rushed outside toward her brother.

Ray waved at her to slow down. "It's okay," he said. "Just a trio of punks with nothing better to do. I scared them away."

Nora stopped when she saw they'd left an open can of black paint and a paintbrush by the garage. They'd dripped and splattered paint on the driveway, but at least they hadn't knocked over the can. On the garage door, they'd scrawled in big letters: JAP TR—

"I heard the sneaky bastards whispering out here and caught them in the middle of this paint job." Ray nodded at the garage door as he rubbed his bare arms from the chill. "*Jap T-R*. What do you think they were going to write?"

Neither Nora nor Chris said anything. She was still catching her breath.

Ray shrugged. "Hey, on the plus side, we got a free can of black paint and a paintbrush out of the deal."

Chris moved past Nora. "Yeah, at least they didn't spill too much." Squatting, he carefully picked up the lid and pressed it in place on top of the paint can.

"*Jap Trap!*" Ray declared. "I bet you that's it. You had that Japanese-American couple living here a while back . . ."

Nora just rubbed her forehead.

"Mom, it's going to be okay," Chris said. He set the paint can and brush by the door to the garage. "If I spray the garage door with the hose right now, I bet it'll wash off completely."

"You heard him, Nor." Ray put his arm around her. "I scared the crap out of the three of them. Believe me, they won't be back anytime soon."

Nora nodded. "You're right. I should be glad. Thank God, you're here, Ray. It's good to have a man around. Maybe now they'll leave us alone." She looked at the big black letters on the garage door and then cringed. "I hope it washes off. We have company coming on Sunday . . ."

"I'll get the hose," Chris said, heading toward the side of the house.

"The guys looked around your age, Chris," Ray called.

His back to them, Chris stopped for a moment.

"Did you see or recognize any of them?"

"No, sorry," Chris replied, not turning around. Then he continued toward the water spigot at the side of the house. "You guys can go back to bed. I'll clean this up."

"Thanks, Chris," Nora said. She turned to her brother. "Why don't you come in for a nightcap, Ray?" She gave him a look. "Please?"

Nora started back inside, but held the kitchen door open for Ray. "All I have is crème de menthe," she said.

"Is it the same bottle—which was opened and recorked—you've had for about eight years?" he asked warily.

"That's the one." She closed the door after him.

"I'll pass." He sat down at the kitchen table and pulled a little pinball puzzle out of his pants pocket. Nora had seen him playing with it earlier. The game was about the size of a pack of cigarettes, only thinner. Ray stared at it and gingerly moved the pinballs around on a baseball diamond, trying to fill each of the four bases with a tiny silver pinball. GET A MAN ON EACH BASE! it read in small letters under the glass. Ray had said the game helped him relax.

At the sink, Nora filled two glasses with cold water. She glanced out the window at Chris, hosing down the big garage door. "Was one of those hooligans tonight a blond boy with a distinctly Aryan look?" She set a glass of water on the table in front of Ray.

Ray didn't look up from the pinball game. "One of them had light brown hair. The other two were darker haired. Why?"

Nora paused at hearing the toilet flush upstairs—followed by Jane's footsteps as she padded back to bed—and then Nora sat down at the kitchen table with her brother. "Chris's only friend is this towheaded creep named Earl, who constantly picks on him," she whispered. "I've always had a feeling he might be in on these night raids."

"I thought all that vandalism nonsense ended after your friends got relocated to the Jap internment camp."

Nora sipped her water and sighed. "It tapered off for a while but seems to have started up again. Tonight wasn't an isolated incident. They broke a window in the front door on Sunday night. I'm pretty certain some of Chris's classmates are responsible."

"You said this Earl guy is his only friend, and he picks on him?"

Nora nodded. "I'm really worried about him, Ray. He used to be such a happy-go-lucky kid. But all that has changed. And it's not just the war. He's been miserable for a while now. His grades have gone downhill. I can't get Chris to admit it, but I think he's being pushed around at school. Pete said it was a teenage boy's rite of passage or something. I know I shouldn't meddle, but I just want to help him . . ."

"I'll tell you what's not helpful," Ray said, sitting back in his chair. He still seemed half-interested in the little puzzle. "Having his mom say right in front of him tonight, 'Thank God you're here, Ray . . . at last, we have a man around . . .' "

"That's not what I said—"

"Words to that effect, Nor."

"Well, it's not what I meant," she said, flustered. "I meant I was glad we have a man staying in the garage apartment to discourage those little bastards . . ." She trailed off, shook her head and then got up. Nora went to the window again. She looked out at Chris, still washing the graffiti off the garage door. "You're right, I'm sure that's how it must have sounded to him. I should go out there and explain . . ."

"Let it drift," Ray advised. "If you try to explain or apologize, you'll only make it worse."

Nora knew her brother was right about that, too. She turned away from the window and sat down with him again. "Ray, could you do me a favor? Be a friend to Chris and maybe find out what's going on with him. He's so damn secretive. His bedroom window looks directly out at the garage. I'm pretty sure he knows who's been vandalizing the house. He must have seen them tonight. But he's afraid to say anything. Last Sunday, he snuck out in the middle of the night, and when I caught him trying to sneak back in, I'm almost certain he lied about where he'd been . . ."

"Nor, he's seventeen," Ray said, finally setting the pinball game on the table. "There's stuff he doesn't want to tell his mama. You need to stop mothering the guy, give him a little elbow room."

She nodded. She knew her brother had a point. With Pete

gone, she depended on Chris for so much. At the same time, she didn't want him to grow up.

"Do you think maybe he resents you for something?" Ray asked.

"Like what?"

"I don't know. Pete joined the Army Medical Corps, and now you've joined the *women's workforce*." Ray said it with a trace of sarcasm. "Maybe Chris feels like his parents have deserted him, like he doesn't matter anymore . . ."

Nora scowled but said nothing. Ray was the one who felt deserted. Her brother still hadn't forgiven her for going off, getting married and leaving him with their grandparents when he was eleven.

"Maybe he feels like he can no longer depend on you," Ray went on. "After all, you're not home half the time now. Looking at it from his point of view, it's not like you really needed to take this job at Boeing. It's men's work, Nor. If you're really so worried about Chris—"

"What do you mean, *it's men's work*?" Nora interrupted. "You sound just like Larry, this jerk at the plant. '*A woman's place,*' and all that garbage. Just a minute ago, you said I was mothering Chris too much. And now, I should stay home and bake victory fudge for him. Which is it?"

"Hey, don't get your knickers all in a twist," Ray said. "I'm just telling you what I'm picking up from your son. First, you tell me you need to know what's bugging him, and as soon as I throw out a few possible explanations, you don't want to hear about it. I can tell you one possible explanation that'll annoy the hell out of you, Nor. Are you ready for it?"

She let out a wary laugh. "I'm not sure, but go ahead."

"Do you think he's figured out that, because of him, you and Pete *had* to get married?"

The question hit her like a punch in the gut. She and Ray had never discussed her unexpected pregnancy from eighteen years ago. She had no idea he knew.

Sitting beside her at the table, he seemed to read her mind. "If I figured it out when I was eleven, it's a pretty safe bet that Chris has figured it out by now. And you've got to wonder how a kid might react to a revelation like that."

Nora said nothing. She heard the squeak of the outside water spigot being turned off. She got to her feet and went to the window.

"I said you wouldn't want to hear it," Ray said.

Nora looked out at Chris, standing in front of the garage door, checking his work. She couldn't see the black letters anymore. "Just please, do me a favor and be a friend to Chris," she said. "Find out what's wrong. Will you do that for me, Ray?"

# Chapter 10

*Sunday, April 11*
*7:27 p.m.*

"Ye gods, Nora, Fran—I almost forgot to tell you . . ." Connie set down her drink. She'd had a few cocktails before dinner and was a bit tipsy. She looked at Nora at the end of the table and then at Fran, seated across from her. She nudged her date, Roger Tallant, on her right. "Roger has a good friend on the police force—in the homicide division . . ."

Neatly dressed in a tan suit and a bow tie, Roger, an engineer at Boeing, had thick, wavy black hair. Nora figured he was about thirty and that he'd probably once been the cute boy-next-door type, but now was a bit past his peak. He'd brought Nora flowers, and from what she'd seen so far, he seemed like a nice guy.

"Roger has all the latest on the murder," Connie went on excitedly. "You know, the girl who was strangled . . ."

"What murder?" piped up Jane, seated on Connie's left.

"Oops," Fran said, cracking a smile.

Wide-eyed, Connie turned to Nora again. "Don't your kids know about it? Oh, God, did I say the wrong thing?"

Nora caught Chris squinting at her as if baffled. Seated between Fran and his uncle at the other end of the table, he shifted in his chair.

Nora gave Connie an offhand shrug. "It's okay. I didn't mention it to anyone because I didn't really know the poor woman—"

"What poor woman?" Jane pressed. "What happened? Who was strangled?"

"Should I tell?" Connie asked Nora. "Or would you rather I just drop it?"

"Well, after this buildup, you can't leave us hanging," Ray said over his highball glass. "Please, one of you has to spill your guts about this. Who got murdered?"

Nora worked up a smile for Connie and finally nodded. "Go ahead. You can tell them." Then she shot Jane a look. "But if you get nightmares tonight, don't blame me."

"I won't," Jane promised. She turned to Connie. "What happened?"

"Well, this girl from Arkansas who worked with her sister in the wing assembly section, her name was Loretta Bryant . . ."

Connie seemed to relish holding court as she explained who Loretta was, though she admitted to knowing her only slightly.

Nora sat back and observed her dinner guests—to make sure everyone seemed to be enjoying themselves. She'd made chicken fricassee, which was relatively easy to throw together. Looking at the empty plates around the table, Nora assumed everyone was happy with the meal. Ray had bought the liquor, set up the bar and kept the refreshments flowing. Connie was the only one who had obviously imbibed too much, and even then, she wasn't a sloppy drunk. She was just having a good time.

The only glitch in the evening—so far—had happened right

before Fran DeLuca and her son had arrived. Jane had discovered that the flusher to the powder room toilet wasn't working. The rod connected to the chain had broken. They were able to take the lid off the tank and flush the toilet manually. But for the party, they kept the powder room door closed and sent everyone upstairs to use the bathroom. Nobody seemed to mind. Nora told herself, if that was the worst thing to happen at the dinner party, then she'd be lucky.

For Nora, it was a novelty to see her work friends "all dolled up." Wearing dresses, and with their bandanas off and hair coiffed, Fran and Connie said they almost didn't recognize each other.

The kids were on their best behavior, and Ray hadn't offended anyone—yet. In fact, he was very charming and funny. From the way Connie laughed at all his jokes and flirted a bit, she seemed quite taken with him. Her date, Roger, didn't seem to mind. He laughed at all of Ray's wisecracks, too.

The only guest not having fun was Fran's son, Marty, who sat at Nora's left—and beside his mother. He was shy and awkwardly self-conscious. And who could blame him? Fran had told Nora this would be his first social gathering since his release from the navy hospital. Marty was a good-looking, baby-faced Italian boy with curly black hair, a chiseled jawline and a cleft in his chin—but then there was the ugly pink scar around his left eye. And his artificial eye was so obviously glass—and cheap-looking—that it seemed to desecrate his face.

Nora had assured Fran ahead of time that Marty shouldn't feel ill at ease about his eye. This was a doctor's house. She and the kids had seen all sorts of scars, cuts and injuries. Whenever there was an accident in the neighborhood, they could count on a visit from the victim. Nora had gotten used to cleaning up the blood.

And just in case Chris and Jane had forgotten how to act around someone with an obvious injury, she'd reminded them: "Don't make a big deal of it, okay?"

When Fran and Marty had first arrived, bringing along the apple pie Fran had made for dessert, Nora had mentioned to them that Connie and her date hadn't shown up yet.

"Well, I'll keep an eye out for them!" Marty said, and then he chuckled. "Don't worry, I don't mean that literally!"

Everyone had laughed—although with a trace of uneasiness. But the joke had broken the ice, and Nora had figured it would be smooth sailing after that.

But she was wrong.

Marty had tried to talk with Chris about the University of Washington Huskies upcoming football season, which was like talking physics with a cocker spaniel. Chris's lack of interest in sports made it a strained, one-sided conversation—until Chris finally told Marty: "I'm really sorry, but I don't follow college football much . . ."

After that, Marty seemed to quit trying. He clammed up, and no one could really bring him out again. Nora hoped she and his mom were the only ones to notice. He smiled his polite smile—and quietly answered all questions in a sentence or two. He ate his dinner and complimented Nora on her cooking. But she could tell he didn't want to be there. Or maybe he just wanted to be invisible.

He seemed temporarily content while Connie had everyone's attention—and no one was looking at him.

"I'm not saying they were a couple of floozies," Connie pointed out. "It's just that the sisters were fresh off the farm and living it up now that they were out on their own. Anyway, like I say, the older sister, Jo Ellen, she'd brought this sailor home, and they discovered her sister dead . . . strangled. So, the police think maybe Loretta had brought someone home, too. I should let Roger explain. His friend, Phil, is the one who's a detective with the homicide division. He said the killer didn't have to break in. There was no sign of a . . . a pressured door . . ."

"*Forced entry*," Roger corrected her.

"Okay, okay, I'll let you tell it," Connie said.

"Well, the police figured it was about an hour between the time Loretta left her sister in the bar and when Jo Ellen found her dead in the apartment's upstairs bedroom at twelve forty-five," Roger explained. "They're pretty certain Loretta met her killer on her way home from the bar. Either he offered her a lift or volunteered to walk her home. A neighbor heard her chatting and laughing with someone by the front door around a quarter to twelve. So . . . the killer was either someone Loretta knew or had just met that night. Anyway, there was no forced entry. She'd willingly let him inside the apartment."

"She had to know him from before," Jane said. "Who would bring a total stranger into their house?"

"Well, he'd probably made her feel safe while he'd driven or walked her home, and then he managed to talk his way inside," Roger said. "The sister, Jo Ellen, said she'd let the sailor who had walked her home come in for a cup of coffee."

"A couple of floozies," Fran remarked.

"Or just very trusting," Nora offered.

Roger nodded. "We think he must have been a good-looking guy, a real smooth talker. He charmed her and put her at ease—"

"Sounds like our bartender tonight!" Connie said, flirtatiously smiling at Ray. "I'm not sure I feel very safe. Where were you a week ago tonight? Do you have an alibi?"

Ray smirked at her. "I was laid up in a naval hospital in San Diego. I still have a couple of bedsores to prove it. You're welcome to check—"

"Ray, do you mind?" Nora cut in. "Some of us are still eating." She turned to Roger. "You were saying that the killer must have used his charm to put her at ease."

Roger nodded. "The neighbor didn't hear any screams. The police are pretty sure he snuck up and surprised Loretta while she was changing her clothes in the bedroom."

"They think the guy might be like a Jekyll and Hyde character," Connie said.

"That's just Phil's theory," Roger said.

"Phil said it's possible the killer might not even remember strangling her," Connie went on. "One minute, he's a perfect gentleman, and the next he's a raving lunatic." She shuddered. "It gives me the heebie-jeebies just thinking about it. I mean, what if the guy works alongside one of us at the plant? How would we know? He could be—"

A loud pop of glass shattering interrupted her.

Startled, Nora turned to see that Marty had dropped his water glass. It had broken against his dinner plate. Shaking uncontrollably, he sat hunched over the table. Shards of glass rested on the soaked tablecloth. "I-I'm so sorry," he gasped, grimacing at Nora.

She put a hand on his shoulder. She could feel him trembling. Heat radiated through his shirt. "Oh, Marty, please, it's okay," she whispered. "Don't worry about it . . ."

"I'm sorry, everybody!" he announced, a tremor in his voice. His one good eye welled with tears. He couldn't stop shaking.

Across the table from him, Roger immediately stood up.

"He gets these spells," Fran said, her hand on Marty's other shoulder. "The doctors at the navy hospital said they'll go away eventually . . ."

Roger came up behind Marty and pulled at his chair. "Hey, c'mon, buddy, let's go outside and grab a smoke." He pulled out the chair, helped Marty to his feet and started to lead him toward the front door. Marty was still shuddering and seemed to lean against the other man as they stepped outside together.

"I'm so sorry," Fran murmured. "Nora, your beautiful tablecloth, and the glass . . ."

Nora carefully picked up the pieces of broken glass and set them on Marty's plate. "Oh, please, Fran. The water won't leave a stain, and the glasses were cheap." She got to her feet. "I just hope Marty's going to be okay."

"It's some form of battle fatigue," Fran explained. "He gets these shaking spells. They just sneak up on him . . ."

"I don't know if Nora told you," Ray piped up. "But I was in an accident and ended up in the naval hospital in San Diego for nearly a month, and I saw some guys with the same condition, guys who'd come back from combat with injuries. In the first war, the Brits called it shell shock. In the air corps they say the guy is *flak-happy*. But in the navy, I don't think they have a name for it."

"If we just leave him alone for a little while, I think he'll be okay," Fran said. "The idea that people are watching him when it happens, that's the worst part for him." She looked across the table at Connie. "Thank God for Roger. He was so quick to react. He's a real sweetheart. You hang on to him, honey."

Nora could see both Chris and Jane were a bit unnerved by what had just happened—and all the murder talk preceding it hadn't done much good either. "Jane, could you help me clear off the table?" She got to her feet. "Everyone else, stay put. We have ice cream and Fran's apple pie coming up for dessert."

Picking up Marty's plate, Nora stole a glance toward the front door, which was open. She saw Marty and Roger sitting and smoking on the front stoop. Maybe it was the distance, but it looked like Marty had stopped shaking. Roger was patting him on the back and whispering to him.

"The apple pie is better heated," Fran said. She turned to Jane. "Honey, don't get up. Let me help your mom . . ."

Once Nora and Fran had collected the dishes and silverware, Fran slipped the apple pie in the oven. Then she put on an apron with a daisy pattern. "This apron is awfully cute," she remarked as she moved over to the sink. She turned on the water.

"Fran, you're not going to wash the dishes," Nora protested, reaching in front of her and turning off the water. "It's enough that you made dessert. You're supposed to be my guest tonight."

Fran turned the water back on. "I have to do something or I'll go crazy," she whispered, tears in her eyes. Grabbing a plate, she held it under the water and started to clean it with a dishrag. "Did I tell you how it happened, how he lost the eye?"

Standing next to her, Nora stacked the dinner plates. She shook her head.

"He was on a destroyer in the Solomon Islands," Fran said. "Martin and some friends were having coffee in the break room. He'd just given up a sofa seat to a fellow crew member when a shell hit. Marty was grazed with shrapnel, and the other sailor—the one who'd just sat down in Marty's spot—he was killed." She stopped scrubbing the plate for a moment. "He and Marty were friends. The last thing Marty saw with his two eyes was his friend getting blown apart."

Taking a deep breath, Fran rinsed off the plate and set it in the drying rack. "Anyway, I want to thank you for having us tonight. I know we aren't exactly a perky pair, but I'm really glad he got out of the house. In a weird way, I'm even glad he had one of his episodes in front of everyone. Now he knows it's not the end of the world if somebody sees. He's so afraid people will think he's a coward."

"Nobody was thinking that tonight," Nora said.

Fran shrugged helplessly. "He hardly leaves the house at all—except late at night. Then he goes out driving, God knows where. He won't say. That scares me because of the blackout. It's not so easy to see things after dark. And, of course, he can't make out distances. Plus, he's using up all our gas ration points." Standing over the sink, she seemed to work up a smile for Nora. "Anyway, honey, I hope we didn't foul up your party. But I'm sure glad to be here. Thank you."

"Perfect timing!" Fran declared.

She and Nora had just finished passing out dessert when Marty and Roger returned to the table. Nora had replaced Marty's water glass.

Fran's son wouldn't look at anyone. He took his seat next to

Nora and picked up his fork. His hand still had a slight tremor. "I'm sorry about earlier," he muttered to everyone.

"Listen, Marty, don't worry about it," Nora said.

"Yeah, c'mon, it's no big deal," Ray chimed in.

Marty turned toward Nora but wouldn't look her in the eye. "Sorry that I broke one of your glasses."

"Hey, I've broken at least five from this set," Chris announced, holding up his water glass. "So you've got a ways to go before you can catch up with me. I'm still the champ."

"Yeah, champion klutz," Jane said.

Everyone laughed.

Nora patted Marty's arm, and he seemed to work up a smile. Then Connie started talking about work. Marty didn't say anything after that.

Just fifteen minutes later, once they'd finished dessert, Marty whispered to his mother. Then Fran announced that it was time for her and Marty to head home: "I don't want to even think about work tomorrow. And four fifteen seems to roll around faster on Monday mornings."

Connie and Roger stuck around for only a few minutes once Fran and her son had left.

At the front door, Nora shook Roger's hand. "You saved the party tonight," she said. "I'm very grateful. So was Fran; she said so. The way you helped Marty, you were so kind and considerate. You knew just what to do."

"Well, thanks," Roger said. "They release these guys from the hospital or from the service, and the poor guys aren't really healed yet—at least, not in their minds. I think—"

"You know, I'm going up and powder my nose before we head out," Connie interrupted. She'd had "one more for the road" after dinner and was now pretty drunk. She'd just been upstairs to get her coat off the bed in the master bedroom. "Nora, could you come up with me?"

Nora turned to Roger, who just smiled patiently and nodded.

"Excuse me, Roger," she said.

Connie teetered slightly as they headed upstairs together. In the hallway, she hooked her arm around Nora's, and they turned into the bedroom. "I really don't have to use the bathroom," she whispered. "I just wanted to ask if you think your brother might want to go out with me."

Nora was thrown for a loop. "Well, Connie, he's only here until Thursday. Then he's going back to his unit in San Diego, and they ship out after that. What about Roger? He's such a sweet man. I thought you and he—"

"Yes, yes, yes, he's nice and sweet and handsome. But I'm not his type. Believe me, I've tried. I'm giving up on him." She let out a sigh. "You know, I have a brother in Walla Walla. If I want to be treated like somebody's sister, I'll move to Walla Walla." She let out another sigh and then nudged Nora. "Meanwhile, speaking of brothers, yours is cute, funny, and I get the distinct impression he's interested in me—and not as a sister-type pal. Would you put in a good word for me—and give Ray my number? I really like him, Nora."

Nora hesitated. "Well, I'm not sure it's such a great match, Connie. Don't get me wrong. I'd like to see Ray with a girl like you. He's my brother, and I love him. But he's kind of irresponsible and reckless. I'm just afraid he'd cause you some trouble . . ."

"*Trouble* I could use right about now," Connie said. "I'm so tired of Roger *respecting* me. It's been months and months and months since I've actually been with a man. And I like your brother. I'm not looking to marry the guy. I just need some male company. Are you shocked?"

"No, I understand completely," Nora said, with a glance over at the double bed. She knew exactly what Connie was talking about. "I-I'll talk to Ray tonight, feel him out and see if he's interested. Then I'll let you know at work tomorrow."

Connie gave her a sloppy kiss on the cheek. "Thank you so much!"

Nora couldn't help feeling strange about what Connie wanted her to do. This wasn't quite matchmaking. Nora knew the word for her role in this kind of setup, and it wasn't used in polite society.

After saying goodbye to Connie and Roger, she kept wondering why the two of them didn't click romantically. She mentioned it to Ray: "I don't understand. They seem so right together, and Roger's a terrific guy . . ."

"He's a Section Eight," Ray said.

He was disassembling the makeshift bar he'd set up on the kitchen counter. Nora was drying off the last of the pots and pans. She could hear the radio in the family room. Chris and Jane had finished their homework, so she'd let them listen to the *Edgar Bergen and Charlie McCarthy Show.*

"What's Section Eight?" Nora asked, pausing in her work for a moment.

"It's the military status for mental cases and homosexuals," Ray answered, putting the bottles of liquor away in the cabinet. "And he's not a mental case. So you do the math."

"Oh, come on . . ." Nora shook her head.

"Hey, I could tell the guy was queer the minute we met. The way he looked at me—and Chris even. Then he was all over that poor guy with the shakes. I caught a glimpse of them outside on the front stoop. I thought he was going to end up kissing him."

"Oh, you are so wrong," Nora argued. "He was being considerate—"

"You're just naïve," Ray said, brushing past her as he emptied an ashtray in the garbage. "I've been around, Nor. Guys like him are on the make for me all the time. No big deal. Comes with the territory when you're good-looking. But I know whereof I speak. And he's a homo."

"Good Lord, you're so conceited," Nora said, drying a saucepan. "You think *everyone's* interested in you."

"Your friend, Connie, certainly was. And her 'boyfriend' couldn't have cared less."

"Could you please get over yourself? I mean, try it for just twenty-four hours."

He laughed. "He and your friend, Connie . . . I could see there's nothing going on between them. Ask her. She'll tell you that he's been 'a perfect gentleman.' I'd make book on it."

Nora put the saucepan away. What Ray said made sense in light of what Connie had told her earlier. He was probably right. But she'd be damned if she'd tell him and give him the satisfaction.

She was equally reluctant about fixing him up with Connie. She'd wait until work tomorrow and talk to Connie when she was sober. If her friend still wanted to get together with Ray, then Nora wouldn't stand in their way.

She started drying another pan. "Anyway—Roger's an engineer at the plant. He's got an essential war job. He's not a Section Eight."

"Fine, but he's still queer either way," Ray said. He put the lid back on the cocktail cherries and took the jar to the refrigerator. "Not that I care. To each his own, y'know? It's just, you asked me what I thought, and I told you."

Closing the refrigerator door, Ray turned to her and rubbed his hands together. "Listen, Nor, I know you have work in the morning and need to hit the sheets early. But for me, the night's still young. Do you think I could borrow the Packard and see what Seattle has to offer after dark?"

Nora woke up to the sound of the car pulling into the driveway.

Ray was returning from his exploits. Nora had been wary about letting him take the Packard to go out carousing. But she didn't want him stuck in that garage apartment with nothing to do.

She rolled over and squinted at her alarm clock: 2:10.

Nora remembered thanking the kids for being so much help with the dinner party, and then she'd gone to bed before them. She'd fallen asleep around ten fifteen.

Now she thought she heard murmuring—and a high-pitched giggle.

Staggering out of bed, Nora threw on her robe and headed out to the hallway. She padded down the corridor to the window. Moving aside the blackout curtains, she peered out toward the backyard. The Packard was parked in the driveway.

A light was on in the living room window of the garage apartment. Ray hadn't closed the blackout curtains. *Typical,* Nora thought.

Hunched close to the window, Nora watched as a petite blonde teetered toward the sofa. She threw off her coat and started unbuttoning her blouse. Ray staggered in after her. He already had his shirt off. He must have taken it off in the stairway.

"Oh, God," Nora groaned. It dawned on her that Chris had a perfect, unobstructed view of the garage from his bedroom window. If he was up, he could see all this. She glanced toward his closed bedroom door. She didn't see a strip of light at the threshold. But that really didn't mean anything. He'd keep the lights off so that he couldn't be seen watching from his window.

Across the way, the blonde took off her brassiere and playfully flung it in Ray's face. Naked from the waist up, she stood in front of him and waved her arms above her head. Nora could hear the muffled laughter.

The woman plopped onto the sofa. Ray came toward her. He started to unzip his pants.

Nora stepped back from the window and pulled the curtain back in place.

Part of her was outraged and disgusted. Another part of her

was jealous that her brother was having a good time. Okay, but did he have to do it with the curtains open? And did he have to do it with some drunken stranger? God only knew what he might end up catching from that floozie—or what she'd catch from him.

As she wandered back toward her bedroom, Nora muttered to herself, "He's leaving on Thursday. Just four more days . . ."

# Chapter 11

*Tuesday, April 13*
*3:48 p.m.*

Her arms ached. As Nora walked the last block home, the grocery bag seemed to get even heavier. She was lugging twenty-two ration points' worth of food.

Nora had once again stopped by the Safeway after getting off the bus from work. She'd been in there longer than usual. She blamed her brother for the extra trip and the extra time in the store. Thanks to Ray, she had an extra mouth to feed.

She found herself blaming Ray for just about everything. It really wasn't fair to him. Yes, her brother was driving her crazy. But Nora knew she'd miss him terribly once Thursday rolled around and he was gone. The kids would miss him, too—especially Chris. Ray had made good his promise to become a friend to Chris during this visit. And Chris happily lapped up the attention.

As she approached the house, Nora saw the car in the driveway. At least, Ray wasn't using it again. She wondered how much gas he'd left in the Packard after taking it out the last two nights.

Once inside the house, Nora headed straight to the kitchen with the groceries. She recognized Earl's voice coming from the backyard: "God, Kinney, you dummkopf! I passed it right to you!"

"Oh, goodie, he's back," Nora muttered to herself.

"Yeah, pal!" she heard Ray yell. "Yeah, 'right to him!' Maybe if he was eleven feet tall, he could have caught it! You're lucky the ball didn't end up in the goddamn ravine, because I'd have made you shag it . . ."

Setting the bag on the counter, Nora peeked out the window. Ray was tossing around a football with Chris and Earl. Nora couldn't help smiling. Every petty little complaint she'd stored up about her brother suddenly vanished. Ray was defending Chris and putting that obnoxious brat, Earl McAllister, in his place.

From the distance, it looked like Ray had some dirt on his face. Had they been playing tackle football?

Earl muttered something Nora couldn't quite make out. She started to put away the groceries. Except for that one outburst, it sounded like Earl was more subdued than usual—thanks probably to the presence of Chris's Uncle Ray.

Nora stashed the empty grocery bag under the sink, then straightened up and took one last peek out the window. Ray seemed to have things under control.

In the front hall, she checked the mail. Nothing from Pete.

She headed upstairs. Passing through the master bedroom, Nora started to unbutton her work blouse. But then she stopped abruptly in the bathroom doorway. She saw a piece of paper taped to the mirror above the sink. It was a note she'd left for Ray early this morning as she'd started off to work. She'd taped it to the inside of the door to the garage apartment—so he'd notice it on his way out. Obviously, Ray had seen the note, and he'd written a response right below it.

> *Dear Ray,*
> *I wanted to have a chat with you yesterday, but never got a chance. It's important that we talk in private today, preferably this afternoon before dinner. Thanks!*

> *XXX—N*

> *HI, NORA—YES, I NEED TO DISCUSS SOMETHING WITH YOU, TOO ... IN PRIVATE! SEE YOU THIS AFTERNOON.*

> *AFFECTIONATELY YOURS, YOUR HANDSOME BROTHER, RAYMOND*

Nora had wanted to talk with him about the woman he'd brought home in the wee hours of Monday morning. She hadn't been able to fall asleep after seeing the two of them. At around four in the morning, she'd heard some murmuring and giggling as they'd climbed into the Packard and driven off. At least Ray hadn't let her spend the night. Nora had had nightmarish visions of him bringing her into the house for breakfast—while Chris and Jane were there. Ray had returned with the car and gone to bed by the time Nora left to catch her bus to work.

At lunch on Monday, she managed to find Connie in the cafeteria line. It was easy to spot the pink and black polka dot bandana she often wore.

"That was a great little party last night," Connie said as Nora approached her.

The woman behind Connie gave Nora a dirty look.

"I'm not cutting in line," Nora assured her. She held up her lunchbox to show the woman. "I'm just talking to my friend." She turned to Connie and lowered her voice. "I didn't speak to Ray yet because something happened last night that I thought you should know."

Connie squinted at her like she didn't understand. The line shifted, and they both moved up.

"Remember, you wanted me to talk to Ray for you?" Nora asked.

"Oh, yeah, sure," Connie nodded.

"Well, I thought you might want to know," Nora whispered. "He went out to a bar and picked up some woman last night. He took her back to the apartment and . . . well, if you're still interested in getting together with him, that's the kind of guy Ray is. And God knows what he might have picked up from this stranger . . ."

Connie laughed. "Well, gosh, I guess I should thank you for the warning! You know, I'm not sure exactly what I said to you last night. I was pretty blotto. And I was mad at Roger about some silly thing." She shrugged. "Anyway, I'm glad you told me. And I'm glad you didn't say anything to your brother."

"So . . . you and Roger, you're dating . . ."

Connie hesitated, and then she nodded. "Yes. He's a sweetheart. Don't you think so?"

Nora remembered how certain Ray had been that Roger was a homosexual. She didn't want to press the matter with Connie. She didn't even want to approach it. "I think he's a real catch," Nora said. "It's just that you seemed kind of frustrated with him last night."

"Yeah, well, it wasn't anything, really," Connie said. "Roger's a perfect gentleman."

Nora just smiled and nodded. She hated it when her brother was right.

Connie moved forward with the line. "Can I get you any-thing?"

"Maybe some Jell-O," Nora whispered. "I'll pay you back. Fran and I will save you a spot at our usual table . . ."

As she made her way through the crowded cafeteria toward the annex, Nora wondered if it had ever occurred to Connie that her boyfriend might be a homosexual. Wouldn't a girl-friend know? Then again, some people could blind themselves to the obvious. Nora figured, either way, it was none of her business. And it was really none of her business who Ray had brought back to the garage apartment last night. She didn't want to be a prude. But she still wanted to speak with him, tell him that he should have been more discreet about it, and maybe lowered the blinds, at least. If nothing else, he'd violated the blackout rules.

But Nora had never had the opportunity to talk to him alone last night. After dinner, she went down to the basement to do a load of wash. When she'd come back upstairs, both Ray and the car were gone.

"Uncle Ray said he didn't think you'd mind if he took the car out again," Chris told Nora. "He said we shouldn't wait up. He might not be back until late."

Ray still hadn't returned when Nora went to bed at ten fif-teen. But the Packard was in the driveway and the lights in the apartment were out when she woke up in the morning. Nora reminded herself that she had to put up with only two more nights of Ray's thoughtlessness. Still, they were allowed only a certain amount of gas per week, and she had a right to know where Ray had been going with her car.

Nora had scribbled the note to him and taped it to the inside of the garage apartment door. Then she'd left for work.

It had been a long day. And now that she was home again, Nora just wanted to unwind in the shower for a few minutes.

Taking the note down from the medicine chest mirror, she wondered what Ray needed to discuss with her. Or was he being sarcastic—and making fun of her message? Nora figured, before taking her shower, she might as well get this talk with Ray over with.

Buttoning up her work blouse again, she headed downstairs. Before she reached the kitchen, she heard Ray's voice, droll, but still ominous. "Hey, you're lucky my nephew is such a peaceable guy, because he could easily beat the crap out of you, kid. Don't push your luck."

Nora hurried to the window in time to see Ray with the football, standing on the other side of the yard from Chris and Earl, who were a couple of feet apart. All at once, Earl cocked back his arm and then punched Chris in the shoulder. Even at a distance, Nora could tell it had hurt.

Wincing, Chris staggered to one side. "God, cut it out!"

But Earl just snickered and hit him again in the same spot.

Ray dropped the football. "Chris, you don't have to take that shit!" he yelled.

Earl gave Chris a forceful shove. "Yes, he does, because he's a chicken!"

"C'mon, stop it!" Chris protested, raising his voice.

Earl seemed to think this was hysterically funny. He made another move toward Chris like he was going to hit him in the shoulder again.

Suddenly, Chris hauled back his fist and punched Earl in the face.

Watching from the kitchen window, Nora was stunned—and for a second, strangely elated. But then, to her horror, she saw blood streaming from Earl's nose.

And Chris didn't stop after one punch. Unhinged, he knocked Earl down onto the grass and pounced on him. Chris was like a crazy man. He hit Earl in the face over and over—until Ray pulled him off.

For Nora, it was frightening to see Chris go berserk like that. For so long, she'd wanted to see him stand up to Earl, but not this way.

Ray held on to Chris, who was crying and trembling, yet still crimson-faced with rage.

Nora had seen her son get angry before—even to the point of tears. But she'd never seen him become violent.

Bloody and battered, Earl rolled over on the grass.

Even through the window, Nora could hear him whimpering and moaning in pain.

It was obvious that Earl's nose was broken.

He also had a split lip, and his left eye was swelling shut.

Nora couldn't get ahold of Earl's father, so she decided they should take Earl to the hospital. She scribbled a note to Jane, who was still at school, working on one of her many afternoon projects.

> *Jane—*
>
> *Earl had an accident & we've taken him to the hospital. He'll be OK, but we might be a while. Hold down the fort until we get back.*
>
> *Love, Mom—4:20*

She left the note on the kitchen table, where Earl was seated with his head tilted back. Nora had wrapped some ice in a dishtowel for him, which he was holding to his face.

Chris was cleaning up the blood around the kitchen sink. He was still shaking a bit.

Ray glanced at Nora's note and chuckled. "He had *an accident*?"

Nora frowned at him. Amid all the chaos, she had just now noticed that the "dirt mark" on Ray's left cheek she'd seen earlier from a distance was actually a bad bruise. It looked like Ray had recently been in a fight, too. Nora automatically glanced down at his hands. They were scratched and battered-looking. "Good God, what happened to you?" she gasped.

He seemed to wave off the question. "It was nothing. I just got into a scrap with this loudmouth at a bar last night. The other guy ended up looking almost as bad as Earl here."

"That's not funny," Nora muttered, glaring at him.

They all piled into the car to take Earl to the hospital. Chris sat up front with Nora, while Ray shared the back seat with Earl. His head tipped back, Earl kept the blood-stained dishtowel with ice to his face. He didn't say a word.

Chris didn't say anything either. At a stoplight, Nora stole a look at his reddened knuckles. She couldn't help feeling that he and his uncle were two of a kind.

Forty-five minutes later, the three of them sat in the emergency room waiting area while the doctor treated Earl. Silent, Chris occupied the chair beside Nora. Ray sat across from them, absorbed in his pocket-size baseball pinball game again.

Nora noticed tears in Chris's eyes. "I hope you remember how crummy you feel right now," she told him. "Because violence never solves anything. There's a happy middle point between letting yourself be bullied and becoming a bully yourself. It really scared me to see you go crazy like that."

"I'm sorry," Chris whispered, slouching more in the chair.

"Oh, c'mon, give him a break," Ray sighed, looking up from his pinball game. "He feels bad enough. Why make a federal case out of it? Y'know, it's not like the little shit is in a coma right now. Chris busted his nose. And the kid had it coming. They'll probably reset his nose, bandage him up and give him back to us . . ."

And Ray was right, of course—at least about what the doctor did for Earl.

It was nearly seven o'clock when they brought Earl home, his nose reset and bandaged. Chris stayed in the car while Nora and Ray walked with Earl to the McAllisters' front door. Nora explained to a gruff, apathetic Mr. McAllister that the boys had gotten into a fight. Earl's stocky, gray-haired father had come to the door with his suitcoat off, his tie loosened and a newspaper in his hand.

"Maybe it's a good idea that Earl and Chris stay away from each other for a while," Nora told him. "In fact, I don't want Earl coming over to the house anymore."

"That's fine with me, I don't care," the boy's father grumbled.

Earl was about to step inside when Ray put a hand on his shoulder to stop him. Ray whispered something into the battered boy's ear. Then he patted him on the arm.

Earl brushed past his father and ducked into the house.

Nora and Ray headed back toward the Packard, parked in the McAllisters' driveway. Chris had climbed out of the car and was waiting by the passenger side.

"What did you say to Earl?" Nora asked her brother.

"I told him to let it drift, y'know? Let bygones be bygones. And I said it was nice knowing him." Ray furtively winked at Nora.

He rubbed Chris's head, messing up his already tousled hair. Then he climbed into the front passenger seat.

"What did you really say to Earl?"

"What do you mean?" Ray asked.

"When we dropped him off at his house earlier tonight, you whispered something to him," Nora explained.

She and Ray were in the garage apartment, sitting at the

kitchen table. It was an old, oak card table that used to be in the family room of the house. With a pencil-compass point, Chris had carved his initials in one corner of the tabletop ages ago. The garage apartment had been rented partially furnished and was full of old furniture that had long since been exiled from the main house. Tak and Miko had added enough of their own touches to make the place seem cozy and quaint. But now, the apartment looked somewhat stark. The kitchen's green-tile countertop was empty. The garish green, yellow and rust wall-paper seemed to compensate for the bare walls. And the hot-water tank in the corner loomed over the apartment-sized refrigerator and oven/range.

Nora had made it clear to Ray that she still wanted to talk with him in private. Since he was staying only one more night after tonight, she no longer felt the need to admonish him about using the car or bringing strange women home. But she did want to know about the fight he'd been in. And in his response to her note, he'd mentioned needing to talk with her, too.

Returning from Earl's house, she'd thrown together "break-fast for dinner": pancakes, eggs and bacon. Jane had made her save the bacon grease to give to the butcher on her next trip to the Safeway. It was used for explosives. If there were a wartime use for eggshells, Jane would have had her saving those, too.

After dinner, Ray had grabbed a bottle of bourbon left over from the party, and he and Nora had retreated to the garage apartment for some privacy. He'd fixed them each a bourbon and water, which Nora had needed at that point—almost as much as she'd needed a shower. She still hadn't changed out of her work clothes.

"I got the distinct impression you didn't really tell Earl 'Let bygones be bygones,' or some such drivel," Nora pointed out. "So . . . what did you actually say to him?"

"I told him that if he ever touched my nephew again, I'd hunt him down and kill him," Ray replied. He raised his glass as if to toast with her.

"That's horrible!" But Nora laughed and clicked her glass against his. "And thank you."

She sipped her drink and then, for a moment, studied the bruise on the side of his face. "What happened last night? What was this fight about?" she asked, pointing to the bruise.

Ray frowned. "It's not worth going into—just some loud-mouth asshole in a bar. He wouldn't stop bothering this gal. So I made him stop. In your note, is that what you wanted to talk to me about—my nighttime activities?"

Nora nodded and then shrugged. "I just wish you'd be more careful."

"Duly noted." He leaned back in the chair and sipped his drink. "I thought you might have wanted to talk about Chris and what's bugging him."

"Has Chris said anything to you?"

"Yeah, but in confidence," Ray replied. "So don't go blabbing to him what I'm about to spill here, okay? Because you're not supposed to know any of this . . ."

Wide-eyed, Nora stared at him. "I won't breathe a word."

"Well, I don't think he's completely over his girlfriend's suicide. What's her name again?"

"Arlene," Nora answered. "According to Pete, she and Chris were just friends."

"Yeah, well, Chris wanted to take it up a notch. But old Arlene, she wouldn't even let him kiss her. At the same time, she wouldn't leave him alone. Chris was like her boyfriend—with all the responsibilities and none of the perks. She sounds like a cock-tease to me—and a first-class snob."

"Did you tell that to Chris?"

"In so many words, yeah. But he didn't need anyone telling

him. He knew. He said that she alienated everyone at their school. Chris didn't do himself any good pairing up with her. When Arlene blew her brains out, none of her classmates gave a rat's ass. It was around this time that Earl McAllister seemed to target Chris. To hear Chris tell it, the whole thing is kind of perverse. Earl wouldn't leave him alone. He coerced Chris into being his lab partner in biology class, but then half the time during class, he picked on him. It's like he wanted to be his friend and torture him at the same time."

"I knew that kid was screwed up," Nora said quietly.

"Chris is pretty sure Earl is the one who spread it around school that a Japanese-American couple lived here. And, of course, it's no help that Chris cuts the lawn for the rich, old Kraut lady who lives at the end of your block—"

"But she's Jewish," Nora argued. "She and her husband fled Germany when—"

"What, are you kidding?" Ray interrupted. "That doesn't matter. Hell, for some of those kids, her being Jewish is one more reason to hate her—and hate the kid who mows her lawn. As far as his classmates are concerned, with his ties to the Japs and the Krauts, Chris might as well be an enemy agent. And Earl is the one who put the word out. Chris says that Earl has a lot of influence over the cool crowd at school, only none of them will be friends with him because he's too much trouble. They think he's amusing and edgy, but absolute poison. Chris can't stand him, but he can't stand *up* to him either—at least, not until today. All this time, Earl has practically bullied Chris into hanging out with him. But outside of biology class and bad-mouthing him to the other guys, Earl doesn't have any-thing to do with him at school. Chris is persona non grata there. He's miserable. He's been getting by one day at a time, trying to avoid a couple of bullies. Chris is pretty damn sure it's his classmates who've been vandalizing the house and this garage—especially the more recent occurrences. He confessed to me that he recognized those three guys I chased away the other night."

"I had a feeling he knew who was behind all those incidents," Nora said—almost to herself.

Ray added a splash of bourbon to his glass. "Anyway, that's what I was able to get out of Chris. But I'm almost positive there's something he's not telling me, some big secret."

Nora's eyes narrowed at him. "What do you mean?"

"When Chris was baring his soul to me yesterday, I could tell he was holding back. I think he almost spilled his guts a couple of times—like he wanted to say something. But then he suddenly clammed up."

"Well, maybe he's worried about college—or getting drafted," Nora said, groping for an explanation.

Ray shook his head. "No, he mentioned that. This is something else. And whatever it is, it seems to be eating him up inside."

Bewildered, Nora just stared at him. She wondered about what this secret could possibly be if Chris wouldn't even share it with his uncle, in whom he'd already confided so much. But her hands were tied because she wasn't supposed to know that he'd unburdened himself to Ray.

She gazed down at Chris's initials in the corner of the tabletop. "Do you think it might have anything to do with what you mentioned the other day?" Nora asked. "You know, about how Pete and I *had* to get married?"

Ray shook his head. "Now that Chris has taken me into his confidence, I don't see why he wouldn't ask me—I mean, if that's what's bugging him."

"The other day, you seemed pretty sure—"

"Yeah, well, that was before he poured his heart out to me. I think he probably did the math and figured it out a few years ago and just hasn't said anything." He gave her a sidelong glance. "Speaking of family skeletons, do he and Jane know about their grandmother? Have you told them that she died in an insane asylum?"

Nora sighed. "I think I called it an *institution*. But yes, I told them a while back. And if he's worried about Mom's condition being hereditary, I'm six years older than she was when she died, and I'm still functioning—more or less. If Chris was really concerned about it, I don't see why he wouldn't say something to me or you."

Ray got to his feet, went to the refrigerator and pulled the ice tray out of the freezer. He took it to the counter and cracked the tray lever. "Well, whatever it is that's gnawing away at him, Chris needs to work it out himself." Ray dropped some ice cubes into his near-empty glass. Then he added a couple of cubes in her drink. "Same thing goes for the bullying. I know you want to help, Nor, but you can't. I mean, he'll be in college or the service next year, and if they start treating him rough, he can't expect Mama to bail him out. He'll have to handle it himself." Ray put the tray back in the freezer, returned to the table and poured some more bourbon into his glass. "For a change, I actually agree with old Pete when he said the bullying thing is a rite of passage for a lot of teenage boys. I told Chris the same thing happened to me when I was in high school."

"It did?" Nora asked, "You were bullied? I had no idea . . ."

"Well, how could you, Nor? You weren't around."

There was only a trace of accusation in his tone and his look. Nora shifted in her chair.

He picked up the bottle again and went to top off her drink. But Nora put a hand over her glass and shook her head.

"Anyway," Ray sighed, putting the bottle down. "I think things may turn around for Chris. I chased away those three little pricks the other night, and maybe now they'll leave you alone. And once the other guys at school see what Chris did to that little son of a bitch today, they'll leave him alone, too. It's something I figured out during my own rite of passage. Beat the crap out of one bully, and the rest of them will fall into line."

Nora nodded pensively, and then she remembered something. "The night before my first day at work, a Sunday night, Chris snuck out after I'd gone to bed . . ."

"You mentioned something along those lines the other night."

"Well, when I caught him coming back at three in the morning, he told me he and Earl had gone to see some battleships in Elliott Bay. But I'm not sure I believe him. Did he say anything to you about it?"

Ray shook his head. "Not a peep." He reached into his pants pocket and took out the little pinball-in-the-bases game he was so fond of.

"Well, maybe he was telling the truth." Nora sighed. Then she reached over and patted her brother on the hand. "Listen, thank you for being a friend to him these past few days, Ray. It means a lot to me—and to Chris. I don't want to think about you leaving the day after tomorrow. What are we going to do without you?"

Ray glanced up from the pinball game and gave her a strange look. "Maybe I won't have to go," he finally said. "Maybe something can happen that makes it necessary for me to stay here a while."

"I don't understand," Nora said.

He set down the little puzzle and took a swig of his drink. "I don't want to go, Nor. The idea of returning to San Diego and my new unit—it makes me sick, literally sick. I hate those guys. They're strangers to me. I spent a few days with them when I was out of the hospital and still recovering—before they gave me this leave. No one even tried to get to know me. They kept mistaking me for this other guy, Jackson, who's a complete moron. He doesn't even look much like me. Oh, maybe a little, I guess. My buddies in my old unit, they were the best. I think I told you, they shipped out to Guadalcanal not long after my accident. At least seventy percent of them ended up dead or wounded. The scuttlebutt is that my new unit will be shipping out soon, God knows where. But these new guys aren't my friends. I don't have anyone looking out for me. If we get into any kind of scrape, any kind of attack, I'm on my own. I won't be protected, because they don't give a shit about me. I know I'm going to die. I just know it . . ."

"Don't say that," she whispered, squeezing his hand. "Listen, Ray, you aren't alone in feeling this way. Pete went through the exact same thing the night before he had to report for duty. It's okay to be scared—"

"I'm not just scared," he said, cutting her off. "I'm *certain*. If I ship out with these guys, I won't be coming back. I fucking know it. I'm going to die. But I . . . I don't have to. There's a way out . . ."

"What do you mean, 'a way out'?"

"If I had another accident and was laid up in the hospital again, maybe they'd let me finish recuperating here in Seattle. If the injury was bad enough, maybe I could sit out the rest of the war stateside. I could get an honorable discharge, like your friend's son got."

Nora let go of his hand and pulled away. "Are you crazy? You want to lose an eye? For God's sake, Ray . . ."

"No, you don't understand," he said, shaking his head. "It's simple. Listen. At one of the bus stops on my way here from San Diego, I saw a stand with these Indians selling fireworks. I thought about how easy it might be to blow off a finger or something like that—"

"Ray, would you listen to yourself? You can't—"

"The navy wouldn't want me after I've been maimed," he interrupted. "Don't you see? I'll be honest with you, Nor. You know the fight I was in last night? I started it. I kept hoping I'd get injured in front of a bunch of people. I know now that it was a dumb move. Something like that is impossible to control. But it got me thinking, it would be so much better—more precise—if I got you to slam a door on my left hand."

"*What?* Ray . . ."

"Or I could just stick my hand in the hinge crack while you slam the door. It'll only hurt for a few seconds. You can tell everyone it was an accident—"

"My God, that's insane! And it wouldn't 'only hurt for a few seconds.' It'll hurt like hell for days! I could permanently maim you, Ray. I can't believe you're suggesting this."

But she could see he was dead serious, and it left her frightened and disillusioned. "Ray, when you had that fall a couple of months ago, was that on purpose?"

He hesitated before answering, and his eyes wrestled with hers. "No, but . . . but I have to admit, it gave me the idea for this."

"Are you sure it wasn't a *convenient accident*?" she pressed.

"You think I'd put myself in the hospital for over a month?" He shook his head. "Listen, I loved the guys in my old outfit. I was ready to go fight and die with them. I would have given up my life for any of them. And they'd have done the same for me." His voice started to crack, and he grabbed her hand. "But it's a whole other ball game with this new unit. I'm friendless there. Please, Nor, you can't let me go off and fight with these strangers. I'll get killed. I only have one way out of this. I'm begging you to help me pull this off."

"You're asking me to hurt you, maybe even permanently maim you."

"You'd be saving my life."

"I won't do it," she said firmly. "And, Ray, don't even think of asking one of the kids to be part of this ruse. They'd be so disillusioned. They idolize you—"

He sighed. "I wouldn't dream of involving Jane or Chris."

"Well, at this point, I don't know what you're capable of," she replied. Nora rubbed her forehead. "Ray, listen to me. Don't you understand that, if you have another 'accident,' the navy is bound to investigate it? You could end up court-martialed. We could both end up in jail."

His chair made a loud scraping noise against the linoleum floor as he suddenly pushed away from the table and stood up. "Fine," he growled. "Fuck it. You can take that thank-you for talking to Chris for you—you can take that and shove it, sis. I should have known you wouldn't help me. This isn't the first time you've hung me out to dry. You ditched me when I was eleven years old, and I haven't been able to depend on you since. I don't know why I even bothered to come here."

Wounded, Nora just stared up at him and said nothing. Tears welled in her eyes. She couldn't help thinking what he said was at least partially true.

Ray trudged over to the apartment door—at the edge of the kitchen, by the living room—and he flung it open. Then he swiveled around to glare at her. "This is your place, and I can't really kick you out, but I wish like hell you'd leave—right now. Will you do that much for me?"

Nora got to her feet and started across the room. Brushing past him, she headed out the door and started down the stairs.

"I know I was supposed to stay until Thursday," he called down to her. "But I can't stand the idea of being here any longer than I have to . . ."

Nora turned and looked up at his silhouette in the doorway. "Ray, please . . ."

"I'll get myself on a bus to San Diego tomorrow. When I ship out in a couple of weeks and end up blown to pieces or lost somewhere at the bottom of the Pacific Ocean, just remember, it's your goddamn fault."

Nora stared up at him. "For God's sake, Ray, please don't be this way. You're angry right now. Let's talk tomorrow. You can't go away mad at me . . ."

He reached over and snapped off the stairwell light.

Then he shut the door, leaving Nora standing there alone in the dark.

# Chapter 12

*Wednesday, April 14*
*3:19 p.m.*

"Turn green, damn it," Nora muttered.

Waiting at the traffic light, she had a white-knuckle grip on the steering wheel. Nora squirmed restlessly in the driver's seat and checked her wristwatch. She was still several blocks from the Greyhound terminal, and Ray's bus was leaving in eleven minutes.

Just a half hour ago, she'd come home from work and read the note Ray had left on the kitchen table:

*Dear Chris & Jane,*

*Well, something has come up & I have to leave for San Diego this afternoon. Looks like I'll miss saying goodbye to you guys. It was great spending time with you both! I'll be better about writing, I promise. Miss you guys already! Keep your powder dry.*

*Love, Uncle Ray*

Nora had immediately called the downtown Greyhound station. The ticket agent had told her that the bus to San Diego was scheduled to leave on time at three thirty. Nora hadn't been sure she could make it to the station by then, so she'd asked the woman to page Ray Shannon. While anxiously waiting for the page to go through, Nora had thought about how she could have been in the car and on the way to the bus terminal already. Five more minutes had ticked by before the woman had finally come back on the line to say that no one was answering the page.

Nora had thanked her and hung up. Grabbing the car keys, she'd run outside and jumped into the Packard. There hadn't been any time to leave her own note for the kids.

The light finally turned green, and traffic started moving again—but far too slowly for Nora. She'd still need to find a parking spot once she reached the terminal. She tried not to ride the bumper of the slowpoke in front of her.

"You're never going to make it," she said under her breath. Then she started to cry.

There was a chance Ray somehow hadn't heard the page. Maybe he was on the bus already. But more likely, he knew it was her having him paged, and he just didn't want to talk to her.

She couldn't bear the idea of her brother going away angry at her. She kept thinking, *What if he's right? What if he ships out and then gets killed?*

He'd asked her—begged her—to *save his life*, and yet she'd refused to help him.

But his scheme had been crazy—and criminal. She'd been so disillusioned that Ray wasn't ready to fight and possibly die for his country. But really, who was she to pass judgment? No one was making her go into the armed forces and fight. Most men didn't have any choice in the matter.

Even if Ray sat out the war loading supply ships in San

Diego, Nora still hated the idea that his last words to her had been so bitter. Before taking off for work this morning, she'd left him another note on the inside of the garage apartment door:

*Dear Ray,*

*Please don't leave today. You can't go away angry.*
*Let's talk and try to figure out some options for*
*you. Stay put . . . PLEASE!*

*I love you.*
*Nor*

At the plant, they'd paired her up with Warner ("I'm not one for small talk") Nash as her bucker again. She'd dubbed him "Laughing Boy" and prayed the arrangement wasn't permanent. During the break, an exasperated Nora had gone to the cafeteria to fuel up on some much-needed coffee. There, she'd spotted Roger and some of his friends at a four-top table. The men ranged from their late twenties to midforties. They were nicely dressed in shirtsleeves and ties. Nora assumed they were Roger's fellow engineers. Connie had recently said that she'd first met Roger through one of these coworkers. She said their group of five or six was like a little fraternity. "I had a date with this fella," she'd explained. "And, of course, it didn't work out. But he ended up introducing me to Roger, and we immediately hit it off."

Nora had wondered what Connie had meant by "of course it didn't work out." Had she meant it was just her dumb luck, or was there something else to it?

"Well, there's the hostess with the mostest," Roger called, getting to his feet.

"Hi, Roger," she said, approaching their table. "How are you?"

His friends all stood up, too.

"Please, everyone, sit," she said.

"I almost didn't recognize you in your work gear," Roger said. He and his friends sat back down. "Guys, Nora had me over to dinner at her beautiful home on Capitol Hill. Best chicken fricassee ever."

"Well, I'll need to get the recipe," one of the men piped up — with his hand on his heart. He was very animated. Husky and balding, he was clearly the oldest one there. "I love a good fricassee!"

Another man at the table laughed.

Roger shot them both a crooked smile before he turned to Nora again. "How are your kids — and your brother?"

"They're great, thanks," she said.

He stood up again. "I'm sorry. Where are my manners? Would you care to join us?"

She shook her head. "Oh, no, thanks. My break's almost over. I should get back. But it was great seeing you again, Roger."

"Well, thanks again for a terrific Sunday night. And I know you'll be seeing Connie at lunch, so say hi for me."

"Will do," Nora replied. She nodded and smiled at his friends, and then moved on. Closer to the cafeteria exit, she glanced over her shoulder at them and almost walked into Larry Krull.

"Hey, watch it!" he barked, dodging her.

Nora stopped abruptly. "Pardon me."

He chuckled. "I see you were conversing with the *Swish Delegation*. That's some company you keep."

She narrowed her eyes at him. "Pardon me?" she repeated, only with a much different tone this time.

"I'm not sure how you know those guys, but you were talking to a tableful of pansies just now." He snickered again and shrugged. "But hey, I guess it's none of my business if you want to associate with a bunch of queers."

"You're right," Nora said, her heart starting to race. "It's none of your damn business, Larry. Excuse me."

She brushed past him and headed for her locker. It wasn't until she was back at work—and getting the usual frosty treatment from Laughing Boy—that Nora started to breathe easily again. She didn't like confrontations, especially at work. And Larry could probably get her fired if she really crossed him.

She couldn't help replaying in her mind the brief exchange with Roger and his buddies. He was such a nice man. Yes, in fact, a *gentleman*. She didn't care what Ray—or Larry—had said about him. He seemed decent. She kept thinking about the husky, effete man who had asked for her chicken fricassee recipe and his friend who had thought that was so amusing. Maybe it was an inside joke she didn't understand. Or was Larry right about them? Were they all homosexuals? Then again, jumping to that conclusion—just because one of them asked for a recipe—was a pretty big leap. Nora told herself that it was really none of her concern—even if her friend Connie was probably wasting her time pining over one of them.

Then again, maybe Connie already knew. Maybe that was what she'd meant when she'd said "of course, it didn't work out," referring to a date with one of Roger's friends. Perhaps Connie's relationship with Roger was strictly platonic.

It got Nora thinking of what Ray had said about Section 8— the classification for homosexuals and psychological cases rejected by the military. If her brother was so anxious to get out of the navy, he could always claim that he was a Section 8. Of course, knowing Ray, he'd probably step on a landmine before telling anyone he was what Larry called a "pansy." It was doubtful anyone would believe him anyway. But Ray could always claim to have psychological problems. After all, their mother had died in a mental institution. Nora had the medical records in storage at the house. She'd collected them when their grandmother had died years ago. Ray could go before the navy board with the doctors' reports on his mother and say he'd inherited her acute melancholia, her insane paralysis or her manic depression. Her mother had been diagnosed with all three conditions over the years.

As Nora worked her rivet gun on the B-17's tail section, she couldn't believe she was even thinking about becoming complicit in Ray's deceptive scheme. Besides, would he want it on his permanent record that he'd left the navy because he had psychological issues? But was that any worse than possibly going through the rest of his life with a mangled left hand?

At lunch, Connie and Fran kept asking what was bothering her. They could tell she was anxious and distracted. But Nora couldn't talk to them about Ray.

Actually, two things were gnawing at her. Besides Ray, she was worried about Chris. Would he face any retaliation at school for breaking Earl's nose yesterday? Would he come home this afternoon all beaten up? Or had Ray been right about the other bullies falling into line now that Chris had finally stood up to Earl?

She also couldn't help obsessing over her son's apparent secret. Had Ray been right about that, too? Nora wondered if it had anything to do with Arlene's death—or perhaps something Earl had made him do. Of course, being a teenager, if he had a shameful secret, odds were that it was probably something sexual—and perfectly normal.

But what if it wasn't so *normal*?

At this point, Nora just wanted her son to survive the day at school and come home in one piece this afternoon. She also hoped to find her brother still there.

Instead, all she'd found was Ray's note to the kids. He hadn't even left a note for her. He'd said his goodbye to her last night.

She was coming up to the Greyhound terminal on the next block.

"Oh, my God, is that a parking spot?" she said out loud.

Nora sped through a yellow light to grab the parking place before someone else got to it. She'd always been adept at parallel parking, but suddenly, now, she was a complete klutz. She was so flustered it took three tries before she finally got it right. And for the last two tries, the driver in the car behind her kept honking the horn, unnerving her even more. The front of the Packard was still sticking out into the street when she left it, but at that point, Nora didn't give a damn.

By the time she made her way inside the crowded terminal, the boarding announcement for the bus to Los Angeles and San Diego was booming over the public address system. The art deco station was wall-to-wall people—with at least seventy-five percent of them in the armed forces. Nora had figured Ray would be in uniform, but everywhere she turned, she saw guys in sailor caps. Frantic, she threaded through the crowd, making her way toward the departure gate, hoping to catch her brother before he went beyond the placard that read PASSENGERS ONLY. She kept thinking every sailor she passed might be Ray. But there was no sign of him. The big clock by the departure gate showed it was a little past three thirty.

"Ray?" she finally called out. "Ray?" Tears in her eyes, she kept glancing around as she struggled toward the gate. "Ray?"

A few sailors nearby seemed to think this was funny, and they called out "Ray," too, one of them in a falsetto.

Someone tapped her on the shoulder, and Nora, startled, turned.

It was her brother—in uniform. Nora let out a grateful cry. She threw her arms around him and held him tightly. "Oh, my God, I thought I'd missed you," she said into his shoulder.

Ray gave her a couple of perfunctory pats on the back and then pulled away. He chuckled and shook his head. "Well, it was real decent of you to come see me off."

She almost couldn't hear him over the noisy crowd swarming around them. Nora held on to his arm so they wouldn't be separated—and so he wouldn't walk away. "Please, stay until tomorrow," she begged. "You can't go away mad at me, Ray. I want to help you—"

"You'll help me?"

"Not like you asked, but we'll figure something out. If you just stay . . ."

He shook his head again. "I already got my ticket, and—" He stopped talking as an announcement came over the speakers: the last call for passengers leaving for Los Angeles and San Diego. "Did you hear that? I've got to shake a leg."

"Ray, I'm so sorry," she gasped, squeezing his hand.

He gave her a wry smile. "Yeah, but not sorry enough to help me out like I asked." He sighed. "Listen, forget about it, Nor." He started to step away.

But she held on to him. "Would you call me or write to me when you get there?" She had to yell because the crowd grew noisier near the gate. "The last address I have for you is the hospital, and I don't know your new unit."

"I'll write!" he said, impatiently. Then he kissed her on the cheek.

"Please, don't do anything foolish!" she cried. "I love you, Ray!"

But he'd already turned around and hurried toward the PASSENGERS ONLY sign. Within seconds, the crowd closed in behind him, and her brother was lost in a sea of sailor caps.

Nora stood there in the rush of people moving toward the gate. She tried to catch one last glimpse of Ray, but it was impossible. He must have already moved through the gate.

Nora couldn't help feeling she'd never see her brother again.

# Chapter 13

*Thursday, April 15*
*10:50 p.m.*

When Roger Tallant stepped out of the Mecca Café with Connie, he thought he saw Nora Kinney's teenage son watching them from across the street.

The café was a perfect halfway point between Connie's and his apartments in the Queen Anne neighborhood. The restaurant was a bit of a dive, but it stayed open late, the cocktails were good, and it was one of the few spots that allowed women to wear slacks, which Connie liked to do—even after work. Occasionally, she also liked to stay up late during the workweek, tonight being a perfect example. They both had to be up in six hours.

Roger had cut Connie off after four gin and tonics, because she often became argumentative or sometimes overly affectionate after one too many—and Roger wasn't a fan of Connie in either mood.

"Say, isn't that your friend Nora's son?" he asked her, pausing under the Mecca Café sign, unlit because of the blackout. He started to wave to the boy but then turned to her. "What's his name again?"

"You mean Chris?" Connie asked, buttoning up her coat. "Where?"

Roger pointed across the street. But when he looked in that direction, Nora's son was gone. "Well, he was there a second ago. I could swear it was him."

"What would he be doing out this late on a school night?"

"I don't know, maybe following you around," Roger answered. "I noticed the way he was looking at you the other night. I think he might have a crush on you."

"Ha, I think you might have a crush on him," she scoffed.

"I got over teenage boys back when I was a teenager," Roger replied. "And I don't think Chris plays on my team."

Roger took another long look across the street, but it was as if Chris had vanished.

They started walking west—toward Connie's duplex, about six blocks away. Though chilly, the night was clear with a beautiful full moon. Connie was wobbling a bit and put her arm through Roger's.

"I'm surprised you even noticed Chris on Sunday night," Connie said. "You were so busy making goo-goo eyes at Nora's brother."

"I don't think he plays on my team either" was all Roger said. Connie was the one who had flirted shamelessly with Nora's smug, handsome brother. But Roger decided not to argue with her. Connie seemed to be in one of her belligerent moods tonight. She often taunted him about his sexuality whenever she wanted to tussle with him.

"By the way, did Nora mention that she saw me in the cafeteria yesterday?" he asked.

"Yeah, she said something about that," Connie sighed.

"I was sitting with the guys during our break, and Wendell

was camping it up," Roger said. "I was ready to strangle him. I'm sure Nora noticed. Did she say anything to you? I mean, do you think she's figured out about me?"

"Ha, it's not too hard to figure out. Not everyone is as dumb as I was about you."

Roger said nothing. He was imagining what could happen if Nora Kinney put it together that he and his little clique of engineer buddies were *queer*. All she had to do was say something to the wrong person at the plant, and he and his friends could lose their jobs. He was always worried about Boeing cracking down on "deviants" in their ranks. He could end up exposed— with his name in the newspaper and his parents finding out that he was a homosexual.

Connie tightened her arm around his. "You know, if you're so concerned about people knowing . . ."

Sometimes, it was like she could read his mind. And he could read hers, too. She didn't even have to finish her sentence, because he knew what she was about to suggest. She'd suggested it several times before. As if the two of them getting married would dispel any rumors. A couple of his gay friends were married and living a double life. But they were just as vulnerable as he was. Besides, he wouldn't do that to Connie. She deserved a husband who genuinely loved her in every sense.

"Please, let's not start talking marriage again," he groaned.

"But we're already friends," she whined, playfully bumping her hip against him as they walked. "In fact, we *like* each other more than most married couples I know."

He chuckled. "If we got married, we'd end up killing each other."

"You could change, you know."

"For years, I told myself the same thing: 'I just haven't met the right girl yet.' And, Connie, honey, you're as right a girl as I'll ever meet. We've known each other for months, and as much as I wish I could please you, I haven't changed one iota."

She released his arm and shoved her hands in her coat pockets. "You're not even trying . . ."

"If you have to *try* to be attracted to somebody, then the whole relationship is in trouble. I'm not going to change, Connie. I've tried. And all I've gotten out of it over the years is several frustrated, baffled women whom I've hurt. Then I end up feeling like a heel."

"Well, you are a heel," she argued. "You weren't honest with them. You never should have asked them out."

"Hey, most of them asked me out."

"Oh, yeah, you're irresistible . . ."

"Well, apparently so," he shot back. "Because you're fully aware of the fact that I like guys, and yet you still want to marry me." He heaved a sigh and muttered, "Nag, nag, nag. God, I feel like we're married already."

She stopped in her tracks and scowled at him.

Roger stopped, too. "I'm sorry, okay? Come on, it's late . . ."

They both started walking again.

"You don't have to walk me home," Connie said coolly. "I'm not helpless."

"I know, but I want to." He started to put his arm around her but thought better of it.

They walked in silence for a couple of minutes. Roger saw her duplex up ahead. The building was completely dark. There wasn't even a sliver of light peeking out at the edges of the blackout curtains.

"I'm not like those other women you went out with," she said. "I know about you. If we got married, we'd have an understanding."

"Oh, please, Connie," he groaned. "Those kind of arranged marriages hardly ever work." He tried to laugh. "I mean, you and I have the same taste in guys. If one of us got lucky, the other one would be so damn resentful and jealous. It's a recipe for disaster."

"OH, FINE!" she bellowed, stopping at the end of her walkway.

He shushed her.

"No! God, why do I waste my time with you? I'm sick of this whole thing! I keep all your secrets and listen to all your stupid problems. Thanks to me, people don't know the truth about you. I'm your smokescreen. You're just *using* me . . ."

"Connie, the neighbors," he whispered.

She marched up the walkway to the front stoop. Searching in her purse for her keys, she obviously didn't see the lights go on behind the black curtain in the front room of her downstairs neighbor, Myrtle. Roger could never remember the old woman's last name. Connie called her Myrtle McSnoop because the lady was such a busybody. She always complained that Connie made too much noise. She'd sometimes pound on her ceiling with a broomstick or whatever—just to get her point across. She'd even called the police on two occasions—most recently when Roger and Connie were just talking at a normal volume on her living room sofa at one in the morning.

"You can go now," Connie announced at the front door. Her back was to him as she continued to rummage through her purse. "I'm fine. You've done your *manly* duty walking me home!"

Roger saw the curtain move. "Connie," he whispered again. "McSnoop's on the warpath. You need to quiet down . . ."

"I don't care!" She pulled her keys out of her purse and held them up. "Found them! You can go now. Good night!"

She unlocked her door, ducked inside and then practically slammed the door in his face.

Roger stood there for a few moments. He saw Myrtle's blackout curtain move again. With a defeated sigh, he retreated down the walkway. He took one more look at Connie's duplex and saw a light go on behind the second-floor window blinds.

Connie could be such a pain in the ass at times, especially

when she had too much to drink. But she was also a loyal friend, and she knew him very well. Practically everything she'd said at her front door was true. She listened to his troubles, they had fun together, and people thought they were a couple. Since he wasn't the most masculine guy around, it was nice to have the "smokescreen" she provided. And he loved her—as much as he could, just not in the way she wanted.

Roger grew up thinking he was the only homosexual in Colfax, Washington. It wasn't until after college, when he moved to Seattle, that he started meeting other men like him, and he wasn't so alone anymore. He actually started having sex once in a while, but not nearly as often as some of the guys he knew. He still wasn't completely comfortable in that "gay" underworld. And, of course, on the outside, he tried his damnedest to come off as "normal."

After Pearl Harbor, like every other red-blooded American male, Roger and his closest "bachelor friend," Stan, wanted to do their part for the war effort. Built like a linebacker and hairy, Stan was almost as effective a "smokescreen" as Connie would end up being. Roger was amazed how easy it seemed for his friend to carry on a double life. Most people didn't have a clue Stan was "that way."

He and Stan were determined to join the army, but that meant lying about their sexuality during the physical exam. Roger was terrified of being found out. At the same time, he knew his country was under attack, and he wanted to do something. He also had a peculiar notion that the army might help him become more of a man. They might not "cure" him, but maybe they'd make him less of a sissy. Still, he was conflicted and filled with dread for days before he and Stan went to join up.

Roger shouldn't have worried. The army doctors found he had a heart murmur. He was rejected before he even got to the psychological part of the induction exam. Stan, on the other hand, effortlessly lied his way through the procedure and was accepted.

Stan had been like Roger's guide in Seattle's homosexual underworld. He'd shown him the ropes and where to meet other men: bars like the Casino and the Double Header, located in Pioneer Square, also known as "Skid Road" or "Fairyville." Without his friend, Roger was a bit lost. But he made new friends at Boeing—a small clique of engineers, a couple of whom didn't seem discreet enough for Roger.

He stayed in touch with Stan, who was having the time of his life in the army. Writing in code, he referred to other homosexuals as "Cougar fans," after the Cougar football team of Roger's alma mater, Washington State University. Stan said he was meeting a lot of Cougar fans at the army training camp in Mobile, Alabama. In a long-distance phone conversation, where Stan could be more candid, he told Roger about life in a barracks full of men in peak physical condition, all the new friends he'd made, and all the places he'd had sexual adventures.

Roger was jealous, but he also had a feeling that Stan was pushing his luck.

And Roger was right. Once there was no longer a critical shortage of inductees, the army started cracking down on homosexuals in their ranks. All it took was one soldier to say another guy was queer, and the suspect would be hauled in front of an inquiry board and made to name any fellow soldiers who were homosexuals or suspected homosexuals. They were classified as Section 8 and locked up in makeshift mental wards along with the "basket cases." That was what happened to Stan.

Roger found out about it when one of Stan's army pals called him to explain why Stan hadn't returned his letters. Stan's friend recommended that Roger not contact Stan again. It would only make things worse—for both of them.

Roger felt like his friend had been killed. It was as if Stan had died in disgrace.

Roger was heartbroken, and angry at Stan for being so reckless. He was also terrified. What had happened to all the letters he'd written to Stan? What if the army made Stan tell them about his homosexual friends in civilian life? What if the news got to Boeing, and the company forced Roger to name all his friends who were "degenerates"?

He didn't talk about these fears with his other buddies — only with Connie.

With Stan gone, she was his closest friend and confidant. So Roger felt awful whenever she was mad at him.

The last three blocks to his apartment building were halfway up the steep incline of Queen Anne Hill. Roger always took it slow, mindful of the strain on his heart. But tonight, he hadn't paced himself. By the time he reached his brownstone, he was exhausted. He would have stopped to catch his breath at the front door, but he heard the pay phone ringing in the hallway just beyond the lobby.

Unlocking the door, he flung it open and ran up the five steps from the vestibule to the lobby. He hurried past the mailboxes to the pay phone on the wall opposite the landlady's apartment. Just as Roger grabbed the receiver, his landlady opened her door. She poked her head out and frowned at him. She had bobby pins in her gray hair and wore a threadbare pale-blue robe.

"Hello?" Roger whispered into the phone. He tried to get his breath.

"Well, I was pretty awful, wasn't I?" Connie said on the other end of the line.

With the receiver to his ear, Roger looked at his landlady. "I'm sorry, Mrs. Mousel. It . . . it's kind of an emergency."

Clutching the lapels of her robe together, she glared at him and then nodded down the hall, where another neighbor, old Mr. Snyder, had his head out the doorway.

"It's always an emergency with her," the landlady grumbled. She'd answered the phone one too many times late at night when Connie had called for him. "Do you know what time it is? It's eleven fifteen . . ."

"Yes, I know. I'm so sorry," Roger whispered.

"Tell that old witch you own a wristwatch," Connie was saying on the other end of the line. "You know what time it is . . ."

"No consideration!" Mrs. Mousel hissed. Then she stepped back and shut her door. Roger heard the chain lock rattling on the other side. Down the hallway, Mr. Snyder closed his door, too.

Roger sighed. "I swear, one of these days, you'll get me kicked out of this place," he whispered into the phone.

"Serves you right for living in a building with a bunch of old fuddy-duddies," Connie said.

He kept his voice low. "Speaking of old fuddy-duddy neighbors, did you have any problems with Myrtle McSnoop?"

"Nope, not a peep out of her," Connie replied. "You know, if we were married, we could have our own house with our own phone, and no old biddies telling us what to do. You haven't even stopped to consider all the practical advantages to a marital arrangement. And with our stylish tastes, we'd have a really beautiful place. We'd give the best parties . . ."

Hovering by the pay phone in the hallway and still trying to catch his breath, Roger thought about how late it was. And his landlady was probably listening at her door. "Connie, honey," he said under his breath. "Are we really having this conversation *now*?"

There was no response.

Roger figured he'd made her mad again. "Connie?"

After a moment, he heard her voice, muffled: "Is somebody there? Hello?"

"What is it?" Roger asked.

"Sounds like somebody came in downstairs," she said.

"Your downstairs entrance? Did you lock the door after you came in?"

"I can't remember. Wait, just a sec . . ." Then she called out again. "Who's there?"

Roger had been in Connie's apartment enough to know the layout. Her telephone was on a built-in phone stand between the living room and kitchen. She would have to put the phone down to go to the door to check the private stairwell up to her apartment.

"Is your upstairs door locked and bolted?" he asked. Sometimes she left the door wide open when he was there. "Connie?"

"I'm not sure. I think somebody's coming up the stairs . . ."

"Well, maybe it's Myrtle—"

"She never comes up to talk to me. She always calls." Connie raised her voice again. "Hello? Who's there?"

"Listen, put the phone down and go bolt the door!"

"Roger, I'm scared."

"What—is this a joke or something?" he whispered.

"I'm serious!"

"Connie, put the goddamn phone down and go bolt the door!"

"Okay." He heard her set the phone down, and then her distant voice: "Is somebody there?"

Roger waited for a response, but all he could detect was a slightly muted noise—like a piece of furniture being kicked across the floor. Then he heard Connie—maybe closer to the phone now—letting out a strange, frail moan. It wasn't a scream or a cry. But the sound still frightened him.

"Connie?" he whispered. Then louder: "Connie, are you there? Can you hear me?"

Then there was a thud—like something had fallen on the floor.

"Connie? What's going on?"

He heard a click on the other end, and the phone went dead. Roger jiggled the receiver cradle, but the connection was lost. "Jesus," he murmured, frantically digging into his pants pocket for a nickel. He put it in the coin slot, waited for the tone and dialed Connie's phone number. He got a busy signal.

"Shit!" he hissed.

Mrs. Mousel's door flew open, and she glowered at him. "Mr. Tallant, people are trying to sleep . . ."

"I know, I'm sorry, I'm sorry," Roger said.

He hung up the phone and, without collecting his nickel, hurried toward the lobby. Running out the front door, he headed down the street. He figured he could be at Connie's place in less than fifteen minutes. But he couldn't race down the dangerously steep hill without stumbling or falling. Roger walked downhill as fast as he could. All the while, he thought of Connie in trouble, eleven blocks away. He should have called the police, told them what he'd heard and sent them to her address. But he couldn't be sure that Connie wasn't playing a prank on him. After all, she was tipsy and mad at him. Maybe this was her warped way of getting even. But would she have really done that?

He finally reached the bottom of Queen Anne Hill and headed west—running now, though his legs felt wobbly. He kept thinking of the faint rasp he'd heard over the phone—as if Connie was struggling to breathe.

That hadn't been faked.

He wished he'd known Myrtle's last name or phone number. He could have called her and asked her to check on Connie. Maybe she'd already done that. She was such a busybody. The old biddy had already sicced the cops on Connie twice. If something had really happened to Connie, if she'd been attacked, certainly the old lady would have called the police. Roger wondered if he'd see a squad car in front of Connie's duplex when he finally got there.

With five blocks to go, he felt his lungs burning. He started to slow down as he passed the Mecca Café. Sweat covered him, and he thought his heart might burst. Connie knew about his condition. She knew he didn't have a car, that he'd have to run to her place if she were in trouble. This wasn't a joke—as much as he wanted it to be.

He started to pick up the pace again. He was close enough to her duplex now that he should have seen police car lights or heard sirens. He wasn't sure what to think.

Roger rushed toward the duplex. It looked the same as when he'd left. The place was still dark, but he could see slivers of light around the edges of the curtains in the first-and-second-floor windows. From the end of the walkway, he thought he saw a curtain move in Myrtle's window. As he staggered up the walkway, he noticed something else—hanging from the front doorknob was a pair of Connie's work slacks.

The door was open a crack.

He swallowed hard and tried to catch his breath. Then he pushed open the door. "Connie?" he called. He paused for just a moment but didn't hear anything—except the faint, distant sound of a siren. At the top of the stairs, Connie's door was open, and light spilled out onto the narrow staircase. Roger bolted up the steps.

Stopping in the doorway, the first thing he noticed was that nothing seemed disturbed in the apartment. Connie wasn't the tidiest person in the world, but there was no sign of a struggle. If what he'd heard on the phone earlier had been a piece of furniture getting knocked over, it had been put back in its place.

"Connie?" he called with uncertainty. He stepped into the living room and glanced over toward the kitchen. That was where he saw her, sprawled on the tiled floor with her face turned to one side. Her hair was in her eyes. Someone had drawn a clownlike smile with lipstick on her mouth. Stripped of her slacks, she wore a pair of panties and an apron that was askew. A nylon stocking was tied around her neck—so tightly that it looked embedded in her flesh. A kitchen knife stuck out of her chest. One wound, but it had bled profusely, creating a crimson puddle beneath her body.

Horrified, Roger hurried toward her and slipped on the blood. He hit the floor with a thump and banged his knee. He smeared blood across the black and white tiles. It was on his hands and down the front of his clothing. His trouser leg was soaked.

As he got to his feet, Roger heard the siren become louder and louder. He knew Connie's neighbor must have called the police after all. But they were too late. And he was too late.

Roger started crying. After a few moments, he realized Connie's killer could still be inside the apartment. Unwittingly, Roger tracked blood toward the bathroom as he checked it. He noticed what he'd done as he went to check the bedroom. He felt so stupid.

Suddenly he heard a car come to a screeching halt in front of the duplex, and then Myrtle's frantic voice. But her words were undecipherable. There was the clatter of footsteps on the stairs, and a man calling out: "This is the police! Is everything okay up there?"

For some crazy reason, all Roger could think of was that Connie wouldn't want anyone to see her like this. He stood over her body, wondering what he could cover her with. But once again, he was too late.

He heard the police officer at the top of the stairs now. Roger turned around and reached inside his coat to get his wallet—to show the cop his identification.

The cop was in the doorway. "Hold it!" he yelled, pulling out his gun.

"No, I—"

That was all Roger could say before two shots rang out. The first shot missed him.

The second shot hit Roger Tallant in the throat.

Nora woke up to the sound of someone coming up the stairs.

She squinted at her alarm clock. It was a quarter to one.

Chris and Jane had still been awake when she'd gone to bed at nine fifteen. For a few nights, while Ray had been staying above the garage, she hadn't worried about noises in the middle of the night.

But her brother was gone, and the sound she heard was from someone *inside* the house. She heard the floorboards in the hallway creaking.

Nora kept her bedroom door open most nights, and because of the blackout curtains, she had a night-light in the hall. She saw a shadow moving across the hallway wall.

A panic swept through her. Throwing off her covers, she scurried out of bed and ran to the door. She saw Chris in the hall, creeping toward his bedroom.

He was dressed and wearing his blue jacket. He froze the moment he saw her.

Even in the shadowy hallway, Nora could see the guilt on his face.

She'd been so relieved when he'd come home from school yesterday without a mark on him. And yet, here he was, up to his old tricks, sneaking out at night again. She couldn't imagine that Earl had put him up to it—not after he'd broken Earl's nose just two days ago.

"What in God's name are you doing up?" she whispered.

"I . . . I heard a noise out near the garage and went to check," he said, sounding slightly winded. "That's all. But it was nothing."

Standing in her bedroom doorway, Nora looked him up and

down. "You got completely dressed to go check on a noise outside?"

Chris nodded. "If someone was out there, I didn't feel like—y'know, confronting them in my underwear."

She frowned. "Are you sure you didn't sneak out to meet Earl again?"

He sighed. "Mom, I can't stand Earl. And besides, he doesn't want to have anything to do with me now. He even switched with someone in biology class, so he isn't my lab partner anymore. I swear, I was asleep only ten minutes ago and got up to check on a noise out by the garage."

"And it was nothing," she said tentatively.

He nodded. "Yeah. Must have been a raccoon."

"Well, thanks for checking, honey," she said, patting his shoulder. "Go back to sleep."

"G'night, Mom," he whispered. He headed down the hall toward his bedroom. The door was closed and the light was off.

As Chris walked down the hall, Nora noticed the bulge of his wallet in the back pocket of his jeans. He'd brought his wallet with him to check on a noise outside? And why had he bothered to close his door?

It didn't make sense.

Nora watched her son step into his bedroom and quietly close the door.

And she knew he'd just lied to her about where he'd been.

# Chapter 14

*Saturday, April 17*
*8:51 a.m.*

Nora barely glanced at the small headline on the left side of the front page of her morning *Seattle Times*:

### QUEEN ANNE WOMAN SLAIN

Strangler Shot Dead by Police at Murder Scene

Victim, 27, Knew Her Killer

There were no photographs of the unfortunate woman or her slayer. Nora was more interested in the latest war news—especially in North Africa. Seeing nothing along those lines on page one, she started making her coffee and toast.

The house was quiet. Jane had gotten up and left early for some rubber scrap drive, one of her many extracurricular activities. Chris was still asleep. He'd asked Nora to make sure he was awake by nine thirty because he had to mow Mrs. Landauer's lawn today. Nora was dressed in slacks and a sweater. She planned to catch up on laundry and housework.

Just as she sat down with her coffee and toast, the telephone rang.

"Oh, spare me," she muttered, getting to her feet. She headed into the hallway to answer the phone. "Hello?"

"Nora? Hi, it's Fran. I didn't wake you, did I?"

"No, I was just about to have my breakfast."

"You don't know about Connie, do you?" Fran asked warily.

Nora and Fran had wondered why Connie hadn't shown up at lunch yesterday. In fact, while they'd been sitting in their usual spot in the cafeteria, Larry had strutted by the table. "Where's your friend with the big mouth?" he'd asked. "I hear she's AWOL today." Not waiting for an answer, he'd kept on walking.

Nora had figured Connie must have taken the day off and given herself an extended weekend. But obviously, Fran knew something. And from the tone of her voice, it sounded like something serious.

Nora felt a sudden tightness in her gut. She sat down in the hardback chair by the phone stand. "What happened?"

"It was in this morning's paper," Fran said.

"I haven't read it yet. I was just about to. What happened?"

"It's bad news, hon, really bad. Brace yourself . . ." Fran's voice cracked a little. "She's dead, Nora. They're saying Roger—that nice Roger—they say he killed her."

Stunned, Nora sat there with the receiver to her ear. "Fran, what are you talking about? That's crazy . . ."

"It's here in the *Times*," she said, sniffling. "I didn't want to believe it either, honey. Not our girl, not our Connie. It couldn't be. They say Roger strangled and stabbed her in her kitchen. The downstairs neighbor—that Myrtle woman Connie told us about, the nosy one—she heard arguing and then it turned into a scuffle or something. Anyway, she called the police. When they arrived, they found Roger, covered in blood, standing over Connie's body. The cop said it looked like Roger was reaching inside his jacket for a gun. So he shot Roger and killed him."

Nora started to cry. She couldn't believe Connie was dead. None of what she heard made any sense. "Roger had a gun?" she asked.

"They discovered later that he was unarmed. Apparently, he was going for his wallet when the cop shot him."

"Then how can they be so sure he killed Connie? The two of them were friends. You saw how they were together . . ."

"The police went through Roger's apartment afterward and uncovered evidence that he was a pervert."

"A *pervert*? They said that in the newspaper?"

She heard Fran blow her nose. "Maybe they said 'deviant,'" she answered, her voice a little raspy. "I'm not sure. Anyway, the gist of it is the police say Roger killed her."

"Well, the police are wrong," Nora protested. "Fran, the other night, my brother guessed that Roger was a homosexual. Connie must have known. I think they were good friends. I'm pretty sure there was nothing sordid or sexual about their relationship, certainly nothing that would lead to a violent murder." Nora wiped away her tears. "She was stabbed and strangled? Can you picture that nice man doing such a thing to Connie—or to anyone for that matter?"

There was a long silence on the other end.

"Fran?"

"He did seem very decent," she said finally. "So . . . you're telling me that he was a homosexual and Connie knew? Because she gave me—along with the rest of the gals in our section—the distinct impression that she and Roger were dating. Did Connie actually tell you that Roger was *that way*?"

"In so many words," Nora answered. "Remember how

Connie was three sheets to the wind at the party? Well, after you left, she pulled me aside and asked me to set her up with my brother. She pretty much admitted that she was love starved and her relationship with Roger wasn't romantic or sexual. I was disappointed to hear it because he seemed like such a catch. He was so nice . . ."

"I thought so, too. I won't forget how kind he was to Martin."

Nora wiped her eyes again. "Poor Marty, how did he take the news?"

"He—well, he was pretty tired when I told him. It was about an hour ago. I was sitting in the kitchen, reading about it, when he got back from one of his evening prowls. He saw I was crying—"

"I'm sorry," Nora interrupted. "I remember you said that Marty goes out some nights. But I didn't know he stays out *all night long.* What does he do until seven thirty in the morning?"

There was a pause, and Nora immediately regretted her tactlessness. "I'm sorry, Fran. It's none of my business. Please, forget it."

"No, it's a good question," Fran said glumly. "Sometimes, he goes to one of those all-night movie houses. In the dark, people don't notice his eye or the scar. He can be out and about without feeling self-conscious. Or he'll drive to the beach to sit there alone and think. At least, that's where he says he's been. Often, when he's been out the entire night—like last night—he has breakfast someplace before he comes home. For a while, I was worried he was out getting drunk somewhere, maybe getting into trouble. But I don't think so. Like I say, he's still not comfortable around people. You saw that the other night. I tell myself, he's twenty-three years old. As long as he stays out of trouble, he should be allowed to go out wherever he wants— and whenever he wants. But I still worry . . ."

"Well, of course you do," Nora murmured. Suddenly Chris

sneaking out for a few hours on the occasional night didn't seem all that bad.

"Anyway, when Marty came in, I told him about Connie and Roger. I told him how it didn't make any sense to me."

"What did he say?" Nora asked.

"Well, like I mentioned, he was tired. He . . . he said something like, 'The whole world's gone crazy. Nothing makes any sense anymore.' Then he went up to bed. He's asleep now. He'll probably sleep all day—until four or five this afternoon. He does that sometimes."

Nora had thought Marty would be more upset—considering how Roger had come to his rescue at the party. And Connie had been very sweet to him, too. Then again, Nora realized she really didn't know Fran's son.

But he was right. Nothing made sense anymore.

On the other end of the line, she heard Fran clear her throat. "Do you really believe the police have it wrong about Roger?"

"I guess I shouldn't be so sure until I've read more of the details," Nora admitted. She started to cry again. "But I can't believe he would have murdered Connie. They were *friends.* I don't care what the police say about him. Roger was a *gentleman . . .*"

Nora couldn't eat anything. But she had a cup of coffee while she read the newspaper account of Connie's murder.

The *Times* article didn't give many details about what the police had uncovered in Roger Tallant's apartment. The so-called evidence that had practically convicted Roger as far as they were concerned was described as "*salacious materials that seemed to fit with the deviant nature of the crime,*" whatever the hell that meant.

Yes, they'd found Roger, covered in blood, standing over Connie's dead body. But what murderer, caught in the act, reaches for his wallet to show the cops his identification?

Nora noticed the clock on the stove panel read nine thirty-five. She splashed some water on her face and then went upstairs to make sure Chris was awake.

She knocked on his door. "Are you up?" she called.

"Yeah, thanks!" he replied.

Nora leaned closer to the door. "Honey, after you get dressed and before you go over to Mrs. Landauer's, I need to talk to you about something."

"Am I in trouble?"

"No, I just—"

"Is it Dad?" he interrupted. "Is that why I heard the phone ring?"

"It's not Dad, Chris. But this *is* something serious."

"I can barely hear you through the door, Mom. Come on in . . ."

She opened the door and saw him sitting up in bed, his brown hair a mess of cowlicks. Squinting at her, Chris scratched his chest through his T-shirt. "What is it, Mom? You might as well tell me now."

Nora remained in the doorway. "I guess this shouldn't affect you as much as it has me." She shrugged. "You only met them once. But my friend, Connie, and her friend, Roger . . ."

"You mean, from the party?"

She nodded. "They—ah, they're both dead. Connie's neighbor called the police about a disturbance. When the police arrived, they found Connie on the floor, dead—with Roger standing over the body. They shot him."

Chris didn't say anything. He just kept squinting at her like he didn't understand.

"The police say he strangled Connie. But I don't think he could have done it . . ." Nora felt her throat tightening, and she thought she might start to cry again. Something about telling Chris made the whole horrible thing so undeniably real. "Anyway, the story's in the newspaper down on the kitchen table—if you want to know more."

Chris covered his face with his hand and slouched back on

his pillow. "Could you—could you please leave me alone for a while?"

Nora almost instinctively went to comfort him, but she held back. She retreated to the hall and closed the door.

"Mom?" she heard him call in a shaky voice.

"What is it, honey?" she replied through the door.

"Mom, I'm so sorry about your friend."

# Chapter 15

*Monday, April 19*
*8:50 a.m.*

In the cafeteria on her coffee break, Nora noticed Roger's friends at the same four-top table they'd occupied last week—only most of them looked pretty somber this morning. It was hard to miss the one who had asked about her chicken fricassee recipe. The tall, heavyset man wore a flashy red tie almost as loud and flamboyant as he was. He seemed to be holding court, while the others, more subdued, sipped their coffee and smoked their cigarettes.

Nora suddenly felt nervous as she approached their table. They seemed so cliquish. And maybe she was imposing on their grief.

They all looked up at her, the big man rather imperiously.

"Hi, I'm Nora," she said with a hesitant smile. "We met here last week when I stopped by to talk to Roger."

They stared at her and said nothing. One of them at least nodded. Unlike last week, without Roger leading them, no one bothered to stand up.

"I'm Connie Wiedrich's friend," Nora went on. "I knew Roger through her. I just wanted to say how sorry I am about Roger. I know he was your friend, and I think he got a raw deal."

One of them stubbed out his cigarette and stood up. "I've got some stuff to do," he muttered to his buddies. "See you guys back in the salt mines." Then he walked off.

A second man quickly got to his feet. "You've got the wrong idea, lady. I barely knew the guy outside of work. None of us did." Then he headed toward the exit, too.

Nora wasn't sure what she'd said wrong. She'd figured these guys—more than anyone else—would agree with her that Roger had been framed. She looked at the two remaining men: the big one, who curled his lip at her, and a skinny, balding man in his late thirties whose eyes kept darting back and forth from her to the stocky guy.

"I'm sorry," Nora said. "I got the impression from Connie that you fellas and Roger were all pretty close. She said your little group was almost like a fraternity. And, well, I just wanted to say, it doesn't make sense to me that Roger would've murdered anyone, especially his dear friend. I'm pretty sure that's what he and Connie were—good friends."

The two men said nothing. The skinny one rolled his eyes, and the hefty man kept sneering at her.

"Listen, I don't want to invade your privacy or make trouble for anyone," she explained, exasperated. "It's just that I couldn't think of anyone else who might stick up for Roger. You can't possibly think the police are right about what happened. Roger couldn't have—"

"*Invade my privacy?*" the large man interrupted. "You don't even know me. What are you insinuating?"

"Oh, calm down, Wendell," the other one said under his breath.

Nora realized she must have crossed a line. Maybe Roger's

friends didn't want to admit they were close to him because he was an accused murderer and exposed as a homosexual. A follow-up story in the Sunday newspaper actually used the word *homosexual.* But there were no new developments in the case—beyond the police force's complete certainty that they'd caught and killed Connie's murderer just minutes after he'd strangled her and plunged a knife into her chest.

"So you're trying to tell me that you weren't friends with Roger Tallant?" she pressed. "The same guy who was sitting at this very table with you last week? This is crazy . . ."

With a theatrical flourish, Wendell stood up, pulled out his wallet and showed Nora a photo. It was of a slightly frumpy woman, seated, and two unsmiling teenage boys standing behind her. "This is my wife, and these are our two sons," he announced. "The taller one on the left is the star of his high school football team." He shut the wallet and tucked it into his back pocket. "I don't associate with perverts—or killers. I have an essential job here. I'm important to this plant. Who are you but some dime-a-dozen riveter? If you want to keep your job, sweetie, you better stop nosing around here, asking people stupid questions. You can start right now by leaving me the hell alone. I barely knew the guy."

He walked off in a huff.

The skinny man put a hand behind his ear—like he was listening to something. "That's three denials. I think I just heard a cock crow." Then he sat back and, once again, rolled his eyes at her. "Lady, you sure know how to break up a party."

Nora sighed. "I'm sorry. I figured you guys were Roger's friends—just like I was Connie's friend. I thought you'd be as upset as I was to hear what happened . . ."

"You meant well," the man said, frowning.

Nora shrugged. "Thanks."

"Don't thank me. It wasn't a compliment. It's something you say about someone who's being a pain in the ass or stupid.

Wendell's right. You shouldn't be asking about Roger around here. Right now, any one of us could lose his job just for knowing Roger outside of work."

"I really am sorry," Nora said, feeling very stupid indeed. "I guess I fouled that up."

He gave her a sad smile. "I liked Connie a lot. And I agree with you. I think Roger got a bum rap."

"Does his friend Phil agree with you? What does he think?" Nora asked.

The man's eyes narrowed at her. "How do you know Phil?"

"I don't," Nora answered. "But when Roger was at my house for dinner, he was telling us what his policeman friend, Phil, had found out about the girl who was murdered two weeks ago. She worked at Boeing as well. None of the newspapers have mentioned the other murder. Isn't it possible they're connected?"

The man just frowned at her and shifted in his chair.

"Do you know Phil?" Nora pressed. "As I mentioned, he's on the police force—in the homicide division, I think."

The man cleared his throat. "Tell you what, if you want to talk about Roger, come by the Double Header in Pioneer Square on Thursday around nine o'clock. Some of his friends will be having a little memorial for him. Phil should be there, too."

"Thursday, nine o'clock at the Double Header in Pioneer Square," Nora repeated, nodding. "Thank you . . ." She realized she didn't know the man's name.

"Richard," he said. "The neighborhood's a little sketchy, so be careful around there. But being a lady, you'll be absolutely safe with the men once you're inside the bar. Meanwhile, do me a huge favor—don't go talking about Roger with people at work anymore. And don't tell *anyone* about Phil. That's very important. Do we understand each other?"

Nora nodded. "Absolutely."

# Chapter 16

"Jane!" Nora called, stepping out to the hallway for a moment. "Honey, when you finish getting dressed, could you please come here?"

Nora ducked back into her bedroom and, once again, started searching through her dresser drawers. Her makeup and hair were done, and she had her black dress laid out on the bed. She didn't have time to paint her legs, so she'd decided to wear nylons to Connie's wake.

She had exactly three pair, two of which she'd never worn. They were still in the box. She felt like a hoarder. It was no longer possible to buy nylons anywhere, except on the black market. Months ago, she'd given Jane all of her old silk stockings and nylons with runs. Jane had been collecting for one of her war material drives at school. In addition to parachutes, the old silk stockings and nylons were used for mosquito netting, flak jackets and glider tow ropes.

Nora was saving the three pair of nylons for an emergency—
and this was an emergency.

"I'm all dressed and ready, Mom," Jane announced, appear-
ing in the doorway of the master bedroom. She wore a dark
blue dress with a white Peter Pan collar and a chapel veil.

"You look nice, honey," Nora said hurriedly. "But you
don't need the veil. We're not going to a church. The wake is at
a funeral home." She pointed to her dresser—with the drawers
partially open. The middle drawer stuck out more than the others—and all the clothes inside it had been rifled through. "Did
you by any chance take my nylon stockings or move them? I
had three pair in this drawer, and now, they're gone."

Jane shook her head as she removed the bobby pins holding
her chapel veil and took it off. "I didn't touch them."

"Are you sure?" Nora pressed. "You didn't take them for
one of your scrap drives?"

She shook her head again. "I swear, Mom. I wouldn't have
taken them without asking first."

"Well, I know they were here in the middle drawer two
weeks ago," she muttered—almost to herself. "They were
under my nightgowns. I don't understand how they could simply vanish. I must be losing my mind." She sighed. "Fine, I'll
just go bare-legged . . ."

"I'm not lying!" Jane snapped, looking wounded. "I swear
on a stack of Bibles, I didn't take them!"

Nora turned to her and gave her a quick hug. "I'm sorry,
honey. I believe you. I-I'm just going a little crazy here." She
grabbed her dress off the bed and carefully stepped into it.
"Listen, you look really nice. Why don't you go downstairs
and wait for me? I'll be ready in a couple of minutes . . ."

Her daughter let out a dramatic sigh and headed down the
hallway.

Jane had eagerly volunteered to go to the wake with her.
This was typical of her. Jane was *involved* in everything—and

maybe, in this case, a bit ghoulish, too. She'd already told her friends at school she was attending the wake of the Queen Anne woman who had been strangled and stabbed. And she kept wondering out loud if the wake would be open casket.

On the other hand, Chris had apologized for not wanting to go. Unlike his kid sister, the last thing Chris wanted was for anyone in his class to know that the much-talked-about murder victim and her homosexual killer had recently been to dinner at his house. He just wanted to keep a low profile.

Once she was dressed and ready to go, Nora found Chris at the kitchen table, doing his homework. "Where's your sister?" she asked.

"Waiting in the car for you," he said, leaning back in his chair. "I think she's actually looking forward to this."

"Chris, I know this is a ridiculous question," she said, putting on her gloves. "But did you take some nylon stockings out of the middle drawer of my dresser?"

"Yeah, and I also borrowed a pair of your earrings," he replied.

She stared at him and blinked.

"Jeez, no, Mom," he said, looking at her as if she were crazy. He tapped his pencil on the cover of his history book. "What would I be doing with your nylon stockings? And why in the world would I be going through your dresser drawers?" he asked testily.

"All right already," she said. "Don't bite my head off. I told you it was a ridiculous question. Listen, we should be back in time for dinner. But if you get hungry, there are some cold cuts in the fridge."

"I'm fine," he said. "Listen, I'm sorry I'm not going to this thing with you."

"It's okay, honey," she reassured him. "I didn't expect you to. She was my friend. You only met her once. We'll be back around six thirty, seven at the latest." She was about to head out the back door, but she hesitated. "You aren't planning to go out, are you?" she asked.

He shook his head. "No."

"Good," she said. Then she stepped outside and closed the door behind her.

On their way to the funeral home, Jane asked once again if the casket would be open or closed. She seemed nervous, conflicted and almost obsessed about it.

"I'm pretty sure it'll be a closed casket, honey," Nora answered with her eyes on the road. She remembered Pete, when he'd started out as a resident, saying they'd brought in a strangulation victim, and her face had been horribly bruised and discolored. He'd said it was typical in strangulations. So Nora figured the casket would be closed. Then again, maybe some morticians would consider that a challenge. "If the casket is open," Nora said, "and you don't want to look, you can stay on the other side of the room. No one's going to make you go up there."

The casket was open.

Nora could see the casket from across the semicrowded room when she and Jane arrived. Flower arrangements decorated every table. Nora thought she recognized a few women from the plant among the mourners. Then she spotted Fran; Marty was with her. Dressed in a navy-blue suit, he looked like he was dying to leave. He kept his hands clasped in front of him and nervously tapped one foot. He nodded and mumbled a shy "hello" to her and Jane.

Fran made a fuss over Jane and her dress. Then she pulled Nora aside and whispered in her ear. "They did a lousy job on our girl. She looks terrible." Fran nodded toward the small group standing to the left of the casket. "That's her family over there—from Olympia and Walla Walla. You can't miss the older sister. She looks just like Connie—minus the sparkle."

Nora turned to Jane and put an arm around her. "Moment of truth, honey," she said under her breath. "You can come with me and meet Connie's family, then kneel in front of the casket and say a quick prayer—or you can stay put here. No pressure."

"You're welcome to hang back with us, hon," Fran offered.

But Jane surprised Nora and decided to accompany her. She was polite to Connie's family and quietly reverent as she knelt in front of Connie in her casket.

But for Nora, it was a shock. The bruises on Connie's face from strangulation were shoddily covered with makeup, and her skin was a ghostly gray. A frilly, high-collared, periwinkle-blue blouse may have hidden the garrote marks around her neck, but it made her look like a grandmother. And the hair was all wrong. Gazing at her, Nora thought Connie would have looked better and more like herself in her pink and black polka dot bandana—with a cigarette or a drink in her hand instead of that rosary. It broke Nora's heart to see her young friend in that casket.

As she and Jane walked away, she put an arm around her daughter's shoulder again. "I'm proud of you, honey," she whispered. But she could barely get the words out.

When they met up with Fran and Marty again, Nora noticed that Fran was teary-eyed, too. "I was just looking at all the flowers," Fran said. "I remember how Connie always complained about having to donate money for a floral arrangement every time someone at the plant lost a loved one in the war. I'd have been so mad if there weren't a lot of flowers here."

Nora hugged her, and they held each other tightly.

"Listen," Fran said, finally pulling back. "We've been here for forty-five minutes, and that's about forty minutes more than Marty can handle. So we're going to scram."

"It's drizzling out," Marty said. "I'll get the car and pull up to the front door, Mom. Take your time." He nodded at Nora and Jane. "Nice seeing you again." Then he hurried toward the exit.

"See what I mean?" Fran asked. "He's just so afraid he's going to get the shakes in front of all these people."

"Do you think it would be awful if we left, too?" Nora asked. "We've already given our respects to the family. And we don't know anyone else here besides you—and Connie."

"I'm sure no one would mind—or notice," Fran assured her. "And if she could sit up and talk, Connie would tell you she doesn't mind either."

The three of them started toward the funeral home's richly appointed lobby. It looked like the living room of an old estate—complete with a fireplace. After collecting a holy card, Jane whispered to Nora that she needed to use the restroom and headed off in that direction.

Nora stood by Fran, who watched through the windows in the double-door entrance for Marty to drive up in the car.

"Listen, I'm glad we have a couple of minutes alone here," Nora said quietly. "I didn't want to tell you in the cafeteria because there are always so many people around, but I'm going to an informal memorial for Roger on Thursday night. Some of his friends are getting together at a bar in Pioneer Square."

"Pioneer Square?" Fran repeated. "Honey, that's Skid Road . . ."

Nora grimaced. "I know. I'm a little nervous about making the trip by myself at nine in the evening. I was wondering if you might want to go with me. I figure there's strength in numbers."

She imagined that Richard and his buddies wouldn't be too thrilled if she showed up to the bar with a friend, especially after she'd promised she wouldn't talk about Roger with anyone from work. But she could always explain that Fran and she had already discussed Roger at length. And Fran had been there at the dinner party when Roger had mentioned his policeman

friend, Phil. Besides, Fran had been closer to Connie than anyone else at work. Didn't she deserve to hear what Roger's
friends had to say about Connie's murder?

But Nora could tell from Fran's expression that she didn't
want any part of it.

"Oh, hon." She slowly shook her head. "I'm sorry, but I
think you're crazy. I'd rather be shot out of a cannon. And it's
not just the trip at night to that part of town. I can't believe you
still think he's innocent."

Fran glanced toward the people in the viewing room, and
then her voice dropped to a whisper. "Haven't you been paying attention to the newspapers? The police are certain he
killed Connie. And you want to go to some memorial service
for him?"

Nora nodded. "I figure Roger's friends might confirm for
me what I feel in my gut. But I can't approach them about it at
work. They're all afraid of losing their jobs. So I'm going to
talk with them on their home turf, where they're more likely to
open up about Roger. And yes, I still think he didn't do it. He
cared about Connie."

"Okay, granted, on the surface, he came across as a very nice
man," Fran said, frowning. "But we have no idea what kind of
sick things the police discovered in his apartment. You think
they assume he's guilty just because he was a homosexual. But
what if they found out something else about him, something
they haven't printed in the newspaper—or *can't* print. We just
don't know."

"That's the point," Nora said. "We don't know. That's why
I want to talk to his friends, people who know things we'd just
be guessing at . . ."

Marty pulled the car up in front of the funeral home's entrance.

"Let's talk about this at lunch tomorrow, hon," Fran said,
touching Nora's arm. "But I'm not likely to change my mind."

"Okay, that's fine. But meanwhile, ask yourself, 'What about the other plant worker who was strangled two weeks ago?' How come there's been no mention of her murder in the newspapers?"

Fran stopped short of turning away and stared at her. "You mean Loretta Bryant?" She shrugged. "Well, I thought of her, too. But certainly, if there was a connection between the murders, the police would have mentioned it . . ."

"Or maybe the police simply couldn't connect Roger to that other murder," Nora said. "Maybe that's why they're not saying a thing about it. I'm sorry, I know I'm being a pain about this, but I can't help feeling that they shot an innocent man. Don't you see? Connie's killer is probably still out there. I think he might have murdered Loretta Bryant, too. I mean, two assembly-line workers both strangled within two weeks of each other. What are the odds? It's probably the same killer. And he'll do it again."

With a sigh, Fran patted her shoulder. "I'm pretty sure the police know what they're doing. We'll talk tomorrow, hon. You're working yourself into a tizzy over this. Try not to think about it for a while."

Fran headed outside. Through the rain-beaded windows, Nora watched her duck into the car.

She took a deep breath and released it slowly. When she turned back to the lobby, she saw Jane coming from a hallway off the lobby. Nora worked up a smile for her daughter.

Just then, a couple came out of the viewing room. Nora didn't get a good look at them, but she heard the man talking to the woman as they passed by her.

"I'm just glad they shot that goddamn degenerate," he muttered.

# Chapter 17

*Thursday, April 22*
*9:09 p.m.*

As she parked in front of a pawn shop down the block from the Double Header tavern, Nora wondered if the Packard would be safe in this neighborhood. She was especially worried about the tires. Rubber had become scarce since the war started. A good set of tires were like gold. She wondered if the car would even be there when she got back.

The citywide blackout took effect at eleven every evening. Nora planned on being home long before then. This section of Second Avenue was seedy enough with the lights on. There wasn't a lot of neon, but she could hear music blaring from the various bars. The place was hopping. Nora figured if someone tried to mug her, at least there were a lot of people around—not that it guaranteed anyone would actually help her.

Although she saw plenty of normal-looking individuals strolling along the sidewalks, Nora automatically focused on the more colorful characters. Drunken servicemen staggered past drifters asleep in doorways. A hooker leaned against a lamppost. Nora noticed another lady of the evening screaming at a derelict who, apparently, was curled up in her usual spot.

*Welcome to Pioneer Square*, she thought.

She made sure the doors were all locked as she climbed out of the Packard. Tightly clutching her purse at her waist, she hurried down the sidewalk.

Nora had been in various cocktail lounges and hotel bars; but she'd been inside a tavern only once. When Pete had been in medical school, she and Pete and some of his friends had gone to a speakeasy. Nora remembered being nervous the entire time they were there. She'd worried the place would be raided and they'd be hauled off to jail in a paddy wagon.

Now she was worried the same thing could happen at the Double Header tonight. Nora had already put it together that the bar catered mostly to homosexuals and lesbians. And such establishments were frequently raided by the police. The customers were arrested, and their names were printed in the newspapers the following day—for their unsuspecting families and employers to see.

That was another reason Fran hadn't wanted to accompany her tonight. They'd discussed it earlier at lunch. But mostly, Fran simply didn't buy into Nora's hypothesis that the police had pinned Connie's murder on Roger as part of a cover-up.

The more Nora thought about the young Boeing worker who had been strangled just two weeks before Connie, the more certain she was that both murders had been committed by the same person. Didn't anyone else see a connection there? Both women were assembly-line workers at the same plant, and both were strangled in their apartments at night. Was it the start of something—some kind of Jack the Ripper killing spree?

Nora remembered when she'd first moved to Seattle in 1927, she'd read about a string of strangulations—mostly up and down the West Coast: San Francisco, Portland and even one in her Capitol Hill neighborhood of Seattle. Most of the twenty-odd victims of this killer were middle-aged landladies, but there were exceptions, including a young mother and her baby strangled in their home. The newspapers called the killer The Gorilla Man because various witnesses had described seeing a swarthy man with long arms and large hands outside the apartment houses of these women shortly before they were murdered. Apparently, he talked his way into their homes on the pretext of renting a room.

Nora remembered Chris had been barely a year old at the time, and she'd been alone at home a lot because Pete had been putting in long hours at the hospital. Eventually, the killer was arrested in Canada. He was tried, found guilty of two murders there, and executed. Nora still remembered his name: Earle Nelson.

Perhaps Loretta Bryant and Connie would end up being the first two in a series of killings—like The Gorilla Man murders. Or, for all she knew, there may have been other female war workers strangled before Loretta Bryant. She remembered that apartment break-in near Chris's high school. Wasn't that woman a riveter? Could she have been an intended victim?

Perhaps the police weren't merely looking to cover their own hides by saying they'd shot Connie's killer. What if they were also trying to prevent a citywide panic—especially among female war workers?

"Honey, you've been giving this way too much thought," Fran had told her during lunch. "You only knew Connie for two weeks. And you met Roger—what—twice? I knew Connie and worked with her for months and months, and I grieved her death. I'm brokenhearted about it. But I haven't allowed myself to become obsessed with it. I don't have all these wild theories about what *really* happened. I believe what Connie told me about her and Roger being a regular couple. And I believe what the police and the newspapers say about her murder."

"Well, what if another woman riveter gets strangled?" Nora had asked pointedly. "Do you think then you'll change your mind?"

"Of course, I will," Fran had answered. Then she'd shrugged. "But is it okay with you if I hope that doesn't happen?"

Nora didn't know what to think anymore. Perhaps her so-called wild theories about the murder were her way of dealing with the loss she felt. If she seemed fixated about Roger's innocence, it was because that was what Connie would have wanted. Yet Nora had so many questions.

Maybe one of Roger's friends could give her some answers. She hoped his policeman buddy, Phil, would be there tonight.

Stepping into the small, cozy tavern, Nora was greeted by the voice of Carmen Miranda on a jukebox, singing "South American Way." The chirpy music didn't seem to go with the dark, smoky, wood-paneled room and those deer heads on the wall. Except for a WAVE on a barstool, surrounded by a bunch of men, there weren't any women seated at the bar. Down at the far end, someone dressed like Carmen Miranda twitched and danced. But the impostor was so tall and burly that, even at this distance, Nora could tell it was a man. As "Carmen" performed, some men sang along with the record: "*Ai, ai, ai, ai, have you ever danced in the tropics?*" Nora didn't see any other women in the saloon.

A fiftyish man with a thin mustache and even thinner hair seemed to emerge from the shadows to meet her at the door. He was nicely dressed in a brown suit. "May I help you?" he asked. "Are you meeting someone?" Despite his polite tone, he was definitely blocking her way.

Nora hesitated. She remembered Connie once mentioning that some taverns didn't allow unaccompanied women. Nora figured that was doubly true for a bar like this. "I was a friend of Roger Tallant," she said.

He smiled and nodded toward the other end of the bar,

where the Carmen impersonator was still dancing. "They're all down there. Welcome."

"Thank you," Nora said.

Heading in that direction, she noticed several uniformed servicemen among the patrons. And once she got closer to the WAVE, Nora noticed her five-o'clock shadow and realized the woman was actually a man. Nora felt conspicuous, but invisible. She didn't belong in here, and yet hardly anyone seemed to pay attention to her. But then she passed a booth with three women in it, and one of them nodded and smiled. Nora politely nodded back and moved on.

As Nora approached the end of the bar, Carmen Miranda stopped shaking his maracas for a moment and glared at her. Past the lipstick and heavy eyeshadow—and under the tutti-frutti hat—Nora recognized Wendell from the plant, the engineer who had shown her the photo of his wife and two sons and insisted he didn't associate with "perverts."

Nora also spotted the two men who wouldn't talk to her the other day in the cafeteria. Now seated at the bar, they noticed her and then did their damnedest to ignore her.

"Nora? Hello . . ."

She turned to see Richard seated at a table with another man. They both stood up. Richard wore a jazzy orange silk shirt. The other man was more conservatively dressed in a blue blazer and tie. He was handsome with a solid build and slicked-back blond hair. "You made it to Fairyville, I see," Richard said, waving her over. "I'm glad your visa was in order."

She smiled nervously. "Thanks for inviting me."

Richard pulled out a chair for her. Their table was directly under a mounted stag head on the wall. Richard nodded toward his friend. "This is Phil, and he's a cop, so no funny business."

Phil reached out and shook her hand. "Roger mentioned you. He liked you a lot, Nora. And all of us here, we were big fans of Connie. She was a sweetheart."

Nora sat down. "Thank you. I was a big fan of hers, too."

Richard sank down in his chair, but Phil remained standing for a moment. "Have you told anyone that you were coming here, Mrs. Kinney?" he asked.

"My kids think I'm out with my work friend, Fran. She knows where I am."

"Did you tell her about me?" he asked warily.

"No, but Roger did—over dinner at my house a couple of weeks ago."

"He didn't use my last name, did he?"

Nora shook her head. "And Fran doesn't know I'm meeting you now."

He looked relieved and finally sat down. "Good. I'm sorry, but I have to be really careful. I could lose my job if they found out that I travel in the same circles that Roger did. Thank you for not talking about me to anyone."

Nora shifted in the chair. "I hope you don't mind my asking, but if you're so worried about losing your job, aren't you taking an awfully big risk being here?" She turned to Richard. "Aren't you afraid the bar might get raided?"

"The owner pays off the cops not to raid the place or harass the customers," Richard explained over his cocktail. "This is the safest bar in Seattle—along with the Casino, a dance club in the basement of this building. It's kind of quiet right now. But in an hour, the joint will be jumping. The boys call it 'Madame Peabody's Dancing Academy for Young Ladies'—for short."

Phil laughed. "The funny thing is he's not kidding."

"The place is big with the drag queens, too," Richard explained. "Wendell will be down there shaking his maracas pretty soon. I have a feeling you recognized him."

Nora glanced over her shoulder. The record on the jukebox had switched to a far more mellow tune: the Mills Brothers singing "Paper Doll." Wendell had stopped performing. He leaned on the bar, smoked a cigarette and nursed his cocktail. His tall tutti-frutti hat was slightly askew.

Nora looked at Richard. "So . . . is he really married with two sons?"

"Yeah, it's one for Ripley's, isn't it?" Richard answered. "Going on twenty years now. But that doesn't mean Wendell hasn't picked up more drunken sailors than the shore patrol. His poor, pathetic wife."

"Roger tolerated him," Phil explained. "But he was never a fan. Can we buy you a drink, Mrs. Kinney?"

"As long as we're avoiding last names, why don't you call me Nora?" she said. "And thank you, yes. I'd love a bourbon and water."

"I'll fetch it," Richard volunteered, getting to his feet. "You two get acquainted." He headed toward the bar.

Nora took another glance at Wendell and his group and then turned to Phil. "So . . . I hear this is sort of an informal memorial service for Roger . . ."

Nodding, he gave her a sad smile. "Very informal." His smile faded. "Actually, this is the closest thing to a funeral Roger will get. Once his parents found out he was a homosexual, they were quick to believe he was a murderer, too. They aren't claiming the body. I think Roger will end up in a potter's field or God knows where." Phil took a last swallow of his drink, draining the glass. "Listen, I want to thank you again for being discreet about my friendship with Roger. And by the way, that's all we were, friends. Anyway, I hope you'll go on being discreet, Nora. Otherwise, I can't take any chances talking with you."

"I understand," she said. "After approaching Richard, Wendell and their friends at work, I learned pretty quickly that a great deal of discretion is necessary."

He nodded. "There's a lot at stake for us—our jobs, families, everything. To be honest, I wouldn't have wanted to talk with you. Only Richard said you already knew about me, and you were asking some pretty on-target questions about Connie's murder."

"Well, in an unguarded moment, Connie told me she and Roger were just friends. Yet she led most of the other girls at work to believe she and Roger were dating."

Phil nodded. "Yes, some of that was wishful thinking on Connie's part, but mostly, she was helping Roger maintain a 'straight' reputation at work. They were good friends. Connie knew the truth about Roger. He even brought her here a few times."

"So . . . there's no way Roger could have killed her in some kind of lovers' quarrel or a . . . a sick, sexual rage. And he wouldn't have killed her because she'd discovered his secret."

"No, that's garbage the police and the newspapers want people to believe." With a sigh, he leaned back in his chair. "In fact, a lot of information has been suppressed that would exonerate Roger. For example, Connie's downstairs neighbor became the police's best witness. She heard Connie and Roger arguing outside her door at eleven o'clock last Thursday night. Fifteen minutes later, Roger's landlady chewed him out because he was using the phone in their lobby, right outside her apartment. She said Roger claimed it was an emergency. Both ladies are certain of the time because it was late and they were peeved about the noise. So we know Roger walked home after this 'heated argument' with Connie at her front door. And then he must have run back to Connie's, because he'd been on the phone with her, and he knew she was in trouble. Connie's downstairs neighbor telephoned the police at eleven seventeen, and she reported hearing a fracas upstairs. I think she called it a 'scuffle.' She'd figured Roger was up there with Connie. She didn't know he'd left Connie at her front door and gone home. This same neighbor had already called the police about Connie on two separate occasions, and both times it had turned out to be nothing. So the cops took their sweet time responding to her call. Roger got there before the police . . ."

"They said he was covered in blood," Nora interjected, remembering the newspaper account. "I'm guessing he'd discovered Connie dead and had been trying to resuscitate her when the police arrived . . ."

Phil nodded. "Yeah, it looked bad. Then Roger reached for his wallet, and the rookie cop thought he was going for a gun. So he shot Roger. It all seemed pretty cut and dry—until they discovered Roger wasn't armed. But when detectives searched his apartment for clues and found Roger's stash of racy material—that was enough to convict him in their eyes."

"The newspapers made a big deal out of what the police found—like it was something vile and disgusting."

Richard appeared at her side balancing three drinks. "Oh, please, some sketches of male nudes and a collection of French postcards—only with men posing instead of women." He set the drinks on the table and sat down. "Roger showed them to me once. They were in a shoebox hidden under his bed. He had postcard photos of Eugen Sandow, for God's sake. You know, the strong man who posed with a fig leaf—back at the turn of the century? Talk about corny. Harmless stuff. Yet the way the newspapers reported it, the cops might as well have uncovered the private library of the Marquis de Sade."

"But it was all the police needed to convince the general public that he was guilty," Phil said. "After they found Roger's stash, it was easy to ignore the testimony of his landlady. The powers that be on the force figured the public would easily buy into the theory that most homosexuals hate women. So as far as the press was concerned, the police caught a deviant killer moments after he'd committed his crime and shot him on the spot. Under those circumstances, the little misunderstanding about the absence of a gun can easily be written off. We cops end up looking like heroes—a lot better than we'd look if it ever got out that we shot an innocent man. It was actually a brilliant move my superiors made. And in time, if Roger is proven innocent, well, no one will raise too much of a fuss because it's all old news."

"And he was just a queer anyway," Richard added cynically. He sipped his cocktail.

Nora looked at the two of them. "But you were his friends—both of you were. How could you let that happen and not say anything?"

"Because we like our jobs and our families," Phil said. "We don't want our lives ruined."

"At this point," Richard explained, "anyone sticking up for Roger or claiming to be his friend might as well wave a big pink flag that says *I'm One of Nature's Mistakes.*"

Nora winced at the phrase.

"We're powerless here," Phil explained. "Richard's absolutely right. If I defied the department's official stance on this and tried to get the truth out there, it wouldn't do Roger or Connie any good. I'd just end up exposing myself."

"I keep asking Phil to expose himself to me, but he won't," Richard quipped.

Phil let out a weary laugh. "Oh, shut up." He took a swig of his drink.

Richard looked at Nora. "You haven't touched your bourbon and water."

Nora sipped it. The drink was strong, but she really needed it at the moment. "Very good, thank you." She turned to Phil. "When he and Connie were at my house for dinner, Roger told us that you were working on the other murder case—the one from almost three weeks ago. Loretta Bryant. I think her murder is still unsolved."

"Actually, a friend of mine in Homicide is investigating the case. But you're right. It's still unsolved. Maybe you noticed some similarities to Connie's case."

Nora nodded emphatically. "Two women, both assembly-line workers at the same plant, both strangled in their homes within two weeks of each other."

"And that's not all. In both murders, there was no sign of rape. But the victims had been somewhat mauled. Here's the really strange part. It looked like the killer had stripped off their slacks. With Loretta, her work pants were found in the hallway outside her bedroom—where the body was. In Connie's case, her slacks were left hanging outside—on the front doorknob of her apartment . . ." He glanced up at the stag head on the wall. "Almost as if the killer wanted people to see the slacks hanging there, like a trophy."

Wide-eyed, Nora stared at him. She felt a shudder pass through her.

"That's another thing that gets my goat with this 'Let's Blame the Queer' tactic," Richard said, frowning. "They want us to think Roger killed Connie, took off her pants, and then went downstairs and hung them on her front door—and after all that, he went back upstairs again."

"Richard has a point," Phil sighed again. "It makes a lot more sense that the killer would have hung the pants outside as he was leaving the crime scene."

"I was talking to my friend Fran about the similarities between the two murders," Nora said. She took another sip of her drink. "I thought it was pretty odd that none of the newspapers reporting Connie's murder even bothered to mention the Loretta Bryant case. But I'm guessing the police couldn't connect Roger to it, and that's why it never came up in any of the articles."

"You're a smart lady," Phil said, raising his glass to her. "On the night Loretta Bryant was strangled in her apartment near downtown Seattle, Roger was three hundred miles away, visiting his parents in Colfax. He came home by train late Monday afternoon. The police couldn't link Roger to the earlier murder, so why bring it up? Why raise any doubts or speculation?"

Staring at him in disbelief, Nora shook her head. "How can

they do that? The killer of two women is still out there. He could kill again . . ."

Phil nodded glumly. "I know. But to be fair to my fellow police officers, there were enough differences in the two crime scenes to indicate that it might not have been the same killer. Loretta was strangled with a lamp cord, while Connie was strangled with a nylon stocking. Connie was also stabbed in the chest, but Loretta was only strangled. The killer put an apron on Connie and drew a wide smile on her mouth with lipstick . . ."

Nora cringed. "They didn't say anything about that in the newspapers."

"I know. Loretta's corpse didn't have those perverse little flourishes. Those were exclusive to Connie."

"Well, maybe the killer simply didn't have time to do that to Loretta," Nora argued. "Didn't her sister practically walk in on him?"

"Yeah, after killing Loretta, he'd stopped to have a snack in the kitchen, the sick bastard. The sister and some sailor missed him by seconds. They heard him run out the back door."

"He could have originally gone to the kitchen for an apron and a knife," Richard offered. "Only he got distracted and decided to raid the icebox."

"Those are good theories," Phil said. "But the cops deal in facts and evidence. There were just enough differences between the two murders to conclude it wasn't the same killer. They made a big deal about his choice of weapons, too. There's usually a consistency with these repeat offenders. The belief is, he wouldn't have used a lamp cord on one victim and a nylon stocking on the other."

"Did they look into any other strangulations or similar cases before Loretta?" Nora asked.

"The last one that went unsolved was over a year ago, a sixty-two-year-old widow who was robbed and strangled in her Mount Baker home. The police didn't see any similarities at all."

Frustrated, Nora took another swallow of her drink. The jukebox was playing Glenn Miller's "Chattanooga Choo Choo." The bouncy tune did nothing to lift her spirits. She glanced over her shoulder at Roger's other friends. Someone must have made a joke, because they were all laughing. Wendell's cackle was louder than the others'.

Nora shook her head over and over. "You've explained it to me, and I completely understand why you can't say or do anything. But Roger was your friend. How can you just accept what the police have done?"

Richard put down his glass—almost banging it on the table. "Please, don't tell us that you plan to raise a big stink about this . . ."

Leaning forward, Phil eyed her intensely. "If you're compelled to do something like that—maybe tell *The Seattle Times* or *The Star* that you were friends with Connie and she told you about her 'special friendship' with Roger—that's fine, do that, Mrs. Kinney. It might clear his name of her murder, but I doubt it. His parents and most of the people who knew him—his friends outside of this bar—they'll still want nothing to do with him or the memory of him. You go ahead and do that if you want. But don't drag any of us into it. And if you do, I'll deny everything I've just told you."

Nora squirmed in her chair, but she wouldn't stop looking at him. "I don't have any plans of betraying your confidence," she said with certainty. "I told you, I completely understand the spot you're in. It's just that I was at Connie's wake two nights ago, and I met her grieving parents. I can't help wondering what would happen if someone told them what you've just told me. If they knew the truth, don't you think they'd pressure the police to start looking for other suspects and maybe find their daughter's killer?"

"Seriously?" Richard asked. "How do you think Connie's parents would act if they were approached by a friend of the degenerate who supposedly strangled their daughter? Do you think they'd listen to anything I'd have to tell them?"

Nora said nothing because she knew he was right. "I'm sorry," she murmured.

Phil took a sip of his drink. "Connie's parents probably want to believe the police explanation even more than the police do," he said. "For them, the case is solved, and the pervert who murdered their daughter is dead."

"So we don't do anything," Nora said.

Both men just nodded.

Nora felt defeated. She wanted to scream. Instead, she took a last swallow of her drink and gave a helpless shrug. "It's just all so wrong. How can you stand it? How can you sit there and put up with this awful injustice?"

Phil gave her a sad smile and patted her hand. "You're not used to it." He glanced around the bar for a moment. "Injustice, lies and keeping your mouth shut . . . that's just another day for guys like us."

As she drove home, Nora thought of what she'd asked Fran earlier in the day: "What if another woman riveter gets strangled? Do you think then you'll change your mind?"

That was all she could do right now — just wait for someone else to die before people realized that Connie's killer was still out there. It was maddening. But when Phil and Richard had walked her to her car, she'd promised them once again that she wouldn't *raise a stink* — as Richard so eloquently put it.

Earlier in the week, Jane had wondered out loud — with a bit of frustration — why the newspapers hadn't contacted them. After all, both Connie and her accused killer had been to dinner at their house just a few nights before the murder. Why didn't the newspapers want to talk to any of them? Jane reveled in the sensationalism of the case — and her small association with it.

Nora hadn't shared her daughter's desire to be in the spotlight. But now, she wished the newspapers had asked her for a statement a few days ago. Her knowledge of the case had been limited. Still, with what she'd known then about Roger and Connie's friendship, she might have been able to convince the newspapers that Roger had no reason whatsoever to murder his dear friend. But now, she felt stymied. Fran was the only person she could talk to about this, and even then, Nora couldn't implicate any of Roger's friends.

She thought of the letter she'd written to Pete about what had happened—a soft-peddled version of the truth. As usual, the last thing she'd wanted was for him to worry about them. Nora had tried to play down how much the murder had distressed her. But she knew Pete would read about it in gory detail in a letter from Jane—and perhaps less so in a letter from Chris, who didn't write as often as Jane did.

"Just let it go," she whispered to herself as she turned down her block. The police had deliberately ignored vital information that would have exonerated Roger. There was nothing she could tell them that they didn't already know. And there was nothing she could do to help Connie or Roger.

Until the real killer was caught, she would make sure the doors and windows were all locked at night when she went to bed. And she'd keep the fireplace poker at her bedside.

Turning the Packard into the driveway, Nora noticed the curtains open and the lights on in the front windows of the house. She glanced at her wristwatch: ten twenty-five; still thirty-five minutes until the blackout. The kids would still be up because tomorrow was Good Friday, so neither one of them had school.

Pulling up to the garage, Nora climbed out of the car to open the big door.

The back lights went on, one by the kitchen door and another light just above her—on the garage. One of the kids must have noticed the car. Glancing toward the house, she saw the kitchen door open.

Chris came down the five steps of the back stoop. He had a

piece of paper in his hand. Jane followed him, but she suddenly stopped on the bottom step and clutched the wrought iron railing. She was crying.

Nora felt a sickening dread sweep through her. Even at this distance, she could see Chris was holding a telegram from the War Department. Nora put a hand on the front hood of the car to brace herself.

"We called your friend Fran," Chris said in a broken voice as he came toward her. "She told us you were on your way home. That was almost an hour ago . . ."

"What happened?" she asked, hardly able to get the words out.

This close, she could see the tears in Chris's eyes.

"This telegram arrived at around nine thirty. We . . . we opened it, Mom. We couldn't wait. We had to know . . ."

Nora held out her hand for it. She was shaking.

"There was a-an accident at Uncle Ray's base in San Diego," Chris said. He held on to the note and started to sob. "It was an explosion. I'm so sorry, Mom. He's dead . . ."

# Chapter 18

*Friday, April 30*
*9:15 p.m.*

*My dearest Pete,*

*Jane is at a slumber party at Susan's house. Chris is listening to the radio and working on his comic strip in the family room. And me, I'm in the dining room again. With Jane gone, it was "Every Man for Himself" for dinner tonight. Chris made a grilled cheese sandwich, and I opened a can of clam chowder...*

"Shit," Nora muttered to herself. Annoyed, she tossed the fountain pen on the dining room table and slumped back in her chair.

As if Pete wanted to read about what she and Chris had eaten for dinner on this meatless Friday night. He was probably half-starved and living on K rations or something just as awful. She knew letters brimming with little familiar details of home were morale boosters for lonely servicemen overseas. But this day-to-day stuff was so mundane, and she felt like such a phony, trying to be upbeat in her letters all the time.

In truth, she felt miserable, sad, lonely and disgusted.

But she was in no position to complain to Pete, whose "day-to-day stuff" included mangled bodies and death, unbearable heat, primitive conditions and sleep deprivation.

Tonight, she was in one of those moods in which she resented him a bit. No one had asked Pete to leave his family and go off to be the hero doctor. But mostly, she just missed him. She wished she could at least talk to him on the phone and hear his reassuring voice. Her brother was dead. And no one was around to console her—except maybe Chris. But he and Jane had lost their only uncle, and Nora had felt it her duty to be the consoler.

Chris took Ray's death especially hard. He was quiet and withdrawn in his grief. Nora had heard him crying alone in his room a couple of nights. But when she'd knocked on his door and asked if he was okay, he'd called back to her, "I'm fine. I just need to be alone for a while."

Jane had been up and down, fine one moment and bursting into tears the next. When her daughter was alone in her room, Nora would sometimes hear the *ding, ding, ding* from Ray's wind-up cymbal-playing Scottie. Jane had wanted Nora to put a gold star flag in the window so people would know someone in the family had died in service to the country. Nora had had a hell of a time convincing her that uncles didn't count. Jane had worn her black dress to Easter Sunday Mass. She'd had the week off from school for Easter vacation but intended to wear her black sweater over her uniform or a black ribbon in her hair all next week at school.

Nora had written to Pete on Good Friday, the night after she'd received the telegram. She'd sent him another letter on

Tuesday. Of course, Pete probably wouldn't see either for at least a week or so. Nora wondered if he'd even care very much that Ray was dead. He and Ray had never really gotten along. They'd merely tolerated each other. She didn't dare tell him too many details about Ray's death—or what she suspected might have really happened.

The telegram read:

NAVY DEPARTMENT REGRETS TO INFORM YOU THAT YOUR BROTHER, SEAMAN RAYMOND FRANCIS SHANNON, USN, WAS KILLED WHEN EXPLOSIVES AT A MUNITIONS SITE WERE UNINTENTIONALLY DETONATED AT THE US NAVAL TRAINING CENTER, SAN DIEGO, CALIFORNIA ON 22 APRIL 1943. THE CIRCUMSTANCES OF THIS INCIDENT ARE BEING INVESTIGATED. A REVIEW OF THE FINDINGS WILL BE FURNISHED TO YOU IN A SEPARATE CORRESPONDENCE. NOTIFICATION REGARDING THE TRANSPORT OF THE BODY AND PERSONAL EFFECTS IS FORTHCOMING. THE DEPARTMENT EXTENDS TO YOU ITS SINCERE SYMPATHY FOR YOUR GREAT LOSS. YOUR BROTHER DIED WHILE SERVING HIS COUNTRY.

VICE ADMIRAL MATTHEW B. LEONARD, CHIEF OF NAVAL PERSONNEL

Nora didn't need any more details to figure out what must have happened. She hated that her mind immediately went there and prayed that she was wrong. But she kept replaying what Ray had said the night before he'd left for San Diego, when he'd begged her to help him arrange an "accident" that would maim him and excuse him from active service. "At one of the bus stops on my way here from San Diego," he'd told her, "I saw a stand with these Indians selling fireworks. I thought about how easy it might be to blow off a finger or something like that . . ."

The last thing she'd said to him was "Please, don't do anything foolish." But by all indications, he must have tried to arrange some sort of accident for himself—only he'd botched it. There was an unofficial expression in the military that Pete had shared with her on the phone: FUBAR—Fucked Up Beyond All Recognition. That must be what happened to Ray with his final scheme.

Hoping to be proven wrong, Nora had called in sick on Good Friday and spent the day on the telephone with the navy's personnel office, trying to attain more information about the explosion at her brother's base. She'd gotten the runaround from the special assistant to Vice Admiral Leonard. All she'd been told was that when servicemen were killed stateside, the body and personal effects were usually sent to the next of kin within a week of the serviceman's death—the body by train, the personal effects by mail. "But there may be a delay in this case because an investigation is pending," the special assistant had told her. "You'll be notified when you can expect the remains, ma'am."

More than anything, Nora wanted to know if there might be a chance her brother wasn't at fault for the explosion. Was there some explanation for what had happened that would completely exonerate him? And if not, had anyone else been killed or wounded when Ray's plan had gone wrong?

Nora wondered just how horrible she should feel about this.

It was bad enough that her kid brother was dead. She'd been a mother to him from the time he'd been a baby until he'd turned eleven. For so many years, they'd only had each other. No one knew her better. Nora couldn't help feeling partially responsible whenever Ray got into trouble. And it seemed, this time around, he'd done something unforgivable.

Nora spent more than an hour on the phone with various personnel at the Naval Training Center in San Diego before she got some answers from a sympathetic ensign. "They're still trying to determine exactly what happened, Mrs. Kinney," he said through some long-distance static. "But I can tell you this much off the record. Your brother had guard duty in a restricted area by the munitions dump on Thursday morning. The place blew sky high when everyone was at lunch in the mess hall. If it had been any other time, a lot of people would have been killed. It was a hell of a blast, did a lot of damage . . ."

"Was anyone else killed?" Nora asked anxiously. "The telegram didn't say . . ."

"A couple of petty officers are in the hospital with burns. They helped put out the fire. They should be okay. It was a real inferno. I tell you, it's a miracle more people weren't hurt."

"Do they have any idea what might have caused the explosion?" Waiting for his answer, Nora bit her lip and tugged at the phone cord.

"They don't know yet," he replied. "It could be anything from a stray cigarette butt to sabotage. I hear they had an incident similar to this one at an army base somewhere in Texas last year, and it's *still* being investigated. If you're anxious about your—um, your brother's remains, there may be a delay delivering the body to you. They might want to hold on to it as part of the investigation."

"Yes, I understand." Nora sighed. "Is there . . . is there anything left of him?"

There was a silence on the other end of the line for a moment. "They were able to identify him by his dog tag, Mrs. Kinney," he said finally.

"And they don't have any leads as to how this happened," she said. "No inkling at all—off the record?"

"Well, another seaman in your brother's outfit cleaned out his locker and snuck off the base at the time of the explosion. No one saw him in the mess hall. They haven't been able to track him down yet. Considering the timing of his disappearance, I can't help thinking he might at least know something."

Nora wondered if Ray had asked this seaman to help him in his scheme. Then when things had gone haywire, maybe the seaman had gotten scared and taken off. Or maybe this missing sailor had been wanting to desert and decided to jump the fence during all the confusion from the explosion.

There was another explanation—and it said something about her faith in Ray that she didn't think of it until last. Perhaps this missing seaman had set off the explosion, and Ray had been a completely innocent victim. But it was hard to imagine Ray the innocent victim of anything.

Nora had thanked the ensign for his help. He'd told her he was sorry for her loss and then hung up.

Nora knew it would make a huge difference to the navy's investigation of the incident if she shared with them some of what Ray had said to her the night before he left. But what if he was actually blameless? She'd be exposing him as a coward for no reason. Then, even if he was innocent, there would always be a cloud of suspicion that Ray had committed sabotage to avoid active duty.

Nora realized that, if the navy discovered Ray was responsible for that explosion, she'd know soon enough.

Maybe cowardice ran in her family.

Nora was pretty disgusted with herself. But she wanted to protect her brother—and what people thought of him. And her kids felt bad enough that they'd lost their beloved uncle. Did they have to feel ashamed, too? She felt enough shame for all of them.

Work had been awful lately, too. It seemed so insignificant compared to her brother's death, but her bucker for the entire week had been irritating. A large redhead in her late thirties, Edna wouldn't stop talking. Past the noise of the rivet gun and all the machinery, Nora hadn't been able to hear her most of the time. After a while, she'd given up asking Edna to repeat things—especially since everything Edna said was of no importance whatsoever.

Last Monday, Edna had asked Nora why she'd been absent on Friday. "They told me I'd be working with a new girl, and then you didn't show up," Edna had said over the din. "Was it because of the religious holiday or something?"

"No, my brother was killed," Nora had yelled back, working her riveting gun. It had sounded so strange saying that out loud in such a casual way. "He was in the navy. There was an accident at his base."

"Oh, that's terrible!" Edna had replied. And two minutes later, she'd started talking about her neighbor's cat—while Nora had pretended to listen.

At lunch earlier today, Nora had spotted Edna sitting by herself in the cafeteria. She'd looked pathetic. Even though Nora didn't like her, her heart had gone out to her. She'd thought that a nice person would invite Edna to come eat with Fran and her. *I'm not a nice person*, she'd decided.

Edna made her almost miss Laughing Boy, Warner Nash. *Almost.* She hadn't seen him at all since working with him the previous week. In the cafeteria, she'd been on the lookout for Marge and Willie, but hadn't seen them either. It was such a big plant. She knew these people were still around, but she just didn't run into them. She continued to work near old Ned's station, and they'd politely nod to each other occasionally, but that was about it. Their last real conversation—about her working with Willie—had, obviously for both of them, put the kibosh on their budding friendship.

Nora felt the same awkwardness whenever she saw Roger's friends at their usual table during her break period. She'd nod in their direction and get a furtive little wave from Richard, a sneer from Wendell, and the other two would always ignore her.

If it weren't for Fran, she would have felt completely friendless at work.

When Nora hadn't shown up to lunch last Friday, Fran had telephoned the house. "I kept thinking about what happened the last time one of us wasn't at lunch," she'd told Nora. She'd dropped off a casserole on Saturday night. And at lunch on Monday, Fran had brought her a tin of home-baked cookies. After the casserole, Nora hadn't been expecting another kind gesture and she'd burst into tears.

She'd been off her game at work all week, too. And it wasn't merely because she'd been working with that annoying chatterbox bucker, Edna. Four times, supervisors had found her rivets weren't uniform, and each time, the whole line had to be ripped out and re-riveted. Larry had actually cut her some slack because word had gotten around that her brother had been killed. But it was so much more than that.

Yet, she couldn't tell a soul what was really bothering her.

She was the keeper of the secrets.

It had been a week since her brother's death, and she still hadn't heard from the Department of the Navy yet. And it had been over two weeks since Connie's murder, and as far as the police were concerned, the case was closed.

She gazed down at the letter she'd started to Pete. She wouldn't be telling her husband about how Roger Tallant had been framed or that her brother had probably committed sabotage.

Instead, she'd write about what they'd had for dinner, all of Miko's flowers blooming in the yard (*"It's a miracle!"*), and her plans to rent out the garage apartment to a couple. She'd already bought the APARTMENT FOR RENT sign and planned to post it near the end of the driveway tomorrow morning.

Picking up the fountain pen, she got ready to write again. But something occurred to her as she looked at the empty chairs around the dining room table. That little dinner party she'd had less than three weeks ago—eight people had attended. And now three of them were dead.

But she wouldn't mention that to Pete in her letter.

Nora would keep it to herself.

# Chapter 19

*Saturday, May 1*
*3:11 p.m.*

Nora plugged in the iron and then took a few T-shirts off the basement clothesline. She'd let the laundry pile up this week. Before washing anything, she had to make room on the two clotheslines that stretched across the basement. The heavy-duty cord was still moving as Nora set aside the clothespins. The shadows of the remaining garments danced on the dingy gray walls.

Nora usually didn't mind being down in the gloomy unfinished basement, except when she was alone in the house—like now.

The basement was one big room—including Pete's work area with a workbench and cabinets, and her laundry nook with the big electric washer and the ironing board. Nora had tried to cheer up the space by tacking travel posters to the wall above the laundry sinks—all those places she'd probably never visit.

But the large room still seemed sinister—what with the storage closet and a couple of shadowy nooks that seemed like perfect hiding spots for a would-be intruder. A huge octopus furnace with its many ducts and a water heater occupied one corner of the room, right by the coal window. The place was cluttered with junk—including Jane's childhood dollhouse, a stack of old shutters and some yard equipment that Jane was itching to donate to a scrap drive.

Nora was touching up one of the T-shirts with the iron when she heard a creaking above her. She glanced up at the ceiling and the cobweb-draped pipes. *Just the house settling*, she told herself. Though it was the middle of the day, Nora had locked the front and back doors before she'd gone down to the basement. She wasn't usually that cautious, but there was nothing usual about someone strangling female riveters in their homes.

She touched up the second T-shirt. Then she pulled one of Jane's school uniform blouses off the line, sprinkled some water on it and went to work with the iron. She did her best to ignore the shadows swaying on the wall again.

This morning, Chris had helped her post the APARTMENT FOR RENT sign at the end of the driveway. Nora had included their phone number on the placard. With the lack of traffic on their street, she didn't expect to hear from anyone until an ad ran in tomorrow's *Seattle Times*.

Chris had forgotten he had to do "volunteer work" today at a scrap repurposing center in South Seattle, part of a school project "to ruin my Saturday," according to Chris. So this morning, at the last minute, she'd had to drive him to the industrial district. At least Chris would be bussed back to the school, and he could walk home from there. He would be back in time for dinner, he'd said.

As for Jane, she'd returned from her slumber party, ate lunch and then asked to be driven to her friend Doris's house. She'd call when she needed to be picked up—probably sometime before dinner. Nora, for her part, didn't have a clue what she was cooking for dinner tonight.

It was a typical Saturday—chauffeuring the kids around, cooking meals and ironing. How did everything go back to normal so quickly after Ray's death?

Early last week, she'd reserved a plot in Lakeview Cemetery. She'd figured Ray was better off buried here than in Chicago beside their mom and dad. With him in Seattle, at least she and the kids could visit his grave. The plot was there, waiting for him—once the Department of the Navy decided to send Ray's remains. She hadn't received his personal effects yet either.

Nora heard another noise, and this time, she set down the iron. It seemed to come from somewhere near the front of the house.

The doorbell rang.

She almost jumped out of her skin. She turned off the iron and unplugged it. Then she hurried up the stairs. In the front hallway, she stopped dead. She wasn't expecting anyone. All she could think about was another telegram—this time regarding Pete.

The bell rang again.

Catching her breath, she headed for the door and moved aside the blackout curtain to glance out the window. The stranger outside wore a dark gray suit. He was handsome and looked a couple of years younger than her. Through the glass, he gave her a friendly smile. "Hi, I'm here about the sign out in front!" he called.

Nora nodded, but hesitated. He was still a stranger. And there was still a murderer on the loose in Seattle, seemingly targeting female war workers. Not only that, she suddenly remembered all the landladies The Gorilla Man had strangled years and years ago. He'd worked his way into their homes by pretending that he wanted to rent a room.

She took a deep breath. "Chris!" she called, turning toward the stairs for a moment. "You and Ray are going to be late for football practice if you don't shake a leg!"

Nora unlocked the door and opened it. "Sorry to keep you," she said, working up a smile. "I was in the basement, and I thought my son was going to answer the door. Typical teenager, he's with his buddy upstairs and they can't be bothered..."

She wondered if he could see through her ruse about her son being home.

"That's okay," he said. "Is the apartment still available?"

He had a nice smile, and his manner was charming. He reminded her of William Holden, the young actor from *Golden Boy* and *Our Town*. But she was reminded of something else, what Roger had said about Loretta Bryant's killer: *"He must have been a good-looking guy, a real smooth talker..."*

"Ma'am? You haven't rented out the apartment yet, have you?"

Nora quickly shook her head. "No, it's still available."

"Is it the apartment over the garage?"

"Yes, but I was hoping to rent it to a married couple," Nora said, keeping her stance in the doorway. What she'd said was true. She wasn't just trying to get rid of him. She'd thought a married couple would be quiet, stable and dependable. A single man might be coming and going at all hours and inviting friends over.

"Well, I'm married," he said. With a shrug, he chuckled and held out his right hand to shake hers. "I'm sorry, I was so excited to see the sign, I haven't even introduced myself. My name's Joe Strauss."

Nora shook his hand. "Nora Kinney."

He leaned forward. "I'm sorry, I didn't get that. I have a hearing problem in my left ear, a perforated eardrum from an accident I had as a kid. It's kept me out of the service."

"I'm Nora Kinney," she said, a bit louder.

He glanced at the blue star flag in the front window. "Is that for your husband, Mrs. Kinney?"

She nodded. "Yes, he's in the Army Medical Corps, stationed overseas." Nora stole a glance at his left hand. She didn't see a wedding ring, but she knew that not all married men wore them. "You said you're married?" she asked.

He nodded. "Going on a year and a half now. My wife and I are from just outside Albany, Oregon. We got a nice offer on our little house and decided we'd had enough of the country. We've been staying with friends in Ballard for the last few weeks, and it's getting kind of old. Would it be possible for me to look at the apartment now? Do you have time?"

Nora hesitated but then finally nodded. "Let me get the keys," she said. "Excuse me." She gently closed the door and called out again: "Boys, you need to get a move on!"

As she dug the spare key out of the junk drawer in the kitchen, Nora told herself that if she was this nervous about strangers coming to the door, she'd have a hell of a hard time of it tomorrow—after the ad ran. And this Joe Strauss seemed perfectly nice.

Still, when she took him up to the garage apartment, she left the apartment door open—and immediately went to the living room window and opened it wide. That way, if she screamed, maybe a neighbor would hear her.

But Joe seemed more interested in the apartment than in her. He kept saying that his wife would love it. He seemed to appreciate the furnishings, the view of the ravine and the quiet neighborhood. He thought the forty-five dollars a month was more than reasonable. He explained that he was a commercial artist, and he'd probably be home working most days: "So . . . if you happen to be out during the day, I'd probably be around to sign for packages, keep an eye on the house or whatever."

Nora told him about her job at Boeing. He asked if she had any other kids besides her teenage son. And he asked about Pete—what kind of medicine he practiced and how long he'd been away. He showed just enough interest that he came across as polite instead of prying.

"I think I should tell you," Nora said. "The previous tenants here were a very nice Japanese-American couple. They've been relocated. But once in a while, the place gets vandalized—someone breaks a window or paints something nasty on the door. About three weeks ago, my brother chased away some teenagers who were up to no good. We haven't had any problems since then. But I feel it only fair to warn you."

"Well, I appreciate your honesty, thank you," Joe said. "And I'm sorry you've had to go through that. But it doesn't change my mind about the apartment. I still love it."

"Good," Nora said. She figured, since he was a little over six feet tall and broad-shouldered, he'd easily scare away any potential vandals.

"So does your brother live here, too, Mrs. Kinney?"

She'd just mentioned him, and yet the question still took her by surprise. Like so many of her crying jags lately, the reality of Ray being dead snuck up on her again. Nora felt a tiny ache in her throat. "No, he—ah . . . he was killed. He was in the navy . . ."

Joe shook his head. "Oh, God, Mrs. Kinney, I'm really sorry."

"Thank you," she whispered, a quiver in her voice.

"And he was just here visiting you three weeks ago?"

Nora told herself she wasn't going to cry. "There was an accident at his base in San Diego. It happened last week . . ." She couldn't help it, she started crying—in front of this stranger. "Excuse me, I'm sorry," she managed to say, covering her face. Her nose started running.

He pulled a handkerchief from his suit-jacket pocket and handed it to her.

"This is so embarrassing." Nora wiped her tears with his handkerchief and then tried to hand it back to him.

He gave her a sympathetic smile and shook his head. "You can keep it. Go ahead and blow your nose. I know exactly how you feel. I lost my kid brother not too long ago. He was in the navy, too. He got it in Guadalcanal."

Nora blew her nose. "I'm sorry for your loss," she murmured.

"Thanks," Joe said. "It was tough. He was my only sibling and our parents are dead, so . . ." He shrugged.

Nodding, Nora wiped her tears again. "That's exactly how it was with Ray and me."

He gave her a sad smile. "I guess we're members of the same club."

Nora looked at the handkerchief in her hand. She tried to laugh. "Well, one of my first duties as your new landlady will be to launder this and give it back to you."

"*My new landlady?* Really? Do you mean it?"

She nodded again.

He smiled. "That's terrific. Thank you, Mrs. Kinney. How soon could I move in?"

"Don't you think your wife should look at the apartment first?"

He seemed stumped for a moment. "Um, of course. Will you be around later this afternoon? I could come back with Veronica in an hour or so—if it's convenient for you. I know she's going to love the place."

Nora told him that she'd be home, ironing. She promised not to rent the apartment to anyone else in the meantime.

When Joe returned with Veronica ninety minutes later, Nora was thrown for a loop. Looking at the two of them on her front porch, Nora wondered, *What does he see in her?* Joe came off as polished and smooth in his gray suit, so handsome and kind. He'd won her over in record time. But his wife wore a clingy garish blue dress that made her seem kind of cheap. She looked older, wore too much makeup, and her hair was an unnatural shade of red. She must have done something wrong with a henna rinse, because the color was sort of a murky maroon.

Veronica seemed painfully shy during the introductions, but as they headed toward the garage apartment, she started going on and on about Miko's gardenwork. "I just adore flowers," she said. "So many colors! You have a beautiful yard—and the house, too, real elegant."

After that, as they went through the apartment, Veronica said the kitchen was elegant, and the view was elegant. Everything was elegant.

Actually, it was kind of endearing. But Nora couldn't imagine becoming friends with this woman the way she'd been friends with Miko. Joe was the main reason she was willing to rent to them. As a couple, they seemed woefully mismatched.

Joe gave her two references, and Nora wasted no time calling them after he and Veronica drove off in their LaSalle. The Ballard couple, Dante and Pattie Bellini, were longtime friends of Joe and said he and Veronica were ideal houseguests. The wife, Pattie, described Veronica as "sweet," but she said it in such a way that Nora got the impression she was groping for something nice to say. The other reference was Joe's friend and representative with an artists' agency in San Francisco. Along with two months' rent in advance, Joe promised to reimburse her for the long-distance call to the man's home. Nora had a bit of trouble pronouncing his last name correctly: Ken Hotopp. But Ken sang Joe's praises. He said Joe was a successful commercial artist, going on nine years now. "You know that cute ad for Baby Ruth—with the kid and his kite and the dog?" Ken asked. "The kite's in the tree, and the kid's got the kite string in one hand and the candy bar in the other? And he's smiling? Joe illustrated that. It was a national campaign."

Nora remembered seeing the ad in a recent issue of *Life* or *Look*. In fact, she was pretty certain she still had the magazine.

When she phoned the Bellini residence again, Joe had just returned, and Pattie Bellini put him on the line. Nora told him that he and Veronica could move in whenever they wanted.

"Veronica's at the grocery store right now," Joe said. "But she'll be thrilled when I tell her the news. We'll see you tomorrow around noon—if that's okay. Would that be convenient for you, Mrs. Kinney?"

"That would be fine," she replied. "And I really wish you'd call me Nora."

After she hung up the phone, Nora didn't go back to her ironing in the basement.

Instead, she went into the family room and started paging through the old issues of *Life* and *Look* that were in the magazine rack. She was searching for Joe's Baby Ruth ad. It took nearly a half hour to find it—in a month-old issue of *Life* with Stalin on the cover. The cute, homespun, colorful illustration was lifelike and exceptional in its detail—like something Norman Rockwell might create.

Nora sat there on the family room floor and studied it. She was in awe of how talented Joe was—on top of everything else. She noticed his initials in the corner of the picture and touched the letters with her fingertips.

"What are you doing?" she whispered to herself.

With Pete gone for nine months, Nora had almost gotten used to the loneliness. Now, she was acting like a schoolgirl with a crush. In a weak moment, she'd felt a connection with this stranger. Based on that—and his smooth good looks— she'd rented out the garage apartment to him and his wife. And she didn't even like the wife.

Shaking her head, Nora closed the magazine.

"What are you doing?" she rebuked herself again.

# Chapter 20

*Sunday, May 2*
*12:19 p.m.*

When Nora opened the front door, she found Joe Strauss standing there alone.

Once again, she was the only one home. She still had on the pretty green dress she'd worn to church earlier. Jane had gone off with her friends after Mass. Chris was down the block, mowing Mrs. Landauer's lawn. He'd just left twenty minutes ago. Nora wasn't sure how much work he'd get done. The sky had turned dark and she could feel a storm coming—not the usual Seattle drizzle, but a potential downpour.

"Well, I picked a terrific day to move in, didn't I?" Joe said, with a look up at the ominous clouds. "Is it at least a good time to pick up the keys?"

"I've got them for you right here," Nora answered with a polite smile. She decided he wasn't quite as handsome as she remembered from yesterday. Then again, he was dressed more casually in a wide-collared blue shirt, pleated trousers and a gaberdine jacket, so some of that polish was gone.

Nora grabbed the keys from the table in the front hallway and then handed them to him.

"Will the moving truck be coming by later?" she asked.

"No, we have what's called a partial load," he explained. He shoved the keys in his pocket. "As of this morning, the truck with all our furniture was in Salt Lake City. Don't ask me what it's doing there. The moving company told me it'll be another two weeks before our stuff will be delivered. That's one reason I'm glad the apartment is partly furnished."

"Well, if you or your wife need anything in the meantime, please, let me know."

"That's the other thing. It looks like I'll be by my lonesome for the next few days—maybe even longer. Veronica had to leave for Albany this morning. Her mother's sick . . ."

"Oh, I'm sorry," Nora said. "Nothing too serious, I hope."

He shrugged. "My mother-in-law gets sick a lot. Not to sound uncaring, but I have a feeling a lot of it is in her head. She'll probably outlive us all." He gave her a lopsided smile. "Anyway, it'll just be me for a while."

Nora found herself staring into his brown eyes. She realized that she'd been wrong before. He was just as good-looking as she'd remembered—maybe even more so.

"I'm parked on the street right now," he said. "Is it okay if I pull into your driveway to that bay to the left of your garage while I unload my car?"

Nora was still gazing at him, thinking how, for the next few days and nights, he'd be alone in that apartment over the garage. Maybe she should invite him to dinner tonight.

"Nora?" he said. "I won't be blocking anyone there, will I?"

She quickly shook her head. "No, that's fine. In fact, you can make that your regular parking spot. Do you need any help moving in?"

"No, thanks. Some of the boxes are dirty from being in my friends' basement. You look so pretty in that dress. I wouldn't want you to mess it up. It'll only take me a few trips anyway."

Nora couldn't tell if he was flirting with her or just being nice.

"Before I forget . . ." He reached into his shirt pocket and pulled out some money, folded up. "This and next month's rent in advance, plus what I owe you for that long-distance call . . ."

The telephone rang.

"Pardon me," Nora said, stepping back. "It's been ringing all morning. The ad for the apartment was in the Sunday *Times* . . ." She walked down the hall to answer the phone.

Sure enough, it was some man calling about the apartment. Even though Nora told him the place had already been rented, he was one of those people who needed to hear exactly what he'd missed out on. "Well, was there a dining room? I wouldn't have wanted it if there wasn't a dining room . . ."

Joe sheepishly waved at her from the doorway, took a few steps inside and left the money on the third step of the front stairs. Then he backed up, ducked outside and quietly closed the door behind him.

By the time Nora got off the phone and opened the door again, she saw Joe climbing inside his car.

Leaving the front door open, she took the money off the stair step: one hundred dollars in cash. He'd overpaid her for the call to his agent in San Francisco.

Nora stepped outside, and from the front porch, watched the LaSalle pull into the driveway. She thought about going out there to tell him that he'd overpaid her, and maybe she'd offer him something to drink.

The LaSalle disappeared behind the house, and after a few moments, Nora heard the car door open and shut. She told herself to leave him alone. If he needed anything, he'd knock on the door and ask.

That didn't stop her from peeking out the kitchen window to check on him as he started to unload the back seat of the

LaSalle. Nora knew she wouldn't be anywhere near this attentive or curious if Veronica was with Joe.

Still, when she went upstairs a few minutes later, she couldn't resist peering out the window at the end of the hallway outside Chris's room to check on Joe's progress. He'd opened the garage apartment door and taken another suitcase out of the back of his car. But then he stopped, set down his suitcase and turned to glance up at the house—almost right at her.

Nora ducked away from the window. Had he seen her? She felt like such an idiot.

Five minutes later, she was still chastising herself as she stripped Chris's bed.

Nora hadn't washed anything yesterday. She'd merely caught up on the ironing and made room on the clothesline. Jane kept her busy with laundry, filling the bathroom hamper with clothes and bedding every few days. As for Chris, though he showered every day at school, he wasn't as clean-conscious as his sister. Every week or so, Nora went into his room to strip the bed and go through his closet for the dirty clothes he wore again and again.

She heard a rumbling outside and wondered if it was distant thunder or Joe doing something by the garage. As much as she wanted to look out the window and check, Nora resisted. She tossed the bundled-up bedsheets on the floor and opened Chris's closet. She gathered up his trousers and a couple of shirts he'd worn this week. Then she started working her way toward the back of his closet for more clothes that needed laundering. She found two more shirts. Near the very back of the closet, she discovered a third, a red plaid flannel. Nora started to pull it off the hanger. But it was completely buttoned up—all the way to the collar. With a sigh, she tucked all the dirty clothes in the crook of her arm and unbuttoned the red plaid shirt. As she pulled it off the hanger, something else fell to the closet floor. It must have been on the hanger—underneath the shirt.

It was a lightweight scarf—pink with black polka dots. Nora picked it up.

She recognized Connie's bandana. She even sniffed it to make sure. She could smell Connie's perfume.

Baffled, Nora wandered back to the pile of bedsheets on the floor and dropped the dirty clothes on top of them. But she held on to Connie's bandana and sat down on Chris's stripped bed. She kept staring at the scarf in her hand. How had it ended up in Chris's closet? Connie hadn't worn the bandana to Nora's dinner party. There would have been no reason for her to bring it with her. That was the only time Connie had been to the house, the only time she would have seen Chris.

So what in the world was he doing with her dead friend's scarf?

Nora sat there in a stupor, conjuring up a ridiculous story in which Connie had run into Chris and given him the scarf to remember her by. Maybe Chris had become smitten with her at the dinner party. And in typical teenage crush fashion, perhaps he'd followed her around or even gone to her apartment in Queen Anne. He could have snuck out at night to go there . . .

Chris and his nocturnal disappearances. The night Connie was murdered, Nora had discovered him coming up the front stairs, fully dressed—with his wallet in his pocket. He'd said he'd heard a noise outside. She'd had a hard time completely believing him even then. All she could think now was that, when he'd stepped outside, he'd brought along his wallet because he'd used the car to drive to Queen Anne.

Chris had lied to her.

And on the night that Loretta Bryant was strangled in Belltown, he'd claimed that he and Earl had been to Elliott Bay to watch the battleships. When Nora had mentioned it the next afternoon in front of Earl, Chris's friend had seemed genuinely confused—like he'd had no idea what she was talking about. Chris had lied to her that time, too. He hadn't taken the binoculars to watch the battleships that evening because he hadn't gone to see the battleships.

Nora held up Connie's scarf and stared at it again.

Lately, Chris seemed like a stranger to her. Between what she knew about Connie's murder and Ray's suspicious death, Nora had felt like the keeper of secrets these past few weeks. But she had nothing on her son. There was so much about his daily life that he wasn't telling her—and so much about what he did at night, when she was asleep, that she didn't know.

She had to hear from Jane about the police questioning Chris after someone had broken into a woman riveter's apartment near Chris's school. Chris had tried to dismiss it as nothing, but he'd practically bitten off his sister's head for bringing it up.

Nora heard a knocking downstairs.

With a gasp, she got to her feet and quickly stashed Connie's scarf under Chris's mattress. *Hiding the evidence*, she thought. She almost tripped over the pile of laundry on the floor. Regaining her footing, she hurried out of the bedroom, down the hallway and then down the stairs and around to the kitchen. She could see Joe on the other side of the window in the kitchen door. A few raindrops hit the glass. Nora's heart was racing as she fumbled for the lock and opened the door. "Hi, is everything okay?" she asked, breathless.

"I'm sorry," he said, giving her a questioning glance. "Did I get you at a bad time?"

Standing in the doorway, she managed a smile. "No, I'm fine. I was just upstairs. What can I do for you?"

"One of the kitchen cabinet doors is loose, and a drawer is stuck—"

"Oh, Chris was supposed to fix those," she said. She still couldn't quite catch her breath. "I'll have him come over later tonight."

"That's okay. I can do it. I just need to borrow a screwdriver and a hammer—and maybe some small screws."

She nodded a few more times than necessary. "Sure, just give me a minute . . ."

Nora almost closed the kitchen door but thought that was too rude. Still, she left him standing out in the drizzle. A half hour ago, she'd had to force herself to leave him alone, and now, she couldn't get rid of him fast enough.

She headed down the basement stairs. At Pete's workbench, she gathered up a hammer and screwdriver and an old applesauce jar full of various nails and screws. Her hands were shaking. Just the thought that Chris might have had anything to do with the murders made *her* feel guilty—as if she were the one with something to hide. One more secret she'd have to keep.

She hurried back upstairs, where Joe patiently waited outside the door.

"I didn't mean to leave you standing out in the rain," she apologized. She handed him the tools and the jar of screws and nails. "I should have invited you to come in."

"It's okay," he said. His shirt was already wet around his broad shoulders. "Thanks, Nora. I'll bring these back as soon as I'm done."

"Why don't you hold on to them until tomorrow? You never know what else we missed that needs repairing."

"Well, thanks . . ."

Nora nodded and closed the door. She still couldn't breathe right—and didn't think she would again until she got the truth out of Chris about Connie's bandana.

It was like the mole on her shoulder she'd noticed last October. She'd broken out Pete's medical books and confirmed that the brown and black irregular mark looked like the deadly melanomas pictured in the texts. She'd felt this awful dread in the pit of her stomach, but kept reminding herself that Pete would have seen the mole two months before and said something. Still, she'd felt doomed and hadn't been able to calm down until she'd gone to a doctor, who had checked the mole and said it was nothing.

As she headed up to Chris's room, she kept reminding herself that she knew Chris was incapable of hurting anyone deliberately. Yet, everything seemed to fall into place too perfectly—like her mole matching the ones pictured in the medical book. Everything matched: the timeline, her missing nylons, the police questioning him, and now, Connie's scarf.

She lifted Chris's mattress and carefully pulled out the polka dot bandana.

If he'd murdered her friend and took the scarf as a souvenir, he hadn't been very careful about hiding it. Chris knew she sometimes went into his closet to collect his dirty clothes. He wouldn't have left evidence of a murder someplace where she could have so easily found it.

Another thing, she'd just looked through his entire wardrobe. None of Chris's clothes were bloodstained. You don't stab someone in the chest and not get spattered with blood.

And why would she automatically assume that one of her missing stockings was used to strangle Connie? There was nothing in any of the newspaper accounts to indicate the stocking wasn't Connie's.

Nora placed the scarf on top of the bed and ducked back into Chris's closet. She started searching through every piece of clothing. Maybe he'd hidden her nylons the same way he'd concealed Connie's bandana. While she went from hanger to hanger, Nora wondered, if one of her nylons was actually used to strangle Connie, would the police be able to trace it to her?

She went through all the clothes in Chris's closet and checked a large Sears box on the shelf. It was full of Chris's old drawings and the comic strips he'd created. He also kept several board games stored up on the shelf: Monopoly, a checkers set, Camelot, Sorry! and several other games. She checked inside each box.

Opening the box for the Melvin Purvis "G"-Men board

game, Nora finally found something: pictures of nude women—mostly Varga girls torn out of *Esquire*. There were also some black and white nudes that seemed to come from an art book. And she found Chris's own drawings and sketches of nude women. In one picture, Nora was pretty certain he'd put Paulette Goddard's face on Venus de Milo's body—only he'd given Venus arms and bigger boobs. Nora told herself it was typical teenage boy stuff.

For a few moments, she felt relieved. She carefully put the pictures back in their place inside the board-game box and then returned it to the shelf with the other games.

Straightening up the closet, Nora stepped back into the bedroom. She frowned at the scarf on Chris's stripped bed. It didn't make sense that he had Connie's bandana.

She started rifling through Chris's desk drawers. In the back of the second drawer down, she found a barrette, decorated with a row of different-colored little rosebuds. It took Nora a few moments to remember where she'd seen it before. Arlene had worn it in her wavy brown hair.

Another souvenir from another dead girl.

In the back of her mind, Nora had always questioned the circumstances of Arlene's suicide. The girl had broken Chris's heart and then, after months of ignoring him, had invited him over. Chris had told Arlene he wasn't going to see her, and then she'd shot herself hours later—apparently. Nora couldn't say for sure that Chris hadn't snuck out that night, too.

Hadn't Ray told her that Chris was harboring some dark secret?

Setting the barrette on his desktop, Nora continued to hunt through the drawers. She kept searching—even as she started to cry. She found something else: a distinctly feminine, lacey-edged handkerchief with a baby blue *M* monogram. It couldn't have been Connie's or Loretta Bryant's or Arlene's. Was there another victim she didn't know about?

Nora heard another rumble of thunder. The rain was coming

down hard now and lashing against the window. She wiped her tears and, more determined than ever, finished looking through Chris's desk. She didn't find the nylons or anything else of interest.

Before she moved on to Chris's dresser, Nora glanced out the window. Through the rain-beaded glass, she could see the side of the garage apartment. She spotted Joe in the window across the way. Had he been watching her?

She immediately lowered the shade.

She wondered how much Joe had seen. Then she told herself he probably had no idea what she was doing in here. He didn't even know whose room this was. He'd probably just been looking at the rain.

Then it occurred to her. Why wasn't Chris home yet? He couldn't be mowing Mrs. Landauer's lawn in this downpour.

She grabbed Connie's scarf, Arlene's barrette and the handkerchief belonging to "M." Then she headed down the hall to her bedroom. She stuffed what she was beginning to think of as "evidence" in her purse.

Downstairs, she pulled her raincoat and an umbrella out of the hall closet.

Three minutes later, she was walking in the thunderstorm, listening to the rain beating against the umbrella over her head. She clutched her purse close to her side. Nora could see the closed front gate to Mrs. Landauer's mansion at the end of the block.

She didn't want to think these crazy thoughts for one more minute. She needed to talk to Chris now. She needed her son to assure her that all of this "evidence" wasn't what it looked like. She needed to know that their lives weren't ruined.

Nora reached the gate and found it locked.

The lawn looked untouched. Down the driveway, the mansion was dark. Not a single light was on in the windows.

Nora rang the intercom anyway and waited in the rain. But there was no answer.

She wondered if Chris had even come here today.

Walking home in the rain, she still couldn't breathe right. Her stomach felt tight with dread. Nora kept telling herself she was crazy to jump to such wild conclusions. But glancing down at her purse, she thought about what was inside it, and she just felt sicker.

Once inside the house, she peeled off the wet raincoat and set it aside with the umbrella. She carried her purse with her into the kitchen, where she glanced out the window in the kitchen door.

Joe's car was gone.

She set her purse on the kitchen table and plopped down in a chair.

She was relieved that Joe had left for a while. She didn't want him dropping by right now.

At the same time, that left her all alone—with her thoughts.

And that was the last thing she wanted.

# Chapter 21

*Sunday*
*1:07 p.m.*

Eleven blocks from Nora's house, in the Roanoke neighborhood, two women in their early twenties shared a garage apartment. They both worked as ship welders at Todd Dry Dock and Construction on Harbor Island.

Anne Farnsworth was married with a husband in the navy, currently stationed in Australia. Her roommate, Gloria Dunbar, dated a lot of different guys. One of them was due over at any moment to take her out for lunch. Gussied up in a flowerprint dress that Anne had loaned her, Gloria stood in front of the bathroom mirror "putting her face on."

"You're gorgeous," Anne said, leaning against the bathroom doorframe. She wore a bathrobe, and her long auburn hair was piled up on her head, secured with clips and bobby pins. "Now, may I please get in there so I can take a shower? The bond rally starts at two thirty, and I want to get a good spot."

Gloria rolled her perfectly made-up eyes. "In this rain? If it doesn't get canceled, I'm sure the rally won't start on time. Those movie stars are always late anyway." She carefully applied some rouge to her cheeks. "Just give me another sec here. Not everyone is a natural beauty like you, Annie."

"Oh, give me a break," Anne groaned.

The doorbell rang.

"Ye gads, that's Bert! Be an angel. Go down and let him in."

"You're completely ready, and I'm in my bathrobe," Anne pointed out. "Are you nuts? Let him in yourself . . ."

With an exasperated sigh, Gloria tore herself away from the mirror and wordlessly brushed past Anne.

"Have fun!" Anne said, ducking into the bathroom and closing the door. She locked it.

"And you have fun at the bond rally!" Gloria called back. "Say hello to Bob Hope for me!"

Anne could hear her trotting down the stairs to the garage apartment's front door.

It seemed as if a different guy—usually a serviceman—dropped by every day for Gloria. This was especially true since the landlords, Mr. and Mrs. Alford, had gone to visit their married daughter in St. Louis ten days ago. The older couple, who lived in the main house, usually watched all of Anne's and Gloria's comings and goings. They were pretty strict with their house rules, which irked Gloria. "A couple of drips from Dripsville," she'd once said, describing the Alfords.

Gloria was taking full advantage of the Alfords' absence. Earlier in the week, she'd even had one of her dates spend the night on the living room sofa. With all the visitors, Anne felt like a USO hostess. She couldn't wait for Mr. and Mrs. Alford to get back from their trip next week.

Anne took off her robe and hung it on the hook on the back of the bathroom door. Past the rain outside, she could hear Gloria downstairs opening the front door to the apartment. Then Anne heard Gloria let out a strange, startled yelp.

Anne figured Bert or whatever-his-name-was must have jumped out and surprised Gloria or grabbed her as a joke.

Before she turned on the shower, Anne waited for the sound of her roommate's laughter. But all she heard was the front door shutting—and the steady rain outside. Anne wondered if they were necking at the bottom of the stairs. It was one of Gloria's favorite spots for that. Or maybe they'd left already.

Anne turned on the water, stepped under the shower and pulled the curtain shut. She decided Gloria and her date couldn't have left already. Not enough time had passed for them to come back up to the apartment so that Gloria could grab her umbrella and purse. With some guy Anne didn't know in the apartment, she was glad for the lock on the bathroom door.

Soaping herself under the warm spray, Anne decided to take her time. She didn't want some stranger gaping at her when she emerged from the bathroom in her robe. Maybe by the time she finished showering, Gloria and her date would be gone.

Anne's friend, Tess, was due over at one thirty. They were going to the bond rally in Victory Square—at University and Fourth downtown. Anne had heard that Bob Hope and Irene Dunne would be there, selling war bonds. She'd set aside twenty dollars for the rally and hoped to talk to Irene when she bought a bond—if the event didn't get canceled because of the rainstorm. Then again, maybe the downpour would keep the crowds away, and she'd have more time to converse with Irene or Bob. It wasn't patriotic to hope for a poor turnout, but she wanted to ask Irene Dunne what brand of shampoo she used and what it was like kissing Cary Grant.

The ceiling light flickered in the bathroom.

Anne paused, hoping the storm wouldn't knock out the power.

Past the sound of the shower, she thought she heard Gloria laughing. Or was she screaming? What was going on?

Poking her head outside the shower curtain, Anne listened

for a few moments. But she didn't hear anything—just the
rushing shower water. Then, as soon as she closed the curtain
and stepped back under the spray again, Anne could have
sworn she heard a rumbling noise somewhere inside the apartment. Was it Gloria and her date running down the stairs? Or
maybe it had been a clap of thunder outside. Under the shower,
sounds played tricks sometimes.

The light flickered again.

"Damn it," Anne muttered. It was unsettling. If they lost
power, how long would it be before the lights came back on
again?

She turned off the shower, and the pipes let out a squeak. All
the rumbling she'd detected earlier suddenly stopped. Pulling
open the curtain, Anne grabbed a towel off the rack and started
drying herself off.

As she stepped out of the tub and onto the bathmat, she
heard the floorboards creaking outside the bathroom door.

*Swell, they're still here*, Anne thought, frowning. She tried to
remember if she'd met this Bert person before.

The bathroom doorknob rattled.

Naked, Anne automatically pulled the towel in front of her.
"I'll be out in a few minutes!" she called.

There was no response from whoever stood on the other side
of the door. But someone was still standing there; Anne could
feel it.

"Gloria, is that you?"

Again, no answer.

Anne listened to the footsteps retreating. Was it Gloria's
date? How weird that he'd tried to open the bathroom door
without knocking first. He certainly must have heard the shower
earlier. He had to know someone was in here.

Uncertain, Anne stood perfectly still and clutched the towel
in front of her.

Now it sounded as if someone was moving something around

in the living room—and then in the kitchen. She didn't hear any talking. Gloria was usually such a chatterbox. Why were they being so quiet? All Anne could hear was the rain starting to let up.

She quickly finished drying herself off and grabbed her robe off the hook on the back of the door. As she put it on, she heard footsteps outside the bathroom again. Anne backed away from the door. Her hands were shaking as she tied the sash to her robe. She stared at the doorknob.

She watched it turn from one side to the other. It didn't make a sound this time.

"Gloria!" she yelled. "Gloria, are you out there?"

No response. The doorknob stopped moving.

"Who—" Anne was about to ask who was out there, but the words caught in her throat. All she could think was that Gloria and her date must have left, and someone had broken into the apartment. It would be just like Gloria to forget to lock the front door.

Anne stared at the bathroom door as it seemed to give a little—like someone was leaning against it on the other side. The door panel groaned under the pressure. The knob rattled and clicked.

"Gloria?" Anne called out, her voice quivering. "John's due over any minute! Would you listen for him? Will you do that for me?"

Again, there was no response.

Anne kept a hand over her mouth. She wanted to scream. She wondered if the intruder believed her lie.

Or would he kick the door down?

Anne watched and waited.

Whoever was on the other side of the door stopped leaning against it. The panel let out one last squeak. The doorknob stopped turning. Past the sound of the rain, Anne listened to the footsteps retreating again.

For another five long, grueling minutes, Anne stood there in the bathroom, paralyzed with fear. She finally heard someone lumbering down the steps, and then the lock on the front door downstairs clicked. Anne could barely hear it. Was he leaving?

It was another minute before she heard the door shut.

Still, Anne didn't move. She kept waiting for the next telltale sound. Had the intruder just pretended to leave in order to lure her out of the bathroom?

She had no idea how long she stood there. The rain seemed to die down.

Taking a few deep breaths, she warily moved to the door and then unlocked and opened it. The hinges yawned. The cool air hit her and a bit of steam escaped from the bathroom as she poked her head out into the now-vacant hallway. With trepidation, she moved to the top of the stairs and saw no one. The front door was closed.

Anne crept toward the living room and spotted her flower-print dress—the one she'd loaned to Gloria—in a heap on the living room floor. As she stepped closer to it, she noticed the garment was torn.

Then she saw something out of the corner of her eye—on the kitchen floor. It was Gloria's shoe.

Anne headed toward the kitchen but recoiled in the doorway.

Gloria lay on the linoleum floor, her head propped up against the refrigerator. With her eyes closed, she might have been asleep—except for her bruised, purplish face and the strange lipstick smile smeared around her open mouth. A nylon stocking was tied so tightly around Gloria's throat that only the tail ends from the knot were visible.

After tearing off her dress, Gloria's killer must have tied the pink gingham apron around her waist. It was slightly awry—barely covering her tan-painted legs.

With its siren blaring and lights flashing, the first police car pulled up just short of the driveway to the Alford house. The girl was waiting there in her bathrobe, barefoot and crying in the slight drizzle. She'd been hysterical over the phone. She must have been screaming when she'd run outside, because a couple of neighbors anxiously hovered around her.

Officers Konradt and Cegielski in the first car would take care of her and get her statement.

The second cop car, followed by the ambulance, turned into the driveway and headed toward the garage. Officer John Martinsen was at the wheel. Sitting up front with him, twenty-seven-year-old Officer Christopher Lahart had been on the lookout for anyone suspicious in the area. As his partner brought the squad car to a quick stop, Officer Lahart noticed that the girl in the bathrobe had left the door open to the garage apartment. And past the slashing windshield wipers, he noticed something else.

There, by the door, on what must have been a flagpole holder, someone had hung a pair of slacks.

# Chapter 22

"Where is he?" Nora muttered to no one in particular.

Hunched over the washing machine, she fed the wet clothes—one piece at a time—through the wringer. She had the hose hooked up to the laundry sink and could barely hear herself over the noise from the agitator.

She'd been in a stupor, sitting in the kitchen for twenty minutes before deciding she'd better get busy or go crazy. She'd changed from her church clothes into her blue housedress and then finished collecting the dirty laundry, two wicker basketfuls. She'd taken them down to the laundry room and gotten to work.

There had been several interruptions—including more phone calls from people who had seen the newspaper ad about the apartment. Nora had rushed up the basement stairs each time, thinking it might be Chris. On two of those trips, while by the phone, she'd tried calling Mrs. Landauer's house. No one had picked up. She'd also run upstairs twice, thinking she heard someone coming through the front door. But she'd been wrong both times.

After one of those false alarms, she'd brought her purse down with her to the basement. With Connie's scarf, the barrette and the handkerchief in there, she wasn't about to let the purse out of her sight.

Jane had returned home about a half hour ago. The mother of one of her friends had dropped her off, God bless the woman. Nora had asked Jane to handle the callers about the garage apartment and to let her know the minute Chris came home. Jane had given her two more blouses to wash.

Keeping busy helped Nora put things into perspective. She decided she'd gone a little haywire in her thinking earlier. Maybe her poor mom wasn't the only crazy one in her family. There was probably a perfectly innocent explanation for why Chris had Connie's bandana. And yes, he had a barrette that had belonged to Arlene—so what? The two of them had been inseparable for months. Nora had no idea who "M" was. But she was sure Chris would tell her when she asked. He would tell her everything—and she'd know whether or not he was lying.

Her thinking was all fouled up because she'd become obsessed over Connie's murder. She felt guilty for not doing anything to clear Roger's name. And if another riveter was strangled, that would be on her conscience. Finding Connie's scarf hidden in Chris's closet had simply pushed her over the edge. And she'd jumped to all sorts of crazy conclusions.

She would ask Chris why he had the bandana—just as soon as he got home from wherever he was. The rain had let up a while ago, but he couldn't be cutting wet grass. He'd probably driven Mrs. Landauer somewhere. Chris had chauffeured her around before. For all Nora knew, the poor old lady might have had a medical emergency and Chris drove her to the hospital.

The washer's agitator finished its cycle, and Nora hung up some damp clothes. With the sudden silence, she heard Jane upstairs talking to someone. Nora thought her daughter must be on the phone. But then she heard another voice.

Tossing a blouse onto the clothesline, she quickly wiped her damp hands on the front of her housedress and hurried upstairs. She followed Jane's voice to the family room, where she found her daughter, sitting on the sofa with Joe.

Jane had the family photo album open between them. "He sent us this picture after he joined the navy," she said, pointing to a photograph.

"You must really miss him," Joe said.

"Oh, and here's another one of me," Jane said, pointing again. "Don't look, it's horrible!"

"What's this?" Nora asked, stopping in the doorway.

Joe looked up, noticed Nora and smiled. "Well, hello . . ."

She was certain it was all quite innocent. But she couldn't help feeling skittish about the fact that, while she'd been downstairs, Joe had come into the house and gotten very chummy with her daughter. On his first day as her new tenant, he'd entered her home without her knowing.

"I'm showing Mr. Strauss some photos of Uncle Ray," Jane explained. "Don't you think he looks like Uncle Ray?"

Nora didn't answer right away. Considering her stupid infatuation with Joe up until now, Nora didn't want to think he resembled her brother in the least. But she suddenly saw a vague similarity in their features.

"I'm very flattered," Joe said. His whole body seemed sort of clenched as he sat there on the sofa with Jane. He smiled at Nora again, but he still looked uncomfortable. "A little while ago, I got back with some groceries and supplies, and Jane was nice enough to help me carry them up to the apartment. Then she wanted to show me some pictures of your brother. I hope you don't think I just let myself in . . ."

"Of course not," Nora murmured.

"Can Mr. Strauss come to dinner tonight?" Jane asked.

He got to his feet and gave Nora a contrite look. "Again, not my idea," he said. Then he turned to Jane. "I told you not to put your mom on the spot by asking her in front of me. And you're supposed to call me Joe, remember?"

"Okay, *Joe*," Jane answered with a giggle.

"I still have some things to unpack. Thanks for your help, both of you." Heading out of the family room, Joe paused in front of Nora. "I left the tools and the jar of nails and screws on your kitchen table. Thanks again, Nora." He started down the hallway toward the kitchen.

Nora followed him. "I hope Jane didn't bother you too much," she whispered.

"Not at all," he said under his breath. "She's very sweet." He stopped in front of the kitchen door.

Nora opened it for him. "Well, if you ever feel she's invading your privacy, please, let me know."

"Will do," he said, nodding. "Take care."

"You too, Joe," she said.

Then she watched him take the short walk to the garage apartment door.

She thought it had been tactful of him not to bring up Jane's invitation to dinner again. Nora hadn't really invited him or uninvited him. No doubt, Jane had foisted herself upon Joe and insisted he come over to look at photos of Ray. And no doubt, he'd ended up being shown photos mostly of Jane. It certainly hadn't been Joe's idea, like he'd said.

But it still bothered her that in the middle of his moving day, he'd willingly gone along with Jane's proposal.

"You didn't tell me how dreamy he is!" Jane sighed, leaning against the laundry sink. She'd followed Nora down to the basement. "And I still think he looks like Uncle Ray. Why can't Joe come to dinner tonight? He's all alone, and it's his first night in a new place. He could probably use a home-cooked meal."

"I told you, *we'll see*," Nora said, emptying the washer. "I don't want you going over there, bothering him. It was very nice of you to help him with his groceries. But before you drop in on him again or invite him into the house, I want you to check with me first. How's the homework situation?"

The telephone rang upstairs.

"Saved by the bell!" Jane declared, and she ran for the stairs.

"If that's Chris, I need to talk to him!" Nora called.

After about ten minutes, Nora realized Jane probably wasn't coming back downstairs—most likely to avoid any further questions about her homework. Nora started washing another load, and with the rushing water, the hum of the automatic wringer and the churning agitator, she couldn't hear a thing.

Standing over the washing machine, she kept glancing at her purse, on the ironing board where she'd left it. If her hands weren't wet, she'd probably take out Connie's bandana, Arlene's barrette and M's handkerchief, just to study them again. She'd acted the same way back when she'd had that melanoma scare. She couldn't stop looking at that mole, and each time she'd tell herself a different story: it wasn't that bad; no, it was inoperable—certain death. With each look, she bargained with God or told herself this couldn't be happening or wondered who would end up taking care of her kids.

Looking up from her work, Nora was startled to see Chris coming down the basement stairs. He'd already reached the bottom few steps. It looked like he was trying to say something to her.

Nora turned off the agitator. "I couldn't hear you over all this noise," she called out over the dying mechanical din.

"Jane said you wanted to talk to me," he said, coming into the laundry nook. The ironing board was between them. "What's going on? Is everything okay? It's not Dad, is it?"

Nora shook her head. She told herself not to get all accusatory. She took a deep breath. "Where were you?" she asked calmly.

"I told you this morning, I was going over to Mrs. Landauer's to cut the lawn."

"In that monsoon earlier?" she asked.

He didn't quite look her in the eye. "No, you're right. I never got around to it. She just had me running errands."

"Well, I called over there twice, and no one answered."

He nodded. "Yeah, I know, one of the errands was driving her to Rhodes so she could go shopping. We were in that stupid department store for at least three hours. She'd walk maybe twenty feet and then have to sit down for ten minutes. It was heinous. We must have gone through the entire store, every floor, and all she got was birdseed for her parakeet. But at least I got paid—ten bucks." He paused and then leaned against one of the support posts. "Is the guy renting the apartment all moved in?"

"Yes, you might meet him at dinner," Nora answered. "But I'm still not sure yet if I'm going to invite him over." She took another deep breath. "Listen, Chris, I stripped your bed and went through your closet for dirty clothes." She pointed to his plaid shirt, drying on the clothesline. "I was taking that off the hanger and found something . . ."

He stared at the shirt and then gave her a wary look. "What are you talking about?"

She stepped closer to the ironing board and opened her purse. She took out Connie's scarf. "I can't help wondering where you got this—and why it was in your closet."

He let out a nervous laugh and quickly shook his head. "I don't know what that is . . ."

"Well, I do," Nora said. "It's Connie's scarf. She used to wear it to work. How did it end up in your closet?"

He took a step back and shrugged. "I've never seen that before."

Frustrated, Nora reached inside the purse and took out the barrette and the handkerchief. She set them down on the ironing board. "I found these in your desk."

"You went through my desk?" he asked indignantly. "Y'know, there aren't any dirty clothes in my desk, Mom. Don't I get any privacy?"

"Not when I find my murdered friend's scarf hidden in your closet!" she shot back. Nora remembered Jane upstairs, and she lowered her voice. "What are these?" she asked, nodding at the rosebud barrette and M's handkerchief.

Chris heaved a sigh. "I forgot I even had those," he said, frowning at her. "You must have really dug through every drawer."

"What are they?" she pressed.

He gazed at the items on the ironing board. "The hair clip belonged to Arlene. She took it off one night in my room and forgot it, so I stuck it in my desk. I think that was one of the last times we got together. Otherwise, I'd have given it back to her. And the handkerchief is Nana's. Back when she died, I asked Dad if I could have something of hers, and he gave me that handkerchief."

Nora felt like an idiot that she hadn't picked up on the fact that the handkerchief had been her mother-in-law's. And what Chris said about Arlene's barrette made perfect sense. He seemed to be telling the truth, too.

But there was still Connie's scarf.

Nora picked it up and showed it to him again. "What about this, Chris? It didn't just magically transplant itself onto the hanger under your plaid shirt. What are you doing with Connie's scarf?"

His face turned red. "She dropped it."

Studying him, Nora shook her head. "Connie wasn't wearing it the night she and Roger were here, and I don't think she brought it with her—"

"No, she dropped it outside her apartment—in Queen Anne," he murmured. "It fell out of her coat pocket."

"When?"

"The Tuesday afternoon after the party," he answered, still unable to look at her. "I skipped study hall and went to her place."

"You skipped school again?" Nora asked, raising her voice.

"Mom, it was study hall. Everybody skips study hall."

"Well, what in the world were you doing at Connie's place?"

"I just wanted to see her come back from work, that's all." He shrugged. "I wanted to see where she lived. I wasn't going to bother her or anything. I liked her. She was nice to me at the party."

"How did you know where she lived?"

"She's listed in your address book."

"Did you talk to her?" Nora pressed.

Chris shook his head. He had that sad, lost-lamb look on his face. "No, I chickened out. I watched her from across the street. Once she went inside, I picked up the scarf and—well, I was going to knock on her door and give it to her. But I was worried she'd think I was some kind of weirdo creep, so I . . . I kept it."

Nora stared at him. He seemed to be telling the truth.

She remembered how hard he'd seemed to take the news when she'd woken him up and told him that Connie and Roger were dead. Chris had been infatuated with two girls, only to have each one come to a gruesome end: first Arlene and then Connie.

*The poor kid*, Nora thought.

But it still didn't feel right. "So you're telling me that you had a crush on Connie," she said. "And you were following her around . . ."

Chris slouched against the post again. His eyes avoided hers, but he nodded.

"Were you following her around the night she was killed?"

He restlessly shifted from one foot to the other. "Yeah," he said, barely audible.

"So when I ran into you in the hallway late that night, and you said you'd heard a noise outside, you were lying to me, weren't you?"

He nodded again.

"The truth is, you waited until I'd gone to bed, and then you drove to Queen Anne . . ."

He shook his head. "I walked. I brought the scarf with me. I was going to give it back to her."

"When was this?" Nora asked.

"I left around nine fifteen," he mumbled. "I didn't get to her place until ten—"

"Chris, you'll have to speak up. I can't hear you."

He looked skyward and nervously cleared his throat. "I got to her place around ten," he said, more clearly this time. "It didn't look like she was home. Then I remembered her and Roger at the party saying that sometimes they liked to go to the Mecca Café in their neighborhood. So I walked there, peeked into the window and saw them. I stuck around until they came out. But I was pretty sure they spotted me, so I stopped following them after that."

"What time was it when you last saw them?"

"Almost eleven."

"Chris, I caught you sneaking back in at about a quarter to one in the morning. That's almost two hours later."

"Yeah, I know, I went to a park near there and just sat for a while. Then I walked home."

She studied his face, uncertain about his story. "Honey, you must have been one of the last people to see Connie alive—Connie and Roger."

He nodded glumly. "I guess so."

"Why didn't you say anything to me?"

"Because I figured you'd be sore at me for sneaking out again and then lying to you about it." He shrugged helplessly. "And it's not like I really saw anything. I'd remember if there was something weird or suspicious. I couldn't have told the police anything that would have helped their investigation."

Exasperated, Nora shook her head. "I can't believe you're doing this, Chris, this—this slinking out until one in the morning on a school night—like it's nothing. How do you manage to stay awake for your classes? No wonder your grades are slipping."

"I'm sorry," he muttered. "It's just that I can't sleep at night sometimes, so I go out."

"You realize how this looks, don't you?" She picked up the black and pink polka dot bandana. "You have Connie's scarf. You were sneaking around, following her, watching her apartment. You said you thought Connie and Roger saw you the night Connie was murdered. What if someone else saw you that night? How do you think it looked?"

"I hadn't thought of that," he said, a sudden, anxious look on his face.

"Chris, I have to be honest with you," she whispered. "I'm scared. This behavior of yours, I feel like I don't know you anymore. When I found Connie's scarf hidden in your closet, I couldn't help thinking the absolute worst."

He stared at her as if he didn't understand.

"Chris, it looked like you were hiding evidence."

"You mean, you thought I'd killed Connie?" He let out a stunned, wounded laugh. "Is that what you think of me? Are you serious, Mom? Do you actually believe I could strangle and stab someone?"

"I didn't know what to think," Nora said. "You're so secretive lately. And if I dare ask you about anything, half the time when you answer me, I can tell you're lying."

He picked up the rosebud barrette. "What about this? Do

you think I killed Arlene, too? Is that why you're asking me about it?"

Nora said nothing.

Chris set down the hair clip, swiped up the handkerchief and shook it at her in his fist. He laughed again. "What? Do you think I killed Nana, too?"

"I didn't recognize her handkerchief," Nora admitted quietly.

"But you actually thought I might've murdered Arlene—and your friend, Connie."

"I told you, Chris, I didn't know what to believe."

"You're my mom," he said. "You're supposed to believe in me. Am I really such a freak that even my own mother thinks I could be a murderer?"

"Chris, give me a break," she said. "I'm tired. My brother died last week. I hate to use that as a 'Get Out of Jail Free' card, but I'm still kind of a wreck about it. And I'm not over what happened to Connie. It gnaws away at me that the police blame Roger for that—"

"So instead, you blame me," he grumbled.

"I'm not blaming you. It just looked bad when I found Connie's scarf—and I got scared. I thought the unthinkable might have happened."

He just stared at her with a hurt expression on his face.

"Chris, don't turn this around and get all upset with me when you've been so secretive and so dishonest lately. I love you. I don't think you're a *freak*. But you leave me in the dark, and I'm always second-guessing what's happening with you. I worry about you, honey. And yes, sometimes I think the worst."

He grabbed the scarf, the barrette and the handkerchief off the ironing board. "Well, I don't want anyone else thinking the worst," he muttered. He started to walk away.

Before Nora realized what he had in mind, he'd already

marched to the big furnace and opened the trap door. "Chris, wait! No!"

Chris seemed to burn his hand on the trap door handle, but that didn't stop him. In one pitch, he threw everything into the furnace fire: Connie's scarf, Arlene's barrette and his grandmother's handkerchief. He slammed the furnace trap door shut and then shook out the pain to his hand.

"My God, Chris, what have you just done?"

Her motherly instincts kicked in, and she reached for his wrist to check his hand.

But he pulled away. "I'm fine. It was just a little hot. Now, maybe nobody else will think I'm a murderer."

"I can't believe you just did that!" she whispered. "Grandma's handkerchief . . . Connie's scarf . . ."

He just stared down at the floor.

"You know, Connie would've been flattered if she knew you had a crush on her," Nora pointed out. "She'd have wanted you to hold on to her favorite bandana. God, how could you just . . ." She trailed off and shook her head at him. All she could think was that he'd just destroyed evidence. Or did he know that?

"If you didn't want the scarf, fine," Nora went on. "But did it even occur to you that I might have wanted to hold on to it? She was my friend. For God's sake, Chris, you do something like that—it's just what I was talking about. What am I supposed to think?"

He frowned. "I already know what you think of me, Mom."

She nodded emphatically. "Yes, and this isn't helping your case one bit." She put a hand to her forehead. "I wish your father were here—or your uncle. Maybe they could talk to you, because I give up."

"So does that mean you're finished asking me questions?" Chris said tonelessly. "Because I'm tired. I'd like to go up to my room and take a nap."

Nora sighed. She took a moment before answering. "I stripped your bed. If you give me a few minutes, I can make it up for you again."

"It's okay, thanks," he mumbled, turning away. "I can make it myself. I know where the sheets are."

Nora watched him trudge up the stairs. "Put some ointment on that hand!" she called.

He didn't answer.

She felt horrible—because she'd hurt him. But worse, because she wasn't sure she completely believed him. He might not be a murderer, but he was still hiding something.

Nora glanced over at the big, octopus-like furnace. She really wished Chris hadn't—in a fit of anger—burned those things.

Then again, maybe he knew exactly what he was doing.

# Chapter 23

Nora rang the doorbell by the garage apartment's entrance. Then she adjusted the wax paper barely covering the dinner plate in her other hand. She missed tin foil, which was rationed because of the war—along with just about every other metal product.

She could hear Joe coming down the stairs, and then the door opened. He wore a T-shirt and pleated pants. He smiled at her. "Well, hi again . . ."

Nora lifted up the wax paper for a moment to show him the plate of food. "I hope you haven't had your dinner yet," she said. "It's ham, scalloped potatoes and green beans. I feel bad I didn't follow through on Jane's invitation. But the timing is off. I have a son who isn't talking to me right now, and it's been kind of a rough day." She re-covered the plate and handed it to him.

"Well, thank you. And actually, I think your timing is perfect." He folded back the wax paper to peek at the food again. "I haven't eaten yet, and this looks delicious."

"I promise, we won't make a habit of dropping by like this," Nora said. "I spoke to Jane about respecting your privacy from now on."

"You know, I felt kind of funny about coming into your house without you inviting me. But Jane insisted I look at some photos of your brother. And she wouldn't take no for an answer."

Nora was relieved to hear him say that. She laughed. "Yes, Jane can be very persuasive."

He turned his head to one side. "I'm sorry, I didn't get that . . ."

"I said, Jane can be very persuasive," she repeated—a bit louder.

He nodded. "Well, I hope you didn't feel obligated to feed me just because she invited me to Sunday dinner."

Nora shook her head. "No, not at all. In fact, it just occurred to me that you're probably better off eating alone tonight. The last time I had Sunday dinner guests, it was a party of eight— and now, three of them are dead."

Joe looked slightly taken aback. With his bad ear, maybe he thought he hadn't heard her right.

Nora felt stupid for telling him that. She came off as flippant. "I don't mean that the way it sounded." She shrugged. "It's just that—well, this was three weeks ago, when my brother was visiting. He was one of the guests—along with a friend of mine from work, Connie Wiedrich, and her friend, Roger Tallant. She was killed a couple of weeks ago. You might have heard about it. She lived in Queen Anne. She was strangled . . ."

"Oh, yeah," Joe said, wincing. "I read about that. *Roger Tallant*, he's the guy the police say killed her. They shot him. They said he had a gun, but then, apparently, he didn't—something like that. It was kind of muddled. They were friends of yours?"

Nora nodded. She wasn't sure why she'd brought it up—except that she couldn't very well talk to the kids about how much she missed Ray and how shaken up she was about Connie's murder. The only other adult she could talk to about it was Fran, and that was during their lunch break. Forty-five minutes in a crowded, noisy cafeteria didn't allow her much time to bare her soul. Joe's very presence made Nora realize how starved she was for adult companionship—and how much she missed being near a man.

He was staring into her eyes. "Oh, Nora, I'm so sorry about your friends—and your brother. You've certainly had a rough couple of weeks. And having to shoulder that by yourself while your husband's away . . ." His voice trailed off. "Listen, if there's anything I can ever do to help out around here, just let me know."

Nora smiled at him and let out a nervous laugh. "You wouldn't care to talk to my son for me, would you?"

"You mean, like a peace negotiator?"

Nodding, she crossed her arms to fight off the chill. "Tell me, when you were seventeen years old, did you sneak out at night and then lie to your parents about where you were?"

He chuckled. "Yeah, often enough."

"Well, I feel better hearing that. Maybe the situation isn't as bad as I thought." Nora smiled at him. "I mean, you turned out pretty nice . . ."

Joe smiled back, and Nora felt a sort of connection between them. She sensed he felt it, too. Or was she reading something in the way he gazed at her? Was it just wishful thinking? For a moment, Nora couldn't say anything.

She finally took a step back and then cleared her throat. "Well, listen, your wife—if you ever want to call her or she needs to call you, please, feel free to use our phone."

He nodded. "Thanks, I might take you up on that sometime. And thank you for dinner."

"You have knives, forks, napkins and all that?" she asked.

He nodded again. "I bought some today. Thanks again, Nora."

"Good night, Joe," she called. Then she headed for the back door.

Nora knocked on Chris's bedroom door. "I fixed you a plate of food!" she called. "I left it down on the kitchen table. I decided you shouldn't go to bed hungry—or mad."

The bedroom door swung open. Chris stood there with his hair mussed from his nap. Once again, he wouldn't quite look at her.

Nora could see into the room behind him. He'd made his bed.

"I've also decided that you can't be upset at me for thinking the worst," she continued. "You're the one who's been so secretive, Chris, not to mention dishonest with me. You created this atmosphere of distrust . . ."

Chris had his hand on the doorknob. He stared down at the threshold between them.

"We've both had a rough couple of weeks," Nora went on, thinking of how Joe had put it earlier. "We need to give each other a break—and be nice to each other."

He nodded. When he finally lifted his head and looked at her, Nora saw the tears in his eyes. "I'm really sorry, Mom," he whispered. "I don't know why I burned up that stuff. I really wish I hadn't now. I've done so many stupid things lately. I don't know what's wrong with me. But I could never kill anybody, I swear . . ."

He hugged her and started crying on her shoulder.

Nora patted him on the back. "I know, honey. I know. I'm sorry, too . . ."

Nora wasn't sure what woke her.

She glanced at the clock on her nightstand: ten fifty. She'd been asleep for only an hour or so. Chris had eaten his dinner, and both kids had still been up when she'd gone to bed.

Nora lay there in the dark, listening.

If a noise had woken her, she didn't hear anything now. Still, Nora knew she had to get up and make sure everything was all right; otherwise, she'd never fall asleep again.

Throwing back the covers, she crawled out of bed. She didn't bother to put a robe over her blue gingham pajamas. Poking her head out into the hallway, she noticed Chris's door was closed. She padded down the hall and paused outside his door. She didn't see a strip of light at the threshold. She didn't want to knock and wake him up. But she didn't want to barge in on him either.

Yet she wouldn't sleep a wink if she didn't make certain he was in bed.

Nora tapped lightly on the door. No response. She waited a few moments and opened the door a crack. "Chris?" she whispered.

In the darkness, she noticed the same body-shaped lump under the covers she'd seen in his bed the night before she'd started her job.

"Chris?" she said, a little louder.

The "lump" in his bed moved. Chris pushed back the sheets and sat up. He squinted at her. "Hey, Mom, what's going on?"

"Nothing, honey. I'm sorry. Go back to sleep."

He nodded and then pulled the bedding back over him. "G'night," he mumbled.

Nora quietly closed the door.

The house was still. She didn't hear anything outside.

Nevertheless, she moved the blackout curtain and peeked out the window at the end of the hallway. No one was in the backyard.

The curtains weren't drawn in the windows of the garage apartment, and the light was on in the living room. It wasn't quite eleven o'clock yet, so Joe wasn't breaking the blackout regulations. Nora didn't spot him anywhere in the apartment, but she noticed, in the living room, he'd set up an easel with a canvas on it and a small table nearby, cluttered with a palette, paint tubes, rags and a jarful of brushes. The front of the canvas was facing the other way, so she couldn't see what he was working on. She had a limited view of the floor but could see that he'd put down a drop cloth.

It was comforting to know that, while she slept, he was quietly at work next door, watching over the place.

Joe stepped into view—apparently from the kitchen, because he had a bottle of beer. He was shirtless and wore a pair of paint-stained khakis that rode low around his hips. After taking a swig of beer, he put down the bottle and picked up his palette and a paintbrush. Then he started to work on his painting.

Nora stood on her tiptoes and noticed he was barefoot. She felt like she could almost reach out and touch him. She could see a yellow paint smear on his trim stomach and another splotch of pale blue on his hairy chest. Different paint colors were smeared on his muscular arms and those beautiful hands. His thick brown hair was a mess.

Mesmerized, Nora stood by the window, watching him.

Every movement he made seemed so unselfconsciously erotic—even something as simple as wiping his hand on his pants before reaching for a different brush. She could have stared at him all night.

Joe picked up something from the little table. It took Nora a moment to realize it was his wristwatch. He glanced at it and put the watch back down on the table. Then, wiping his hands again, he moved over to the window and pulled the blackout curtain closed.

Nora's heart sank.

She watched him methodically close all the other curtains.

# Chapter 24

From down the block, Nora could see people waiting at the bus stop on Broadway. That was a good sign. She hadn't missed the bus to work.

This morning in bed, she'd turned off her alarm and fallen back asleep—for only twenty-five minutes, but it had been enough to throw her into a panic. She'd barely had time to dress. She'd had to forgo her coffee and cornflakes and the usual quick glance at the newspaper. In fact, she hadn't even had time to bring in the paper. She'd left it on the front walkway as she'd run out the door to catch her bus.

Nora was relieved the bus was running a bit late.

Catching her breath, she slowed down and continued toward the stop at the end of the block. About six people were standing there, Boeing assembly-line workers like her. She was too far away to see their faces, but after so many trips on this same bus, she was beginning to recognize some of the regulars at her stop. Not that she actually knew any of them yet. It wasn't a very chatty bunch. But considering it was barely light out, most of them—like her—were still half-asleep.

She glanced over her shoulder—and just then, the bus sped past her.

*Damn.*

Nora started running.

Up ahead, she saw the bus pull up to the stop, and people started boarding. Frazzled, she broke into a sprint. "Hold the bus, please!" Nora screamed, waving.

But no one seemed to notice her.

The last passenger stepped onto the bus. Then it started to move.

"Please!" Nora cried, running even faster, pushing herself until her lungs burned.

She caught up to the bus and was racing alongside the big vehicle when it came to an abrupt stop. She heard the doors flap open. Reaching them, she staggered on board, thanked the driver and showed him her pass. The bus started moving again. Nora made her way down the aisle and plopped down in a seat. She tried to catch her breath.

Then after a few moments, she started wondering if she'd locked the front door. She'd left in such a hurry. But she was almost certain she'd locked it. Still, it hadn't been smart to leave the newspaper outside. If one of the kids didn't bring it in, somebody casing the neighborhood would see it sitting out there all day, and they'd know no one was home.

Then Nora remembered Joe. He'd said he would keep an eye on the place during the day. He'd be there in the apartment above the garage, painting the artwork for some national ad—probably while shirtless. Nora almost giggled at the thought. The image of him last night still lingered in her memory.

In her loneliness, especially over the last few weeks, there were times when Nora just wanted to be near a man. She'd developed little crushes on certain nameless guys she recognized—like the sweet, bookish-looking blond man who occasionally rode the same bus home with her, and the tall, Robert Taylor look-alike who often sat at a neighboring table in the cafeteria during her lunch hour. She loved her husband and missed him terribly. But he was in North Africa, and she had no idea when—or if—she'd ever see him again. Meanwhile, just glimpsing these strangers gave her a secret thrill—something to look forward to as she headed for the bus home or into the cafeteria for lunch. They were safe little infatuations. She'd probably never talk to them or know their names.

But she knew Joe, and he was just fifty feet from her kitchen door. Already, her feelings for him were so much stronger than anything she'd harbored for the others—and that scared her. He wasn't a fantasy man. He was real.

The bus pulled over to another stop, jarring Nora out of her daydream.

The man across the aisle from her was reading *The Seattle Times*. As he held the paper open in front of him, Nora noticed one of the headlines on the front page:

## CAPITOL HILL WOMAN, 25, STRANGLED IN HOME

### Victim's Roommate Hid in Locked Bathroom

### Killer Eludes Seattle Police

Stunned, Nora leaned across the aisle to read the subheadings. She'd been waiting for something like this to happen—and dreading it. She wondered when the woman had been killed. Had it happened last night?

The newspaper rustled as the man across the aisle lowered it and glared at her with annoyance.

"I'm sorry," Nora said meekly. "But I think there's a story

on the front page about someone I know. Would you mind if I took a quick look?"

With a sigh, he set the newspaper on his lap, pulled out the front section and handed it to her. "I'd like it back, please," he grumbled.

"Yes, of course," Nora said. "Thank you."

She anxiously scanned the article. The murder victim, Gloria Dunbar, lived in a garage apartment, which immediately struck Nora as a weird coincidence. From the Roanoke neighborhood address, she guessed it was only a mile or so from her house. Gloria and her roommate worked as welders in the shipyards on Harbor Island. The poor woman was the third Seattle war worker strangled in the last month. Yet there was no mention of that in the article, no mention of Loretta Bryant or Connie. Nora skipped ahead, searching for their names, but didn't see them.

She went back to the first couple of paragraphs. Gloria Dunbar's "partially clothed body" was discovered by her roommate, who had narrowly escaped the killer by hiding in a locked bathroom. The roommate didn't see the killer or hear his voice. Gloria was strangled with a nylon stocking at approximately one thirty on Sunday afternoon.

Nora's stomach turned as she read the time—just about when Chris was supposed to have driven Mrs. Landauer to Rhodes department store.

Nora replayed in her mind the conversation they'd had in the basement yesterday. At first, Chris had said he'd been cutting Mrs. Landauer's lawn; but then, no, he'd been running errands for her at her home; and finally, he'd claimed to have chauffeured the old woman to the department store downtown.

Had he even been with Mrs. Landauer at all yesterday afternoon?

Nora kept asking herself that for the next three hours—

while she riveted B-17 tail sections with Chatterbox Edna again. It was unnerving. She was so worried about Chris, and this woman wouldn't stop talking *at* her—mostly regarding things Nora didn't give a hoot about. With all the noise, Nora was never certain if Edna was telling her about the alignment of the rivets or something as inane as her nephew and his girlfriend coming in third for the Skagit County Dipsy Doodle Dance Contest.

At one point, during a routine on-the-spot inspection, Larry discovered the configuration of rivet heads was off. He screamed at the two of them, calling them "worthless bubble-brains." They had to rip out all the rivets in one row and start over again. Nora didn't blame Larry for being furious.

During her coffee break, as much as she needed a cup, Nora bypassed the coffee line in the cafeteria and ducked into one of the phone booths. She'd left her address book at home. But the booth had a phone book, and she found the listing for *Landauer* on Summit Place East.

Would the old lady even know where Chris had been yesterday afternoon? Nora had a feeling he'd borrowed Mrs. Landauer's car to get to wherever he'd gone. He was the only one who ever drove it. He had a set of keys with the understanding that he could take Mrs. Landauer's Duesenberg whenever he needed it. While he'd been out, it had rained steadily for almost two hours—and yet Chris had come home relatively dry. He couldn't have walked to his destination without getting soaked. Did Mrs. Landauer even know he'd taken her car?

Nora jotted down Mrs. Landauer's number, dropped a nickel in the slot and then dialed. While the phone rang, she impatiently counted the ringtones. After four rings, Nora wondered if eight fifty in the morning was too early to call someone—especially an elderly woman.

Through the window in the phone booth door, she spotted Roger's friend, Richard, moving toward the coffee line. She hung up the receiver but remained in the booth.

Nora wondered if Richard had read about the woman strangled yesterday. Had he talked to Phil, his cop friend, about it?
With this new murder, the police could no longer blame Connie's death on Roger. But did they have any new leads or suspects?

Nora knew she couldn't ask Richard now, not in front of
Wendell and the others.

Lifting the phone receiver, Nora tucked it between her
shoulder and jaw and jotted down the number that was on the
little round plate. Then she hung up the receiver again, stepped
out of the booth, and noted that it was the fourth booth from
the right. She hurried over to the coffee line and found Richard,
waiting behind two people.

The last time she'd spoken to Richard, she'd been determined to confirm her gut feeling about Roger's innocence.
Now, her reason was much more personal and dire: she needed
to prove to herself that her son had nothing to do with these
murders.

Richard rolled his eyes at her as she approached him. "Oh,
good God, I had a feeling you'd be all over me today—like
stink on a monkey. I'm sure you want to talk, and I can guess
what you want to talk about, but I've already told you—"

"I know, you don't want me asking you a lot of questions
here at work," Nora interrupted him. "But I thought of a way
around that . . ."

The cafeteria worker handed Richard a cup of coffee and he
gave her a dime. While he did that, Nora dug some change out
of her purse.

"I'm not having coffee with you," he said, turning away
from the counter. "Wendell would blow a gasket if he saw me
talking to you. And he's right over there . . ." Richard nodded
in the direction of their usual four-top table. He started to walk
that way.

"Yes, I know, I understand," Nora said. "I just have a few
questions—and a request." She glanced over toward Roger's

friends' table. Wendell seemed to be holding court with the two others who always ignored her. They hadn't yet noticed her and Richard.

She gave Richard a nickel—and the piece of paper with the booth's phone number on it. "That's the number you can use to call me. I'll be waiting for you in that booth—if someone else doesn't grab it before me."

"Oh, good God," he muttered again. "This is the craziest thing. You want me to do this now? This very minute? My coffee's going to get cold."

"Please, it's important," Nora whispered. "I can't tell you how important it is to me . . ."

He let out a dramatic sigh and then shoved the change and the phone number in his pants pocket. "All right, all right. Give me five minutes, and I'll get you on the Ameche. Now, take a powder before they see me talking to you."

"Thank you," Nora said.

Heading back to the phone booths, she spotted another woman zeroing in on the fourth booth from the right. In a burst of speed, Nora ran ahead of her, nearly knocking her down. "Excuse me! Sorry!" she cried, ducking into the booth and shutting the door. Nora picked up the receiver, but held the cradle down so that the line remained open. She caught her breath while pretending to chat away on the phone—to no one.

She didn't know how long she waited for Richard to call, but she glanced at her wristwatch and realized she didn't have much break time left.

At eight fifty-five, the phone finally rang, and she quickly took her fingers off the receiver cradle. "Hello?"

"Hello, Nancy Drew," Richard said. "I hope you appreciate that I had to guzzle my coffee and lie to the fellas about having to call my mother. So . . . what do you want to know? Make it snappy. My break's almost over."

"Mine too," Nora said. "Thanks for calling. I'm wondering what you might know about this new murder—if it's like the others. The newspapers didn't say. The *Times* didn't even mention the other murders. Have you talked to your friend Phil?"

"We talked briefly last night," Richard said. "And yeah, from what he told me, it was the same setup—with all the flourishes: the apron, the lipstick smile and the girl's pants hanging by the front door. Only this girl wasn't strangled and stabbed like Connie. She was just strangled—with a nylon stocking."

"Do the police have any leads?" Nora asked anxiously.

"The cops aren't changing their stance about Roger. They don't want to admit they made a mistake and shot an innocent man. A bunch of them were at the Double Header and the Casino last night, harassing the customers with questions. Their theory about this new murder is that some homosexual copycat pulled it off. Either that or the killer was one of Roger's lovers, and they had a Leopold and Loeb thing going on."

"What does that mean?" Nora asked.

"You know, the two college students in Chicago who were boyfriends? They kidnapped and murdered a kid for kicks . . ."

"Yes, I remember the case. I was living in Chicago at the time. But what does that have to do with Roger?"

"They're saying Roger could have had a partner, a lover who's carrying on some killing spree they'd both planned out."

"That's crazy . . ."

"I'll say," Richard agreed. "The cops are really making our lives miserable. I heard just now from one of the fellas that some detective might even be questioning us here at work. We're all trying to keep a low profile, so you really need to leave us alone."

"I will," she said. "But if I gave you my phone number, do you think Phil could call me at home tonight? I have some questions only he could answer."

The break bell sounded. Through the phone booth's window, Nora watched everyone starting toward the cafeteria exit.

"That's the bell," Richard said. "I need to shake a leg. Okay, give me your number, but I can't guarantee Phil will call you tonight . . ."

By lunchtime, it occurred to Nora that she hadn't eaten anything since dinner last night. She hadn't even had a sip of coffee today. But she bypassed the cafeteria lines and went directly into a phone booth. She put in her nickel and dialed Mrs. Landauer's number again.

It rang three times before a woman with a thick accent picked up. "Hullo? Lindahower redescent."

It took Nora a moment to realize she'd meant to say, "Landauer residence." Mrs. Landauer had a live-in housekeeper, a middle-aged Swedish woman who had taken the place of the Japanese-American nurse-housekeeper, Sono Nakai.

"Hello, this is Nora Kinney," she said carefully. "I'm Chris's mother. May I please speak to Mrs. Landauer?"

"Oh, Chris's *mor*, yeah!" She seemed delighted at the mention of his name. "Yeah, you wait . . ."

Biting her lip, Nora listened. It sounded like the housekeeper said, "Chris's *mor*" again—loudly. After a few more moments, Nora heard the receiver being picked up, and then a slightly frail voice on the other end: "Hello, Mrs. Kinney?" The old woman had a German accent, but her English was precise and comprehensible.

Nora had had the last two hours to decide exactly what to say to Mrs. Landauer. She didn't want to come out and ask if Chris had driven her to Rhodes department store yesterday. The old woman had such a high opinion of Chris, and if he'd lied about where he'd been, Nora didn't want her to know.

"Hello, Mrs. Landauer," she said. "I'm sorry to bother you. I just wanted to double-check that it was all right with you that Chris took your car yesterday afternoon."

There was a pause on the other end.

"Mrs. Landauer?"

"Of course, absolutely," the old woman finally answered.

"Did Chris tell you why he needed to use your car yesterday?" she asked.

Another pause. Nora waited, hoping to hear her say, "Well, yes, in fact, he took me shopping downtown. I bought birdseed for my parakeet."

But Landauer finally answered, "No, but Chris knows he's welcome to take the Duesenberg whenever he needs to use it. I've told him so. He's a good driver . . ."

*He lied*, Nora thought, devastated.

Either that, or the old woman was senile. But no, Mrs. Landauer still seemed pretty sharp. Nora didn't have to wonder what Chris was covering up. He had a different lie for his whereabouts when each of those women had been strangled.

"I trust him," the elderly woman went on. "Chris is a very responsible young man."

"Yes, he's responsible," Nora repeated, the words sticking in her throat. She just wanted to cry. Her eyes teared up.

"Are you all right, Mrs. Kinney?"

She cleared her throat. "Yes, I'm fine, thank you. I'll let you go now. Thank you for letting Chris use your car, and thanks for your time."

"You're very welcome, Mrs. Kinney. Have a nice day."

"You too, Mrs. Landauer," she said in a shaky voice. "Goodbye."

After she hung up, Nora lingered inside the booth for another few moments so she could wipe her eyes and blow her nose.

She had no idea what she was going to do about Chris.

She'd just have to wait for Phil to call her tonight. She needed some inside information about the cases that only a cop could provide. Was it too much to hope that, sometime before dinner, Phil would call her and say they'd nabbed someone for all three murders—and gotten a signed confession? Then she could have a good laugh at herself for even thinking that Chris could have ever hurt anyone.

But there was no denying he'd lied to her about yesterday.

As Nora stepped out of the booth, her head started throbbing. She probably needed some coffee and solid food in her stomach.

She waited in line and bought a cup of coffee and a turkey and Swiss sandwich. Her mind was a blur as she took her lunch tray to her usual spot.

"There you are!" Fran declared, setting down her fork and leaning back in her chair. "I'd just about given up on you. Honey, you look a little peaked. Are you okay?"

Nora sat down across from her. "I'm just tired." She sipped her coffee.

Fran shook some ravioli out of her thermos into the cup. It was another one of her inspired thermos lunches. She stabbed a piece of the pasta with her fork but paused to look at Nora. "Would you like some, hon?"

Nora worked up a smile and shook her head. "No, thanks, Fran."

Ordinarily, Fran's homemade lunch would have smelled delicious to Nora. But not now. Her headache was making her nauseous. At this point, she didn't think she could even eat her sandwich.

"I figured you wouldn't want anything to do with me today," Fran said, dabbing her mouth with a napkin. "I'm sure you know about that poor girl who was strangled. I read about it in the newspaper this morning and said to myself, 'Well, Nora told you this was going to happen.' I was so sure of myself, so quick to believe that Roger killed Connie. Now I feel horrible—about this girl, about Roger, about not listening to you. I'm sorry, Nora. I deserve a kick in the pants and a great big *I Told You So.*"

Nora took another sip of coffee. "It's okay." She rubbed her forehead. "I knew this was going to happen. I just keep thinking I could have done something to prevent it."

"Like what?" Fran asked. "Didn't the police already know everything you knew? Who would have listened to you, hon? I didn't even listen to you, and I'm your friend—at least, I hope I still am."

"Of course, you are," Nora murmured. She took a bite of her sandwich.

"Well, at least the police can't keep blaming Roger for Connie," Fran said.

"I have it from a reliable source that they're sticking to their theory that Roger is guilty."

"Your source being one of Roger's engineer friends?"

She nodded. "But I can't talk about it."

"Well, even though this new victim worked at the shipyard, everyone's talking about these murders. That's all I heard about during my break."

"The newspaper story this morning didn't connect them," Nora said.

"Yeah, but it's as plain as one, two, three," Fran said. "That's three Seattle women war workers, all strangled within the last month. He's like Jack the Ripper. It's obvious this guy has a grudge against Rosie the Riveters."

Nora managed another bite of her sandwich. "I still don't understand why the newspapers are almost intentionally ignoring a connection."

Fran shrugged. "Maybe it's like you were telling me at Connie's wake. They don't want to contradict what the police are saying. Or maybe it's bad publicity for war production, so they're not going to write about it."

"I don't understand," Nora said.

"It's like the accidents in these plants—with all these new, inexperienced workers. They don't talk about the everyday casualties in the newspapers. But I hear, since the war started, about *ten thousand* people have died in accidents in war plants, nationwide. I'm serious. But the newspapers don't write about that stuff because it would discourage girls from signing up for war jobs."

Nora squinted at her. "Where did you hear this?"

"I have my own sources around here, too, you know." She sipped her coffee. "Anyway, maybe they're not mentioning the other murders because it might put the kibosh on recruiting more women war workers. But like I say, people are figuring it out—and some of the girls are really terrified. George, one of the busboys, he was just telling me a few minutes ago that there's a slight shortage of forks and knives today. Believe it or not, the girls are stealing them and hiding them in their purses for protection during the trip home this afternoon." Fran sighed. "It won't even be dark out. But this last girl was killed in the middle of the day, so no one wants to take any chances. This guy seems to go after the young, pretty ones, doesn't he? So I guess I'm safe. But you need to be careful, Nora. Maybe you should steal a knife or fork . . ."

Staring blankly at her lunch tray, Nora had stopped eating. It seemed unfathomable that her son could be the one behind the murders.

"Nora?"

She looked up.

"I was saying you should take a knife or a fork for the walk home later—just for insurance. You can always return it tomorrow."

"I think I'll be okay," she said. "It's only a few blocks home from my bus stop."

Fran ate a ravioli. "Well," she said, her mouth half-full. "Be sure to lock your doors tonight. Hopefully, this will all be over soon. You know, it's only a matter of time before this killer trips up and the police catch him. They always do . . ."

Nora took another bite of her sandwich, but she had to force herself to swallow it. A disturbing thought hit her as she listened to her friend. And she hated herself for it.

Suddenly she was glad Chris had burned Connie's scarf yesterday.

# Chapter 25

Lugging a grocery bag from the Safeway, Nora turned into the driveway. She still had on her blue bandana from work. She could hear someone talking and water running from somewhere near the back of the house. As she moved farther down the driveway, she spotted Joe and Chris washing Joe's LaSalle in the parking bay by the garage.

Chris worked the hose while Joe, with a rag, squatted down to clean a rear tire. They both wore T-shirts, and their trousers were splashed with water. The two of them were chatting and hadn't noticed her yet.

Obviously, they'd finally met, and seemed to be getting along fine. In fact, working alongside each other, they could have been father and son. For some reason, seeing them together made Nora uncomfortable.

Maybe she was simply afraid that Joe, practically living with them now, would find out what she'd discovered about Chris.

She remembered what Fran had said about the police catching up with the strangler eventually. Nora's maternal instincts had her wanting to protect her son—even from himself. The notion of Chris murdering anyone seemed impossible. Preposterous. But she couldn't deny the circumstantial evidence, or the fact that Chris had repeatedly lied to her.

She wanted to confront him over his latest falsehood. But she knew he'd only deny it and make up another tale about where he'd been yesterday afternoon. Or he'd act all hurt again. She didn't want a repeat of yesterday. She would wait until she spoke with Phil before she took any action. She hoped he'd call before dinner, so maybe she could eat. Her stomach was still on edge.

"Hey, Mom!" Chris called. He wasn't smiling.

Neither was Joe, who looked her way and straightened up. He wrung out the wet rag.

They'd both seemed happy just a few moments ago—until they'd noticed her.

Chris dropped the hose, then moved over to the spigot on the side of the house. The pipes squeaked as he shut off the water.

*Something happened*, Nora thought.

Chris sheepishly approached her and took the grocery bag out of her hands. "A package from the Navy Department arrived for you," he said solemnly. "Joe signed for it. He gave it to me. I think it's Uncle Ray's stuff. I left the box by the table in the front hallway for you."

Nora was relieved the bad news had nothing to do with Pete. She nodded. "Thank you, honey."

"Do you want me with you when you open it up, Mom?" he asked. "Or would you rather be alone?"

Her eyes wrestled with his. *Please, don't try to be nice to me right now*, she thought. After all his lies—and quite possibly much, much worse—she couldn't stand it if he was sweet to her.

Chris seemed to sense her hesitation. "It's kind of heavy," he said. "I can carry it up to your room if you want to be alone."

She worked up a smile and nodded. "That would be nice. Thank you, Chris."

He started toward the back door with the groceries, and Nora followed him. She glanced over at Joe and nodded cordially.

With a somber look, he nodded back.

Nora ducked inside the back door.

She unloaded the groceries. Then Chris hauled the box up to her bedroom for her. After setting it on the bed, he went down the hall to his room and returned with his Swiss Army knife to cut open the top of the box. Then he left her alone.

Nora took a deep breath and opened the box. A folded U.S. flag rested on top of everything else. Below it, she found a sailor hat and several envelopes, each containing a few items—some of them carefully wrapped in cellophane. One was Ray's dog tag, slightly singed and warped from the fire. She also found Ray's little pinball baseball game. For a few moments, Nora tried to maneuver a silver ball into one of the diamond bases. But a wave of sadness overwhelmed her, and she put the game down.

She went through more envelopes. She wasn't sure what she'd do with Ray's sunglasses, a pair of cufflinks, or the wristwatch that had been her father's. Chris would probably love to have them, and Nora knew Ray would have approved of that. But she wasn't sure she wanted to give anything of Ray's to the kids, not when she thought about how he'd killed himself in a botched attempt to avoid active duty. The destruction he'd caused was enormous—and costly. Obviously, Ray hadn't intended to commit sabotage. But that was what had happened because of his cowardice.

Then Nora found his wallet with photos of Chris, Jane and

her — along with some ticket stubs, his Illinois State driver's license, and his social security card.

There was one more envelope, and below it, the rest of the box consisted of neatly folded clothes and two pair of shoes. Nora recognized a few of the shirts Ray had worn on his recent visit.

The last envelope was full of photos, some of which Nora hadn't seen for ages or had never seen: pictures of her parents; photos of her, Pete and the children; and of her and Ray when they were growing up. In one slightly blurry shot, they were standing in their grandparents' backyard. It was summer. Nora was a fresh-faced sixteen-year-old, just emerging from her adolescent gawkiness, her hair down past her shoulders. She remembered the blue shorts and matching striped short-sleeve blouse. Ray was seven; standing beside her, he came up just above her waistline. He was hugging her, with his little arms around her thigh and his head resting on her hip.

Nora began to cry. She kept thinking of how he'd died. Maybe if she'd raised him differently or hadn't left him when she had, Ray wouldn't have come to such a shameful end. She was still dreading the call or telegram from someone in the Navy Department, informing her that they'd concluded their investigation and that her brother was to blame for the explosion at the base's munitions site.

Wiping her eyes, Nora put the photos back in the envelope and set it aside on her bed. She stuffed everything else back in the envelopes and then back in the box. She slid the box into the corner of the bedroom. She would sort through it later and decide what to do with everything. She didn't want to think about it now.

She was too worried about the other boy she'd raised — and the impending call or visit from the police regarding what he'd done.

* * *

For dinner, Nora stretched out another meal by chopping up some leftover ham, tossing it in with leftover macaroni and cheese and a beaten egg, and then baking the concoction in a casserole dish. The kids loved it, but Nora didn't eat much— not with her stomach still in knots. And going through Ray's things this afternoon had made her feel even more emotionally fragile. Before dinner, she'd let the kids see Ray's little collection of family photos. Jane had been itching to see what else was in the box the navy had sent—almost as if it were a Christmas package or something.

"I'm still going through that stuff, honey," Nora had explained. "I'll let you and Chris see what's in there soon enough. I don't think there's anything that will interest you."

Through dinner, Nora didn't say much, and neither did Chris. He seemed to sense her mood. He didn't mention yesterday's strangulation. He must have figured she still believed his lie about chauffeuring around Mrs. Landauer all afternoon, and the less said about the latest murder, the better.

Jane, however, wouldn't stop talking about it. The young woman was killed just eleven blocks away—*walking distance*. And the killer was still out there on the loose. Jane was genuinely scared. Her bedroom was practically at the top of the stairs. If someone snuck into the house, he'd probably kill her first. She'd already seen how easy it had been to break the window in the front door. Once he broke a window, then all the killer had to do was reach through the opening and unlock the door and he'd be inside.

"I'm sleeping with a whistle under my pillow tonight," Jane announced, "that metal one that's so loud . . ."

"I'm sure the police have increased their patrols of the neighborhood," Nora tried to assure her. "We've got the block's air raid warden, Mr. Weiss, doing his rounds. Plus, there's Joe right next door, and your brother's here, too. We'll be fine, honey. If you get really scared, you can always crawl into bed with me tonight."

Jane was also keyed up about an overnight field trip her class was taking to Orcas Island on Wednesday: a whale-watching excursion. Once reassured that she'd probably survive the evening, Jane wondered aloud what she should pack for the impending two-day trip. She started to name every piece of clothing she intended to bring. "And, of course, I'll need a sweater, but my dark blue cardigan is so boring," she'd prattled on. "Can you wash my light blue, Mom? It would be so much prettier, and—"

"God, would you shut your trap for just two minutes?" Chris had interrupted. "Hedy Lamarr on a cross-country USO tour wouldn't give her wardrobe as much thought as you're giving your clothes for this stupid, two-day whale-watching thing. And, y'know, Mom's not your personal slave . . ."

This led to an argument—and some tears on Jane's part. But the kids quickly made up. After dinner, Jane pulled her usual disappearing act to avoid KP duty. ("Our daughter has chronic dishpan diarrhea," Pete had once observed.) But Chris stuck around and offered to wash the dishes for Nora.

"Thanks, honey, but I've got it covered," she answered, not quite looking at him as she tied an apron around her waist. "But I'll tell you what you could do. Could you listen for the phone for me—and see that Jane doesn't tie up the line? I'm expecting a call about work."

He was being way too kind and considerate toward her tonight—almost as if he was sorry for something.

*Stop it*, she told herself. *You still don't know for sure.*

While Nora started on the dishes, the kids settled in the family room to listen to the radio and do their homework.

Nora heard the phone ring—and Chris answering it. Turning off the water, she quickly dried her hands and hurried to the front hallway.

Chris held the receiver out for her, his hand over the mouth-piece. "It's a Mr. Phillips," he said. "Do you want me to turn down the radio?"

"That's okay, honey," she whispered, grabbing the phone and receiver. "I'll take it into the broom closet."

Bringing the phone across the hall, Nora set it down on the floor of the large broom closet. Then she pulled the string for the overhead light and carefully closed the door over the phone cord. Ages ago, Jane had dragged their metal step stool out of the kitchen and put it in the closet for one of her marathon tele-phone chats, and the step stool had remained there ever since. Nora sat down on the stool amid the cleaning things, coats, umbrellas and galoshes. "Hello, this is Nora," she said into the phone.

"This is Phil," Roger's friend on the police force an-nounced. "Richard gave me your number. He said you wanted me to call you."

"Yes, thank you so much." She hesitated. "*Mr. Phillips*? Is your name really Phillip Phillips?"

"No, I just figured you'd catch on it was me," he explained. "I'd like to remain semi-anonymous, if that's possible. Speak-ing of which, Richard told me about your phone booth shenanigans in the cafeteria today, shades of Mata Hari. So . . . you have some questions for me about this latest murder? Richard's hoping once I answer them for you, you'll leave us alone. I'm kind of hoping the same thing."

"I'm sorry to be a pest," Nora whispered. "But I have a the-ory about the murders. It might help with your investigation. Richard told me what the police are doing. Do they really be-lieve the killer in yesterday's strangling is a friend of Roger's?"

"A friend or lover, yeah."

"And there are no other suspects or leads?" she pressed.

"None. They think it's quite possible that two guys were in on Connie's murder, both woman-hating homosexuals. One got away unnoticed, and the other got killed."

"But you told me last week that the police talked to Roger's landlady," Nora said. "And if she's right about the time he was talking on the phone in her lobby, then he couldn't have killed Connie. The police know that. How could they keep perpetrating this lie that Roger's guilty?"

"Well, if Roger had a partner doing the killings with him, then that explains it. This new theory works with the story they've already put out there. It's typical. Once you lie, you have to keep building on it with more lies. And then you start to believe it's true. Anyway, that's what my fellow officers seem to be doing."

Phil paused, and Nora could hear the radio in the family room.

"They have a psychiatrist on the case," he continued. "The doctor says these killers—or I guess it's just one killer now—the psychiatrist says the strangler's going after women war workers because he doesn't like to see them taking on men's jobs or being in positions of power. That's why he's taking the victims' work slacks and putting them on display. Then he dresses the victims in aprons and puts lipstick on their mouths. The last two corpses were dragged into the kitchen—where, apparently, women belong."

Nora immediately thought of Larry—and so many men like him at the plant. They made life hell for the women working there.

Nora also remembered something Ray had said about Chris possibly resenting her for taking on the riveter job. And the first murder had been the night before her first day of work. Was that just a coincidence?

"This is all inside stuff," Phil said. "Off the record, you understand."

"Of course," Nora said, anxiously tugging at the receiver cord. "Do the police know if the nylon stockings used in the killings belonged to the victims?"

"You're quite the detective, aren't you?" Phil remarked,

sounding genuinely impressed. "They went through Connie's dresser—and Gloria Dunbar's, too. It looked like the killer didn't break up a pair. Gloria didn't have any nylons, and Connie had one pair. The shade and brand didn't match what was around her throat. They figured out this morning that the stockings used to strangle Connie and Gloria were the same brand and type. The color is beige, and the brand is called Purple Something . . ."

"Royal Purple?" Nora heard herself ask.

"Yeah, that's it. How did you know?"

Nora's stomach felt as tight as a fist. The stockings she regularly wore were beige Royal Purple brand from Sears, Roebuck and Company. She swallowed hard. "It's a pretty common brand," she said, her voice quivering a bit. "Do you know if there's any way they might trace those stockings to the person who bought them?"

"If the case goes to the FBI, yeah," he answered. "Especially if the purchaser charged the stockings to a Sears account or paid with a check. But if they paid in cash, I doubt it."

Nora was almost certain she'd paid in cash.

"Homicide figured out that the lipstick used on both victims didn't belong to them either," Phil continued. "The shade didn't match anything they had in their purses or on their dresser tops."

Nora hadn't thought about the lipstick. And Phil's bringing it up was like a sudden punch to the gut. Was it too much to hope that the killer hadn't used her brand and shade? She wore Scarlet Kiss from Dorothy Gray. She had a tube in her purse and another in her dresser drawer. The one in her dresser was unused. She'd purchased it—with cash—a couple of weeks ago. She hadn't been keeping track of it. She'd have to check whether the lipstick tube was still in the drawer.

"Have they figured out the particular color or brand of the lipstick?" she asked warily.

"Yeah, they narrowed it down to two different shades, Blushing Something and Scarlet Something."

Nora said nothing.

"So . . . you said you have a theory," Phil continued. "Does this information help you any? Do you suddenly have a big breakthrough you'd like to share—anything that might help Roger's case?"

"No, I . . . I was mistaken," Nora murmured. "I thought I had something that would be useful to you, but I was wrong."

"Well, please, keep all this under your hat, Nora," he said. "As far as I'm concerned, we've never had this conversation. And please, don't bug Richard or any of the other guys at the plant about this. They have enough to contend with right now—thanks to my comrades on the force."

"Yes, I understand," Nora replied. "Thank you for calling . . ."

After she hung up, Nora turned off the closet light and then returned the phone to the stand in the hallway. She climbed the stairs and headed into her bedroom, where she opened the top drawer of her dresser. She already figured the lipstick wouldn't be there, but that didn't stop her from rifling through the drawer for it.

Her search was in vain.

Nora reminded herself that, according to Phil, they probably couldn't track down whoever had purchased the stockings and lipstick used in the last two killings, not if the items had been paid for in cash.

At this point, there was no way they could suspect Chris at all.

She still didn't want to think it was true—even though everything she'd just learned from Roger's cop friend seemed to confirm her worst fears.

Nora stepped into the bathroom and splashed water on her face. In the mirror over the sink, the woman staring back at her looked haggard and lost. After drying her face with a towel,

Nora returned to her bedroom and straightened up her dresser drawer.

Starting down the hallway, Nora paused outside Chris's bedroom and stared at the closed door. She wondered if her lipstick and the remaining nylons were hidden somewhere in his room. But she'd already searched through his closet and desk. Maybe he was just too clever for her—and for the police.

*You still really don't believe it's possible*, Nora thought.

What mother would?

Almost in a trance, Nora headed down the stairs to finish washing the dinner dishes. She passed by the family room. She heard Chris and Jane laughing at *Fibber McGee and Molly* on the radio.

Her heart ached. It seemed like nothing would ever be normal again.

In the kitchen, she went to the sink and turned on the water. But she just stood there, staring down at the dirty dishes. She felt another teary breakdown coming. Nora turned off the water, untied her apron, draped it over a kitchen chair and quietly ducked out the back door. She didn't want the kids to hear her crying.

The chilly night air was bracing. She stood on the back stoop, rubbed her arms and gazed up at the stars.

"Hi, Nora. How are you doing?"

She heard gravel crunching underfoot and saw Joe emerge from the shadows by the garage. He wore a jacket over a casual, open-collar shirt. "I'm sorry," he said, coming closer. "Did I scare you?"

She had a hand over her heart. "No, I just didn't see you there."

He turned his head slightly. "Pardon, what did you say?"

"Nothing," she said—a bit louder. "I didn't see you there. That's all. How are you?"

He leaned against the wrought iron banister for the steps up to the kitchen door. "I came out for some air," he said.

"Me too," she replied.

"To be honest, I'm feeling kind of blue," he admitted. "You probably came out here to be alone. Maybe I should scram . . ."

"No, please, don't go," Nora said. She went back to massaging her arms to keep warm. "You're right, I came out here to be alone. But I . . . I really don't want you to leave."

Unzipping his jacket, Joe took it off and then came up the few steps and placed the jacket around her shoulders. It was lightweight but warm from his body. She could smell his subtle, spicy aftershave on it. "Thank you," Nora said, pulling the jacket tighter around her.

Joe moved down a step so that their eyes were level. He leaned against the side of the house. "I've been thinking about you all day," he said.

"Really?" she murmured shyly. "You have?"

"Yeah, ever since I signed for that package this morning," he said. "I know what it's like. I went through the same thing after my brother died. It's pretty devastating. You hear your brother's been killed, and it's awful. It doesn't make any sense, doesn't seem real. But then they send you his stuff, and suddenly it's all very real and undeniable."

"I'm still waiting for them to ship me Ray's remains," she said, glancing down at her feet. "Sounds gruesome, but apparently, he's awfully burned up." She thought of his singed dog tag and tried to put the image out of her mind. She looked at Joe again. "Did they ship your brother's body back home?"

He shook his head. "No, the Pacific got him. What was he like, your brother?"

A melancholy smile passed over her face. "Charming, irresponsible, sweet . . ." She shrugged. "You probably heard enough about Ray from Jane. What about your brother? What was he like?"

"Oh, you don't want to hear about it," he muttered.

"But I do," Nora said. She meant it, too. She wanted to stop thinking about Ray and Chris for a few minutes. "I don't even know his name."

"Andy," Joe said.

"I can't remember if you said he was older or younger."

"Younger."

Nora nodded. "That's right, you mentioned that you took care of him. You and I have that in common. How many years younger was he?"

"Just four years," Joe answered. "But the thing with Andy was—he was a little slow, mentally—not so much that we needed to send him to a special school or anything. But in hindsight, I think it might have made life easier for him if we had. Still, he could read and write, and he was a great athlete. It's just that he had a hard time keeping up with his classmates. They teased him at school all the time, but he was too sweet to lash out at anyone. I got in so many fights with guys in school over the way they treated him. Some of the girls were just as mean . . ."

As Joe talked about his brother, Nora couldn't help thinking of Lenny in *Of Mice and Men*. And she couldn't help feeling even more drawn to Joe for being a protective big brother. She noticed his eyes tear up a little, but he was smiling.

"Andy was a good kid," Joe went on, "a hard worker, very responsible. The only times he ever got into trouble were when someone took advantage of his good-natured, trusting innocence. He was also really good-looking, so he attracted people, and some of them weren't especially nice. I ran interference for him the best I could." He sighed. "I was my brother's keeper, and it sometimes felt like a full-time job. I guess you know what that's like."

Nora nodded.

"Anyway, after Pearl Harbor, Andy joined the navy without telling me. I did my best to get him out of it. But he'd passed all his tests, and they wouldn't release him. And he was so happy the navy had taken him. Andy always loved the water. He told me more than once he wanted to be buried at sea. He had this weird romantic notion about it. Anyway, I couldn't join up and serve alongside him, because of my ear. So, Andy was on his own for the first time in our lives. While he was stateside, I tried to keep tabs on him and make sure he didn't fall prey to any Allotment Annies or other unscrupulous types."

"Were you and Veronica married by then?" Nora asked.

Joe nodded. "Yeah, I hate to admit it, but I know it was easier on her with Andy away. Anyway, he shipped out last year, and we were writing pretty regularly until Guadalcanal." He worked up a smile. "Anyway, that was Andy. It was sweet of you to ask about him, Nora."

"I'm glad you told me, really," she assured him.

"Well, it was a few weeks ago when I found out about him. I can only imagine what you're going through now. I'm not sure how I'd handle the one-two punch you had recently. First your friend, and then your brother. Or was it the other way around?"

Nora stopped to put together the timeline. "Let's see," she thought out loud. "They were both here for dinner on Sunday the eleventh. On Wednesday afternoon, Ray took a bus back to San Diego. And I was pretty blue about that. Then the next night, Connie was murdered. But I didn't find out about it until Saturday. Ray was killed on Thursday. I got word about it that night." She sighed. "That was eleven days ago . . ."

"I'm so sorry," he said quietly. He started to reach out to touch her arm, but then he seemed to change his mind and pulled his hand back.

Nothing about the abandoned gesture was lost on Nora. She wanted so much to bury herself in his arms.

Instead, she cleared her throat and brought up his wife again. "You know, my offer still stands. Any time you'd like to phone Veronica, you're welcome to come in and use our phone. You must be wondering how she is."

"She's fine," he said. "I grabbed a fistful of change, went up to the drugstore and called her this afternoon. She'll be with her mom for at least another week."

"I'm sorry to hear that," Nora lied.

Maybe she was reading too much into it, but Joe seemed to speak of his wife with nowhere near the same degree of love and devotion he'd had talking about his brother.

"I didn't tell her that we had a murder in the neighborhood yesterday," he said. "I didn't want her to worry or change her mind about the apartment. I wouldn't bring it up now, only I'm sure it's quite disturbing for you—especially after you lost your work friend in a similar way. But if it makes you feel any better, I'm a night owl. I stay up until two or three in the morning sometimes. And my hearing isn't all that bad. So it's almost like you have a nightwatchman living next door."

"It's comforting to know that," Nora said. "I was just reminding Jane tonight about that."

"Listen, speaking of Jane," Joe said. "Please, feel free to say no. But I'm wondering if I could borrow a photograph that I saw in your family album. Jane showed it to me. It was a picture of her and your brother—at a picnic, I think. She said it was about three years ago during one of his visits. She looked so cute in the photo, and I thought I'd use her face for a peanut butter ad I'm painting. It's a national campaign. I'd take it to a photographer and have a copy made for me. Anyway, don't answer right away. Sleep on it."

Nora laughed. "Well, that would certainly please Jane. In fact, it would make her impossible to live with. She's a big fan of yours. We have a *Life* magazine with your Baby Ruth ad in it, and Jane brought it to school this morning to show her friends and brag that we have a celebrity living above our garage."

Joe chuckled. "Well, thank you. That makes me feel like a big shot."

"Do you want the photograph now?" Nora asked.

"It can wait. I should leave you alone. I've imposed on you enough."

Nora shook her head. "You haven't imposed on me at all, Joe. Just the opposite. When I first stepped out here, I was feeling lonely and very sorry for myself. But you helped turn that around for me."

Joe gazed into her eyes and then opened his mouth as if he were about to say something. But he hesitated.

In that moment, Nora got scared. She took off Joe's jacket and handed it to him. "I should get back inside," she said. "I need to finish up a letter to my husband. I try and write a little something every night."

"Thanks for the talk, Nora," he said.

She opened the kitchen door. "Good night, Joe," she replied.

Then, with reluctance, she turned away from him and stepped inside.

# Chapter 26

*Tuesday, May 4*
*5:07 p.m.*

Nora was in the basement, washing Jane's baby-blue cardigan.

She'd last seen Jane, up in her bedroom, packing for her class trip to Orcas Island tomorrow. Nora was looking forward to a brief break from her daughter's incessant talk about the murders. Not that she blamed Jane for fixating on the strangulations. It was scary for a young and vulnerable girl—especially with the most recent slaying happening right in her neighborhood, and the victim in the previous murder having been her mother's friend and a dinner guest in this very house. Small wonder she was slightly traumatized.

An overnight field trip was probably the best thing for Jane right now. She'd gone to bed last night with her father's hammer under her pillow. And she'd given Nora her whistle. "I think you should have this in your purse for the walk to the bus stop tomorrow," Jane had told her. "It's still awfully dark when you leave in the morning, Mom. If somebody tries to attack you, the whistle's loud as all get out, and it'll scare them away. Practically everyone within a block will hear it . . ."

Nora had been touched that her typically self-centered teenage daughter was actually concerned about her. And it wasn't just Jane. Chris had left his Swiss Army knife and a note on the kitchen table this morning:

*Dear Mom,*

*Wake me up so I can walk you to the bus stop! If you decide not to, I'd feel better if you carried this with you tomorrow to & from work. Just to be on the safe side. Be careful with the blade. I sharpened it for you.*

As Nora had slipped the note and the knife inside her purse this morning, she asked herself: *Would a killer do this?*

Everything she felt in her gut clashed with the overwhelming circumstantial evidence. Nora knew her son, and even at his worst, she couldn't imagine him intentionally hurting anyone. Then again, she'd seen him attack Earl. But hell, that kid deserved to have his nose broken.

She was so stymied about what to do. Confronting Chris again didn't seem like an option—not unless she was absolutely sure of his guilt. In the meantime, what if another female war worker was murdered? It would be on her conscience. How soon before the police started to suspect him? Chris was seventeen years old. Maybe they'd try him as an adult and give him the electric chair. Or did they hang convicted killers in Washington State? She didn't know.

At work today, everyone seemed to be talking about the murders. A few of the women called the killer "The Rosie Ripper," which really didn't make much sense to Nora, since he was strangling his victims, not slashing them to pieces. Besides that, one victim had been a bucker and another a welder.

Nora wasn't the only one concealing weapons in her purse. Fran had said that other women were arming themselves with sharp-tipped nail files, knitting needles and scissors. Some of them were pairing up for the trip home this afternoon. Even though the strangler had obviously planned to kill two women in his last attack, the women at the plant seemed to feel there was still safety in numbers. "One good thing to come out of this," Fran had told her at lunch. "Marty stayed home last night for a change. He's worried about me . . ."

Earlier, during her break, Nora had spotted Richard, Wendell and the others at their usual table. They hadn't seemed to notice her, and she'd kept her distance. She wondered if the police had come to the plant and spoken to each of them individually—as Richard had said they would. Had any of them told the police about her keen interest in the case? Would Phil end up informing his fellow police officers about her incessant questions? Phil and Richard had asked her not to repeat anything they'd told her. But she hadn't asked them for the same kind of discretion. For all Nora knew, she may have already inadvertently alerted the police about her connection to the killings. By now, the cops might even have Chris's name and description on file. After all, they'd questioned him about the break-in at the Boeing worker's apartment near his school.

The very thought of it made Nora's stomach lurch.

"Hey, Mom!" Chris yelled from the top of the basement stairs.

"Yes?" she called back, hovering over the sink.

"I'm going to the store now!" he shouted. "Is it okay if I pick up a carton of Coke, too? We're running low, and it's not on your list. It's only two bits!"

"That's fine! Don't forget the ration book!"

"Got it! See you in about an hour!"

She heard the floorboards creaking above, and then the back door slammed.

When Nora had returned from work, she hadn't been able to relax until Chris had come home. She had to know where he was at all times now. At three thirty, she'd finally heard him outside talking to Joe. When he'd stepped inside, she'd thanked him for the Swiss Army knife and asked him to make the store run sometime before dinner.

A few minutes later, while upstairs, Nora had spotted Chris and Joe from the hallway window. They'd been in the back-yard, tossing around the football—obviously not Chris's idea—but they'd seemed to be getting along well.

"That's a great spin you've got on the ball," she'd overheard Joe call to him. "I don't know why you said you stink at this. You're good . . ."

Nora had retreated to her bedroom for a nap. Curling up on the bed, she'd fallen asleep thinking what a far cry Joe's encouragement was from Earl's constant goading and criticism. If she'd been uncomfortable seeing Joe and Chris so chummy yesterday afternoon, her feelings had changed. More than any-thing, right now, her son needed a friend, someone who made him feel normal.

Nora had slept for ninety minutes and then taken a shower. She'd actually felt refreshed when she'd gone down to the base-ment to handwash Jane's cardigan.

She made a mental note to lend Joe that photo he'd been ask-ing about, the one of Jane and Ray at the picnic a few years ago. She would bring it to him sometime before dinner. And she'd use the opportunity to ask him—as long as he was up late at night—to keep a lookout for Chris. She had already admitted to Joe that her son sometimes snuck out at night. She wouldn't be asking him to spy on Chris. But she'd sleep easier knowing that someone might be awake to keep tabs on him—and maybe even stop him from going out.

As she hung Jane's sweater on the line with clothespins, Nora glanced over at the trap door to the big octopus furnace. She wondered, once again, if Chris had burned Connie's scarf in an impulsive fit of anger, or if it had been something more calculated. She reminded herself that he'd destroyed his grandmother's handkerchief and Arlene's barrette as well.

In fact, he'd become especially angry and defensive when she'd shown him Arlene's barrette. Of course, Arlene's death had hit him hard. He'd been so close to the girl and had feelings for her. Nora wondered—once again—if Chris had had anything to do with her "suicide."

But Arlene's death was nothing like the recent strangulations. Or was it?

Nora had been so worried about Chris at the time that she'd paid no attention to the details. Apparently, the girl had snuck down to her father's study late at night, taken a gun out of his desk and shot herself in the head. Now Nora couldn't help wondering: When they'd found Arlene's body, how had she been dressed? Had her face been made up in any unusual way? Had any articles of clothing been found hanging on the Drummonds' front door?

Nora remembered reading about Arlene's death in *The Seattle Star*. But she hadn't been looking for clues back then.

Nora wished she could get her hands on that newspaper again.

Taking off her apron, she hurried up the basement stairs— and then up to the second floor. She poked her head into Jane's room, where she found her daughter still fussing over a half-packed small brown suitcase on her bed.

"Listen, honey," Nora said, a bit out of breath. "I need to step out and run an errand. Chris should be back in about forty-five minutes. I may be gone for a while. But I think Joe's next door. Will you be okay by yourself?"

"I guess," Jane said, holding a hanger with a blouse on it. "Did you wash my blue sweater?"

Nora nodded. "It's drying on the line right now. If I'm not back by dinnertime, and you get hungry, in the refrigerator there's some—"

"I'll make that Chef Boyardee spaghetti dinner in a box!" Jane interrupted. It was some new, low-ration-points, easy-fix dinner kit Jane had made Nora buy a week ago. Her daughter had been dying to try it. "We'll save you some . . ."

"Terrific," Nora said. "Chris is buying some Coke. Tell him I said it's okay that you each have one—only one."

Nora ran downstairs and fetched her coat and purse. As she was about to head out the door, she heard Jane call to her from upstairs: "Don't forget your whistle!"

"I've got it! Thanks, sweetie!" Nora called back.

It was a clear, lovely evening—and a twenty-five-minute walk to downtown Seattle. Some of the government and utility buildings were still surrounded by sandbags—in preparation for a possible aerial attack. Nora passed through Victory Square at Fourth and University, where rallies, bond drives and memorial services were held. The speakers' stand was shaped like Jefferson's home in Monticello. There wasn't an event going on now, but the square was crowded with people getting off work, servicemen and servicewomen, and tourists. At the other end of the square was a seventy-five-foot replica of the Washington Monument with the names of the local war dead inscribed on its sides.

Nora continued down Fourth to the central branch of the Seattle Public Library. The old, neoclassical building took up nearly the entire block, and inside, featured tiled floors, polished mahogany tables and woodwork, and big, arched windows. Nora walked up to the periodical section on the second floor. For access to newspapers before April, Nora had to fill out a request form and give it to the stocky, middle-aged librarian. The cheerful woman looked like she would have made a good bucker. She moved fast and carried around huge volumes of bound newspapers with what appeared to be no effort at all.

On her way to the library, Nora had figured out exactly when in October Arlene had died. Halloween had been on a Saturday last year, and Arlene had killed herself in the early hours of Sunday morning the previous weekend. The story had been in that Monday's *Seattle Star.*

Nora requested *Seattle Star* and *Seattle Times* editions for October 26, 1942. She figured if one newspaper missed a detail, the other might catch it.

Those editions from last year were already bound. Nora got only one book at a time, which was just as well, because *The Seattle Times* editions for the last half of October were in a huge lime-green volume that weighed about ten pounds. She lugged the book over to one of the long, mahogany reading tables and flipped through it until she found Monday, October 26th. The story was on page three, with the headline:

## HIGH SCHOOL STUDENT DIES IN APPARENT
## SUICIDE

There was a photo of Arlene, and it looked as if she was wearing the same barrette Chris had tossed into the furnace. Then again, it was a slightly blurry black-and-white photo, and the rosebuds on the hair clip could have been a different color than the one Chris had destroyed. Still, it was jarring.

The article mentioned that Arlene was dressed in her nightgown when her parents had discovered her in the middle of the night on the floor of her father's study, his gun nearby. She'd been shot once in the head. While Arlene's parents insisted it must have been an accident, the *Times* reported that "police on the scene indicated that the gunshot wound appeared to be self-inflicted." The newspaper didn't mention any sign of foul play. Nora figured that the Drummonds would have made doubly sure investigators ruled out the possibility of a homicide—anything to avoid accepting that their daughter had killed herself.

Another thing Nora considered: if Arlene had been expecting company that night—say, Chris—she would have at least put on a robe over her nightgown.

Then there was the barrette. Chris had burned it along with his grandmother's handkerchief and Connie's bandana. And just an hour later, he'd admitted that he regretted doing that. He'd been angry and upset. There had been nothing calculated about it. The barrette hadn't been *evidence* of anything—except a close friendship with a disturbed girl.

There was nothing really incriminating about Chris having Arlene's barrette. It wasn't a souvenir of a killing. Could the same be said about the pink and black polka dot bandana? Was it possible Chris had been completely honest with her about how he'd ended up with Connie's scarf—and where he'd gone the night she'd been murdered?

Then again, maybe she was grasping at straws, trying to convince herself of Chris's innocence.

Nora returned the bound *Seattle Times* to the periodicals desk and picked up the bound editions of *The Seattle Star*.

The article in the *Star* didn't offer any new insights into Arlene's suicide. There wasn't even a photo of her. But the news story seemed to confirm for Nora that Arlene's death was indeed a suicide.

She returned the second bound volume to the cheery woman at the counter and thanked her. Glancing toward the large, arched windows, Nora noticed it was growing dark outside. Her feet hurt after a day at work and the long walk downtown. As she ducked into the restroom, Nora decided she'd catch a bus home.

She was washing the newspaper grime off her hands, when, in the mirror, she noticed a handprinted sign on one of the toilet stalls in back of her. She turned to read it: OUT OF ORDER— SORRY FOR THE INCONVENIENCE.

Nora dried her hands on the towel roller and looked at the sign again. Then something dawned on her.

*How could you be so stupid? How could you forget something like that?*

Chris and Jane weren't the only ones who could have gone through her dresser and taken her nylons and the lipstick.

The powder room toilet hadn't been flushing on the night of her dinner party. At different times during the evening, each of her guests had gone upstairs to use the bathroom. Any one of them could have rummaged through her dresser drawers. The coats had been tossed on her bed, too. It would have been simple to smuggle the stockings and lipstick out of the house unnoticed.

Her mind reeling, Nora wandered out of the restroom and then down the stairs and outside. She started walking at a more determined pace as she headed to the bus stop a block from Victory Square. All the while, she considered who had had the opportunity to make off with her stockings and lipstick on the night of the party. Could the police be right about Roger? He'd been in her bedroom that night. And he was still the only suspect in Connie's murder. Maybe Phil didn't know everything his police investigator friends had uncovered about the case. Maybe, like her, he'd automatically assumed that Roger was innocent because he'd been Connie's friend. But who knew what Roger and Connie's relationship had really been like? Some friendships could be as volatile and destructive as love affairs and marriages.

Nora was so focused on suspects from her dinner party that she almost missed the bus to Broadway. With busses coming up to the stop every minute or two, she didn't notice the Number 7 until it was almost ready to pull away. Running to the door, Nora climbed aboard, paid her fare and quickly grabbed a seat.

She thought about the dinner party again and wondered about Fran's son, Marty. No doubt, the poor guy was troubled. And according to Fran, he went out practically every night—

God knew where—and sometimes didn't come back until morning. Marty might have come across as sweet and sad, but Nora didn't really know how his war wounds had affected his mental health.

But she knew her son. And Chris was not a murderer.

The bus came to an abrupt stop, distracting Nora for a few moments. An old lady left by the back door. As the bus started moving again, Nora became aware of a woman's voice, which sounded oddly familiar.

"I just adore your purse!" the seated passenger was saying to another woman, standing in the aisle. They were about two seats in front of Nora. The woman with the purse, which Nora couldn't see, nodded politely at the woman on the aisle seat.

"It's real elegant," the seated woman went on. Nora couldn't see what she looked like. "I love elegant things. Do you mind if I ask where you got it? I could use an elegant handbag . . ."

Nora not only recognized the voice. She recognized the maroon hair.

She got to her feet and leaned to one side so she might get a look at Joe's wife's face. "Veronica?" she called.

But the woman didn't turn around. Nor did she seem to hear her.

"Veronica?" Nora repeated. "Mrs. Strauss?"

The woman with the *elegant purse*—and a few other passengers—looked at her. But the maroon-haired woman didn't turn her head.

Nora thought it was strange that Joe hadn't said anything about his wife coming back to town. In fact, just last night he'd said she would be gone another week.

Nora moved up the aisle until she was beside Joe's wife. "Veronica?" she asked, leaning toward her.

The woman looked up as if baffled. She glanced at the lady seated next to her—and then back at Nora. "Are you talking to me?"

It was the same woman, Nora was sure. She narrowed her eyes at her. "Don't you know who I am? I'm your new land-lady . . ."

Once again, the woman looked at her as if she were crazy. But then a flicker of recognition rearranged her blank stare. She shifted in her seat and quickly shook her head. "I . . . I honestly have no idea what you're talking about." She looked out the window and then got to her feet. "Do you mind? I'd like to get off. This is my stop."

"You aren't married to Joe, are you?" Nora asked. "Do you even know him?"

The bus slowed to a stop. Almost knocking her aside, the woman brushed past Nora and made her way to the back door. It opened, and she hurried off the bus.

Undeterred, Nora followed her. It was still about a mile until her stop, but that didn't matter right now.

The woman was rushing down the sidewalk to get away from her.

"Miss?" Nora called. "Wait up! I just want to talk to you!"

Joe's "wife" glanced over her shoulder and hesitated.

Nora hurried to catch up to her.

The woman stopped. "Oh, what the hell," she said—almost to herself. "I don't know why I'm trying to cover for the son of a bitch, I never heard from him again." She heaved a sigh. "So . . . you've got me. What do you want?"

"Your name isn't Veronica, and you're not married to Joe Strauss," Nora said.

The woman shook her head.

"And you don't even know him," Nora continued.

"He started talking to me outside a drugstore on Broadway on Saturday," she explained. "I thought he was trying to pick me up. I looked at him and figured I could do a lot worse. He told me he'd give me twenty bucks and take me out for a steak dinner if I was a good sport and pretended to be his wife for a half hour."

"And you went along with it?"

She nodded. "Yeah, he gave me the money up front. Then we drove together to see you and the apartment. But he never called me, the rat. If you ever see him again, tell that jerk he still owes me a dinner. On second thought, tell him to go to hell." She started to walk away.

"Wait a minute . . ."

She stopped and frowned at Nora again.

"You never got his name?" Nora asked.

"Joe, like you said earlier. I didn't get a last name. Did you say it was *Strauss*?"

Nora nodded.

"Yeah, well, it's more like *Louse*."

"Did he say why he wanted you to pretend to be his wife?"

The woman rolled her eyes. "He gave me some song and dance about being a cop on an undercover assignment, but he never showed me a badge or anything. Did you end up renting that apartment to him? Because if you did, I wouldn't trust him as far as I could throw him. Hell, I can't believe I gave the so-and-so my number. You tell him for me, I wouldn't go out to dinner with him now even if he begged me. Lots of luck, honey." She swiveled around and headed down the sidewalk.

Stunned, Nora watched Joe's "wife" walk away.

# Chapter 27

Only a mile or so from her regular stop, Nora wasn't about to wait for another bus. She started for home on foot.

It was dark, and the streetlamps were on—at least until the blackout. She and Joe's fake wife had stepped off the bus at the edge of the downtown business district. From the stop on Pine Street, Nora headed north along Bellevue Avenue, past small shops and businesses, many of them with the star flag in the windows indicating a family member in the service. Most of them were closed for the night.

Nora barely noticed. She was too dazed and shaken over the revelation about Joe. She'd just started to let down her guard with him, and her children had already come to like him. Was he really a cop, working undercover? Had he moved in over the garage so that he could watch Chris?

And to think, she'd planned on asking Joe to keep an eye on Chris and make sure he didn't sneak out at night.

Maybe she'd been right with her earlier hunch. Maybe the police had been keeping tabs on Chris since he'd been questioned about the apartment break-in near his high school. And anyone could have spotted Chris following Connie around— right up until the night she'd been murdered. Perhaps the police had somehow figured out who had bought the stockings used to strangle two of the victims.

Yet Nora was almost certain she'd paid for the stockings and her lipstick in cash.

The neighborhood around her became increasingly residential. She passed apartment buildings and houses—with more star flags in the windows. But she encountered fewer and fewer people. Most everyone was already inside, settling down for the night. A gentle breeze rustled the branches and leaves of the trees, casting shadows around Nora as she walked. She was glad to have the whistle and the Swiss Army knife in her purse.

Her mind went back to Joe again. If he was a cop working undercover, then the police must have started suspecting Chris shortly after Connie's murder. Joe had come to her door the day before Gloria Dunbar had been killed.

Strange, Joe had taken up residence in their garage apartment the same day Gloria had been murdered in her garage apartment several blocks away. Joe had taken off for a couple of hours that day. In fact, Joe had been gone around the time Gloria was strangled.

Somewhere behind her, Nora heard a shuffling noise. Glancing over her shoulder, she didn't notice anyone following her. The sidewalk and street were empty of people. She spotted a car in the distance—with blue cellophane over the headlights for the blackout—but then the vehicle turned up a side street. Nora stopped and dug Jane's whistle out of her purse. Clutching it in her fist, she moved on, picking up her pace. She had only a few more blocks to go until she reached the house.

She reminded herself that all of the "Rosies" were murdered in their homes. *He's not going to get you here.*

But she was different from the others. This killer seemed to know her. He'd taken her nylons and lipstick. She still held on to the possibility that someone from the dinner party had made off with them. Or could Joe—if that was even his name—have broken in before he showed up inquiring about the apartment and stolen those items from her dresser? Their house was off the beaten path—with very little traffic. How else had he spotted the APARTMENT FOR RENT sign so soon after she'd put it up? He must have already been watching the house.

She wondered if Chris and Jane were safe with him just next door. Though if Joe wanted to hurt them, he'd had plenty of opportunities over the last three days. Besides, the "Rosie" strangler wouldn't care about anyone but her.

She didn't know what to think. Whoever "Joe" was, he'd completely bamboozled her. Nora wondered if that whole sob story about his sweet, mildly retarded brother was hogwash. Probably.

Yes, he was probably a cop. A murderer wouldn't risk hiring some stranger—a potential witness—to portray his wife in a ruse to get close to his next victim. He wouldn't have friends posing as references over the phone. But an undercover cop might do that.

Nora still desperately clung to the idea that Chris was innocent. But obviously, the police didn't think so.

Just two blocks from home, Nora realized she hadn't seen another soul—not even a moving car—for the last few blocks. The trees and hedges bordering the sidewalk created dark nooks where anyone could be hiding. Nora tightened her grip on the whistle.

As much as she wanted to get home right now, it was no longer a safe haven—not with a deceitful stranger living above

her garage. She felt like such a fool for being taken in by him—
*and* for having been attracted to him.

"All right, all right," she whispered to herself, about to turn
up her block. "What are you going to do about him?"

As Nora walked past a tall hedge, a shadow swept over her
so quickly that she didn't even have time to bring the whistle to
her mouth. She froze.

A man in a dark overcoat stepped out from the walkway that
cut through the hedge.

Nora gasped.

The older, white-haired man looked just as startled as she
was. He stopped for a moment, blinked at her and then tugged
the leash on the miniature schnauzer behind him. "C'mon,
Buster, don't dawdle," he muttered. He nodded at Nora as he
walked around her, pulling his dog after him.

Nora stood there for a few moments to catch her breath,
then, her heart still racing and her legs a little wobbly, she continued on down the block. She could see her house in the distance.

Nora heard a door slam. Once past a neighbor's tree that
blocked her view, she spotted Chris hurrying down the front
walkway toward the street. He had on his gab jacket and carried a small grocery bag. Nora started to wave but realized he
didn't see her.

When he reached the sidewalk, Chris turned and quickly
headed down the street toward the other end of the block.

Glancing at her wristwatch, Nora wondered where he was
going at this hour.

She couldn't believe he'd left Jane alone in the house after
dark with a killer on the loose. As she watched him move down
the street, Nora couldn't help herself: she wondered if she'd
read in tomorrow's paper about a fourth murder.

Shoving Jane's whistle back into her purse, she groped

around for her keys, found them and ran toward the house. She noticed the lights on in the windows of the garage apartment. Nora reached her front door and unlocked it. Swinging the door open, she immediately called out: "Jane! Jane, where are you?"

She heard footsteps above. Then her daughter came to the top of the stairs. "What is it? Ye gods, Mom. You sound like the house is on fire!"

"Where's Chris off to?" she asked anxiously. "Did he say where he was going?"

"There's some emergency at Mrs. Landauer's. He wasn't sure when he'd be back."

"Get your coat. Hurry . . ."

"What?"

"Just do what I say, Jane, please!"

Two minutes later, she and Jane were climbing into the Packard. As she backed out of the driveway, Nora noticed Joe at the garage apartment's kitchen window. He seemed to be looking out at them.

Once out of the driveway, Nora glanced back toward the garage again. She spotted Joe emerging from the apartment entrance. She shifted the car into drive, stepped on the gas and sped down the block. Taking a curve in the road, she pulled into a neighbor's driveway and killed the headlights and the motor.

"What in the world is going on, Mom?" Jane asked. She was sitting on the passenger side, gaping at her mother.

Half-turned in the driver's seat, Nora looked out the rear window at the street behind them. "There was an emergency at Mrs. Landauer's house, that's what Chris said?"

Jane nodded. "Yeah, that's what he told me. Mom—"

"How did he know there was an emergency? Did Mrs. Landauer call him? Did you hear the phone ring?"

"I don't know. It might have. I was in the bathroom with the water running right before he yelled up to me . . ."

Nora watched Joe's LaSalle speed by. The headlights were off. But Nora could still see the vehicle through the trees as it turned up a side street—in search of her, no doubt.

"Mom, wasn't that Joe's car?" Jane asked.

"Yes," Nora replied, turning the ignition key again. "Honey, you need to be my lookout. Let me know if you notice him following us, okay?"

"Okay. But won't you please tell me what's happening?"

Leaving the headlights off, Nora carefully backed out of the neighbor's driveway and then slowly drove down the block toward Mrs. Landauer's mansion. Even at a distance, Nora could see the front gates were open. She pulled over across the street and parked behind a beat-up, older car.

"I just want to check on Chris—and Mrs. Landauer," Nora explained, eyeing the old lady's gated estate.

"But why was Joe following us?"

"I'm not sure," Nora answered honestly. "But I had a feeling he might. Did Chris say anything else to you before he left?"

"He asked if I'd be okay alone and told me if I got scared, I should go next door and stay with Joe until you got home. Hey, we had the Chef Boyardee spaghetti, and it was yummy. We left some for you in the refrigerator . . ."

"That's good," Nora answered absent-mindedly. "Thanks."

She watched Mrs. Landauer's Duesenberg—blue cellophane over its headlights—coming down the long driveway. It was too dark—and Nora was too far away—to see who was behind the wheel. But then the old car moved beyond the open gates, stopped, and Chris jumped out of the driver's seat. He hurriedly shut the gates and then ducked back inside the vehicle.

"Can you see if anyone else is in the car with Chris?" Nora asked her daughter.

"I can't see a thing with this jalopy in front of us."

Nora waited until the Duesenberg started up the road, and then she began to follow it at a distance. Her stomach was on edge. As they headed east on the quiet, residential streets, Nora felt nervous driving with the headlights off.

"Why don't you blink your headlights or honk so Chris can see you?" Jane asked. "Wait a minute, your lights aren't even on . . ."

"I don't want Chris to know we're following him." Nora checked the rearview mirror. "Are you keeping a lookout for Joe's LaSalle?"

Jane turned sideways, her back against the passenger door. "I don't understand any of this," she said, staring out the rear window.

Chris turned up another side street, and Nora followed him.

"Listen, honey," she said, eyes on the road. "When you were alone with Joe on Sunday, did he ask you a lot of questions?"

"What do you mean?"

"Did he seem curious about us—about Chris in particular?"

Jane shrugged. "Not really. When I was showing him photos of Uncle Ray in the family album, Joe asked about him. He asked about Dad, too, I think. But I don't really remember."

Obviously, Joe was being very careful. And he was good. He'd completely hoodwinked her and the kids. Nora wondered if he was even an artist—or was that his "cover" for this covert assignment? Was the Baby Ruth ad really his, or had he just claimed it as his own?

Nora tightened her grip on the steering wheel as she watched Chris turn onto another residential street. He headed east, uphill past Arlene's old neighborhood near Volunteer Park and then past their church.

The three closest hospitals—Seattle General, Virginia Mason and Harborview—were all in another direction. So—if this was really an emergency for Mrs. Landauer, it wasn't a medical one.

Nora checked the rearview mirror. "Have you noticed anyone following us?"

"Nope," Jane answered. "It's all clear."

"Listen, when you were helping Joe carry his things into the
apartment on Sunday, did you see any of his paintings?"

"No, he hadn't unpacked them yet," Jane answered. "Why
do you want to know so much about Joe all of a sudden?"

"I was merely wondering, that's all," Nora replied. She figured Jane didn't need to be enlightened about Joe right now,
not when she was going away on her class field trip. The less
she knew, the better.

Nora slowed down as the Duesenberg stopped at an inter-
section at the bottom of a hill. Chris turned left onto a busier
street. Nora had to switch on her headlights.

"Mom, why don't you want Chris to see us? What's going on?"

"I-I'm worried about this *emergency* . . . and whether Chris
can handle it on his own," Nora lied. "Honey, can you see if
anyone else is in the car with him? I still can't tell . . ."

"Neither can I. We're too far back."

Up ahead, Chris turned right onto Interlaken Drive East, a
downhill winding road through a forest park. If he hadn't already spotted the family Packard tailing him, he might notice it
on this steep, dark, isolated road. Navigating the twisty turns,
Nora tried to lag as far behind the Duesenberg as she could
without losing it. She didn't dare switch off the headlights for
fear of driving off the narrow road and crashing into a tree.

Chris came to a stop and then turned left onto Lake Washington Boulevard East, along the Washington Park Arboretum.
The traffic was light. Nora deliberately let another car come between them. They passed under a pedestrian bridge. Chris was
headed north, seemingly toward the University of Washington.

It dawned on Nora that the Boeing plant and the Harbor Island shipyards were in the opposite direction. Workers at ei-

ther of those plants weren't likely to live too much farther
north than this, not if they could help it. The commute would
be too long and time-consuming. Was it too much to hope that
this clandestine trip wouldn't end at the home of a female war
worker, another "Rosie"?

With a car between Nora's Packard and the Duesenberg, it
wasn't always easy to keep tabs on where Chris was headed.
But Nora followed Mrs. Landauer's car across the Montlake
Bridge and past the university, where the middle car finally
turned onto another street. Nora continued to lag back as Chris
merged onto Erickson Road. It led north to the town of Both-
ell—which eventually became farm and forest country.

"This is crazy," Jane sighed. "Can I stop looking out for
Joe's car now?"

Her eyes on the road, Nora nodded. "Yes, thanks, honey."

"Well, wake me when he reaches the Canadian border," Jane
muttered, tipping her head back and closing her eyes.

Nora wasn't sure if Jane was really asleep or playing possum,
but her daughter didn't say anything for a while. The landscape
around them became increasingly woodsy, but there were still
signs of civilization. Nora passed phone poles, and through the
trees, she spotted an occasional pocket of light from a secluded
home or cabin. She let the gap between her car and the Duesenberg widen as there were so few vehicles on the road.

Nora checked the gas gauge; they still had half a tank. When
she glanced up again, Chris was turning onto a side road.

Switching off her headlights, Nora made a right onto the
same road and then followed the Duesenberg at a distance. Its
taillights were her guide. But then, after what seemed like half a
mile, the lights suddenly disappeared.

Nora went into a panic. Had Chris spotted her and shut off
his lights? Without the Duesenberg's taillights to help her navigate, she was driving in the dark—on another narrow, tree-
lined road.

Then she noticed a one-lane gravel road on her left—and those red taillights again. Nora quickly pulled over. Biting her lip, she peered out her window. Down the gravel lane, she could see Mrs. Landauer's car had come to a stop. Its headlights illuminated a sign on a chain-link gate: PRIVATE PROPERTY—NO TRESPASSING. The whole area appeared to be fenced off.

Chris had already climbed out of the Duesenberg. He unlocked the gate and opened it.

"What's going on?" Jane asked, stirring in the passenger seat.

"Honey, I haven't a clue," Nora admitted.

She watched Chris duck back inside the car, and then he drove down the gravel road. Nora noticed the red taillights bobbing up and down as he hit a few potholes. He'd left the gate open.

Nora took a deep breath and followed him along the road, which wound through some woods. She heard the gravel crunching under her tires until the road became a dirt path. They drove over a few potholes. Once again, the Duesenberg's taillights in the distance helped her navigate through the trees and the blackness.

"God, this is creepy," Jane whispered. "Do you know where we are, Mom?"

"Honey, I haven't a clue," she repeated.

Up ahead, Mrs. Landauer's car reached a clearing, and its headlights swept over a single, large cabin. It was illuminated for only a moment. Then the Duesenberg turned to one side and stopped. Nora could see the car's lights through the trees, but then they went off.

Nora slowed down to a crawl a few yards short of the clearing. With just enough foliage and trees to camouflage the car, she stopped and shut off the engine. She didn't want Chris to hear the motor. Her timing was perfect. In the silence, she heard the other car's door open and shut. Then another door opened and closed. Or was Chris getting something out of the trunk? Nora couldn't tell. Trees and shrubs blocked her view.

But Nora could see the cabin—a log and stone two-story structure with a wraparound porch and a garden. Considering it was in the middle of nowhere, the house and immediate grounds were in pristine condition. Either no one was home, or all the blackout curtains were tightly drawn.

But then, an outside light came on, and the front door opened, letting light from within the cabin spill outside. A young girl stepped out on the front porch. At least to Nora, from a distance, the girl looked young.

From over where the Duesenberg was parked, Chris's silhouette came into view. He had the small grocery bag with him and was patiently walking an elderly, slightly stooped woman toward the cabin's front door. Nora recognized Mrs. Landauer, even though it had been months since she'd last set eyes on her. The thin, tall woman was always smartly dressed and sporting some impressive piece of jewelry—whether it was a brooch, a necklace, or a stunning ring. Chris had told Nora that a beautician visited Mrs. Landauer once a week to color and touch up her platinum hair.

The girl hurried toward them. Over the sound of rustling leaves and an owl's cry, Nora could hear the girl talking to Chris. The words were hard to distinguish, but her tone was unmistakably urgent. She waved Chris toward the cabin. He nodded and ran inside. Then the girl took Mrs. Landauer's arm and carefully walked her toward the front porch.

Apparently, it really was an emergency—of what kind Nora, again, didn't have a clue.

"Stay here," she said to Jane, reaching for the car door handle.

"What? Are you kidding me?" Jane protested. "You're not leaving me alone in these—"

Nora shushed her. "I'll just be a minute. I want a closer look. Please, do me a favor and stay put."

"Fine," Jane said, folding her arms. She shifted nervously in the passenger seat.

Nora opened the car door, climbed outside and quietly shut the door behind her.

The girl stopped on the front porch, turned and looked out in the direction of the Packard.

Nora quickly ducked behind a large evergreen. With the light from the cabin shining on the girl's face, Nora thought she recognized her. She was almost certain that the girl was Ruth, the young daughter of Mrs. Landauer's former Japanese-American housekeeper and nurse, Sono Nakai. Ruth was about Jane's age, petite and pretty with long black hair.

In early February of last year, before the government started rounding up Japanese-Americans and relocating them to internment camps, Mrs. Landauer had supposedly let Sono go. The last Nora had heard, Sono and her daughter had moved east someplace.

The girl motioned for Mrs. Landauer to step inside the cabin. Then she lingered on the front porch for another minute, staring out toward the Packard.

Still hiding behind the evergreen, Nora wondered if Sono's daughter could see the car from where she stood.

At last, the girl retreated inside the cabin and closed the door.

Nora waited a few moments and then turned and gave Jane a little wave—encouraging her to stay put just a little longer. She stepped out from her hiding place and crept toward the cabin.

Suddenly the cabin door opened again, and Chris rushed out onto the porch. He had an old hunting rifle in his hands. "Who's out there?" he yelled. His voice was so intense and threatening, Nora almost didn't recognize it.

She froze. Her hands were half raised.

Chris's eyes met hers. She saw the stunned look on his face.

Nora tried to catch her breath. "Honey, I followed you

here—" she managed to get out. She heard the car door open and shut, and turned in time to see Jane tentatively moving toward them.

Still looking dazed, Chris shook his head at Nora. "Mom?"

"Chris, what's going on?"

"I . . . I need your help in here," he said. "Please . . . I don't know what to do . . ."

Baffled, Nora quickly signaled Jane to join her, and together they hurried toward the cabin.

Chris waited for them to reach the porch and then led the way inside. Nora found herself in a big room with a stone fireplace and rustic furnishings. She was immediately hit with the stench of vomit. Jane had gotten only as far as the front door before staggering back onto the front porch because of the smell.

Ruth stood by the sofa, sobbing. Old Mrs. Landauer didn't seem to know what to do. With a hand over her heart, she hovered over the sofa, where Sono lay under a blanket, shivering violently. She was a petite woman in her midforties with gray streaks in her black hair. Beside her was a wastebasket, the inside splattered with vomit.

"We need to do something," Ruth whimpered, wringing her hands. "She's been sick all night. I think she's going to die . . ."

Nora turned to look at Chris.

"I brought Dad's medical book," he said, handing it to Nora. "But I don't know, Mom. Sono's afraid it's her appendix. Should we get her to a hospital?"

"No, you cannot do that!" Mrs. Landauer cried out in her German accent. "They will arrest her! They will take her and Ruth away to one of those camps. No one will ever see them again . . ."

Nora hurried over toward the sofa, where the stench was even stronger. Setting the medical book on the coffee table, she led the old woman over to a chair and sat her down. "It's going to be all right," she said—even though she had no idea if that was true or not.

Then Nora returned to the couch, where Sono was still shuddering and moaning. The frail woman grabbed Nora's coat. "I'm a nurse," she murmured, her voice raspy. "It's like he said, I'm almost certain it's my appendix. I've never felt this sick before. My stomach's swollen. I have a fever. If you don't take me to a hospital soon, I'm going to die . . ."

# Chapter 28

*Tuesday*
*9:55 p.m.*

Nora tried to give the ailing woman a calm, reassuring smile. "Sono, I'm Nora Kinney. We've met before. My husband's Dr. Kinney. I live down the block from Mrs. Landauer. Do you mind if I take a look at you and ask you some questions?"

She'd seen Pete handle patients in this same comforting manner, whenever neighbors—sometimes even strangers—had shown up at their door with a medical emergency. That had included a few appendicitis cases—or patients with stomach issues symptomatic of appendicitis attacks. If not reassuring someone's worried relative, Nora had often assisted Pete as he'd made his diagnoses. She tried to remember all the steps he'd gone through examining possible appendicitis cases.

She put her hand on Sono's sweaty forehead. It was warm, but not hot. "Did you take your temperature, Sono?" Nora asked.

"No, but I was burning up earlier," the woman gasped. "I could tell I had a fever . . ."

"She wasn't making any sense!" Ruth cried. "I was so scared . . ."

"When did she last throw up?" Nora asked the girl.

"About a half hour ago. There was practically nothing left. She threw up seven times. I didn't know what to do! I called Mrs. Landauer, and she called Chris . . ."

"You did the right thing, honey," Nora said. She nodded at the vomit-splattered wastepaper basket beside Sono. "Could you take that outside, please?"

While Nora peeled back the blanket and pressed her hand on the patient's lower right belly, she asked Chris to open some windows. She applied pressure to Sono's right torso and then again, closer to her navel. Sono stirred and groaned a bit. But most patients with appendix trauma practically hit the roof in reaction to this pressure test. "Did the stomach pain feel better after you threw up, Sono?" she asked. "Or are you feeling worse now?"

Grimacing, Sono said she felt a tiny bit better, but not very much. Yes, she'd had diarrhea earlier. It had hit her at around seven o'clock. Then she'd started throwing up. No, she hadn't eaten anything unusual for dinner—just rice, vegetables and chicken. Ruth had eaten the same thing, and she wasn't sick.

"Well, I don't think you're running a fever," Nora said. "And if this were an appendicitis attack, you'd be feeling worse every minute, not better. Am I right? I mean, you're the nurse . . ."

In response, Sono nodded weakly.

Nora's voice dropped to a whisper. "Have you been able to pass gas?"

Sono sighed and rolled her eyes—as if too dignified to answer such an inquiry.

Still hovering over her, Nora frowned. "C'mon, Sono, you're a nurse. You can answer the question."

She finally nodded.

"Then I'm pretty sure it's not your appendix," Nora said. "What did you eat for lunch? Did Ruth eat the same thing?"

"I had a peanut butter sandwich," Ruth said. "Mama had some canned salmon."

"Salmon," Nora repeated.

Sono nodded. "It was perfectly good when I opened up the can a few days ago. It's been in the refrigerator the whole time."

"Mama, I'm sure that was last week," Ruth piped up. "That open can's been in the refrigerator for at least six or seven days . . ."

Nora let out a long sigh and looked at her patient. "I don't think it's your appendix, Sono . . ."

Chris found some Pepto-Bismol in the medicine cabinet. Sono was able to swallow a spoonful without gagging.

In the kitchen, Jane made herself useful by breaking up some ice cubes with an ice pick. Alongside her, Ruth brewed some ginger tea.

Nora had Sono chew the ice chips to fight dehydration—until Sono was ready for the tea.

Eventually, Nora helped her upstairs, changed her into a nightgown and put her to bed. Mrs. Landauer made it up the stairs with some assistance from Chris. Then he went downstairs to join the girls.

The elderly woman sat next to Nora at Sono's bedside. They plied Sono with more tea and used a cool, damp washcloth to dab her forehead, face and neck.

While their patient dozed on and off, Mrs. Landauer quietly explained that she owned the cabin. Her late husband had bought the two hundred and fifty acres and built the two-bedroom cabin in the woods as a weekend getaway for them. When his health had started to decline, Otto Landauer had had more modern conveniences installed in their vacation home: indoor plumbing, electricity and a telephone.

After her husband died, Mrs. Landauer never had much use for the place—not until early last year. "I saw what was happening to Japanese-Americans in this country," she whispered to Nora while Sono slept. With a bony, wizened hand, she pointed to Nora. "You saw it, too, because you had those nice people staying over your garage. The awful signs, those hateful painted messages on our sidewalk and the front gate, the vandalism. I'd seen it all before—years ago in my homeland, when they started persecuting people of my faith, people like me who considered themselves good Germans. We were beaten up in the streets, and no one tried to stop it. Our businesses and homes were destroyed. That's when my husband and I decided we had to leave Germany. We got out just in time, Mrs. Kinney—before the Nuremberg Laws, while we still had our money and a sponsor here in the United States. Our families and friends who stayed behind weren't as fortunate as we were. By the time they tried to get out, it was too late . . ."

Mrs. Landauer's eyes started to tear up, and she took a deep breath. "I stayed in touch with my relations over there. After the *Kristallnacht*, the 'Night of Broken Glass,' one by one, their letters stopped coming. The paramilitary murdered my brother-in-law, Hans, and my nephew, Jorg. They were shot in the street. My sister, Leni—along with her daughter and grandchildren—disappeared. I heard they were taken out of their homes in the middle of the night and sent to concentration camps. It's the same with all of my family and friends who remained there. None of them are left . . ."

"I'm so sorry," Nora whispered, with her hand on the old woman's angular shoulder. "You haven't heard from any of them?"

Mrs. Landauer shook her head and then pulled a handkerchief from her dress sleeve and wiped her eyes.

"So, when you saw what was happening here to the Japanese-Americans, you decided to hide Sono and Ruth," Nora concluded. "I'd heard they'd moved east someplace."

"That was what I wanted people to think," Mrs. Landauer

explained. "They were staying with me—at my house, hiding up in Sono's bedroom whenever someone stopped by. But then it became too risky. So I moved them here last summer . . ."

"They've been here alone all these months?" Nora asked, incredulous. She took a moment before she said anything. "Mrs. Landauer, taking into consideration what happened to your entire family, I . . . I understand why you'd want to hide Sono and Ruth. I see the similarities, I do. But what's happened here isn't the same thing as what started in Germany ten years ago."

"Isn't it?" Mrs. Landauer asked with a steely look.

"No, not at all," Nora argued. "You haven't heard from your family. But I've been writing back and forth with Miko. It's been a while since the last letter, but as far as I know, she and Tak were getting by all right. Conditions in their camp are far from ideal. I know some of those places aren't much different from prisons—with barbed-wire fences and guard towers. And they're located out in the middle of nowhere. But believe me, the place in Idaho where Tak and Miko are being held isn't as bad as a concentration camp."

Unblinking, Mrs. Landauer kept staring at her.

Nora realized how shaky her argument sounded. But she'd heard rumors that prisoners in the European concentration camps were starving to death and being tortured or murdered. Those were unconfirmed stories, still, Nora was pretty certain nothing like that was happening in the internment camps.

"It's not the same thing," she said adamantly. "It couldn't be. This is the United States. Like I said, I've been in touch with Miko. She wrote that they're trying to make the best of it . . ."

Nora felt guilty for letting five months slip by without writing to Miko—and for not visiting them at their camp in Idaho—and actually seeing the camp for herself so she could tell others what it was like. She'd sent Tak and Miko a Christmas package of socks—along with some trinkets the kids had bought for them. And she'd let Miko know that she'd set aside their advance rent money, so that they'd have it when they came back.

Maybe that was the difference. Nora was certain she would see Tak and Miko again. But Mrs. Landauer seemed to know her family was lost to her forever.

Nora glanced down at Sono, who seemed to be asleep. "I can't believe she and Ruth have been on their own out here since last summer. I see they have a telephone—and a rifle. But still, aren't you worried something could happen to them? Who knows what kind of character could get past the fence around this property—maybe someone with a real grudge against Japanese-Americans? As you're well aware, there are plenty of them. What if tonight had been a genuine medical emergency? The power could go out here, and you'd never know."

Nora put her hand on Mrs. Landauer's arm. "Believe me, I wouldn't want to be in one of those internment camps. But how much worse off would Sono and Ruth be than they are now? At least they wouldn't be alone. The camps have doctors, maybe not the best medical care, but certainly they'd have someone more qualified than my son and me, who live forty minutes away. Miko wrote to me that they have all sorts of group activities. Don't you think Ruth would be better off around children her own age?"

"So she could play with them inside a barbed-wire fence?" the old woman countered.

"Mrs. Landauer, forgive me," Nora said, "but Sono and Ruth are inside a barbed-wire fence now—only they're alone and *hiding*. I can't imagine how awful that must be for Sono—wondering, with every little sound in the woods, if someone is about to discover them. How in the world have they been able to get by these past months?"

Mrs. Landauer squirmed in her chair. "At the start, I drove

here to bring them food and supplies every week. But it was too much for me. I don't see that well anymore . . ."

"Well, then who—" Nora stopped in midsentence. Before she even asked the question, she knew the answer.

Mrs. Landauer nodded. "Chris took over. He's been bringing them supplies for the last seven months. He's been doing it in secret. I'm sorry, Mrs. Kinney. I had no one else I could trust. The grocer delivers my food orders once a week, and once a week, Chris takes my Duesenberg and makes a delivery here. I asked him not to tell anyone."

Nora realized how wrong she'd been about her son.

A few moments passed before she said anything. "Did he make a delivery on Sunday afternoon, when it was raining?" she finally asked.

Somehow, she already knew the answer to that question, too.

The old woman nodded again.

"But most of the time, he makes those runs around midnight or later," Nora heard herself say. "Am I right?"

Mrs. Landauer nodded once more. "Without Chris, Sono and her daughter wouldn't have been able to survive. You might think what Chris did was wrong, because he broke some stupid law. But you should be proud of him. Your son is a re-markable boy, Mrs. Kinney."

"I'm sorry, Mrs. Landauer," Nora said. "But I can't allow Chris to keep helping you with this arrangement, not anymore. He's not an adult yet. It was wrong of you to involve him. He could get arrested for what he's been doing. You could be ar-rested, too."

"What good would it do them to arrest an old woman?" Mrs. Landauer said. She sipped her tea. "Besides, I have an ex-cellent attorney, Alphonse De Klerk. And I'll see that Mr. De Klerk represents Chris, too, should Chris get into any trouble whatsoever."

They were in the living room, drinking what was left of Ruth's ginger tea. Having left Sono sleeping upstairs, Nora and Mrs. Landauer now shared the sofa. The open windows had helped air out the room, but it was chilly, so Chris had made a fire in the stone fireplace. Ruth and Jane sat in front of it. Tapping his foot nervously, Chris occupied a rocking chair.

"I don't mind making these grocery runs, Mom," he said. "In fact, now that you know, I'm kind of relieved—"

She shook her head at him. "I'm sorry, honey. I won't allow it." She turned to Mrs. Landauer. "I know you meant well, and your heart was in the right place. But I think you put Sono and Ruth in a lot of danger—making them hide and leaving them here in these woods alone. The longer they stay out here, the more at risk they are. Sooner or later, someone's going to discover them. And you . . ." Nora wanted to say: *And you better pray that the worst thing they do is report them to the authorities.* But she glanced over at Ruth in front of the fire with a worried look on her face, and Nora decided to keep it to herself.

"What would you have me do?" Mrs. Landauer asked quietly.

"I think you should call Alphonse De Klerk in the morning and tell him the whole story—only leave Chris out of it. If you decide to hide Sono and Ruth in your home again, I won't say anything—and neither will my children." She shot Jane a look of warning and then turned to Mrs. Landauer again. "Whatever you decide, I'd really like you to leave Chris out of it."

Mrs. Landauer reached over and put her hand on top of Nora's. "The last thing any of us want to do is make trouble for Chris. He's been so good."

"He's our hero," Ruth added.

Nora gave the girl a regretful look. "And I feel like your villainess. But I can't let Chris be involved in this anymore. I'm sorry, honey."

A voice came from near the top of the stairs. "Don't apologize..."

Nora—and everyone else in the living room—looked up to see Sono.

Leaning on the banister, she was dressed in a blue suit, something she might wear on a train. She still looked a bit shaky as she cautiously made her way down the steps. "Thank you, Mrs. Kinney—for everything you've done for us tonight. You should know, too, that I agree with you entirely..."

Chris got up and went to help Sono down the rest of the stairs. But as he led her toward the rocking chair, Sono gently resisted as if to show she could do it on her own.

Sinking into the rocking chair, she let out a sigh and turned to her daughter. "Dear, I want you to go to your room and start packing—everything you think you'll need for a long, long trip." She looked at Nora and Mrs. Landauer. "I've been thinking about this for a while. I don't want to stay out here alone anymore. I'm scared all the time...and so lonely. Mrs. Kinney is right about that. And I hope you're right about your attorney, Mrs. Landauer, because I don't want to go to jail. I'm ready to be with my people, whatever that entails. I know it's not going to be easy. And it's not fair. But if that's the sacrifice we have to make—in this time when everyone is making sacrifices—then I'll accept it. That's what my country wants from me."

Sono looked at her daughter again. "Ruth, we're leaving tonight, just as soon as you pack your things. So, hurry—before I change my mind."

Ruth hesitated, but then she nudged Jane. "Do you want to help me?"

Jane nodded. "Sure..."

Then the two girls headed up the stairs.

"Are you sure you feel well enough to travel?" Nora asked Sono. "Rest is what you need most right now. Chris can drive everyone back. I could stay here tonight and call in sick in the morning. Then I'd help you pack and drive you to Mrs. Landauer's."

"Thank you, Mrs. Kinney, but I'm already packed," Sono replied. "I've had a suitcase ready for months. I've always thought I'd need it—in case of an emergency. I threw some extra things in a smaller bag just a few minutes ago." She glanced around the room and finally locked eyes with Mrs. Landauer. "I never intended to stay here this long. May Ruth and I spend the night at the house one more time, Mrs. Landauer?"

"Of course," the old woman said.

Sono turned to Chris. "Dear Chris, would you mind taking my suitcases out to the car? There are two of them, upstairs by my bed."

"Sure thing, Mrs. Nakai," he murmured sadly. Then he went up the stairs.

"You and Ruth can't take just two suitcases each," Mrs. Landauer said. Her old eyes took in the room. "There's so much here that belongs to you now, Sono. You can't just leave it all behind."

"When that notice came out last year for all of us Japanese-Americans to report for relocation, you showed it to me, remember?" Sono shifted in the rocking chair a bit and held her chin up. "In the notice it said we could bring only what we could carry. Two suitcases each is all that Ruth and I can carry."

# Chapter 29

*Wednesday, May 5*
*12:17 a.m.*

With her headlights on for the drive home, Nora found it easier to follow the Duesenberg this time around. Still, nervous and exhausted, she kept a white-knuckled grip on the wheel.

Chris was a few car lengths ahead of her, chauffeuring Mrs. Landauer, Sono and Ruth back to Mrs. Landauer's house. Nora lagged behind to make sure they were okay. She was still concerned about Sono's health. Even a mild case of food poisoning could have complications. And after all those clandestine deliveries Chris had made at night, wouldn't it have been too ironic if the police stopped him on his very last trip—while he was transporting two Japanese-American fugitives? So far, the drive had been blessedly uneventful. But never one to "count her chickens," Nora couldn't relax—not yet. In a few minutes, they'd reach Mrs. Landauer's front gate.

After all her talk about how much better off Sono and Ruth would be in an internment camp, Nora remembered reading that a prisoner at one of the camps had been shot dead during an escape attempt. She'd also heard that in the first weeks of the "relocation" program, some internees had died from malnutrition or medical emergencies the camps weren't equipped to handle. She knew about the ramshackle housing and exposure to the elements. But in the past year, there had been major improvements—mostly made by the camps' resourceful residents. At least, that had been the impression Nora had gotten from Miko's letters. Either way, Nora couldn't help second-guessing the ultimatum she'd practically forced onto Sono and her daughter. But one thing she was certain about: Chris couldn't continue to be their lifeline in Mrs. Landauer's unlawful scheme—even if it did make her son a hero to them.

Only a few hours ago, she'd wondered if Chris had taken off in Mrs. Landauer's Duesenberg with the possible intention of murdering someone. Yet a part of her had always known he was no killer. Here, at last, she had an explanation for all of Chris's lies and the disappearing at night.

Her son would never go back to that cabin on another secret mission.

After dowsing the fire in the fireplace, closing and locking all the windows, and shutting off the power and water, they'd locked up the cabin. Ruth had cried, but Sono had been stoic about leaving behind their home for the past several months. Then again, as Chris had escorted Sono to the Duesenberg, she'd probably been too tired to care about anything except getting some sleep.

Nora had promised she'd drive back to the cabin and collect anything Sono or her daughter might have forgotten. Before climbing into the Duesenberg, Chris had given her the keys to both the cabin and the front gate. With some help from Jane, Nora had locked the gate after following Chris off the property.

Now, forty minutes later, Nora turned onto a very familiar side street, and up ahead, she saw the tall, wrought iron gate to Mrs. Landauer's mansion. She pulled over, while the Duesenberg stopped at the edge of the driveway. Chris hopped out of the driver's seat and unlocked the gate. He waved at her and hurried toward the Packard. Nora rolled down her window.

"You don't have to wait around for me, Mom," he said. "I can walk home. I want to carry their bags up to their room. Plus Mrs. Landauer's housekeeper, Kristina, is home, and we need to brace her for a couple of unexpected guests."

"It's okay, I'd rather wait and drive you back," Nora said.

"Okay, well, you might as well follow us and wait in front of the house." He started to move away from the window.

"Chris?" she asked.

He came closer to her window. "Yeah, Mom?"

"You know, all this time, you've been breaking the law and lying to me . . ."

"I know," he mumbled, frowning.

"I don't want you ever doing that again."

He nodded. "I'm sorry."

"But at the same time, I'm very proud of you. I just wanted to tell you that."

He gazed at her and smiled.

For Nora, it was the strangest feeling, because, suddenly, Chris didn't seem like a boy anymore. He was a young man.

"Thanks, Mom," he said, tapping the Packard's hood. He hurried back to the other car.

Nora followed him down the long driveway. She pulled over in a turnaround while Chris helped Mrs. Landauer to the front door of the mansion. Nora watched Ruth help her mother inside. The curtains in the windows must have been drawn for the blackout, because the only light that came from within the huge, stately house was from the open front door.

For the last half hour, Jane, in the passenger seat, had dozed on and off. Now, she sat up, yawned and rubbed her eyes. "I'm really glad I packed early for the overnight tomorrow," she said.

"Yes, and I'm sure your blue sweater should be dry by now," Nora said—before her daughter could ask about it. "Listen, do you think you're awake enough to remember something important I need to say to you?"

"I guess," Jane said, pushing her hair back behind her shoulders.

"First, thank you for helping me through this ordeal tonight," Nora said, patting her shoulder. "If you weren't here keeping me company, helping me navigate, I'd have completely lost my mind."

"Sure," Jane said. "I'll bet we used up almost a week's worth of gas ration points tonight."

Nora watched Chris take the suitcases from the Duesenberg's trunk and carry them inside the mansion. "I'm not finished," she said. "Second, you can't tell a soul about *any* of this. I mean it, Jane. We could all be in serious trouble . . ."

Jane shrugged. "Okay."

"Honey, I know you. And you're probably thinking, *I'll just tell Doris*. But you can't. You can't tell anyone what Chris did. Believe me, you won't be too popular if it gets out that your brother helped hide some Japanese-Americans. I don't want the house getting vandalized again. And I don't want us getting into trouble with the law—or the federal government. This is a family secret. In fact, I'd rather you not write to your father about it. He'll only get worried and distracted. Do we understand each other?"

Jane nodded. "I get it. *Loose lips sink ships.*"

"That's right," Nora said. "Thanks."

She noticed Mrs. Landauer's front door opening, and the

foyer light spilled out again. She could see—in silhouette— Sono and Ruth taking turns hugging Chris goodbye.

He put Mrs. Landauer's Duesenberg in her garage, closed and locked the big door, and then hurried toward Nora and Jane. Even though he walked at a brisk clip and it was dark out, Nora thought she saw tears in Chris's eyes as he passed her window. He ducked in the Packard's back seat. "Thanks for waiting for me," he said in a low, shaky voice. He cleared his throat and said nothing.

Turning the car around, Nora cruised down the driveway and past the gate, where she stopped. Chris climbed out, shut and locked the gates, and got into the back seat again.

"I can't believe this night," Nora murmured, starting down the block. She realized she had to be up for work in four hours.

She was halfway down the block when she saw the police car parked in front of the house.

"Oh, my God, is this for us?" she blurted out. "Now what?"

Her first thought was that the police had caught on to Chris's weekly trips, aiding and abetting two Japanese-Americans. Or were they convinced—as she'd almost been—that Chris was a murderer?

As she approached the driveway, Nora noticed Joe and a uniformed cop leaning against the side of the patrol car. The policeman was smoking a cigarette. He was about fifty and husky with a heavy five-o'clock shadow on his jowly face. He and Joe looked pretty chummy. Joe waved at her.

Nora stopped the car and watched Joe and the cop walk in front of her headlights. She rolled down her window. "What's going on?" she asked anxiously.

"Someone broke into your house about an hour ago, Mrs. Kinney," the policeman said.

She stared at him. "What?"

Joe leaned closer to the car window. "The block air raid warden, you know, the old guy who looks like Bert Lahr?"

"You mean Mr. Weiss?" Nora nodded. "Yes . . ."

"He was on his rounds and saw a light on in the house. So, he knocked on the front door. When nobody answered, he came and knocked on *my* door. Then he took me around to the front of the house to show me the light—and that's when we heard the back door slam. We caught only a glimpse of the guy. He seemed to be carrying something. He ran into the ravine. Mr. Weiss had his flashlight, but we lost the guy. He was too fast for us. Anyway, I called the police. This is Officer Stoewer."

The cop nodded cordially at her. "Ma'am."

"Mr. Weiss gave a statement and went home," Joe said. "If you'd gotten here ten minutes ago, you would have caught him."

"What was stolen?" Nora asked numbly. "Do you have any idea?"

"That's why we're waiting for you," Officer Stoewer explained. "Maybe you can take a look around the house to see if anything is missing or damaged. And I'll make a report . . ."

While pulling into the driveway and parking the car, Nora tried to pacify Jane, who was convinced the strangler had paid a visit to their house tonight.

Of course, Nora was thinking the same thing—not that she'd share it with her daughter.

But now that she knew how wrong she'd been to suspect Chris, the only connection she had to the killer was that she'd known Connie—and that her stockings and lipstick had mysteriously disappeared.

Had the strangler meant for her to be his victim tonight?

He probably knew her—if he'd been watching Connie before he murdered her, he would have figured out who Connie's riveter friends were.

She couldn't think about that now. She was too tired, scared and confused.

And she didn't want to think about Joe—if that was even his real name. She saw him through the car window, standing there with the cop. He'd lied to her about being married—and God only knew what else. She couldn't trust him. And yet he'd been the one to call the police and chase down tonight's intruder.

As Nora climbed out of the Packard with Chris and Jane, Officer Stoewer approached her. "By the way, Joe and I were wondering where you folks were until this hour."

"We . . . we went to the movies, a double feature," Nora answered lamely. It was the first thing she could think of.

"Until midnight?" the cop asked as they headed for the back door. "Don't your kids have school in the morning?"

"We stayed to watch the newsreel again," Chris piped up. "They showed some of the army medical facilities for the North Africa campaign, and when we saw it the first time, we thought we spotted my dad up on the screen. That's why we stayed so late."

"I'm pretty sure it wasn't him," Nora said, going along with the lie. "But the kids disagree with me." She couldn't help being impressed at how quickly Chris invented the fabrication. Small wonder he'd been able to deceive her for the past several months.

Pausing on the steps up to the back door, she turned to Joe. "Thanks so much for looking out for us, Joe," she said coolly. "We've imposed on you enough. You can go on back to your apartment now. I'm sure Officer Stoewer can handle it from here, can't you?" She smiled at the cop.

"Yeah," the policeman agreed. "I'll swing by if I have any more questions. Thanks a lot, Joe. Nice meeting you."

Joe seemed a bit blindsided to be dismissed. He gave Nora a tentative smile. "Well, I'm just over the garage if you need me. Good night, everybody."

The kids called good night to him, and he gave a shy little

wave as he turned and walked toward the entrance to the garage apartment.

Nora showed Officer Stoewer into the house. They led the way while Chris and Jane lagged behind. The officer noted there was no sign of forced entry and asked if they'd locked the doors before heading off to the double feature.

Nora said she thought she had but couldn't be absolutely sure. That much was true.

Officer Stoewer and she checked the dining room first. Her silver service and candlesticks were still on the side table. All the crystal and china were there in the breakfront. Nothing was missing or out of place in the living room either.

Jane was certain the strangler had targeted her bedroom, but everything was just as she'd left it. It was the same way in every room and closet. Nothing had been disturbed.

When they reached Nora's bedroom, Officer Stoewer asked Nora to make extra sure none of her jewelry was missing. As she stood in front of her dresser, checking the jewelry box, she had to tell the cop what was on her mind. With her back to him, she gazed at his reflection in her mirror. "I know this is going to sound paranoid—and just like my daughter—but two weeks ago, I had a tube of lipstick, a pair of new nylons and another pair of old ones in this dresser. Then, the other day I noticed they were gone." She turned around to face him. "I know that the victims in the last two Rosie killings were each strangled with a nylon stocking. And the killer smeared lipstick on their mouths . . ."

"How did you find out about the lipstick?" Stoewer asked. "That part wasn't in the newspapers."

"I heard about it from one of the women at the Boeing plant where I work," Nora lied. "My point is, do you think it's possible tonight's intruder might have been in here before—and stolen those items out of this dresser?"

Officer Stoewer started to shake his head. "Mrs. Kinney—"

"The stockings were beige, Royal Purple brand," she interrupted. For the last two days, she'd been so afraid the police might connect the stockings and lipstick to her. But now, she needed them to know. "The lipstick shade was Scarlet Kiss by Dorothy Gray. Aren't you going to write that down?"

"Sure," he replied, taking out his notepad. But even as he jotted down the information, it seemed to Nora like he was simply appeasing her. "How old is your daughter, Mrs. Kinney?" he asked, not looking up from his writing. "Thirteen . . . fourteen?"

"Twelve. Why do you ask?"

"Because I have three daughters, and I can tell you, when they were young teenagers, all three went through their mom's dresser, borrowing her jewelry, perfume, lipstick, stockings, you name it . . ."

"I already asked Jane," Nora said. "And she didn't take my lipstick or my stockings."

"Jane has friends over, doesn't she? This room is between Jane's bedroom and the bathroom. Without Jane knowing, any one of her friends could have come in here at any time and absconded with your nylons and your lipstick. As I'm sure you know, both are in short supply right now . . ."

Nora had originally suspected Jane had taken the stockings for a nylon scrap drive. Used lipstick dispensers were in high demand, too, for the metal. Jane's friends were just as involved in those scrap drives as Jane was. Or perhaps one of Jane's friends simply wanted to look pretty, and she couldn't resist raiding Jane's mother's dresser. What Officer Stoewer said made sense.

But Nora didn't feel any better. And why should she? Some stranger had been inside her home tonight, going through her family's things.

Nora and Officer Stoewer finished searching the house and ended up in the front hallway. Jane was still checking every nook and cranny in her room, and Chris was in the upstairs bathroom.

"I'll bet your air raid warden scared the intruder away before he could grab anything," Stoewer concluded. "Everybody's on edge—what with a killer on the loose, going after gals who work on the assembly lines. Joe told me that you knew one of the victims. So, it's hard not to jump to conclusions about this break-in tonight. But we've had a lot of burglaries recently, Mrs. Kinney. The blackouts aren't helping. And these blue star flags in the windows make it pretty easy for crooks to figure out which houses don't have a man around. I think your best defense is making sure all your doors and windows are locked."

Nora nodded and opened the door for him. "I'll make sure to do that."

"Give us a call if you find anything is missing, and I'll add it to my report," he said.

"I will, thank you," she answered, standing by the door. "And will you please pass along that information about my missing stockings and lipstick to the detectives investigating the strangulations? Just in case . . ."

"Of course," Officer Stower said, heading outside.

She knew he probably wouldn't. But Nora thanked him anyway.

She watched the officer walk toward his patrol car. Then Nora closed the front door and locked it. When she turned around, she saw Chris coming down the stairs.

"Nothing's missing?" he asked.

Nora shook her head. "Not that we could tell."

Chris leaned against the newel post at the bottom step. "Are you scared?"

"I'm exhausted mostly," Nora admitted. "On the plus side, I

think we're okay for now. This burglar isn't about to strike twice on the same night. I think everything's all locked up . . ."

She and Stoewer had checked all the first-floor windows to make sure they were closed and secured. She glanced toward the family room, where they'd left the light on. She noticed the binoculars on the shelf. She turned to Chris. "Before I forget, the night before I started working at Boeing, you said you'd snuck out to go watch the battleships at Elliott Bay. Were you actually making one of your deliveries to Sono and her daughter?"

He nodded. "Yeah, I'm sorry I lied."

"But you were telling the truth about the night Connie was killed . . ."

He nodded again. "Yeah, I stopped following her and Roger around when they came out of a restaurant in Queen Anne. I thought they'd spotted me. Like I told you, I ended up going to a park nearby for about an hour before heading home."

It dawned on Nora that Connie's killer could have spotted Chris, too. "And you didn't notice anyone suspicious?" she pressed.

"No, nothing," he answered. "Like I told you, Mom, I'd have said something to you and the police if I had, I swear."

"What about Sunday?" she asked. "Mrs. Landauer said you went to the cabin to make another delivery. But that was in the middle of the day."

"I made an occasional run out there during the day," he admitted. "On Sunday, I told Mrs. Landauer that I had to cool it with the nighttime trips because you were catching on. So, we went out there in the afternoon."

"And yet you lied to me about it—even when you knew I had these horrible notions about what you might be doing. Why, Chris?"

He picked at the newel post's molding. "I didn't want you to get involved, Mom," he said quietly. "I was trying to help Sono and Ruth, and I knew once you discovered what I was doing, you'd have to end it—like you did tonight. I'm not sore at you or anything. You're only watching out for me. I just didn't want to be the one to let them down. At the same time, I'm sort of glad it turned out the way it did tonight."

"So that was the big secret you were holding inside," Nora said, remembering her conversation with Ray the night before he'd left.

"What?" Chris asked.

"Nothing," she said, shaking her head. She let out a sigh and held out her arms. "Just come here . . ."

Chris hugged her. For a few moments, they held each other and said nothing.

Nora still thought that Chris's efforts to help Mrs. Landauer in her misguided plan had been a foolhardy thing for him to do. But what he'd done was also brave, noble and kind.

Nora finally and gently pulled back. "Well, I'm starving," she said, a little quiver in her voice. "I didn't have any dinner. I'm going to make myself a sandwich before I go to bed. Can I make something for you?"

"I'm fine, thanks, Mom. Jane cooked spaghetti tonight."

"So I heard," she replied. Nora reached up and straightened Chris's unruly hair. Then she remembered earlier tonight, realizing he was no longer her little boy.

She stopped fussing with his hair, worked up a smile and patted his arm. "Come and sit with me in the kitchen for a few minutes, will you? I need to talk to you about Joe . . ."

"I thought he might be an undercover cop, trying to keep tabs on you because the police had questioned you about that break-in near your school . . ."

"Mom, the police talked to me that day for only a minute,"

Chris whispered. He sat next to her at the breakfast table, sipping a Coke.

Nora ate cold, leftover spaghetti, which was surprisingly tasty. Then again, she was so hungry, anything would have been delicious. They kept their voices down because Jane had gone to bed about ten minutes ago.

"I figured the police had you under surveillance or something," Nora pointed out. Up until a few hours ago, she'd assumed that since she suspected the worst with Chris, so did the police. "I keep coming back to the notion that Joe might be a cop," Nora went on. "Maybe because he told that woman he'd paid to be his phony wife that he was working undercover. Plus, when we first pulled up in front of the house tonight, Joe looked pretty friendly with that policeman—like they were colleagues. But I don't know anymore. Everything he's told us has probably been a lie."

Chris shrugged. "Mom, have you ever stopped to think that maybe he pretended to be married so he could get the apartment? I mean, you told him you'd made it a requirement. The housing shortage is really bad. He was probably desperate. Maybe he figured he could keep up the charade for a while until we got to like him, and then he would tell us the truth."

"Then why did he try to follow Jane and me when we set out to tail you earlier tonight?" Nora argued. She dabbed her mouth with a napkin. "He must not be a very good detective, because I lost him pretty easily—after one block. It didn't take much. All I had to do was pull into a driveway, and—"

Nora fell silent at the sound of light tapping on the kitchen door. She froze and gazed wide-eyed at Chris.

Getting to his feet, Chris cautiously moved to the door and moved aside the blackout curtain. He turned to her. "It's Joe," he said under his breath.

Nora stood up, stepped over to the door and unlocked it. Chris remained by her side as she opened the door. At this point, she was too exhausted and unnerved to even work up a smile for the guy calling himself Joe Strauss.

"Hi," he said, standing on the back stoop with what looked like a lunch bag in his hand. "Sorry to swing by this late, but I figured you were still up. I saw a sliver of light behind the blackout curtain and thought I heard someone talking in here . . ."

Nora wondered if he'd actually heard what they'd said.

"What's going on, Joe?" she asked.

"Well, considering what happened tonight, I thought maybe you'd feel better if you had this nearby—in your nightstand drawer or someplace." He held out the bag for her. "There's a revolver in here. Be careful. It's loaded."

Hesitating, Nora stared at the paper bag—and then at him.

He pulled the bag closer to his chest. "Then again, maybe you're not comfortable with a gun in the house. I only thought—"

"No," Chris interrupted, reaching for the paper sack. "I think it's a really good idea. Thanks."

"Well, Chris, it's not for you," Joe said. "It's for your mom."

Nora took the bag from Chris. "Yes, and it's a good idea. Chris is right." She nodded at Joe and worked up a smile. "I'll rest easier if I have this for the next night or two. Thank you, Joe."

"You're welcome. And listen, I'll be up for the next few hours, so—like I said earlier—I'm just above the garage if you need me."

"It's comforting to know that," she lied.

"Well, good night," he said.

"Good night, Joe," she replied.

"Night, Joe!" Chris called.

Nora watched him head back toward the garage. Then Chris closed the kitchen door and locked it.

Sitting down at the table, Nora peeked into the paper sack at the revolver.

"Well, what do you think about that?" Chris asked, peering over her shoulder. "Maybe he is a cop—like you say. Or maybe just a really nice guy."

"I keep thinking how there isn't much foot traffic on this street—or traffic of any kind," Nora said. "We're pretty secluded here. And yet three hours after we put up the APARTMENT FOR RENT sign, he was knocking on our front door."

Nora glanced down at the gun again. "He'd been watching our house, Chris," she said. "I'm sure of it."

# Chapter 30

*Wednesday*
*8:49 a.m.*

There was no answer at the Bellini residence. Maybe they were still asleep.

Nora hung up after five rings.

She'd come to work this morning with the phone numbers of Joe's two references. She'd also brought along a coin purse full of change for the long-distance call to Joe's second reference, his "artist's agent," Ken Hotopp—if that was even the guy's real name.

It was her coffee break, and Nora was inside one of the phone booths in the cafeteria. She knew it might be too early to call anyone, but considering these friends of Joe had lied to her, she wasn't too concerned about waking them up.

With her coins ready and the numbers on a piece of scrap paper in front of her, Nora read the San Francisco phone number to the long-distance operator. She felt wide awake, despite only three hours of sleep. She'd gotten by on less when both kids were babies. Slugging down two cups of coffee this morning had helped.

She followed the operator's instructions and deposited eighty-five cents. While it rang on the other end, she checked her wristwatch: only a few minutes left of her break.

"Hello?" a woman answered.

"Hello, may I speak to Ken Hotopp, please?" Nora said.

"I'm sorry. He's left for work. Would you like to leave a message?" The woman on the other end of the line sounded young, maybe in her twenties.

"Well, maybe I should make sure I have the right Ken Hotopp," Nora said. "Is he an artist's agent?"

"Yes, that's right, Masterworks Artists Representation. Would you like the phone number?"

"Yes, please, in just a minute." Nora started digging into her purse for a pencil. "Listen, while I'm looking for something to jot this down, do you know if your husband represents Joe Strauss?"

The young woman chuckled. "I'm not his wife. I'm his daughter, Greta—Greta Hotopp."

"Oh, I'm sorry, Greta—"

"I know several of my dad's clients, but that name doesn't ring a bell."

"There's no *Joe Strauss* on his client list?" Nora pressed. "He was supposed to have illustrated an ad for Baby Ruth candy bars with a child and a kite—"

"You mean Joe Slattery?"

*Slattery?* Nora thought. She still needed to make sure she had the right guy. "He's about thirty, handsome, dark hair, and he has a hearing problem in one ear?"

"That's Joe. My dad has known him for years. He's a friend of the family. How do you know Joe?"

"I'm sorry," Nora said. "I never introduced myself. I'm Connie—Connie Phillips. I met Joe last week. I saw the Baby Ruth ad and thought I'd commission him to paint a portrait of my daughter. I wrote down your father's name and forgot to write down Joe's last name. So silly of me."

"Well, speaking of writing things down, did you find a pencil or pen yet?"

"Yes, thanks, go ahead." Nora had a pen in her hand.

As Ken Hotopp's daughter read off the phone number for Masterworks Artists Representation, Nora wrote it down—along with Joe's real last name.

So, it was obvious now: Joe wasn't a cop. He was an illustrator—just as he'd said. But he'd lied to her about being married and about his last name. Why? And what else had he lied about?

"Got it, thanks," Nora said, finishing her scribbling. "Joe seems really nice . . ."

"Oh, yes, growing up, I had a big crush on him."

"He told me about losing his brother. It's a terrible shame."

"We're still hoping Jackson will turn up somewhere," Greta Hotopp said. "He's such a sweet guy. No one thinks he intentionally went UA."

"*Jackson?* I thought his name was Andy . . ."

"Joe's the only one who calls him Andy. Jackson's his real name. Andy Jackson, get it? It's one of those nicknames between the brothers."

"You said Joe's brother went UA? That's *unauthorized absence* . . ." Joe had told her *Andy* had been killed in Guadalcanal.

"Well, unauthorized absence sounds like he took off for a weekend bender. It's been two weeks, so I guess it's more like he has completely disappeared."

"What exactly happened?" Nora asked.

There was a brief silence on the other end.

"Hello?" Nora said. "Greta?"

"You said a minute ago that Joe told you what happened to his brother."

Nora heard the bell sound, signifying the end of her break.

She glanced at her wristwatch. "Um, no, he merely said he'd lost his brother, *Andy*, who was in the navy, and he used to look after him. I'd assumed his brother was killed in action."

"No, he was stationed at a base down in San Diego," the young woman said. "There was an explosion or a fire or something, and when the smoke cleared, they discovered that Jackson had cleaned out his locker and disappeared. I'm sure he had nothing to do with the explosion or whatever it was. He probably panicked and got confused. My theory is that he must have assumed the Japs were bombing us, and his first thought was that he had to go find Joe and make sure he was okay. The two of them were inseparable . . ."

The operator chimed in and asked for eighty-five cents for an additional three minutes. Nora was already late returning from her break. So, she thanked Greta Hotopp for her help and hung up.

She quickly jotted down some more notes on the scrap paper and then studied it for a moment:

*Masterworks Artists Representation—San Fran—*
*Klamath-7299*
*Joe SLATTERY—Jackson!!!*
*San Diego naval base—Ray?*

Nora circled her brother's name.

She was late getting back to her workstation, and her lead man reprimanded her. Yelling over all the noise on the assembly line, he reminded her that she'd been late returning from a break on Monday, too. "In case you've forgotten, there's a war on," he told her. "Consider this a warning!"

"Honey, you have to be more careful," Fran advised her over lunch, two hours later. With a pair of tongs from her lunchbox, she took a hot dog out of her thermos of steaming water. She carefully set it on a bun. "If this is your second time tardy within a week, you're really pushing your luck. You only get one more. Why were you late?"

"I was on the phone with someone about . . ." she hesitated, "about Ray."

"Well, you should have told your lead man that. They usually give you a break when it comes to losing someone in the service." She was about to take a bite out of her hot dog, but then set it back down on her napkin. "You know, he was quite a fella, your brother. I only met him that one time at your dinner party. But before Marty and I left, he pulled me aside and asked for our address. He wanted to keep in touch with Marty and make sure he was getting along all right. 'One navy man looking out for another,' he said."

Nora gave her friend a melancholy smile. Ray was always full of surprises.

"Isn't that sweet?" Fran said. "I told him that you had our address in your address book." She glanced down at her lunch. "You know, this hot dog could use some ketchup and relish. I'm going to raid the condiment bar. Can I get you anything while I'm up, hon?"

"No, thanks," Nora said.

Wrapping her hot dog in a napkin, Fran headed toward one of the lunch counter side tables.

Nora nibbled at her lunch and thought about Ray and her follow-up calls to his base in San Diego. She remembered what the ensign had told her about a seaman who had vanished around the time of the explosion. Then she recalled what Joe had said about people who took advantage of his trusting, sweet kid brother. Had Ray been one of those people? Had he talked Jackson Slattery into helping him with his scheme to avoid combat duty? And when things had gone horribly wrong, maybe the poor, scared kid had run away.

Or maybe it was just how Greta Hotopp had imagined—with Jackson as surprised by the explosion as anyone else.

Then, thinking they were under attack, he'd cleared out to go search for his big brother.

And his big brother had found her.

Joe wasn't a cop. He hadn't moved into the apartment over her garage to catch a strangler or to keep tabs on Chris. He was there because he thought he knew something about Ray.

Nora was hardly aware of Larry Krull walking toward her—until he was just a few feet away. As he passed by, he smirked at her and then, with his finger, he drew a slash line across his throat.

A chill raced through her. For a second, Nora thought he was threatening her—or maybe even indicating that she might be next in the assembly-line worker murders. She didn't know why her mind automatically went there.

But then she realized that Larry knew she'd been disciplined for returning late from her break this morning.

It was about her being late—and, maybe, how she deserved to be terminated.

# Chapter 31

Joe's LaSalle was still in the driveway. The garage apartment's living room window was open, and Nora could just barely hear Frank Sinatra's crooning on the radio. Every once in a while, she saw Joe pass by a window in his T-shirt and paint-splattered khakis.

On the bus ride home, it had occurred to her that, when Joe had asked to borrow the photo of Jane with her uncle, he hadn't been interested in painting Jane at all. More likely, he'd wanted a good, clear photo of Ray.

One of the first things Nora had done after returning home was check the family photo album for that photograph. But the photo of Jane and Ray at a picnic three years ago was gone.

Nora wondered if one of the kids had already given the photo to Joe. Or had Joe been so eager to get his hands on the picture that he'd snuck into the house and stolen it?

But that didn't make sense. She'd already promised Joe she

would lend him the photograph. Why would he go to all the trouble of stealing it when he didn't have to?

Nora had about a hundred different chores she could have been accomplishing around the house, but all she could do was anxiously pace around the kitchen, knock off a Coke, and keep glancing out the window to see if Joe was still home. She just wanted him gone for an hour. Then she'd use her extra key to get into the garage apartment and search every inch of the place until she found something that might help her figure out what he was up to.

She heard the front door open, and raced into the hallway to see Chris returning from school. She didn't even give him a chance to put down his books. "Hi, honey," she said briskly. "Did you by any chance lend Joe a photo from the family album?"

"Yeah," Chris said, pausing in the hallway. "I gave a picture of Jane with Uncle Ray to him yesterday afternoon so that he can get a copy made. Joe said he wanted to use Jane's likeness for a peanut butter ad." He moved into the family room and set his books on the desk. "Why? Did I do something wrong?"

"No, it's fine," Nora said, standing in the family room doorway. "I was just curious."

She didn't want to tell him that Joe might be investigating Ray. That would have meant admitting to Chris her suspicions about the explosion at Ray's navy base. Nora had no intention of telling anyone about that, not if she could help it.

Chris took off his jacket and flung it on the back of a chair.

"You're a little late today," she remarked.

"Yeah, I swung by Mrs. Landauer's," he said glumly. "She called her attorney this morning. He got on the horn with the authorities. So, a couple of hours ago, they came and picked up Sono and Ruth. Sono was feeling much better today. And they felt okay about what they had decided to do. But everyone cried, I guess. Mrs. Landauer said the guys who came to pick them up were pretty decent about it. The lawyer was there the whole time. I don't think anyone's going to jail or anything. They said Sono and Ruth will probably end up in the Minidoka Relocation Center in Idaho. Isn't that where Tak and Miko are?"

Nora nodded. She felt bad for everyone involved and wondered if Chris resented her for forcing the issue.

With a sigh, he headed toward the kitchen. "Anyway, Mrs. Landauer said my name didn't come up once. Even her lawyer doesn't know about my involvement. So, I guess that's that."

"I'm sorry, honey," Nora said, "*relieved*, but sorry."

He glanced out the window. "So have you decided what to do about Joe?"

"Right now, I wish he'd get lost for about an hour so I could take a look around the apartment," Nora admitted. She leaned against the counter. "I'm sure he has something in there—some clue—that would give us an idea of what he's doing here."

Chris opened the refrigerator. "Can I have a Coke?"

"Sure," she said distractedly.

"We're almost out," he said, taking a bottle from the shelf.

"I know. I'll pick up some more. I need to go to the store later anyway."

Chris took the bottle opener out of the drawer and opened his Coke. He went to the window again and gazed out toward the garage. "Mom, why don't you go to the store now?" he said. A smile flickered on his face. "I have an idea. Give me about forty-five minutes. By the time you get back, Joe and I will both be gone. I'll make sure he's occupied for at least an hour. Does that give you enough time to go through the apartment?"

Nora could see the gleam in his eyes that hadn't been there when he'd come home a few minutes ago. "What are you planning to do?" she asked.

\* \* \*

Chris staggered out the kitchen door and made his way to the garage apartment entrance. He banged on the door.

He'd just spent the last few minutes spinning in a circle in the front hall, where he couldn't knock anything over. As a kid, he used to employ this tactic whenever he wanted to get out of going to school or church. About five minutes of constant spinning was all it took for him to feel and look as sick as hell. Very little acting was required after that. His mother would take one glance at him and put him to bed with a spit-up bowl. An hour later, like a miracle, he'd be fine. It had worked like a charm for a while—until his dad figured out the ruse. That was one of the disadvantages to having a father who was a doctor.

Actually, his mom had been wise to him all along. She'd told him so a few years ago: "I decided, if you wanted to avoid Mass, school or your chores so badly that you were willing to make yourself sick, then what the heck, I'd give you a break."

That was the difference between his mom and his dad. His father was nobody's fool and never let him get away with anything. But his mom let him goof off once in a while—even when it meant letting him think he'd pulled the wool over her eyes.

Chris wondered, if he hadn't really fooled his mom when pretending to be sick as a kid, would he be any better at deceiving Joe now?

Maybe that was why he'd spun around a bit longer than he should have.

With one hand braced against the doorframe, Chris fought the nausea and dizziness. He heard Joe coming down the stairs. The door opened.

His head still swirling, Chris tried to focus on Joe, who was dressed in a paint-stained T-shirt and khakis. He was barefoot.

"My God, Chris, are you okay?" he asked. "You don't look so hot . . ."

"I just threw up," he lied, gasping for effect. "I feel like I'm going to die, my stomach hurts so bad. It's getting worse—especially right here." He pointed to his lower-right belly. "I checked my dad's medical book, and I think it's my appendix. My mom's gone to the store. I don't think I can last until she gets back. Could you drive me to the hospital?"

Joe stared at him. "Don't you have a doctor you can call?"

Clutching his right side, Chris let out a sharp cry and bent forward. "Please, you got to get me to a hospital . . ."

"Okay, okay, hang on, Chris," Joe said. "Let me grab the car keys and put on some shoes. Wait right there!" He turned and raced up the stairs.

Chris straightened up a bit. He was already feeling better.

When he'd told this plan to his mother, she'd had no trouble guessing what had inspired the notion. She'd commended him on his cleverness but hadn't liked the prospect of Joe dangerously racing through traffic to get Chris to a hospital—and then wasting the doctors' and nurses' time with a fake emergency.

She'd suggested that he ask Joe to drive him to the University Bookstore for a book he needed for school. "I don't know when the bookstore closes, but you can tell him it closes at six," she'd said. "After that, you can stall him. That should give me enough time."

His mom had even given him five dollars to buy any book he wanted. "As long as it's believable that you're reading the book for school," she'd said.

After she'd left, Chris had decided there were too many variables with her "bookstore" plan. What if Joe refused? Or he might say, "Fine, take my car and drive yourself." Chris felt the "appendicitis attack" ploy guaranteed Joe's cooperation. And during the car ride, Chris wouldn't have to make small talk with someone he no longer trusted or liked very much. He'd just pretend to be in pain and groan a lot.

Chris decided, when all this was over, he'd give his mom

back her five dollars and apologize for not going along with her suggestion. If the last few days had taught him anything, it was that lying to his mom wasn't a good idea.

He heard Joe coming down the stairs again. Chris clutched his stomach once more.

Joe had put on his shoes and thrown a jacket over his T-shirt. He double-locked his door. As they headed toward the LaSalle, Joe asked him if he'd left a note for his mother. Chris lied and said yes.

Joe got the passenger door for him. "Did you lock both doors to the house?"

Chris couldn't remember. He stared at Joe for a moment.

"Chris, you just had a break-in, and I don't want your mom coming home to any other surprises. Better give me the keys . . ."

Chris waited in the car while Joe locked the back door and went around to check the front. Chris wondered, if Joe was such a bad guy, why would he be looking after them like this?

After a minute, Joe climbed behind the wheel and gave the house keys back to him. He started up the car. "Listen, I don't know where the hospital is," he said, out of breath. "So you'll have to give me directions. Can you do that?"

Chris groaned a little. "I think so," he whimpered.

"That a boy," Joe said. He began to back the LaSalle out of the driveway. "And since you're feeling really sick, can you do me a favor and roll down your window?"

Standing at the top of the narrow stairwell to the garage apartment, Nora realized that, if Joe weren't such a liar, he'd be an ideal tenant. Not only had he locked his door when he'd left, but he was quite tidy, too. The kitchen was spotless, and the only mess in the living room was around where he'd set up his easel, paints and a drop cloth.

Taking a closer look, Nora noticed some tubes of paint that had been left uncapped—as if Joe had left in a hurry. Chris must have caught him in the middle of his work. Nora had a feeling her son had stuck with his original plan to fake an appendicitis attack. If they'd gone to the bookstore, Joe would have stopped to put the caps back on his paint tubes.

Nora stepped around the easel to get a look at the painting.

"My God," she murmured, astonished.

The nearly finished illustration was obviously an advertisement for Spam. It showed an infantry soldier with a tired grin on his face, eating Spam out of the can. He appeared to be in a jungle someplace, huddled under a makeshift tent to keep out of the rain. What was so startling about the painting was the soldier's resemblance to Ray.

Since meeting Joe on Sunday, Jane had mentioned several times how much he looked like Uncle Ray. But the soldier in this ad was like a combination of both men—Ray especially.

Nora spotted Joe's sketchbook leaning against the wall along with some painted canvases. She searched through the book and found pencil drawings that must have been preliminary sketches for more ads. Every ten or so pages she noticed a rendering of the same handsome Ray look-alike—smoking a pipe, eating an ice cream cone or dressed in a snazzy business suit, whatever the ad called for.

Then Nora remembered something Ray had told her, sitting over there at the kitchen table the night before he'd left. "No one tried to get to know me," he'd said of the other men in his new unit. "They kept mistaking me for this other guy, Jackson, who's a complete moron."

Her brother *knew* Joe's brother, Jackson. Ray and Jackson weren't only at the same base; they were in the same unit. In all likelihood, it was no coincidence that Jackson had cleaned out his locker and disappeared at the time of the explosion.

After putting the sketchbook back, Nora moved to the living room's built-in breakfront. On the counter sat a leather carrying case. Inside was a camera and some rolls of film. Nora started searching through the breakfront drawers. She found more tubes of paint, paintbrushes, pencil sets and other art supplies. One drawer held a shoebox full of photographs. She recognized the shots of Jackson that Joe had used for some of those preliminary ads in his sketchbook. Another one of his models was a girl who looked a bit like Rita Hayworth. From the photos, she and Joe seemed to be romantically linked. One of the shots showed them at the beach—with the girl in a polka-dot two-piece suit. Nora found a photobooth strip of the two of them, and they were kissing in one of the frames. On the back, he'd scribbled: *With Carol @ Fisherman's Wharf— June '41.* Nora couldn't help wondering if Joe and Carol were still an item. There were other photos, older ones of the brothers together, growing up. Nora also found a formal studio portrait of Jackson alone—in his sailor uniform. She could see why the guys in their outfit got Jackson and Ray mixed up. Jackson had signed the photograph: *To My Big Brother—Ship Ahoy! Andy.*

Nora placed all the photos back in the shoebox and returned it to the drawer. In the last drawer she checked, under a short stack of folded paper bags, she found some bills, bank statements and letters—all addressed to Joseph Slattery at a Seattle post office box. Some of the mail had been forwarded from 1459 Cole Street in San Francisco.

So, Joe wasn't married and he wasn't from Albany, Oregon. Before moving to Seattle, he had lived in San Francisco.

One of the letters was from an aunt, thanking him and his brother for sending her flowers on her birthday. She mentioned that Jackson had sent her a nice card. Reading between the lines, Nora wondered if this aunt had had a hand in raising them. The same aunt had sent him an Easter card. There were no letters from Carol.

Nora put everything back in its place and closed the drawer. She headed into the bedroom and started going through the closet. It smelled like Joe's cologne. Nora saw a shoebox on the shelf. Inside, she expected to find more photos or some documents. But there was only a pair of two-tone shoes. She noticed the labels on his clothes: The Emporium, City of Paris, and other San Francisco stores.

After glancing under the bed and finding nothing, Nora checked the dresser. In the back of the bottom drawer, under some sweaters, she discovered a thick folder. On top of all the papers and photographs was the photo of Ray and Jane at the picnic. Beneath that, she found a manila envelope addressed to Joe at the Seattle post office box. The return address was *Robert Gold, San Diego, Calif.*

Nora brought the folder over to the bed and sat down. She carefully slid two eight-by-ten photographs out of the manila envelope. A note was paper-clipped to them:

*April 30th*

*Joe,*

> *Hope this is what you were looking for. It's from the San Diego Union-Tribune. You were right about the date: March 21st. Hope you can read this. These photos were the best I could do. Keep me up to date on what you find up there in Seattle. Good luck, Buddy.*

*Bob*

Nora studied the first photo, which was of a newspaper article—with the headline:

## TWO UNIVERSITY HEIGHTS WOMEN BRUTALLY SLAIN

Below the headline were two slightly blurry photographs, each of a young woman, one blonde, one brunette. The caption read: *Phyllis Thorpe, 23 (left), and Elizabeth "Betty" Rodenkirk, 25 (right), were roommates and worked on the assembly line at Consolidated Aircraft Corporation.*

Nora thought it strange Ray had never mentioned that two female war workers had been murdered in San Diego—only two weeks before Loretta Bryant had been strangled in Seattle. He'd been recuperating in the naval hospital on March twenty-first and would have had nothing to do but read the newspaper. The Loretta Bryant murder had come up in conversation at the dinner party—and later, Jane had mentioned it a few times in front of Ray. Why hadn't he said anything about this double murder near where he'd been stationed?

Nora anxiously read the article. The two young women were strangled and stabbed repeatedly. The bodies were found in their hallway outside the bedroom. Both women had been employed at the plant for seven months. They were riveters.

A coworker called their landlady when the roommates hadn't shown up at the plant. The landlady let herself into the apartment and discovered the bodies.

The police were searching for the killer, who might have known both women. There was no sign of forced entry. Neighbors in the apartment house told the police they hadn't heard any screams.

Nora was frustrated that the article didn't go into detail about the crime scene. There was no reference to any of the "flourishes" the "Rosie" killer would later add to his murders—the lipstick smile, the apron, and the work pants on display by the front door of each victim. Then again, for each new murder he seemed to be refining his signature touches.

And with these two poor young women in San Diego, he'd only been getting started.

# Chapter 32

*Wednesday*
*6:09 p.m.*

Marty DeLuca thought he was seeing things. Coming out of the florist shop, he stopped dead. With his one good eye, he was almost certain he spotted Nora Kinney's brother, Ray, across the street. But he knew Ray was dead, so it must have been someone who looked a hell of a lot like him. The guy stepped into the five-and-dime.

Marty had gone to the florist to buy his mom some flowers. It was his dad's birthday. The old man would have been fifty-eight today—if he hadn't drunk himself to death three years ago. At least his dad hadn't been a mean drunk. He used to get quietly sloshed every night and pass out. Marty and his father had never been very close, but he realized he could have done a lot worse. Some of his buddies in the navy had fathers who were absolute monsters. For Marty, his dad had to be dead for a while before he could appreciate him a bit more.

Marty's mom had asked him yesterday if he could stick

around tonight. She wanted to cook a nice dinner, she'd said.
She hadn't said anything about today being his father's birthday, but he knew. Marty had wanted to do something special
for her, but he hadn't decided on flowers until just a few minutes ago.

His mom had left the roast in the oven and walked to the
market for some last-minute ingredients for the sides. Marty
had taken the car and figured he'd be back before she was.

Standing outside the florist shop with a box of a dozen yellow roses, he contemplated going into the five-and-dime to
track down the Ray look-alike. But what for? So he could tell
the guy, "I met someone who looks exactly like you, but he's
dead now"?

Marty started toward the car, parked a block away.

Even before his mother had asked him to stay home tonight,
he'd resolved not to go out on any of his nightly prowls for a
while. Marty didn't want to leave her alone in the house after
dark, not when some maniac killer was on the loose. So far, the
strangler's victims had all been young women. But that could
change.

Two thirtyish women passed him on the sidewalk, and they
stared. One cringed a bit and then tried to pretend she wasn't
looking at him. She whispered in her friend's ear. Marty knew
they were talking about his eye. He still wasn't used to being
gawked at. Stupid little things like that would throw him into a
mood.

Or maybe he was blue because he wasn't seeing Rhonda
tonight. Staying home for his mom was no big sacrifice because
Rhonda was otherwise occupied for the next several evenings.
Her kid sister was in town from Spokane, and she'd be at
Rhonda's house through the weekend.

Marty's mother had asked him many times if he was seeing
someone on his nightly excursions. Marty always lied and said
no, because Rhonda was married with two toddlers at home

and a husband away in the air corps. Marty didn't see her every night, but often enough. On those other nights out, he'd go for a drive or a walk along a Puget Sound or Lake Washington beach. Sometimes, he'd go to a bar, where he'd drink and ruminate on the hopeless situation with Rhonda.

The streetlights went on as Marty walked back to his car. It made him uneasy to think of his mother walking home from the market at twilight. She didn't carry anything for self-defense in her purse—not like so many of the other female assembly-line workers. "I'm an old woman," she'd said, completely dismissing the idea. "What would this so-called 'Rosie' killer want with me?"

But Marty assumed the killer must have been watching Connie for a while. Certainly, he knew Connie's friends. Marty wished his mother was more cautious.

As he neared the family Ford, he decided to swing by the market and see if his mom was still there so he could drive her home.

Marty pulled the car keys out of his pocket. He didn't notice until he was about to climb inside the car that someone had slashed the Ford's tires.

Coming through the back door with a bag of groceries, Fran let the screen door slam shut behind her. "Shit," she muttered. She'd noticed the car was gone.

Marty had promised to stay home tonight. He knew she had a fancy dinner planned. Hell, with the roast in the oven, he could *smell* that she had a fancy dinner planned.

He did this once in a while. He'd say he planned to stay in, and *yes, lamb chops for dinner would be great.* Then, twenty minutes before dinner was ready, without so much as a good-bye, Marty would suddenly take off in the car and not be back until morning. "I'm sorry I disappeared like that, Mom," he'd tell her later. "I just had to get out of the house. I don't know what it is. But sometimes I feel like I'll go crazy if I stay home another minute. It's like the walls are closing in on me or something."

She understood—or at least she tried to.

But she couldn't help feeling let down tonight. Did he even remember it was his father's birthday?

She checked the roast—fifty-nine cents a pound, fourteen ration points, and she'd be eating it alone. After unloading the groceries, she went upstairs to take a shower.

In her bedroom, Fran started peeling off her work clothes. Tossing her pants on the bed, she remembered how her husband, Hank, disapproved of women in slacks. He'd be rolling over in his grave if he knew that his wife had just been out and about in *pants*—for everyone to see.

She was unbuttoning her blouse when she heard a noise downstairs. It sounded like the front door opening.

Grabbing her robe, Fran put it on and headed into the hallway. Maybe Marty hadn't ditched her after all. "Marty? Honey, is that you?" she called. She stopped at the top of the stairs.

Fran looked down at the front door—closed.

"Martin?" she called.

There was no answer.

Padding down the steps in her bare feet, she checked the front door. It wasn't locked. That was unlike Marty. Whenever he left for his nightly wanderings, he always locked up the house.

Fran locked the door.

She couldn't help feeling a little spooked. She was almost certain she'd heard someone come inside the house. She checked the living room, dining room and kitchen—and even the closets, powder room and pantry. Around other people, Fran tried to act as if she weren't scared by the "Rosie" killings—as if she were too old for such nonsense. But she couldn't help feeling jittery at times.

The basement door was beside the kitchen pantry. Fran had no desire to go down and check the basement right now. So, instead, she latched the hook on the basement door into the eye on the doorframe.

Returning upstairs, Fran finished undressing and took her shower.

She wondered where Marty had gone off to tonight. He claimed he wasn't seeing anyone. But Fran suspected he'd found somebody, probably a married woman or a widow. There were so many of them now, lonely women whose husbands were away at war or dead. Fran almost hoped that Marty had found some happiness with one of them. At least, then he'd be with somebody he cared about. She preferred that to him wandering aimlessly alone or drinking in some dive bar every night. She'd lost her husband to alcohol. She didn't want to lose her son to it, too.

Fran lingered longer than usual in the shower. The roast still had at least another twenty minutes to cook. She wasn't even sure she'd eat it tonight. Maybe she'd cook it and stick it in the refrigerator for leftovers, then make herself a sandwich instead. Some special occasion. *Well, Happy Birthday, Hank*, she thought as she shut off the shower water.

She emerged from the bathroom in her robe. In her bedroom, it took a few moments for Fran to realize that something was different: Her work pants were no longer on the bed.

Baffled, she checked her closet to make sure she hadn't hung them up. But the slacks weren't there.

Fran stopped to listen for any sounds within the house. All she heard was the dripping showerhead in the bathroom.

Warily, she stepped into the hallway and listened again. Nothing.

She crept toward the stairs and glanced down at the front hallway. She spotted her work pants draped over the newel post at the bottom of the steps.

A chill raced through her. Nora had told her that the Rosie killer displayed his victims' work pants outside by their front doors.

*He's put them within easy reach*, she thought. *Hanging them outside is probably what he does last.*

For a few moments, Fran stood paralyzed at the top of the steps, uncertain what to do. If she tried to race down the stairs and out the front door, would she make it? Or should she lock herself in the bathroom?

Suddenly, someone pounded on the front door and rang the bell repeatedly.

Panic-stricken, Fran clutched her robe together at the neck. She still couldn't move.

Then she heard a muffled yelling on the other side of the door: "Fran? Fran, are you home?"

She recognized the voice of her neighbor, Lew McFadden, a stocky, balding widower a few years older than her. He'd been drinking buddies with Hank. People always wanted to fix her up with him, but Fran wasn't interested.

She ran down the stairs, unlocked the door and flung it open. "Lew . . . hi . . ." she said, her heart racing.

Fran glanced over her shoulder to make sure nobody was coming at her from behind. She caught another glimpse of her work pants flung over the newel post.

"Marty telephoned me," Lew explained. "He went out for an errand, and someone slashed his tires. He got worried about you and tried to call. When he didn't get an answer, that's when he tried me. I came by about ten minutes ago. I rang and knocked. I thought I heard footsteps in here, but no one came to the door . . ."

Fran nervously fingered the lapel of her robe. "I was in the shower. I—"

The screen door in the kitchen slammed.

"What was that?" Lew asked, startled.

"I don't know." Fran nervously stepped aside. "Could you come in and help me check, Lew?"

With a nod and a determined gait, Lew headed down the hall into the kitchen. Fran trailed after him.

The back door was open—and so was the basement door.

She knew the hook lock on the basement door was flimsy. It was there more for peace of mind than real security. A blade through the door crack was all it took to maneuver the hook out of its eye. That was what her intruder must have done. It was all so clear to her now. She'd heard him sneak in through the front door while she'd been undressing. He'd hidden in the basement, and she'd unknowingly locked him in there. He must have waited until she'd been in the shower before flipping the hook and letting himself out.

Standing at the kitchen door, Lew peered out at the back-yard. "I don't see anybody, Franny . . ."

The telephone rang, giving her another start. The phone was on the wall, by the hallway-kitchen entrance, near where Fran stood. A hand over her heart, she answered it. "Hello?" she said in a shaky voice.

"Mom, is everything okay?"

"Marty . . ." She couldn't quite catch her breath. "Um, Lew's here. Everything's okay now. I just had a little scare, that's all."

"What happened?" Marty pressed.

"I'm fine, honey," she said, watching Lew step outside to the back stoop.

Arms akimbo, he glanced around the backyard.

"Where are you?" Fran asked her son. "Are you all right? Lew said someone slashed our tires . . ."

"Yeah, both tires on the driver's side," he said. "I'm at the Shell station on Empire Way. I had to run an errand, and while I was in the store, someone took a knife to our tires. I tried to call you to say I was going to be late, and I didn't get an answer. I knew you had to be back from the store. So, I called Lew."

"Well, I'm glad you did." Fran looked over at the open basement door and the dark stairway.

"Where were you that you didn't hear the phone?" Marty asked.

"I was in the shower, that's all. Will they be able to fix the tires?"

Fran noticed something on the kitchen counter. It looked like a daisy-patterned blouse, left there in a heap. She reached over and picked it up.

It was an apron. And it wasn't hers.

"I asked them about that here at the service station," Marty was saying. "The car's about two blocks away. The mechanic needs to take a look at the damage. I'm hoping they can patch the tires, because with the rubber shortage right now, God knows how long it'll take to replace them—and how much it'll cost. Even if it's just a patch job, they'll need the car overnight. The mechanic said he'd give me a lift home. I should be there in about forty-five minutes. Mom, are you sure you're okay?"

She stared at the strange apron in her hand.

*He had everything ready*, Fran thought.

"Mom?"

"I'm fine, honey, really," she said carefully. "But don't be alarmed if—when you get here—there's a police car outside . . ."

# Chapter 33

*Wednesday*
*6:42 p.m.*

Sitting on the edge of the bed with Joe's file in front of her, Nora wondered why he was so interested in the "Rosie" killings. The photos of the six-week-old *San Diego Union-Tribune* article had been sent by his friend on April thirtieth. So, obviously Joe had asked his buddy to track down the article days before he'd moved in above her garage. Had he already known that she'd been friends with one of the Seattle "Rosie" victims?

He had a clipping from Monday's *Seattle Times* about Gloria Dunbar's murder—as well as photographed copies of the *Times* and *Star* articles about the murders of Loretta Bryant and Connie. Nora figured he must have taken his camera to the library and photographed the articles there. But she still couldn't begin to guess why Joe was so interested in these killings. And what did the murders have to do with her—besides her association with Connie?

Joe couldn't possibly think Chris was responsible for the

"Rosie" killings, not when the first one had been in San Diego. Nor could he suspect Ray, because her brother had been in the hospital when the San Diego double-murder had occurred. And Ray had been dead for over a week at the time of Gloria Dunbar's slaying.

Nora thought she heard a car. Springing up from the bed, she hurried into the living room and looked out the window at the driveway. No one. *False alarm.* But she noticed it was getting dark out. She checked her wristwatch. Whether he'd made Joe take him to the bookstore or to the hospital, Chris couldn't keep him occupied for very much longer. Nora knew she had to be out of the apartment soon.

Hurrying back into the bedroom, she sat on the edge of the bed and dug deeper into the folder. She knew she was pushing her luck time-wise. She didn't linger over the formal notices from the Department of the Navy regarding Joe's brother:

THIS IS TO INFORM YOU THAT AS OF 27 APRIL 1943 YOUR BROTHER, SEAMAN JACKSON DOUGLAS SLATTERY, HAS BEEN DETERMINED ABSENT WITHOUT AUTHORIZATION FOR A PERIOD OF FIVE DAYS FROM HIS CURRENT POST AT THE US NAVAL TRAINING CENTER, SAN DIEGO, CALIFORNIA. IF YOU HAVE ANY INFORMATION AS TO HIS CURRENT WHEREABOUTS, YOU ARE INSTRUCTED TO CONTACT THE DEPARTMENT OF THE NAVY . . .

Nora didn't read any further. A second message from the Department of the Navy was a letter with the subject matter emblazoned along the top of the page: *NOTICE: SUSPENSION OF WAGES DUE TO UNAUTHORIZED ABSENCE.*

She found a news clipping from the April 23rd edition of the *San Diego Union-Tribune*. The headline read:

## EXPLOSION AT NAVAL TRAINING CENTER

### 1 Dead, 2 Wounded in Fiery Blast

### Sabotage "Not Ruled Out" as Investigation Pending

Nora quickly scanned the article, which mentioned Ray by name as the sole victim of the explosion. But it didn't give any other details about him. There was nothing about Joe's brother, Jackson.

Next, Nora found a piece of notebook paper with a hand-written list of names and phone numbers of naval personnel at the training center. Nora recognized a couple of the names from when she'd made inquiries about Ray. Joe had obviously gone through the same process as she had. There were also names of doctors and nurses at the nearby naval hospital.

Beneath the list, Nora uncovered a few five-by-seven photographs that Joe must have taken on the sly: pictures of the house and the garage apartment, and a photo of her he'd snapped near her bus stop. Her hair was limp and matted down from wearing her bandana all day at work, and she wore a dark green sweater with an embroidered flower above the right breast. It was unsettling to realize Joe had photographed her without her knowing. That sweater had been in the laundry basket since the weekend. So, Joe had been following her around since sometime last week. The photos confirmed her suspicions that he'd been watching the house—and her—for at least a few days before he'd knocked on her door and inquired about the apartment.

Nora knew she couldn't risk staying in the apartment much longer. But there were only a few documents left in the file—

including letters to Joe from his brother. The letters were still inside their envelopes—and sent to the Cole Street address in San Francisco. Jackson wrote on notebook paper in painstakingly neat script. None of the letters were dated, but Jackson wrote the day of the week along the top. In one letter, written on a Tuesday, Nora noticed a passage that was underlined in red—probably by Joe:

> *Our outfit has a new guy Ray who seems very nice. He just got out of the hospital. All the guys say he looks like me & he kind of does! He's a handsome devil, he is! Our CPO keeps getting the 2 of us mixed up.*

Another letter, dated Sunday, had another passage underlined in red:

> *I know you keep telling me I shouldn't lend money to anybody but I let Ray borrow five dollars. I think he's good for paying me back. He's a swell person. He's one of the only guys here who doesn't treat me like I'm stupid. I hope you can meet him on your next visit to the base.*

Nora was putting the letter back into its envelope when she heard a car. Getting to her feet, she knocked over the file folder. The papers and photos scattered across the floor.

"Shit!" she hissed, bolting into the living room. She anxiously glanced out the window.

Another false alarm.

Returning to the bedroom, she decided to pick up the mess, put everything back in the folder and get out of there. She wasn't absolutely sure what order the papers and photographs had been in. But she remembered Jane and Ray's photo was on top, and beneath that, the manila envelope with the photo of the San Diego newspaper article.

Retrieving the strewn papers and photos, Nora still couldn't figure out why documents about Joe's brother were in the same file with a photo of her and newspaper articles about the "Rosie" murders. How were they all connected?

Near the nightstand, she picked up the last stray piece of paper—Joe's list of navy contacts. As Nora straightened up, she glanced out the window. From this spot, she could look down into the ravine. She still had the file folder and the unsorted documents in her hand, but Nora stopped and stared out the window.

In the waning light of dusk, about halfway down the ravine, she spotted a patch of pink amid the trees and dense foliage.

Nora remembered Joe saying that the intruder last night had escaped into the ravine, and it had looked as if he'd been carrying something.

As quickly as she could, Nora tried to put the papers and photographs in order and then placed the file folder under the sweaters in the bottom drawer of the dresser. She made a perfunctory check of the living room to verify that she hadn't disturbed anything, and then she hurried down the narrow steps. Once outside, she shut the door behind her and gave the knob a twist to make sure it was locked.

Nora ran into the house through the back door. After grabbing a flashlight out of the kitchen drawer, she headed outside again.

At the ravine's edge, Nora hesitated. She wondered whether the brown Oxford flats she wore were okay for traipsing down into the wooded ravine. From where she stood, she couldn't spot the pink patch amid the trees and shrubs, but she knew the general direction to take to find it.

Starting down into the ravine, she felt a chill and realized she should have grabbed a sweater when she'd gone in for the flashlight. Pressing on, Nora navigated around the trees, shrubs and small gullies. The deeper she descended into the ravine, the darker and colder it became. She switched on the flashlight. The ground beneath her was muddy in spots, and she almost slipped a couple of times. She could smell the wet earth. Looking up for a moment, she felt as if she'd been swallowed up inside this huge crack in the ground.

In the distance, Nora thought she heard a car—and then maybe a door slamming. Was it another false alarm? She wasn't about to climb back up and check.

Halfway down the steep slope, she guessed the pink patch she'd noticed was someplace in the vicinity. Pausing for a few moments, she directed the flashlight so that its beam swept across the bushes and low-hanging branches around her. She spotted the pink patch on her right—only about thirty feet away.

Threading around shrubs and fallen brushwood, Nora headed toward what she now could tell was a piece of clothing. She had a pair of pajamas the same color, and Jane had a small coverlet that was pink. But what would anyone want with either of those?

She finally zeroed in on the object, which had gotten snagged on a thornbush. Nora shined the flashlight beam on the pink patch of fabric. It was her pink gingham apron.

When they'd searched the house for missing items last night, she should have checked her apron drawer in the kitchen.

Jane had been right about the strangler visiting their house.

He choked his victims with Nora's stockings and painted smiles on their faces with her lipstick. But that wasn't enough. Now he wanted to dress them in her aprons.

She heard a twig snap. Nora swiveled around to see a shadowy figure coming down toward her through the woods. Startled, she dropped the flashlight.

Squatting, she frantically retrieved it. She was about to scream when she heard his voice: "Nora?" he called. "Are you okay? What are you doing down here?"

Nora shined the light on Joe as he continued to move down the slope toward her. Dazed, she stared up at him. "Where's Chris?" she asked warily.

"He's okay. He's in the house," Joe explained. "He thought he was having an appendicitis attack earlier, and I drove him to the hospital. He said he'd left you a note. Didn't you see it?"

Nora shook her head.

"Well, whatever was giving him a stomachache turned out to be nothing. He's fine. We just got back a few minutes ago."

Nora realized she should thank him for taking Chris to the hospital, but she didn't say anything.

"What's going on?" Joe asked. "I looked out my bedroom window and saw someone down here with a flashlight. I thought last night's uninvited guest was making a return visit."

Nora stepped over toward the thornbush and carefully removed the pink apron.

"What's that?" she heard Joe ask.

"The 'uninvited guest' last night must have dropped this." Nora showed him the garment. "I have several aprons. I'll have to check if this is the only one he stole or if he took some others." Brushing past him, Nora started up the slope but stumbled over a tree root.

Joe went to grab her arm. She jerked it away.

"Nora, what's wrong?"

She glared at him and then turned and continued up through the trees and shrubs.

"Why would someone want to steal your aprons?" he asked, trailing after her. "I don't understand. Are you angry at me about something? What did I do?"

She stopped, turned and narrowed her eyes at him. "*What did you do?"* she snapped. "I don't know where to start, *Mr. Slattery!*"

"You've been through the apartment, haven't you? I was wondering why my door wasn't double-locked. I'd made sure to double-lock it before I left with Chris."

"I ran into your 'wife' on the bus yesterday," Nora said. "She told me that you paid her to put on that charade Saturday afternoon. She also said you were a *louse.* I'm inclined to agree with her."

"All right, I'm sorry about that," he sighed. "But I couldn't be honest with you at the time. I still didn't know you, Nora—"

"And I obviously don't know you, Joe," she interrupted. "But I'm catching on. I saw the file you have hidden in the dresser drawer."

Joe frowned at her. "What do you think you know?"

"I should ask you the same thing," Nora replied. "Your brother, *Jackson*—not Andy, but *Jackson*—didn't die at Guadalcanal, like you told me. He went on an unauthorized absence from his base in San Diego. And you seem to think Ray is somehow to blame. What I don't understand is why you thought it necessary to con your way into my home and bamboozle me and my children. I saw that photo you took of me at my bus stop *last week.* How long have you been following me around and watching our house?"

"I arrived in Seattle last Tuesday night," Joe admitted, his frown dissipating. "And I'm sorry I couldn't be more up front with you at the start. I'm especially sorry because—well, it's only been a few days, but I've come to like you and your kids a hell of a lot, Nora. You're good people—decent and kind. Yet I . . . I can't say the same about your brother . . ."

Nora's feet seemed to shift on the muddy ground. She put her hand against a tree to steady herself. "What do you mean?"

"You're right. I think Ray's to blame for what happened to Jackson."

Nora started shaking her head at him.

"Remember how I told you that Andy—I mean, *Jackson*, Andy was my nickname for my brother—remember how I said he seemed to attract unscrupulous types who took advantage of him? Well, I think Ray was one of those unscrupulous types. When you went into my file, did you read my brother's letters?"

"I glanced at a couple," Nora admitted.

"You should have checked all five of them, because he mentions Ray in each one. Jackson thought he'd found himself a new friend. But I could tell, it was more like Ray Shannon thought he'd found himself a sucker with the 'slow guy' who looked like him. I've spent most of my life trying to protect Jackson from people like your brother."

"You have no idea what you're talking about," Nora said.

"But I do. I checked Ray out—even before the explosion. I pulled a few strings and got into the naval hospital. I talked to a couple of nurses who took care of Ray after the accident that laid him up for a couple of weeks—"

"Shows what you know," Nora interrupted. "It was more like a month."

"No, he was laid up in the hospital for exactly two weeks, five days in Hawaii, two on a hospital ship and a week in San Diego," Joe said unequivocally. "It was just long enough for him to miss getting shipped out for active duty with his unit. The San Diego nurses told me the little spill Ray took was way too conveniently timed. They seemed to see right through him. But my poor brother couldn't. He was such a trusting guy. Ray took full advantage. He set Jackson up . . ."

Nora couldn't refute what Joe was saying about the accident, because she'd suspected it herself. Obviously, Ray had exaggerated the severity of his injuries—and lied to her about the length of his hospital stay. Why? To gain sympathy? She remembered how angry and hurt he'd become on his last night here, when she'd questioned him about his "accident." And this was after he'd begged her to help him with another scheme to avoid combat duty.

Nora couldn't look Joe in the eye. "So, Ray borrowed a few bucks from Jackson and didn't pay him back. I'm sorry. I'm really very sorry . . ." She turned and started to make her way up the ravine's slope again.

"My brother never would have deserted," Joe said, following close behind her. "I don't think he cleaned out his locker and took off during the chaos after that explosion. I think Ray's the one who cleaned out his locker."

Nora stopped to stare at Joe again. "Now you're not making any sense. Ray was killed in the explosion. The navy cleaned out his locker for him. You were here when they sent me Ray's things. I have his scorched dog tag, for God's sake."

"I'm saying Ray cleaned out *my brother's locker* and took off—after he'd set Jackson up to burn in that blast."

Bewildered, Nora shook her head again. "That's crazy . . ."

"Ray was supposed to be guarding a munitions dump that day."

"I know that," Nora said impatiently.

"Did you read my brother's letter from two days before the explosion?"

Nora shrugged. "I don't know. The letters weren't dated."

"The envelopes they're in are postmarked. Two days before the explosion, my brother wrote to me about how his new buddy Ray and he pretended to be each other for a night—so they could fool the other guys in their outfit. It was Ray's idea, of course. I spoke with one of the guys in their barracks. He said Ray did a terrific imitation of the way Jackson spoke. He even had Jackson's walk down pat—that same little bounce in his step. In his letter, my brother said the 'old switcheroo' hoax worked and completely fooled the other fellas. Ray and Jackson even swapped dog tags for good measure. That was Ray's idea, too."

Her mouth open, Nora stared at Joe.

"I got that letter the day after the explosion," Joe said. "It was like my brother telling me from the grave what had really happened. I knew right then that Jackson was dead. Their outfit was due to ship out for active duty soon. Your brother couldn't have another convenient accident. And he couldn't desert, not without having the navy searching high and low for his sorry ass. So, when he was assigned guard duty by that munitions site, he talked Jackson into taking his place for him—the 'old switcheroo' again, just for a couple of hours. My brother was probably happy to do it because he thought they were friends. I never met Ray. That's why I asked for that photo of him. But I could clearly picture this guy talking my brother into exchanging dog tags—for good measure . . ."

Nora thought of Ray's dog tag—and the scorch marks on it. The notion that he'd coaxed Joe's trusting brother into wearing the dog tag made her sick.

"I don't know exactly how Ray set off the blast," Joe went on. "One simple way is to stick a lit cigarette in a book of matches. Ray could have checked in with my brother while Jackson was filling in for him on guard duty. All he had to do is toss the little incendiary device into the ammunition dump and then go back to the barracks. The cigarette burns down and lights all the matches, and bang. But that's just a theory . . ."

"It's *all* just a theory," Nora argued. "You don't know if any of it is true . . ."

"Like I say, I know my brother, and he never would have deserted his post. How well do you know your brother, Nora? Is it possible that Ray would go to such great lengths to avoid combat duty?"

Of course. It was more than just *possible*. But she didn't dare answer him.

"The navy's investigators are pretty sure Ray set off that explosion," Joe said. "I got it on the q.t. from one of them. They're just not going public with it . . ."

"That's crazy. What are you talking about?"

"They looked into his previous accident, and then talked to some of the guys in his old outfit," Joe explained. "They figured he tried to set up another accident for himself so he could avoid shipping out for combat duty—only he fouled things up and got himself killed."

Nora frowned. "Then why didn't the navy say anything to me about it?"

"Like I told you, they don't want it going public. They don't want people knowing how easy it was for an enlisted man to commit an act of sabotage. If the news got out, it might give a few disgruntled sailors some ideas. So they're putting a lid on the whole thing . . ."

Nora couldn't believe it. The navy already knew what she'd suspected about Ray's death. And they'd chosen to keep it a secret.

"But the navy investigator I talked to," Joe went on, "I couldn't convince him that Ray switched places with my brother."

"Well, you're not going to convince me either," Nora said. She glanced up toward the edge of the ravine. She felt cold and grimy in the dark, wooded gully.

"Don't you see?" Joe said. "Ray practiced switching places with Jackson. He set him up. Then after the blast, during all the confusion, Ray cleaned out Jackson's locker and disappeared. It was the perfect getaway. Everyone would be looking for Jackson, not him—everyone but me."

"Listen," Nora said steadily. "I'm sorry your brother disappeared. I know you're angry and looking for someone to blame. But you can't expect me to believe this whole cockamamie story you've invented that makes Ray out to be some horrible, manipulative—"

"He's a killer, Nora!" Joe shouted. Tears filled his eyes. "You know what I hate most about that fucking son of a bitch brother of yours? It's because of him that I have nothing left of Andy. His body's burnt to a crisp, and Ray took all of Andy's possessions with him. He probably sold everything or threw it away as soon as he got out of San Diego. There's nothing. The navy won't be sending *me* anything . . ."

Unnerved, Nora stepped back. Her heart ached for Joe. But he was scaring her, too.

Wiping his eyes, Joe took a deep breath. "I'm sorry," he muttered. "I know Ray's your brother and you love him. But he's been lying to you—and not just about how long he was in the hospital or the extent of his injuries. Jane told me when he showed up on your doorstep, it was a big surprise. It was Friday, April ninth, right?"

Nora merely nodded. She had no idea what he was getting at.

"Ray said he'd arrived by bus in Seattle earlier that same day. But, Nora, I talked to some sailors in his outfit. He finagled a two-week leave and on the morning of April third, he caught the bus to Seattle. Ray had been here for five days before he dropped in on you . . ."

"I don't understand," Nora murmured.

"Remember you told me the other night that Ray left town the day before your friend Connie was killed? Well, I checked, and he didn't report back to the base until the seventeenth, two days after Connie Wiedrich's murder."

"That's nonsense. I saw him get on the—" Nora fell silent. She hadn't actually seen Ray board the bus.

"One of the guys in Ray's outfit saw him at the downtown bus station when he got in on the seventeenth," Joe explained. "The bus trip takes thirty-six hours, Nora. It doesn't take three days . . ."

"What are you getting at?" Nora asked.

"Don't you wonder what your brother did during those extra days he was in Seattle?" Joe asked. "Ray was here in town when Loretta Bryant was strangled—and when Connie was killed. But he went out of his way to hide that from you."

"So what? That doesn't mean anything!" she cried.

"It means a hell of a lot, and you know it," he said. "In my file, did you see the newspaper article about two riveters from Consolidated Aircraft in San Diego? They were roommates, both strangled and stabbed . . ."

Nora nodded. "Yes, I saw it. But you can't blame Ray for that because he was laid up in the hos—" She almost choked on the word.

"He was out of the hospital already, Nora," Joe said soberly. "A couple of days after the explosion, they called me to the base about Jackson's disappearance. I got a chance to talk to some of the guys in Ray's and Jackson's outfit; one of the sailors told me something—and an alarm went off inside me. He said that he noticed Ray had a kid's toy in his locker. It caught the sailor's eye because he'd given the same toy to Betty Rodenkirk, one of the girls murdered in San Diego. The sailor had dated Betty for a short while a few months before. He asked Ray where he'd gotten the toy, and they almost ended up in a fight about it. The sailor figured if Ray had a toy that had belonged to Betty, chances are he might have killed her. At the very least, he'd known her and refused to admit it. The sailor was ready to go to the cops about it, too."

"Well, why didn't he?" Nora asked defiantly. "If he was so certain my brother was a cold-blooded killer, why didn't he go to the police?"

"The sailor broke into Ray's locker the next morning, and the toy was gone. Ray denied ever having it. But the sailor was sure it was the same toy he'd given Betty. It was pretty unique—like one of those wind-up monkey dolls that play the cymbals, only it was a black Scottie dog."

Stunned, Nora stared at him. She started to back away. "No, you're lying. Jane told you about the toy Ray gave her, and now you're making all this up . . ."

"Jane has it now?" Joe asked. "Jane has the wind-up toy?"

"You're making this up!" Nora cried, still backing away. "You're lying! Ray didn't kill anybody. My brother's dead . . ." Her foot caught on something and Nora stumbled, the flashlight and the apron flying out of her hands. With a crash she fell into some bushes. Branches and twigs snapped under her weight. Flailing around helplessly, she scratched her face and hands, but was barely aware of it.

Joe grabbed Nora's arms and pulled her up and out of the bushes. "My God, are you okay?"

Nora started sobbing. "I won't listen to this! Do you understand? My brother's dead, and I won't let you—"

"Ray isn't dead, Nora!" he yelled, gripping her tighter. "He's here in Seattle. I think he killed Gloria Dunbar—"

"No!" Nora screamed. She looked up and saw they weren't far from the edge of the ravine. She just wanted to get away from him. "Leave me alone! God, please . . ."

"I've seen Ray watching the house," Joe said, his face inches from hers. "I recognized him—from the photos Jane showed me. I think he might have lightened up his hair. I don't know if he's figured out who I am yet. But he knows something's up. I'm pretty sure it was Ray who broke into the house last night . . ."

"I don't want to hear it!" Nora cried, still struggling to get free of him.

"*Let her go!*" someone shouted.

Nora looked up.

From the top of the ravine, Chris charged down toward them.

With Joe distracted for a second, Nora managed to break

free of him. She pushed him away—and then stumbled back. She grabbed hold of a tree to keep from falling again.

"Chris, wait!" Joe yelled. "Stop!"

But Chris barreled toward him like a crazy man. He lunged at Joe.

"No, honey, don't!" Nora cried, reaching out toward her son. "I'm not hurt! He didn't—"

But she was too late. Helplessly Nora watched as Chris plowed into him.

He knocked Joe off his feet, and for a moment, the two of them seemed to fly in the air. Then, with an awful thud, they landed. Joe remained there amid the smashed, broken underbrush, his face in the dirt. He didn't move at all.

But Chris kept toppling down the muddy, wooded slope—until he slammed into a tree.

Then he, too, became completely still.

# Chapter 34

*Wednesday*
*8:03 p.m.*

As she left the restaurant, twenty-three-year-old Dolores Oberlin—Dolly to her friends—buttoned up her coat. She'd hoped to get home before dark, but it was already too late for that. In the parking lot, Dolly hesitated before unlocking the driver's door of her parents' DeSoto. She glanced inside the car to make sure no one was hiding in the back seat.

Dolly was a riveter at Boeing. And like nearly every woman working an assembly-line war job in Seattle, she was on edge. The "Rosie" killer had murdered three women within the past month—and he was still out there.

No one was in the back seat of the car, thank goodness.

For the last couple of days, Dolly couldn't shake the feeling that somebody was watching her. This was based on nothing. It was just a feeling she'd gotten on the bus from work and late at night alone at home before she closed the blackout curtains. She'd admitted as much to her friend, Grace, over their shrimp cocktails during dinner.

Grace confessed she was scared, too—and she didn't even have a war job.

If Dolly didn't need to be up at four fifteen tomorrow morning, she would have asked her friend to sleep over tonight.

Unlocking the car door, she climbed into the front seat, started up the DeSoto and headed for home—more specifically, her parents' home. Dolly had grown up in that house—along with her older sister, Adele, who was now married and living in Wenatchee, and an older brother, Bill, now in the army, stationed in Biloxi. Dolly had moved back in with her parents last year.

She'd had one of those whirlwind wartime romances. Dolly had met Jim a week before Thanksgiving 1941, and she'd known right away he was the one. He'd enlisted in the Marines shortly after Pearl Harbor, and they'd decided to get married. They'd had exactly three weeks together as husband and wife before Jim left for basic training. Then Dolly had found out she was pregnant. Buying baby supplies had been a welcome distraction when she'd gotten the news that Jim was shipping out for active duty in the Philippines. But Dolly had lost the baby—a girl—after five months.

Not long after that, she'd moved back in with her parents. So much had changed for her in the brief period she'd been out of the house. But suddenly, everything was the same again. She was back in her old room, living with her mom and dad—except now she had a husband risking his life every day somewhere in the Pacific and she still ached over the loss of her child.

Dolly would have gone crazy if she hadn't gotten the riveter job at Boeing. It gave her a sense of purpose. She was doing something to help the war effort—and her husband.

Dolly didn't know any of the women who had been murdered. But her parents' house in Queen Anne was only a few blocks from where a riveter had been stabbed and strangled in her duplex almost three weeks ago. The police had claimed they'd shot and killed the man who had murdered her.

On Saturday, Dolly's parents had gone to Wenatchee to visit her sister. She'd driven them to the train station.

Then on Sunday afternoon, another war worker had been strangled. Obviously, the police hadn't shot and killed the strangler after all. Dolly had heard all about it at work on Monday. Her coworkers talked about stashing knives or knitting needles in their purses to defend themselves against this lunatic.

Neither Dolly nor her mother knitted, so Dolly carried an ice pick in her purse. But every time she reached into her bag, she worried she might stab herself. After she ended up poking a hole through her purse, Dolly put a cork over the ice pick's sharp tip. Then it dawned on her. What was she supposed to do if some maniac attacked her? Ask him to wait a minute while she took the cork off the ice pick? The cork kept falling off anyway—every time she jostled her purse.

Dolly turned into her parents' driveway and watched the headlights sweep over the large Tudor house, set back from the street, surrounded by trees and bushes. She'd left a few lights on inside the house.

Her parents were coming back tomorrow night—and not a minute too soon. She didn't feel safe by herself in the old house at night. She'd always felt that way. The house was too big for one person to be comfortable there. The unfinished cellar was a maze of rooms, all of them gloomy and foreboding. Growing up, her brother had a habit of forgetting his house keys, but he'd easily climb in through a basement window. For the past few nights alone in the house, Dolly kept remembering that. And because the house was set apart from their neighbors for privacy, Dolly figured she could scream and scream, and no one outside would ever hear her.

She'd admitted to Grace tonight that, since her parents' departure, she'd been sleeping with her brother's baseball bat at her bedside. What she hadn't told her friend was that she'd also belted back a couple of bourbon and waters each night before bed so she could relax and fall asleep. This morning, she'd gone to work with a slight hangover.

Dolly pulled up to the garage, which was attached to the house through a corridor off the kitchen. Her garage door key was on the same ring as the car keys, so Dolly had to turn off the ignition before she climbed out of the DeSoto to open the garage's carriage doors. She left the headlights on. It wasn't until she was outside that she noticed the light above the doors was out. She was certain she'd turned it on when she'd left the house earlier. A chill raced through her.

Nervously glancing around, she unlocked the carriage doors and swung them open. Then she hurried back into the DeSoto and started it up again. She steered the car into the garage. On either side of the parking area, they stored yard equipment, tools, bikes, boxes and various castoff junk—all of it briefly illuminated by the headlights. Then as she pulled in closer to the far wall, a large shadow swept over everything again.

Dolly switched off the headlights and the ignition. She was swallowed up in darkness only for a moment. Then she grabbed her purse and opened the car door. The DeSoto's interior light went on. A pull string to the garage light on the ceiling was directly overhead—just outside the driver's door. Dolly automatically reached up to pull it. But her hand grasped at the air.

Baffled, she glanced up. The pull string was out of reach, looped over a pipe that ran across the garage ceiling.

Dolly looked over at the light switch by the door into the house. That was when she noticed the door was open a crack. Something was wrong. She'd definitely locked that door before leaving for the restaurant tonight.

Her first instinct was to duck back into the car, lock herself inside and get out of there. The car door was still open. She shoved her purse straps up her arm and was about to climb behind the wheel.

But then one of the garage's carriage doors slammed shut.

Dolly froze. She saw a man in silhouette dart across the opening.

She let out a scream—just as he pulled shut the other door and rushed toward her.

His face was a blur. But Dolly saw something dangling from his hand. It was a nylon stocking.

Already halfway inside the car, she pressed the car horn on the steering wheel. The ear-splitting blare seemed to reverberate within the confines of the garage. He barely paused in his assault.

Lunging at her, he grabbed Dolly by the arm and threw her against the car, knocking the wind out of her. He pinned her against the DeSoto, his pelvis grinding against hers.

Dolly could smell alcohol on his breath. She screamed out again and desperately tried to fight him off.

But all at once he had the stocking around her neck. His movements were so fast and frantic that Dolly didn't even realize what was happening until he started choking her. She clawed at his hands—to no avail.

Then she remembered the ice pick in her purse.

With the stocking crushing her windpipe, she managed to push him away—just a few inches, but it was enough room for her to thrust her hand inside her bag. She prayed the cork had fallen off the sharp end of the ice pick. She felt the wooden handle and grasped it.

Everything started going black. All the nerves in her body felt on fire.

Dolly pulled the ice pick out of her purse and stabbed him in the stomach.

Her attacker let out a gasp. Spittle sprayed her face. He took a step back and made a grab for her hand.

But Dolly pivoted to one side, raised the ice pick and plunged it into the side of his head.

Blood spurted across the car windows as he staggered back and fell to the cement floor.

In shock, Dolly pried the nylon stocking from around her throat. She could breathe again, but she was hardly aware of it. She didn't even realize that she'd let go of her weapon.

All she could do was stare at the man, twitching and convulsing at her feet. The ice pick handle stuck out of his ear. A pool of blood bloomed under his head.

Dolly accidentally dropped her purse, and several items spilled out. Among them was a cork, which rolled across the dirty garage floor.

# Chapter 35

The soldier in the illustration was crouched down on his knees, covering his head with one hand and clinging to his rifle with the other. YOUR BLOOD CAN SAVE HIM! read the caption for the Red Cross poster on the wall of the hospital emergency room's waiting area.

For the last hour, Nora had been staring at the poster in front of her. She sat at the end of a long, double-sided wooden bench, the kind found in train depots—one of two benches in the big room. A nurses' station and reception desk were to her right. The gray and maroon tiled floor looked freshly waxed. There were only four other people in the waiting area: a woman with two toddlers, who were asleep on the bench, and another woman sitting alone, quietly crying.

It looked like a slow night in the emergency room. But then, the two nurses behind the counter suddenly got up and ran toward the street entrance. From the hallway, a doctor rushed out through a pair of swinging doors to join them. Nora heard some commotion and crying. She glanced over her shoulder to see an orderly pushing a gurney that held a bloody and battered young boy. The banged-up woman who hobbled alongside the semiconscious child was bleeding, too—and weeping hysterically. It looked like they'd been in a car accident. One of the nurses was trying to reassure her and keep her out of the doctor's way as they wheeled the boy into the hallway.

Suddenly, they were gone and it was quiet again, the double doors to the hallway swinging back and forth in their wake.

Nora sympathized with the poor, distraught mother. She'd been that woman just an hour ago when she'd arrived with Chris and the ambulance drivers. She was still covered in dirt, with scratch marks on her face and hands. She must have looked like she'd tumbled halfway down the ravine along with Chris and Joe.

She'd heard enough stories from Pete during his residency days about what a nuisance worried parents could be in the emergency room. And Chris hadn't wanted her in there while they'd cut him out of his clothes. So, Nora did her best to sit quietly and stay out of the doctors' and nurses' way. She also tried not to dwell on what Joe had told her in the ravine—about Ray. She'd seen those letters in Joe's file, and Joe had spotted Ray skulking around the house. Maybe her brother was still alive, but he couldn't be the madman who had been murdering female war workers. It was unthinkable. Yet Nora couldn't completely dismiss the notion. It was still there in the back of her mind, gnawing away at her as she waited for updates on how Chris and Joe were doing.

The last hour and a half were just a blur now.

But Nora remembered feeling swallowed up in the dark, damp ravine. She'd never been so panic-stricken. Fumbling around for the flashlight, she shined it on Chris—a broken, bleeding, lifeless-looking body slouched at the base of a huge evergreen. Nora wasn't sure she'd ever get that image out of her head.

Chris had been at least halfway down the ravine, and yet Nora didn't recall navigating through all the trees and undergrowth. She just knew that, by the time she reached him, Chris was conscious and trying in vain to get up. He had a bloody gash along his jawline and his face was riddled with scratches. Dirt and blood covered his torn clothes. From the impossibly bent angle of his right leg, Nora could tell it was broken. She told him to stay put while she got some help.

"Is Chris all right?" she heard Joe call out weakly from above them.

Nora had lost track of where Joe was. "We're down here!" she yelled. "His leg's broken!"

Chris clutched her arm. "Mom, I thought he was trying to kill you or something . . ."

Nora shook her head. "No, he didn't mean any harm at all. I'll explain later. Just don't try to move." Digging a handkerchief from her pants pocket, she gave it to him and guided his hand up to the cut along his jaw. "Hold that there, honey," she said.

Then Nora headed uphill, moving around the flashlight in search for Joe. She could hear twigs snapping and bushes rustling. She finally spotted Joe making his way down the slope toward her. He was a mess, his clothes torn and filthy. His forehead was badly cut with blood running down the side of his face and neck—under his shirt collar.

"God, Joe, I'm so sorry," Nora said, reaching out to him.

Joe put his hand on her shoulder. "I'm sorry, too," he said. "I'm a little wobbly right now. I don't know if I can make it back up the hill. If you take me to Chris, I'll keep him company while you call for help."

"Please," Nora whispered. "Don't tell him about Ray. I

promise, we'll figure this out. Only right now, I don't want Chris to know."

"Don't worry, I won't say anything," Joe replied under his breath.

"I'm the last one who should be asking you for any favors right now," she said as they headed down the ravine together. "Why are you being so nice to me?"

"I told you—I like you, Nora. I like your family."

Nora asked Joe for yet another favor before leaving him with Chris. She thought it would be easier if they all stuck to the story that Joe and Chris had fallen into the ravine while playing football in the backyard. Explaining anything close to the truth to the doctors might be too complicated.

She gave Joe the flashlight so that the medics or the firemen—whoever arrived first—could spot them in the darkness.

Nora glanced back at Joe and Chris as she started up the densely wooded hill.

Leaning against the tree trunk and each other, they looked like two battered, weary soldiers who had barely survived a battle. Joe directed the flashlight's beam at her so that she could find her way up to the ravine's edge.

It took two ambulances, a fire truck and a police car ten minutes to arrive—and then another twenty minutes for the emergency crew to bring Chris up on a stretcher. Joe made it up the ravine on foot—with the help of one of the emergency crew members. The sirens and flashing lights had attracted a few neighbors, who stood around the vehicles for a better look at what was happening. Considering how far Chris and Joe had fallen down the ravine and how banged up they were, the "football accident" cover story seemed rather feeble. But none of the medics or firemen questioned it. Nora rode in the back of the ambulance with Chris. The other ambulance crew took Joe.

According to the doctor, it was a miracle that Chris and Joe hadn't sustained more severe injuries.

A skinny, fortyish nurse with brassy red hair had taken pity on Nora. Her name was Ida, and she'd given Nora updates on Chris and Joe. Chris had multiple cuts, three of which required stitches—including the gash along his jaw. He'd also sprained his left ankle and his right arm and wrist. But Chris's most severe injury was a displaced fractured fibula in his right leg. The emergency room staff were moving the pieces of broken bone back into place before immobilizing the leg with a temporary splint. There was a possibility he'd require surgery.

In comparison, Joe had gotten off easily with a few bruised ribs. The doctor had also sewn up the laceration in his forehead with six stitches.

Nora glanced at her wristwatch, stood up and went to get a drink from the water fountain by the nurses' station. She sipped her water and was patting dry her mouth with the back of her hand when she overheard one of the nurses talking.

"Ida, you'll never guess what's happened . . ."

"You're right, I probably won't," Ida replied, sounding uninterested.

Passing the counter again, Nora spied the other nurse—young, petite and blonde. She must have come in from another doorway to the nurse's station. She seemed out of breath. "They got the strangler!" she announced.

Nora stopped and stared at them. Neither Ida nor the other nurse seemed to notice her.

"What are you talking about?" Ida whispered.

"That maniac who's been murdering assembly-line workers from the war plants—you know, the 'Rosie' killer," the young nurse explained. "He attacked a girl in Queen Anne tonight, and she stabbed him with an ice pick—right in the ear canal. The police just brought him into the morgue downstairs."

"Well, good riddance to bad rubbish," Ida said.

Nora stood there, frozen. "Do they know his name?" she heard herself ask anxiously. "Do they have any idea who he was?"

Ida and the other nurse gaped at her.

Nora's first thought was that she'd need to brace her children for the headlines in tomorrow's newspapers—making their uncle out to be a sadistic killer.

"Please, I really need to know," Nora said, approaching the counter. She put a hand on the edge of it to steady herself. "I . . . I was friends with one of the girls who was killed. I worked with her at Boeing. Are they sure it's the Rosie killer? Do the police know his name?"

Ida gave her coworker a nod. "Go ahead and tell her, Jeannie. She'll hear about it soon enough anyway." Then she turned to Nora. "We work pretty closely with the cops around here. They let us in on everything . . ."

The younger nurse looked at Nora. "Well, the guy tried to strangle this gal with a nylon stocking, and she's a riveter at Boeing," said the nurse. "So Frank—he's my friend on the force—Frank said they're pretty sure they've got the right guy on the slab downstairs."

"Do they know his name?" Nora pressed.

"Yeah, sure, Frank told me . . ." The nurse made a face, wincing as if she couldn't remember. "It's on the tip of my tongue . . ."

*Was it Raymond Shannon?* Nora wanted to ask. But she bit her lip and remained silent.

"Ronald Lapp!" the nurse exclaimed, obviously proud of herself for recalling his name. "Frank said this Lapp fella was about as low as they go. He was a real bad guy, a drifter—in and out of jail most of his life. The police were already looking for him. He was wanted for murder. He strangled a woman in Portland last year, a clerk at a five-and-dime."

"The woman he tried to strangle tonight, is she okay?" Nora

needed to know before she could feel relieved that it was all over.

"She's shook up, but she'll be okay—according to my friend," the nurse answered.

Nora let out a long sigh and nodded. "Thank you," she said.

But when she returned to her spot on the bench, she really didn't feel any better. She was still uncertain about her son's injuries.

And this news about the Rosie killer didn't explain away what Joe had told her about her brother. Ray was still alive, lurking around the house at night. And Ray had given Jane that wind-up toy that had belonged to a murdered riveter down in San Diego.

Nora wondered about the drifter on the slab down in the morgue. Could it be that the police had the wrong "killer" again?

Overwhelmed and depleted, Nora came home from the hospital by taxi.

As the cab backed out of the driveway, she stood and stared at the dark, empty house. Instead of heading inside, she walked slowly down the driveway.

She glanced toward the ravine and noticed a pink patch by the edge. The pink gingham apron had been left behind in all the chaos. Walking across the lawn, she picked up the apron and then stared down at the shadowy, wooded ravine for a moment.

She would be alone in the house tonight. She still didn't know for sure how serious Chris's leg injury was.

"We'll know more in the morning, after the orthopedic specialist examines him," the doctor had told her. "We're going to keep Chris overnight to make sure he's stable and hasn't suffered a concussion. In fact, you can count on him being here for at least two or three more days. The best thing you can do right now is to go home and get some sleep. Visiting hours are almost over."

Nora had gotten a quick "good night" in to Chris before they'd wheeled him into his semiprivate room. But he'd been groggy from the pain medication they'd given him and barely responded.

She'd also caught a few minutes alone with Joe in the examining room. The doctor wanted to keep him under observation for at least another hour—to make certain he hadn't suffered a concussion. Nora had found Joe sitting on the examining table, buttoning up his shirt. The attending nurse had gone to fetch something. Joe had had a big adhesive bandage on one side of his forehead.

"The nurses here thought it was pretty bizarre we were playing football when we took that half-gainer down the ravine," Joe had whispered to her. "After all, I'd just brought Chris in here a couple of hours ago, claiming his appendix was about to burst. Then again, teenage boys have a way of bouncing back, don't they?"

Nora had thanked him again and apologized. She'd told him about Ronald Lapp, down in the morgue. But Joe had already heard the story from one of the nurses. Apparently, word about it had gotten around the hospital pretty quickly.

"You and I know they don't have the right guy," Joe had said under his breath. "Yeah, he tried to attack a riveter, and was wanted for another murder last year. The police figure they've hit the jackpot this time. But I think he was a copycat. The cops will figure it out when another assembly-line worker gets strangled. And I'm afraid it'll be on our conscience when that happens. We need to talk to the cops about your brother . . ."

Nora had just nodded. She hadn't even tried to argue with him. In her gut, she'd had a feeling he was right. Ronald Lapp hadn't stolen her lipstick and her nylons. And Ronald Lapp hadn't tried to steal her apron last night.

Nora had volunteered to stay with Joe at the hospital until they released him, but Joe had insisted she go home, lock her doors and get some rest. "See you in a couple of hours," he'd said with a tired smile. "Or maybe not. If you're sleeping, I'll try to be quiet."

Now, as she stared down into the ravine, Nora clutched the apron her brother had stolen from her kitchen.

It had been awful enough thinking Ray had caused that deadly explosion in an effort to avoid combat duty. She was almost relieved to hear from Joe that the navy investigators had already figured out Ray had been responsible for the blast. And she was grateful they'd decided to keep it a secret. No one needed to know. She might have been able to forgive Ray, assuming he'd died when his plan had gone horribly wrong.

But his plan hadn't gone wrong. Everything had gone off as Ray had wanted it to. He'd set up Joe's poor brother, killing him. And Jackson Slattery hadn't even been the first person he'd murdered. There had been the two war workers in San Diego. Then later, the three women who worked on the war plant assembly lines here in Seattle. Nora felt sick when she thought of all the dead—and the ripple effect with Roger and the friends and families of all the victims.

Joe had been right. If or when Ray murdered again, the police would realize they had the wrong killer with Ronald Lapp. She would have to tell the authorities about her brother.

She couldn't help thinking about the ripple effect again—and her own family. Chris and Jane would die of shame. Their beloved uncle was a gutless saboteur and a murderer. It would haunt them for the rest of their lives.

More than anything, Nora wished her brother really were dead.

She felt responsible. After all, she'd raised him. It was because of her that Ray had become the monster he was. He'd have been the first one to say so, too. She'd abandoned him when he was eleven years old. He'd never forgiven her for that. Maybe things would have been different if he'd come to live with her and Pete. She should have tried harder to make that work.

How Ray must have loathed her—long before she'd refused to help him in his scheme to avoid shipping out to the Pacific. He'd started killing before showing up at her door. And his victims were women like her, one of them even a friend of hers. He'd stolen Nora's nylons and lipstick while staying with her. He wanted to *involve* her in his killings. Hell, he wanted to rub her nose in what he was doing.

She remembered Ray telling her that Chris might have resented her taking a wartime job. But Ray was the one who had resented it. He'd gone to such great lengths to avoid combat duty. Who else but a coward would take out his frustrations on women doing their part for the war effort? Who else would want to put these "heroines of the home front" back into the kitchen—with their aprons and permanent smiles painted on their faces?

Nora turned and walked across the lawn to the house. Slinging the apron over her arm, she dug the housekey out of her purse and started to unlock the back door. But then she realized the door was already unlocked. Had she left it that way? Probably.

She stepped inside the kitchen and set the apron on the counter. She switched on the light and stood there for a moment, listening. The house was so quiet. Yet Nora couldn't help feeling as if she weren't alone.

"Ray?" she called out warily. But there was no answer.

She looked over at the basement door, open a crack.

Taking a deep breath, she stepped over to the door, pulled it open farther and switched on the light at the top of the basement stairs. Nora crept halfway down the steps and glanced around the shadowy cellar—the clothes hanging on the wash line, the washing machine, Pete's workbench and the octopus-style furnace. "Ray?" she called out again, breaking the silence.

No answer.

Nora retreated upstairs and headed into the front hallway. She stopped at the bottom of the stairs, switched on the second-floor hallway light and gazed up the steps. She almost expected to hear the floorboards creaking—or perhaps Jane's Scottie dog's cymbals going *ding, ding, ding*. Maybe Ray would announce his presence by snickering. That had been how she'd usually found him when they'd played hide-and-seek as kids. He'd always had a tough time stifling his laughter whenever he'd fooled her.

She wasn't scared so much as tormented—and disgusted at the notion that her brother was alive and watching her.

After setting up Joe's brother to perish in that explosion, Ray could have gone anywhere—maybe to the East Coast or to the South, someplace where no one would recognize him. But he'd risked coming back to Seattle, so he could kill again.

Nora had a feeling the San Diego murders were unplanned, the result of rage. But he must have come to Seattle last month intending to kill more female assembly-line workers. Otherwise, he wouldn't have kept her in the dark about when he'd first arrived in town in April. And after "dying," he'd come back to Seattle. For the murders to really matter, Ray needed her to feel their full impact. He murdered women in Seattle because she was there.

And he was going to keep killing until she stopped him.

The phone rang, giving her a start.

Her first thought was that something had happened to Chris, and the hospital was calling. Maybe he'd had a concussion after all, and now they couldn't wake him up.

She grabbed the receiver. "Hello?"

"Nora? Oh, thank God. Honey, where have you been?"

"Fran?"

"I've been calling all night," her friend said. "I was about to phone the police and ask them to check the house. Is everything okay?"

"Yes—well, no," she said. "I was at the hospital. Chris had an accident—"

"Oh, no, what happened? Is he going to be okay?"

Leaning against the wall, Nora rubbed her forehead. "He's in stable condition, but he broke his leg and got banged up pretty badly. They're keeping him at the hospital for another couple of nights. He and our new tenant were playing football in the backyard and . . . well, they started roughhousing, and both of them fell into the ravine."

"Oh, honey, I'm so sorry. What about the other fella? Is he all right?"

"Some cuts and bruises, but he should be okay. I expect him back in an hour or so."

"Good, you won't be alone there too much longer," Fran said soberly.

Nora glanced at her wristwatch. "Shouldn't you be in bed? What's going on? Why were you trying to get ahold of me?"

"Well, I had a little scare here, too," Fran explained. "Someone broke in earlier tonight, while I was alone in the house, taking a shower."

"Oh, no," Nora whispered. "Oh, God—"

"I'm okay," Fran assured her. "A neighbor came by and scared the guy away. The police were here. And Marty's here now . . ."

"Oh, Fran, I'm so sorry." Just as she said it, Nora realized it sounded more like an apology than an expression of sympathy.

Fran let out an uncomfortable laugh. "Well, it's not your fault."

But it was her fault. She couldn't believe that Ray had gone after Fran. And yet, why was she surprised?

She listened as Fran told her about someone slashing the tires when Marty had taken the car to town to buy flowers. Maybe it was a coincidence, maybe not. Whoever had broken into the house had draped Fran's work pants on the newel post and left behind an apron on her kitchen counter. "I couldn't help thinking he was getting everything ready so he could wrap up quickly after he'd finished me off," Fran said. "But the thing is—and I don't want to alarm you—"

"As if I weren't already alarmed," Nora said. "Fran, this is horrible . . ."

"Well, it's about to get worse. The apron he left on the counter wasn't mine. I think it's yours, honey. It has a daisy pattern on it. I remembered, you put it on to wash the dishes at the dinner party. I'm almost certain it's the same one . . ."

Nora swallowed hard. Stretching the phone cord nearly to its limit, she stepped into the kitchen and checked the drawer where she kept her aprons. They were all missing from the drawer—except, of course, for the dirt-stained pink gingham apron her brother had dropped when he'd made his escape down the ravine last night.

"Nora? Honey, are you there?"

She kept staring at the empty drawer. "Are you sure you're all right, Fran? You're safe?"

"Yes, like I said, Marty's here. But I don't think the police took me very seriously. I can't say I blame them. I'm sure they're getting a dozen calls like mine every night now. Everyone's in a panic. And I'm pretty long in the tooth compared to the other strangler victims. So, why would he be going after me, right? But that pair of work pants didn't magically move itself—and then there's this apron. Am I crazy? Is this your apron with the daisies on it?"

Nora hesitated.

"I asked the police if they wanted to take it as evidence, and the cop told me to hold on to it. Like I said, he didn't seem to take me too seriously . . ."

Nora closed the drawer. "Well, that . . . that must be another apron," she said, cringing at her lie, "because I'm looking at my daisy-patterned apron right now. It's here. But—I think the police are right, Fran. You should hold on to that apron just in case . . ."

She'd never told Fran about her missing nylons and lipstick because she'd been worried Chris might have taken them. Now she was protecting her brother—even after he'd broken into Fran's house and tried to murder her. Nora had always been Ray's "little mother" and his protector. And old habits die hard.

She remembered Fran mentioning that Ray had asked for her address at the dinner party—supposedly so that he could keep in touch with Marty. Even as far back as the party, Ray had been planning to kill her. He'd sat at the dinner table with Nora's two friends, plotting how he would strangle them.

Nora was pretty certain Fran would be safe tonight. Ray wasn't about to make another attempt on her life, not when Marty was there. Ray was too much of a coward for that.

He was far more likely to come here tonight—if it was true what Joe had said about Ray watching the house.

After saying goodbye to Fran and hanging up, Nora got a pencil and a piece of paper. She sat down at the kitchen table and wrote a note:

*Ray, I know it's you.*

Then Nora set down the pencil and started to cry.

# Chapter 36

The 1936 Chrysler Airflow coupe he drove was registered to Sidney Garrick, 29, of Bakersfield. That same name was on the driver's license in his wallet. It said on the license that Sidney's hair was blond. That was the only thing he'd needed to change. He'd dyed his hair to match the license description. He and Sidney were roughly around the same age, height and weight. And they both had blue eyes.

Hitchhiking outside San Bernardino, he'd caught a ride from Sidney. In the passenger seat on the way to Nevada, he'd learned that they'd had other things in common: a lack of family, and they'd both been between jobs. Sidney had had no ties. The military hadn't even wanted him because he had asthma.

He'd been in the car with Sidney for a little over three hours when he'd realized no one was looking for Sidney Garrick, and no one would miss him. That had been two weeks ago.

He'd buried Sidney in the desert outside Las Vegas.

Now they were both dead. Yet another thing he had in common with Sidney.

Ray had been living off the one hundred and seventy dollars he'd found in Sidney's wallet—along with some money and jewelry he'd stolen from Gloria Dunbar. Those Rosie the Riveters were never wealthy, but they were usually good for a week's worth of groceries. He always left a few bills in their purses so that the cops—and the press—would know it wasn't money that he was after.

He'd been staying at a cheap hotel in North Seattle, getting by pretty well under his new identity. Ray had always had a talent for getting by between jobs. Maybe that was why he'd never felt motivated to stick with one job for too long. Plus, he got a certain thrill from conning people out of money. And he wasn't past selling himself for sex, rolling the occasional drunk, or house-breaking. He'd been "getting by" like that since his teenage years in Chicago. He'd been arrested a few times, but the stupid cops could never make any of the charges stick.

Ray's background as a petty criminal had been perfect training for his ultimate mission in life, the thing that would make him famous. There was a war going on in Europe and the Pacific. Yet who had made headlines in all of the Seattle newspapers the day before yesterday? Raymond Shannon, that was who—except the papers didn't know his name yet.

He'd hoped to make tomorrow's headlines, too—with the murder of a middle-aged widow and Boeing riveter, Fran DeLuca. That really would have unhinged everyone, because then they'd have realized he wasn't only going after young women. No female working on the assembly line would feel safe. He'd have the whole goddamn city afraid of him.

The last month or so had been a wild ride for him. He'd never felt more important and powerful in all his life.

But things didn't always go his way. Ray had thought he'd

covered all his bases earlier tonight when he'd slashed the tires of the car driven by Fran's one-eyed basket case of a son. Ray had figured no one would be coming to Fran's rescue. But then that nosy neighbor had come by and started banging on the door. What was it with these pain-in-the-ass old neighbors? The woman near Chris's school, Sally What's-Her-Name, had gotten away thanks to the old geezer in the apartment down the hall from her, and Connie's old biddy downstairs neighbor had almost ruined everything for him, tapping on her ceiling with a mop or broomstick the whole time he'd been strangling Connie.

He had assumed Fran's neighbor would be back. So, Ray had decided to abort tonight's mission. He could have easily returned Fran's pants to her bedroom and retrieved Nora's apron from the kitchen counter where he'd left it. No one would have been the wiser that he'd paid Fran a visit. But he'd felt compelled to leave a calling card before hustling out of there. He'd almost wanted Fran to recognize the apron—and tell Nora about it.

He wondered if Nora had figured out by now that her nylons and a tube of her Scarlet Kiss lipstick were missing. Obviously, she had no way of knowing they'd been used in the last two murders. It had occurred to him after killing Gloria Dunbar that maybe the next "Rosie" wouldn't own an apron or keep one in plain sight. So, he'd gotten the idea to steal Nora's aprons and use them in his killings.

And damn it to hell, typical, some old coot civil defense warden on Nora's block had spotted him in the house. Ray had almost broken his own neck escaping down the ravine. That had been a close call.

He wondered if the police might eventually trace the lipstick, nylons or aprons to his big sister. But Ray Shannon was officially dead. So, what would they think?

There were a lot of advantages to being dead.

The idea had first come to him when he'd had a run-in with one of the other sailors in his outfit, Dan Millsap. Ray had had no idea that the guy had dated Betty Rodenkirk at one time. The bitch must have really gotten around. Ray had picked up her roommate—or maybe, technically, it had been the other way around, because the other girl had taken him back to their apartment. Betty had been there—in her work pants, acting like she kept the world safe from tyranny because she knew how to work a stupid rivet gun. Making conversation, Ray had talked about his old outfit and mentioned having seriously in-jured himself in a fall. She'd started giving him shit about his "convenient accident" happening right before his unit had shipped out. She'd heard that a lot of the guys in his old outfit had been killed. She'd started ridiculing him—even worse than those suspicious bitch-nurses at the hospital. She'd really ticked him off.

Well, more than just *ticked him off*. In fact, he'd gone a little crazy and punched her in the face. The roommate had pitched a fit, and he'd had to shut her up. Then one thing had led to an-other.

When he'd finished, he stole close to forty dollars from their purses, a few pieces of jewelry and the wind-up Scottie toy. And he'd felt strangely elated.

How was he to know that Dan Millsap had given Betty the cymbal-playing Scottie? After they'd scuffled about it, Dan had threatened to go to the cops.

Ray had known his luck was running out. And his outfit had been due to ship out to some combat zone soon—probably somewhere around the Philippines. That was when Ray had re-alized he'd be better off dead.

The funny thing about it was that he'd kind of liked the dummy. Jackson Slattery had been a sweet, simple guy who had looked up to him. He'd been like a puppy dog. Such an easy mark. A part of Ray had really regretted setting him up to die like that. But it had come down to either him or the dummy. And who would miss him? Jackson used to yap on and on about a big brother somewhere, but he'd had no other family or friends.

It had been a smart move on his part, "dying" like that.

Ray had decided tonight that, within a week or so, Sidney Garrick would have to take another road trip. It was almost time to leave Seattle. He knew, once again, he'd be pushing his luck if he stayed put. He had good instincts that way. In the meantime, he'd already targeted an attractive young mother who bore a striking resemblance to a WAVE in one of the more popular recruitment posters. She was another riveter at Boeing. Then he might give Fran a second try before leaving town.

But he would miss checking in on Nora. He was on his way to the house now.

"Ray" might have died, but he wanted to keep that connection to his sister alive. Her kids adored him. But it went beyond any of that sentimental garbage. If he continued his campaign somewhere else, it simply wouldn't be the same, because he wouldn't be killing on Nora's turf. It wouldn't affect her at all.

He wasn't too happy that she'd rented out the garage apartment to some stranger. The last thing Ray needed was another pair of eyes possibly spotting him whenever he checked in on Nora and the kids. Because of the coverage from all the trees, along the top of the ravine was the best place for watching what went on inside the house. But with that guy above the garage, Ray had to be extra cautious when spying on Nora from the ravine's edge.

Ray had a weird feeling about the guy.

At the same time, the new tenant was good-looking, and Ray kind of hoped Nora would end up in bed with him. It would be nice to see his Goody Two-Shoes sister knocked down a moral peg or two. Ray never could stand his brother-in-law, Pete. And anything contributing to the erosion of Nora's marriage was fine with him. In his most recent vigils, Ray had hoped to catch Nora and her new tenant in the act. But no such luck yet.

Ray switched off his headlights as he cruised by the house. With the blackout curtains and the late hour, at first glance, it looked like no one was home—in either the house or the garage apartment. But then Ray noticed something in the moonlight, something hanging on the mailbox by the front door.

Driving farther down the block, he parked and then climbed out of Sidney's car. With no sign of the stupid civil defense warden, Ray walked back toward the house. Approaching the front door, he realized what was draped from the latch on the mailbox. It was a pair of women's work pants.

He stopped dead.

He of all people should have recognized what they were—even from far away.

All he could think was that someone had murdered his sister, some copycat "Rosie" killer.

From halfway up the front walk, Ray could see the door was open slightly. A faint light escaped through the gap.

He took a few steps closer to the front stoop and spotted a piece of paper pinned to the work pants. But it wasn't until he stepped up to the door that he could read the note:

*Ray, I know it's you.*

He let out a stunned little laugh. It felt as if Nora had just slapped him in the face.

But he couldn't help smiling. He dared to push the door open farther, and the hinges squeaked.

"The kids aren't home, Ray," he heard his sister say from

within the dimly lit house. "The man in the garage apartment is gone, too. It's only you and me."

Stepping into the front hall, Ray spotted her sitting in a cushioned chair in the darkened living room. She wore a blouse and a pair of slacks. He noticed scratch marks on her face. "You look a little beat-up," he said.

She said nothing for a moment and then finally cleared her throat. "Maybe you should bring my pants inside for now and shut the door before someone notices. I'm sure you don't want my pants out there—not until the right time."

Chuckling, Ray retrieved the work pants, which, he realized on closer inspection, were filthy. It was as if she'd been rolling around in the dirt or something. He draped them over the newel post, then wiped the dirt off his hands and closed the front door.

He stepped back into the living room and smiled at her. "Aren't you glad to see me?" he asked. "How do you like me with blond hair?"

She said nothing.

"Aren't you at least happy I'm alive?"

"No," she whispered, not moving from the chair. "No, Ray, I'm sick about it."

Folding his arms, he leaned against the living room's arched entryway. "How long have you known about me?"

"Someone told me earlier tonight."

"Who?" he asked, his posture straightening.

"I didn't want to believe it, but then it all started to make sense." She shook her head at him. "God, Ray, how could you?"

"Who did you talk to, Nora?" he pressed. "What exactly do you think you know?"

She didn't say anything for a moment—or change positions in the easy chair. Ray couldn't see her hands. They were squeezed between her thighs—as if she were trying to fight off a chill. Her whole body seemed clenched. She glanced down toward the carpet. "You know what happened to Roger Tallant, don't you?" she asked quietly.

Ray shrugged. "Just wasn't his night. No one's going to miss him."

"But you're wrong, Ray. He had friends. All your victims had friends and families who miss them. They're devastated. You've hurt so many people—"

"You're breaking my heart," he sighed. He leaned against the living room entry again. "You don't know much. You've just been guessing. Your friend, Fran, probably called you tonight. Did her son spot me on Empire Way? I had a feeling old Marty might have caught a glimpse of me with his one working eye."

"You left my apron behind at Fran's house."

"But they don't know anything, do they?"

Nora slowly shook her head.

Ray snickered. "I didn't think so. And you wouldn't want her to know anything, would you?"

She didn't answer.

"Of course, you wouldn't," he said. "You wouldn't want anyone knowing what your kid brother has done. I'd be flattered by your loyalty. But I know it's your family and your reputation you're protecting—not me."

Again, she just stared at him. Her silence was beginning to irritate him.

"So, who did you talk to earlier tonight?" Ray asked once again. "Who else besides Fran? Who's this person who knows so much?"

He couldn't have any loose ends. He was sure Nora wouldn't tell anyone about him, because she had everything to lose. But somebody else knew he was alive. And what was keeping that person from going to the cops? Ray knew, even if he left town tonight, wherever he went, he'd constantly be looking over his shoulder. He had to nip this "loose end" in the bud.

"It wasn't just your apron at Fran's house that tipped you off," he said, sitting down across from her in a hardback chair. "What little bits of information have you pieced together? It can't be much. Who else knows about me?"

"I know pretty much everything," Nora said with regret, "more than I want to know, Ray. The only thing I wonder about is how you picked the poor women you've killed. I know you murdered Connie and went after Fran tonight because they were my friends. But the others . . ."

"It's simple," he said—almost boastfully. "I just wait outside the plant at quitting time—along with the rest of the wives and 4-F husbands and boyfriends. The guards don't bug us. I pick a 'Rosie' "—he stopped to smirk at his pun—"and then I take the same bus as her and follow her home. I stake her place out and get to know her routine."

"And then you kill her," Nora said.

He nodded and smiled. "What else are you wondering about? Don't you want to know how I managed to rise from the dead?"

"I already figured out how you deceived Jackson Slattery into switching places with you," she replied.

Ray was dumbstruck for a moment. Nora knew a hell of a lot more than he thought. But then he chuckled. "Well, don't you want to hear how I blew up that munitions dump? It was pretty ingenious . . ."

But she was shaking her head. "I don't care, Ray. I already have a pretty good idea. And anything you say isn't going to impress me. I won't sit here and listen to you brag about how you committed sabotage and killed an innocent man. You disgust me."

"The guy was a nobody—a borderline moron. No one's going to miss him."

"He had a brother," Nora said. "And he misses him."

"The brother, shit," Ray muttered. "You talked to the dummy's brother. Where is he? How did he get ahold of you?"

"What are you going to do, Ray? Kill him, too—after you've killed me?"

He shifted around in the chair, casually slinging one leg over the armrest. "I don't have to kill you, Nora," he said with confidence. "Besides, I want you alive. I want you to feel the brunt of every single thing I do and every life I take. You're as responsible for these murders as I am. And you're never going to tell anyone about me. There might have been a time you'd have kept quiet to protect me. But like I say, it's not about me anymore. You won't say anything because you'd die of shame if word got out about me. It would ruin you and your precious family. You're thinking of Chris and Jane. They'd never live it down. Imagine what those 'patriotic' vandals would do to your place. They'd burn the goddamn house to the ground and dance around the cinders. And if Pete makes it back from the war, no one will want a doctor whose brother-in-law is a saboteur and the 'Rosie' killer." Ray shook his head and chuckled. "No, you won't breathe a word about me . . ."

He suddenly sat up. "But the dummy's brother, that's another story. Where is he? Where can I find him?"

She didn't answer. She just sat there, coiled up in the chair with her hands buried between her thighs.

Ray took a deep breath. "Okay, listen. I already know his name. It's John or Jim Slattery. Just tell me where he is—and if he's talked to anyone else. You do that, and I promise to leave your friend Fran alone. I won't lay a finger on another 'Rosie.' I'll disappear. I'll leave town and you'll never see me again. No one else will know about me. I'll stay dead. Our secret will be safe. Just tell me where he is, so I can shut him up. Then you won't have to worry about me again."

"You act like you're doing me a big favor," she said.

"I am. You have so much more to lose than I do. Now, where is this guy? His brother said he was in San Francisco. Is he still there, or did he come to Seattle looking for me?"

She frowned. "You know, Mom's mental illness was never this bad. She never hurt anyone except herself. Your insanity is so much more—evil and *malignant*."

Her words were like another slap. But he swallowed hard and shook his head. "Sticks and stones, sis. Tell me where I can find Slattery's brother."

"You really are insane, Ray—not just because of the murders, but because you're crazy enough to believe I'd allow you to kill one more human being in some kind of screwed-up bargain to protect my reputation. My God . . ."

He got to his feet. "I could easily kill you."

"Go ahead, Ray . . ."

"So, when Jane comes home—and Chris—they'll find you. I think there's still another apron in your kitchen, one that wasn't in the drawer. And I'll just hang those pants out where you left them."

She gazed up at him. "Go ahead . . ."

"Only Chris and Jane won't be able to tell the police what they found, because I'll fucking kill them, too. They'll have to tell Pete in North Africa that his wife and kids have been slaughtered."

She didn't even flinch.

She must have seen through his bluff about killing his nephew and niece. It was just a threat. Once she was dead, there would be no point in killing Chris and Jane, too. He wouldn't risk sticking around for that. Nora wasn't stupid. She knew the worst he could do was kill her—and she seemed ready to let him do his worst.

Standing in front of her, Ray reached into his jacket pocket and pulled out a nylon stocking. "This was meant for your friend tonight," he whispered. Dangling the sheer stocking above her head, he let it brush against her neck and cheek. "Just tell me where he is, Nora, and you'll never see me again."

She had tears in her eyes, but the way she stared up at him was utterly defiant—almost as if she dared him to kill her.

Ray felt the rage boiling inside him. In his mind, she was no longer his sister. She was just like the other women who thought they were better than him, the other ones he had killed. All he wanted from her was a little bit of information about the dummy's brother. The stubborn, high-and-mighty bitch. She deserved to die—for not helping him, for once again hanging him out to dry.

"You never gave a damn about me," he growled.

Lunging forward, he frantically wrapped the stocking around her neck. Nora let out a rasp and struggled—like they all did. She had that grimace, so familiar to him by now. But strangely, she didn't claw at his hands. He came to expect that from each one—the scratch marks, his version of battle scars.

As Ray pulled tighter on the stocking around her throat, Nora's face turned crimson. She made a gurgling sound he'd heard before.

But she still wasn't fighting him off. She wasn't doing anything with her hands.

Suddenly Ray felt something hard poke into his chest.

His grip on the stocking slackened a bit as he realized she was holding a gun to his heart. She'd been hiding it in the cushioned chair all this time.

Ray let out a stunned laugh. "Nora—"

She had tears in her eyes as she struggled in vain to get a breath. But Ray saw something else in her expression, something besides the usual look of panic they all had on their faces during the last few moments. What he saw in his sister's eyes was pity.

She still had the weapon pressed against his chest.

But Ray pulled tighter on the nylon stocking around her

throat. He didn't think she had the guts to pull the trigger. She'd black out first.

Besides, it would be too ironic if he died here in her living room—especially after he'd gone to all that trouble to avoid being shipped to some godforsaken place where he might get shot. All of it would have been for nothing. He'd have wasted so much—

A shot rang out.

Stunned, he felt a horrible, searing pain in his chest.

With that fatal shot still ringing in his ears, Ray had one last thought.

*Who would miss him?*

# Chapter 37

*Wednesday*
*10:50 p.m.*

As Nora stood up, the nylon stocking fell from her neck and drifted to the floor. She felt as if her windpipe had been crushed, and she started coughing. She dropped Joe's gun onto the chair's seat cushion. Still gasping for air, she stared down at her brother's body.

Sprawled on her living room rug, Ray had a hole in his chest that bled through his shirt. His eyes were open in a dazed, dead stare—as if the shock he'd experienced in his final seconds had been forever stamped on his face.

Nora was in shock, too.

She started sobbing and wasn't sure she could ever stop. But she couldn't afford to fall apart right now. The weeping made her sore throat even worse. With a handkerchief, Nora wiped her eyes and nose. She kept telling herself that Ray had already been dead to her.

The gunshot must have been heard by everyone on the

block. Had any of her neighbors called the police? At this point, answering a bunch of questions from some police investigator would just about kill her. The last thing she wanted to do was reveal all the evil things Ray had done—all his horrible crimes. Yet she had to call the police before someone else did, before someone came knocking on her door about the gunshot.

Making a wide arc around Ray's body, she staggered to the phone in the front hallway. But Nora hesitated before picking up the receiver. She thought about Chris and Jane—and the legacy their deranged uncle had left for them. Ray had been right about that. This would ruin her family.

Why couldn't he have been killed in that explosion? Until this evening, she'd thought her brother had died a coward and a bungler. And she might have been able to forgive him. But that was before she'd realized what he'd done was much, much worse.

She heard a car outside. It sounded like the vehicle was slowing down. Her first thought was that one of the neighbors had indeed called the police about the gunshot.

Nora went to the front door. With a shaky hand, she moved aside the blackout curtain and glanced out the window. A taxi had pulled up to the end of the driveway. Joe climbed out of the back seat.

Nora turned and glanced at her brother's corpse again. She stepped back toward the living room.

For a few moments—maybe longer—everything stood still. The reality of what had just happened started to sink in and it paralyzed her. She couldn't stop staring at Ray's lifeless body.

A gentle knocking on the front door snapped her out of it.

Biting her lip, Nora went back to the door and opened it.

With his clothes still filthy and a bandage over the gash on his forehead, Joe gave her a tentative smile. "I saw the curtain move, and figured you were up. I—" He fell silent and his smile disappeared. "My God, Nora, what happened to your neck?"

She realized that the stocking must have left a mark. "Ray showed up here a half hour ago," she said—in a strained, scratchy voice.

Opening the door wider, she nodded toward the living room.

Joe brushed past her and stopped dead in the living room entryway.

"My God," he whispered again, staring down at Ray's corpse. He stood there and said nothing else for a few moments.

Finally, he turned, took her hand and led her into the front hall. He sat her down on the stairs.

Nora heard herself quietly explain everything that had happened. She knew, if she called the police and they saw this crime scene and the marks on her neck, she could plead self-defense. It would probably be an open-and-shut case.

"But you don't want to call the police, do you?" Joe asked, standing in front of her with his hand on the newel post. "You don't want it getting out about what he's done."

Nora couldn't answer him without crying. She folded her arms and shook her head. "But I have to . . ."

Joe glanced toward the living room and frowned. From where she sat on the stairs, Nora couldn't see into the room. But she knew Joe was looking at Ray, sprawled on the floor.

"Before you shot him," Joe said, "did you at least tell him that he didn't get away with it—that we knew he set up my brother?"

Touching her neck, Nora cleared her throat and nodded. "He . . . he became very agitated about that. He figured out that Jackson's brother must have tipped me off, but he didn't know you were Jackson's brother. He couldn't remember your first name. He kept asking me where he could find you. He wanted to strike a deal with me. He'd leave town and completely disappear if I told him where you were."

"But you wouldn't tell him?"

She shook her head. "I couldn't do that to you, Joe."

He said nothing. But he smiled a little and sighed.

Nora shrugged. "Anyway, then he started to choke me . . . and you know the rest . . ." Her voice started quivering. "Listen, we can't just sit here. I . . . I have to call the police . . ."

"And it'll completely destroy your family, you know it will," Joe said.

Closing her eyes, she nodded. "That's what Ray said. And he was right. But I don't have a choice."

Joe gazed over toward Ray's corpse again. "Yes, you do. He died nearly two weeks ago in an explosion down in San Diego." He turned to her. "You and I are the only ones who know he came here tonight, Nora. If we buried him somewhere, no one would be the wiser. Nobody's looking for him. He already took care of that for us by faking his death."

"I can't," she whimpered, her throat still scratchy. "I need to take responsibility for what happened . . ."

"For killing him in self-defense?" Joe asked. "Or are you assuming responsibility for his crimes, because he was your kid brother? Is it worth ruining your life and devastating your family?"

"The families of Ray's victims deserve to know . . ."

"The police already have their murderer—and he's in the hospital morgue right now with an ice pick in his head. You couldn't ask for a more suitable ending for the 'Rosie' killer. You wouldn't be doing the victims' families any favors by confusing the issue with this revelation about your brother. I talked to one of the cops in the emergency room tonight. They're certain they have the right guy this time—and he got what he deserved. Don't wreck that for the cops and everyone else because you want to punish yourself."

Nora couldn't argue with what he was saying. But she was never one of those people who felt okay about getting away with something. Even if she took Joe's advice and buried Ray somewhere, it would still haunt her for the rest of her life. Yet Joe was right. No one would be the wiser—including her children and her husband. And they wouldn't be hurt by any of this.

"Another thing," Joe said. "It's like I already told you, the navy doesn't want the truth getting out about Ray. They're trying to keep a lid on it. I'd just as soon you keep a lid on it, too..."

"I don't understand," Nora said, bewildered. "I thought you—of all people—would want Ray exposed as the murderer he was."

"Now that he's dead, it doesn't matter so much." Wincing a bit, Joe shrugged. "It's complicated. I can explain later. Basically, I don't want everyone knowing that my poor brother got duped..." He glanced toward the living room again—and then at her. "Nora, I understand that you need to do what you think is the right thing here. But no one wants to know about your brother. It won't help anybody. Don't let Ray destroy you and your family. I can bury him someplace for you. I'll make this go away—and make it right."

Nora gazed up at him. "I couldn't let you do that, Joe..." She reached up toward the newel post and placed her hand on his. "Not alone..."

"Please, God, I hope we're doing the right thing here," Nora murmured—so quietly that she could barely hear herself.

Soaked with perspiration and covered in grime, she was exhausted. She could see her breath in the cold night air. With the back of a shovel, she patted down the rectangle of loose, dark dirt over Ray's grave.

They'd found a tiny clearing between some trees and shrubs. While digging the hole, she and Joe hadn't encountered many rocks or tree roots. Joe had done most of the heavy work and hadn't complained—despite his bruised ribs. Moments ago, he'd gone to collect some branches to cover the freshly turned soil. Nora took this time alone to pray over her brother's grave.

"All the people Ray hurt, please, God, ease their suffering," she whispered. "I hope what we're doing here somehow helps them and the police put an end to all this. Let Joe be right about that. I'm doing this to protect my family. And maybe I'm still trying to protect Ray, too. I'm always going to feel responsible for him—for what he did . . ."

Nora heard twigs snapping underfoot and rustling. Through the trees, she spotted Joe approaching the gravesite.

She realized she'd started out praying and ended up talking to herself.

While she'd dug her brother's grave, Nora had come to the conclusion that burying Ray was more or less the best thing they could do—for everyone. There was no better solution—at least, nothing that didn't involve people getting hurt. But she couldn't shake a few lingering doubts. And she would always be worried that someone might discover the grave.

Two hours ago, Joe had asked if she wanted to bury her brother in the ravine. But Nora knew that if she did that, she'd never be able to look at her backyard without thinking about Ray's body hidden in the gulch below.

She'd had another place in mind.

Before wrapping her brother in an old, paint-splattered drop cloth, Joe had removed Ray's wallet and some car keys from his pants pocket. That was when they'd realized Ray must have robbed a Bakersfield man named Sidney Garrick and assumed his identity. Ray may have even killed him. In all likelihood, Ray had parked Sidney Garrick's car somewhere near the house. But they'd decided that the car would have to remain there for the time being.

Going through Ray's other pockets, Joe had also found a room key to cabin 16 of the Blue Haven Roadside Hotel. "We'll need to check his room and make sure he didn't leave anything there," Joe had said. "This is going to be a long night, Nora. This place you want to bury him, is it close?"

She'd told him that it was a forty-minute drive.

They'd carried Ray out the back door and loaded him into the Packard's trunk—along with two shovels. Nora had remembered to bring a flashlight and the key to the gate marked PRIVATE PROPERTY—NO TRESPASSING. Then, with Joe beside her in the passenger seat, Nora had driven, retracing the route she'd taken the night before to Mrs. Landauer's private woodland retreat.

They'd found this spot in the forest—at least fifty feet from the dirt trail.

Now she helped Joe scatter some branches and leaves over the gravesite. Joe wiped off his hands and then retrieved his shovel. "Before we go, would you like to say a prayer or something?"

"I already did that," Nora replied. She picked up her shovel, too.

"Well, then I'll say my own little prayer." Joe stopped and looked down at the unmarked grave. "God, let no one ever find what we've buried here—at least, not in our lifetime."

"Amen," Nora murmured. "God, forgive him."

Then, dirty and tired, they treaded back to the car.

During the drive home, Nora struggled to keep her eyes open and focus on the road. "I couldn't have done any of this without you, Joe," she told him. "I'm in your debt—and so is my family. As I mentioned earlier, I thought you of all people would want to see Ray exposed as the murderer he was."

"Well, I'm trying to protect my brother, too," he admitted. The breeze through the open window on the passenger side ruffled his hair. "In the long run, it's better for Jackson this way. He was tricked into helping Ray with his scheme—to the point of switching dog tags with him. I think about the investigation and the news stories, and I'd hate to see Jackson put under that kind of scrutiny. People can be pretty cruel and heartless. But when I talked to some of the guys in his and Ray's outfit, none of them had a mean thing to say about Jackson. Maybe it's because they were talking to his brother. But no one accused Jackson of being a coward or a deserter. The general consensus among them seemed to be that, after the explosion, Jackson must have gotten confused and thought they were under attack. So, he threw his stuff together, thinking they'd be shipping out. But then he wandered off base where something must have happened to him. Jackson was actually smarter than that. He would have stayed put and waited for his orders. Still, if they want to think he got confused and wandered off, I guess that's not so bad."

"I should be getting word from the navy any day now about the remains," Nora said, turning onto Erickson Road. "I've reserved a plot and a marker at Lakeview Cemetery, which isn't far from the house. I haven't instructed them yet about what I want on the tombstone. I'll pay for everything, of course. Would you like Jackson to be buried in Seattle?"

A sad smile came to his face. "That's awful nice of you, Nora . . ."

"No, it's the very least I can do," she replied, watching the road ahead.

"Well, I'll have to think about it," Joe said. "Andy—I mean, Jackson—he always wanted to be buried at sea . . ."

It was one fifty in the morning when, on the way home, they swung by the Blue Haven Roadside Hotel, a long, sprawling, cabin-style motor court. Slightly dilapidated, it looked like the place had seen better days. From the rendering of a lumberjack on the road sign, Nora guessed the hotel must have catered to timber workers at one time.

No one seemed to be around when she and Joe let themselves into cabin 16. Joe found a couple of his brother's shirts hanging in the closet. Pulling them off their hangers, he held the bunched-up shirts to his chest for a moment. Nora noticed tears in his eyes. He seemed so grateful to have found them.

Then they went back to searching the cabin for anything that might be traced to Ray, Jackson, or the murders. Nora wondered if Ray had kept any souvenirs from his victims—like the wind-up Scottie with the cymbals. But they didn't find anything. If Ray had stolen something of value from any of the women he'd murdered, he must have sold or pawned it already. They left with only the two shirts.

Twenty-five minutes later, as Nora slowly drove down her block, Joe kept a lookout for a car with California plates. He had her stop alongside a black Chrysler coupe. The key he'd taken from Ray's pocket easily fit into the lock. In the trunk, he found Nora's three missing aprons, a bag containing her nylons and lipstick, and a box of tools—lockpicks, a crowbar, screwdrivers and master keys.

Joe said they looked like a burglar's tools. He said he would dump them off at a scrap drive post, making a few trips so it wasn't so obvious what he was scrapping.

Nora had no desire to hold on to the nylons, the lipstick or the aprons. They seemed tainted now. She would burn them in the furnace before going to bed. She was too tired to do anything about Sidney Garrick's Chrysler. Within the next day or two, she'd drive the car to another part of town, park it, leave the wallet in the glove compartment, and then take a bus home.

After she pulled into the driveway, they unloaded the shovels, Ray's box of tools and Jackson's shirts.

"I need to be up for work in two hours," Nora sighed, grabbing the aprons and the bag containing her nylons and lipstick out of the back seat. She closed the car door and glanced at the house. "It's just two hours, but right now, I really don't want to be alone in there."

"You shouldn't have to be," Joe replied.

She stashed the shovels in the garage. Joe set the box of tools and the shirts on the steps to the garage apartment. Then he closed the door, locked it again and came back to Nora. They headed into the house together.

While Joe washed up in the powder room, Nora went down to the basement and burned the stockings, the aprons and the lipstick in the furnace. Then she scrubbed the bloodstain out of the rug in the living room. She kept thinking there was something else she needed to do.

"We've covered everything," Joe told her. "What you need to do is rest."

He made her a sandwich while she took a shower.

They sat together on the family room sofa. Nora had a couple of bites of her sandwich and half a glass of milk.

Joe didn't say a word. He didn't have to. He was just there, and that was enough.

Nora rested her head on his shoulder—an intimate gesture she'd shared only with Pete. The last time had been months and months ago. Somehow, it didn't feel strange with Joe. Nora was so grateful that she began to cry, but not for long.

She felt his arm go around her shoulders and soon fell asleep.

# Epilogue

*Friday, May 7*
*8:45 p.m.*

*My dearest Pete,*

*Brace yourself, honey, Chris is in the hospital. But he's going to be okay.*

*Wednesday afternoon, he was tossing around a football (yes, our Chris was playing football) in the backyard with our new tenant, Joe. And somehow, the two of them ended up tumbling down the ravine. I had to call an ambulance. They brought Chris up on a stretcher. Both Chris & Joe ended up with cuts, bruises and stitches. But Chris broke his leg. It was a bad break, and they had to operate on him yesterday. He had a great surgeon, Pete, and everything went smoothly. He'll be in the hospital for the next week. With proper healing and physical therapy, he should be able to walk normally in*

*about six months—so the doctor told me. But he
also said that this injury will most likely keep our
boy out of the draft. That's the one silver lining to
all this.*

*Joe, by the way, feels horrible about the accident—
even though it wasn't his fault. I think the two of
them simply got all caught up in their scrimmaging
or whatever they were doing . . .*

Nora stopped writing, sat back and set her fountain pen on
the kitchen table for a moment. It wasn't easy lying to Pete—
even in a letter. She'd have to convince Chris to use that same
cover story when writing to his dad about the accident. She'd
already told Chris that her scuffle with Joe in the ravine had
been a huge misunderstanding.

From where she sat, Nora could look out the kitchen window and see the lights on in Joe's apartment. It made her feel
safe to know he was there.

The house was quiet. Jane was up in her bedroom, doing her
homework and sulking. This afternoon, she'd come home from
her field trip to learn she'd missed all the excitement of Chris's
mishap. She was also furious at Nora for accidentally breaking
and throwing out the cymbal-playing Scottie dog her Uncle
Ray had given her. "Honey, it completely fell apart when I
knocked it off your shelf," Nora had lied. "It was in pieces. I
didn't think you'd want it anymore."

The truth was, early Thursday morning, she'd put the wind-
up toy in a paper bag and furtively tossed it in a trash can near
her bus stop.

Nora had reported to work on time the morning after she
and Joe had buried her brother. She might have phoned in sick
and taken the day off. But as her lead man had reminded her,
there was a war on.

During her break, she'd spoken to him and someone in personnel, asking if, starting that day, she could work half days until her son got out of the hospital. She'd wanted them to know she was serious about her job but needed to put her children first. They'd said it could be arranged.

She'd left work yesterday at eleven o'clock and gone directly to the hospital, where she'd waited it out while they'd operated on Chris. Joe had joined her for a while. Then, with her grateful blessing, he'd gone home and gotten rid of Sidney Garrick's car for her.

"ROSIE" SLAYER DEAD had been the headline for the *Seattle Times* on Thursday. The article had provided details of Ronald Lapp's attack on a riveter at her parents' home in Queen Anne—and how she'd killed him with an ice pick. The riveter, a young woman named Dolores "Dolly" Oberlin, was praised for her courage—a fine example of a home front heroine.

Ronald Lapp had clearly been a miserable excuse for a human being. He'd had a long criminal past and beaten out a rape charge in 1941. The police had been searching for him for the strangulation-murder of an eighteen-year-old girl in Portland last year. The authorities had seemed certain they'd found the "Rosie" killer this time.

A spokesman for the Seattle Police Department had said it "wasn't likely" that Roger Tallant had killed Connie Wiedrich after all. It would probably be as close as they'd ever get to an apology for killing Connie's friend and wrongly accusing him of her murder.

Nora still felt terrible about what had happened to him.

She'd eaten an early dinner in the hospital cafeteria on Thursday. Then she'd finally visited with Chris. He'd been conscious, but still woozy from his surgery. Nora had stayed until visiting hours ended. When she'd come home, Joe had stopped by and they'd had a drink in the kitchen—at the same table where she sat now. She'd barely been able to stay awake.

But they'd needed to figure out a few more details—to answer any questions Chris or Jane might have. They'd decided to go along with the idea that Joe had fibbed about being married so he could rent the apartment intended for a married couple. It seemed forgivable considering the wartime housing shortage. And they would say that Joe had been contemplating a professional name change when he'd signed the lease. He'd wanted to be considered a "serious" artist and briefly rechristened himself *Joseph Strauss* for a few days—before realizing that good old *Joe Slattery* made a decent living as a commercial illustrator, and he didn't want to starve to death. Joe had come up with that idea. Nora figured these cover stories would clear up any confusion and allow Joe Slattery to stay on in the garage apartment. And Nora wanted very much for him to stay.

She had hated the idea of him going back to his apartment last night, leaving her alone in the big, empty house. Nora had been too exhausted to want any kind of intimacy. She'd just wanted to be under the same roof with him while she slept. But at nine forty-five, she'd sent him on his way, locked the doors, and then wearily treaded upstairs to bed.

Now, Nora picked up her fountain pen and glanced toward the kitchen window again. She saw Joe in his paint-splattered T-shirt, passing by the living room window of the garage apartment. He must have been working. It felt as if he was watching over her and Jane tonight. It would always feel that way—as long as he was there.

Nora focused on her unfinished letter. Her husband would never know how much Joe meant to her. She would never tell Pete—or anyone else—about her brother's crimes. That would remain a secret between Joe and her.

She went back to the letter, telling Pete about her arrangement for half days at work. She also told him about Jane's two-day field trip to Orcas Island.

*I'm looking forward to a quiet weekend with just us girls. There's nothing on the docket except visit-*

*ing Chris in the hospital and maybe some tilling around the victory garden. Nothing else is new here besides Chris's terrible tumble. But this too shall pass.*

*Meanwhile, my darling, take care of yourself and stay safe. I miss you.*

*Love,*
*Me*

In the week that followed, Nora stayed busy. She spoke to a representative at Lakeview Cemetery and learned that she didn't need to furnish the cemetery with a body or death certificate to finalize purchasing a plot. Plenty of markers in the cemetery were for soldiers who had died and been buried overseas. So, Nora followed through with the purchase of a plot and a modest tombstone. For the inscription, she confirmed the birth year through Roger's friend, Richard. Though his body may have ended up in the potter's field, Roger would have a marker in a nice spot at Lakeview Cemetery, reading:

### ROGER J. TALLANT
### 1913–1943
### A FRIEND & GENTLEMAN

Nora felt she owed him that much.

Before Chris's release from the hospital, Nora received a mere two days' advance notice from the navy that her brother's remains would be arriving in Seattle by train. But it was enough time for her and Joe to arrange for a crematorium to pick up the remains. They later chartered a boat and sailed out on the Puget Sound, where Joe scattered his brother's ashes over the water. Jackson Slattery got the burial at sea he'd always wanted.

Chris and Jane weren't happy with her for not including them for what they thought was their uncle's sea burial. Jane pointed out that Catholics weren't even allowed to be cremated. And Chris said it was just plain weird that she'd had a burn victim cremated. But Nora insisted that her brother had wanted it that way.

Nora appeased the kids a bit when she gave Chris the Illinois Central Railroad watch Ray had inherited from her dad, and Jane got her brother's sunglasses. Jane thought the glasses were cool. Everything else belonging to Ray that the Navy had sent—except for the family photos—Nora gave to charity.

While laid up in the hospital, Chris started writing to Ruth Nakai at the Minidoka Relocation Center near Jerome, Idaho. They would become pen pals and he'd share some of Ruth's letters with his mom.

Ruth wrote that, during her first week at the internment camp, she and her mother were able to track down Tak and Miko through a directory listing the 120,000 internees. Miko was a teacher at one of the camp schools, and Tak was on the board of the internees' self-governing committee. Ruth wrote that she was better off at the camp than she'd been alone in the woods with her mother. She was making friends there, and they had regular activities. But they were in the desert, and she missed the woods. She also missed having her own room and bathroom. *But the worst part about this place*, she wrote, *is that I'm a prisoner here, and I'm not sure they'll ever let us out.*

By the time Chris was released from the hospital, Nora could tell he'd become more confident and happier. Even as he tried to get around in his clunky cast with his crutches, Chris seemed more comfortable in his own skin. In the hospital, he'd seen so many people who were worse off than he was—including a few wounded veterans not much older than him, overflow from the local army and navy hospitals. Some of them had been crippled or lost limbs. Chris would be taking physical therapy sessions with them, and they treated him like a peer. Suddenly—or maybe not so suddenly—her son had grown up.

As far as Nora could tell, no one picked on him at school anymore. Then again, how low can you go, bullying a kid in a cast? Having kept up with his studies while in the hospital, Chris had to hobble back and forth to classes for only two weeks until summer break. A lot of kids signed his cast—even though he still spent most of his time alone.

That wasn't quite true. He spent a lot of time with Joe.

The vandalism stopped. Ray had initially scared them away. And having Joe in the apartment above the garage had helped deter further trouble.

For a while, Joe became like a member of the family—and a big brother to Chris. As the weather turned nicer, he joined them for dinners at the picnic table in the backyard. True to his word, he used Jane's likeness in an illustration for a peanut butter ad. It was going to run in several national magazines—including *Life* and *Look*—in September, just in time for back-to-school. Nora figured Jane would be impossible to live with.

Returning home from the plant every workday, one of the first things Nora still did was check the mail for a letter from Pete. She continued to write to him two or three times a week. In mid-July, one of his letters started out with his code about being relocated:

> *Hello, Sweetheart,*
>
> *So happy to have gotten your last note & read that all is well. I'm amazed at how well Chris seems to be recovering. Can't believe that Jane had an actual "date." I feel so old! Love to them both. You know how much I miss you all . . .*

So, Nora knew he'd moved onto Sicily for the next big push by the Allies. And she would worry about him again—in the same dangerous situation, only in a different place.

It was around this time, on a warm summer night, she and Joe ended up alone together in the backyard. It was twilight, and they were sitting in lawn chairs near the victory garden by the garage. They sipped ice teas and talked quietly—about nothing in particular, the way married couples sometimes do. Joe had the garage apartment window open and the radio on. Rudy Vallée was singing a schmaltzy version of "As Time Goes By."

Nora felt so comfortable, she caught herself almost reaching out to stroke his arm. Instead, she took a minute. Then she sighed and gave him a sad smile. "Joe, it kills me to say this. But you'll have to move soon. I've become way too attached to you."

"I know," he said quietly. "I feel the same way. And I like you and your family too much to ruin things."

A week later, Joe moved out.

Within a month, two women in their twenties moved into the garage apartment—both riveters, both with Marine fiancés away in the Pacific. The women were nice enough, but they worked swing shift, and Nora didn't see that much of them.

She and the kids each received a couple of postcards from Joe that summer—of the Golden Gate Bridge, the Grand Canyon, and other West Coast attractions. They couldn't write back, because Joe was traveling and didn't give a return address.

Nora never heard from Joe again.

But for years, long after Pete came back safe from the war, Nora would sometimes open a magazine and see an exquisitely illustrated ad for one thing or another, and she'd recognize Joe's work.

Sometimes, there was a character in the background of Joe's various illustrations—a woman who looked exactly like her.

And he always made her look beautiful.

# THE ENEMY AT HOME

## ABOUT THIS GUIDE

The suggested questions are included to enhance your group's reading of Kevin O'Brien's *The Enemy at Home*!

# DISCUSSION QUESTIONS

1. *The Enemy at Home* was researched and written during the COVID pandemic. The author couldn't help comparing how we reacted to this recent crisis and how "the Greatest Generation" reacted to the war with the adjustments and sacrifices everyone had to make. How do you think we'd handle these wartime adjustments, restrictions and sacrifices today? How else would you compare the pandemic to World War II?

2. When developing the characters of Nora and her husband, Pete, the author wanted to create a marriage that has had its fair share of problems and struggles. At the same time, he wanted to instill a sense of 1940s values and gender roles. How do you think Nora and Pete's marriage would hold up after the war? Do you think they make a good couple?

3. The passage of time in the book—from start to finish—is only a month. Do you see a transformation starting in Nora during that time? Do you think she's on her way to becoming more confident and independent? At the end of the war, most "Rosie the Riveters" lost their jobs and were told to go back to their housework. How do you think Nora would have handled that?

4. In several scenes, Nora encounters racism, misogyny or homophobia—all often tolerated (and sometimes even endorsed) at the time. In your opinion, does Nora take any kind of stand against such injustices, or does she do nothing to "rock the boat"?

5. Nora's seventeen-year-old son, Chris, obviously had some problematic friendships and growing pains. His

lies concerning his whereabouts when certain murders were committed eventually make Nora suspect the worst. Do you think there was enough evidence against him to cause Nora distress? Did she take too long to wonder about his role in the "Rosie" murders? Or did Nora overreact? This is something most mothers couldn't even imagine. How would you react in Nora's situation?

6. In her loneliness, Nora clearly becomes infatuated with her handsome tenant, Joe. Did you want her to act on her desires—or stay true to her absent husband? Was Joe too suspicious to be a traditional "love interest"?

7. *The Enemy at Home* might be called a serial killer thriller—set thirty years before the term *serial killer* was even coined. Pre-WW2 murderers Jack the Ripper and Earle Leonard Nelson are both mentioned in the book. But the author based the "Rosie" killer's main motive on theories that Ted Bundy's murder rampage was partly driven by his adverse reaction to the women's liberation movement in the 1970s. In *The Enemy at Home*, the "Rosie" killer feels threatened by women taking on important wartime work. Did you feel there were other factors that contributed to his crimes? Was there a true-life serial killing or murder spree that particularly scared you?

8. Do you think Nora made the right decision after she discovered what Chris was doing in the cabin in the woods at night? Though protecting her son, she also drastically altered the lives of two people (Sono and Ruth). What would you have done in Nora's shoes?

9. Similarly, Nora's actions at the end of the book are "unconventional" at best. Do you think she made the right

choice? Was it an ethical choice? What would you have done in her situation?

10. There are tributes to several old movies in the book. A few references are made to Alfred Hitchcock's *Shadow of a Doubt*, and Nora's brother, Ray, plays with a baseball "pocket puzzle" similar to one Dana Andrews had in *Laura*. Did you notice any other old movie references? Speaking of movies, who would you cast in a current movie version of *The Enemy at Home*? If this was the 1940s, who would you cast?

Visit our website at
**KensingtonBooks.com**
to sign up for our newsletters, read
more from your favorite authors, see
books by series, view reading group
guides, and more!

Become a Part of Our
**Between the Chapters Book Club**
Community and Join the Conversation

Betweenthechapters.net

Submit your book review for a chance to win exclusive
Between the Chapters swag you can't get anywhere else!
https://www.kensingtonbooks.com/pages/review/